# Wicked Ties . . .

"... is a deliciously kinky and naughty thriller ... A satisfying tale of suspense and sexual awakening."
—Joyfully Reviewed

"... absolutely took my breath away."
—Romance Junkies

## MORE PRAISE FOR THE WICKED LOVERS NOVELS

"A wicked, sensual thrill from first page to last. I loved it!"
—Lora Leigh, #1 *New York Times* bestselling author

"Make[s] your toes curl!"
—Angela Knight, *New York Times* bestselling author

"Will . . . have you panting for more!"
—Susan Johnson, *New York Times* bestselling author

"Shayla Black . . . you rocked it!"
—The Romance Reviews

"Thoroughly gripping and . . . so blisteringly sexy."
—Fallen Angel Reviews

"Five-alarm HOT!"
—Books-n-Kisses

"Scrumptiously erotic, sensual, heady, and very arousing."
—*Affaire de Coeur*

"[A] fabulous read."
—Fresh Fiction

"A master of BDSM erotic romance."
—Love Romances & More

# Wicked Ties

SHAYLA BLACK

BERKLEY
New York

BERKLEY
An imprint of Penguin Random House LLC
penguinrandomhouse.com

Copyright © 2007 by Shelley Bradley LLC
Penguin Random House supports copyright. Copyright fuels creativity, encourages diverse voices,
promotes free speech, and creates a vibrant culture. Thank you for buying an authorized
edition of this book and for complying with copyright laws by not reproducing, scanning,
or distributing any part of it in any form without permission. You are supporting writers
and allowing Penguin Random House to continue to publish books for every reader.

BERKLEY and the BERKLEY & B colophon
are registered trademarks of Penguin Random House LLC.

ISBN: 9780425268179

The Library of Congress has catalogued the
first Heat trade paperback edition of this title as follows:

Black, Shayla.
Wicked Ties / Shayla Black.—1st ed.
         p.        cm.
ISBN: 978-0-425-21361-2
1. Sexual dominance and submission—Fiction.   I. Title.
PS3602.L325245W53   2007
813'.6—dc22
2006025689

First Heat trade paperback edition / January 2007
Second Heat trade paperback edition / April 2013
Berkley trade paperback edition / July 2021

Printed in the United States of America
13th Printing

Book design by Tiffany Estreicher

This is a work of fiction. Names, characters, places, and incidents either are the product
of the author's imagination or are used fictitiously, and any resemblance to actual persons,
living or dead, business establishments, events, or locales is entirely coincidental.

# Wicked Ties

# Chapter One

Haye *you ever wanted to put yourself in the hands of a man whose sole purpose is to give you pleasure?*

The words flashed across Morgan O'Malley's laptop screen. She sucked in a sharp, shocked breath. She'd met this man in an online chat room less than three minutes ago. How could he know that?

He must have guessed, had to have guessed. She hadn't told him anything about herself, not one single thing, except her name and the fact that she wanted to interview him for her cable TV show.

But even through her stunned silence, he kept peeling back the layers of her secrets.

*Do you want a man to see inside you, all the way to your fantasies, the darkest ones you don't even tell your friends about, and make every one of them come true?*

A surge of arousal coiled in her belly. Her palms began to sweat. Morgan swallowed hard.

In the silent living room shadowed with the many colors of dusk, Morgan squirmed on the black leather sofa, shoving desires she didn't dare admit to the back of her mind.

This was business. *He* was business. It wasn't a good idea to have the hots for the next interview subject for her show. It might be late-night cable talk, but *Turn Me On* was her job, her brainchild, her little rebellion . . . her life.

Besides, aching for a guy whose real name she didn't know, whose face she'd never seen—whose lifestyle she shouldn't even ponder—was just dumb.

*So, Master J, is that what a dominant does?* she typed in response, determined to keep the conversation light. *Dish out fantasies?*

*One of the things,* he responded at length. *But that would be oversimplifying the relationship. His most important goal is to earn his partner's trust. Trust is important in any relationship, but especially in one involving Dominance/submission. Without that, how can a woman freely put herself in a man's care and know that her well-being and safety will always be first? How can she know her master will understand her so he can make her every wicked fantasy come true?*

Dominance wasn't just about tying someone to the bed and screwing them into the mattress? Surprise wrinkled Morgan's brow. Trust, care, understanding—she had to admit, that all sounded like a fantasy in itself. Certainly, she'd been lacking those qualities in her relationship with her ex-fiancé, Andrew—especially the understanding.

*Trust allows a woman to connect with the primitive part of her that craves the utter surrender of being at her master's mercy, despite not knowing if his plans for her involve pleasure, pain, or both.*

Morgan couldn't deny that Master J intrigued her even more now than when one of the production assistants, Reggie, had given her his bio.

Toggling to her email, she opened the bio she'd been given and scanned it again.

*A member of the BDSM and D/s scene for nearly ten years, Master J is experienced in all facets but continues to learn. He owns a personal security company and has been bodyguard to senators, international diplomats, and athletes. A West Point graduate, he also served in military Special Forces as a team leader before being honorably discharged.*

Morgan clicked the email closed. The paragraph revealed a lot about the man whose words made her shiver with dark fantasies. Self-discipline, honor, strength. Yet the blurb said very little at the same time. Who was this guy? Could he really bind and tease a woman into making her beg?

*Morgan?* Her name flashed across the screen. *You still there?*

*Sorry. Just thinking. Clearly, I have a lot to learn about in order to do the show properly. I guess I thought it was all about velvet ropes and handcuffs.*

*It's about that, too.☺*

She laughed, pushing down the ache curling in her belly . . . and lower. A little curiosity didn't make her depraved. Definitely not. It was just interesting to see how the other half lived.

*But it's also an exchange of power and trust,* he typed. *A woman chooses to give her master dominion over her body and her mind. She surrenders her flesh and free will to anything and everything he desires.*

*What sort of surrender?* a voice inside of her demanded to know. A thousand dark images pushed themselves into her brain from the depths of her fantasies: her kneeling to this stranger's cock, him ordering her to spread her legs wide so he could simply look at her, her bound to his bed as he prepared to take whatever he wanted.

Disturbed by the shocking turn of her thoughts, she shook them away. And ignored her rapid breathing.

Lots of people had bondage fantasies at one time or another, she'd read. Having one or two herself was normal, no matter what Andrew said.

Morgan squirmed against the leather cushions again, ignoring any extra moisture between her legs.

*But a D/s relationship is also about a lot more,* Master J typed.

*How do you put someone in manacles, blindfolds, and dark rooms but still earn her trust? How do you develop an emotionally gratifying relationship when one person has all the power?*

*It's not like that.*

Morgan's gaze stayed riveted to her screen as she waited for more. For a long, silent moment, she held her breath . . . but nothing. Master J wasn't going to reply further. Just like in the bedroom, she supposed. He had the power to give or withhold.

Finally, a longer reply appeared in the little chat room window.

*Sorry, but I've had an urgent call. Have to go. If you feel I have the background to assist with your show, let's meet. I'll answer your questions then. Someplace public, so you don't worry I might be a serial killer luring you into danger. I can talk faster. I've mastered a lot, but not typing <g>. I still hunt and peck.*

Morgan scuttled her impatience. Not hard when the man made her smile at his jokes.

*I understand,* she answered. *Can we meet tomorrow at 3? I Googled and found a place that seems to be popular there in Lafayette, called La Roux. Know where that is?*

*Cher, I'm a native. I know every crack in the sidewalk around here.*

Morgan smiled and typed, *Cher? I'm not that tall or old enough to have had a singing career since the 60s!*

*LOL. It means* dear *in French,* he translated. *I'm Cajun, so I grew up speaking the language.*

Morgan read his reply and ignored the little flutter in her belly. Flirtation was a French thing, and he'd been raised with the culture. It was as natural to him as breathing, no doubt.

*<blushing> I've lived in Los Angeles too long, I guess. I'll see you then?*

*You will. How will I know you? Lots of pretty girls in Louisiana. I want to make sure I reveal my innermost secrets to the right one.*

He was a charmer, Morgan bet. He'd have to be with his interest in wielding whips and chains. Certainly, most "normal" women would run screaming in the opposite direction at the thought of a little pain and a lot of obedience with their sex.

*I'll be wearing a straw hat, sunglasses, and a big, boxy coat,* she answered.

*Sounds more like a disguise,* Master J returned.

He had no idea. And she wasn't advertising the fact she had a stalker. Morgan only hoped the reason she needed a disguise would be caught and start rotting in hell soon.

*See you tomorrow,* she jotted back.

*Au revoir.*

The message on her screen told her moments later that Master J had left the private chat room. With a sigh, she moved to close the chat room window.

Her hand trembled. No, her whole body trembled, despite the heat snaking under her skin.

She was tired, that's all.

*Tired doesn't make you ache in very personal places,* the voice in her head taunted. *Tired doesn't make you wet.*

"Tired makes me hear pesky voices in my head," she grumbled.

She tried to push Master J, the man, aside and focus on the questions she'd ask him tomorrow. The show's outline had to be in soon, and she wanted to be prepared to launch her second season with a bang. Already, she had a growing cult following. With the right material, the show could skyrocket.

Which meant she had to keep her eye on the prize and focus on work.

But after ten minutes of staring at an empty screen, Morgan admitted that Master J wouldn't leave her mind. What was it about him?

*Other than the fact that he lives out the fantasies you've ached about?*

Morgan shook her head, determined to ignore the maddening little voice. She was curious, not deviant. No matter what Andrew said or her mother would think.

With a sigh, she reached for the phone and dialed the number of the production assistant in Los Angeles.

"Reggie," she said when he answered. "Hey, I talked to this Master J guy you hooked me up with, and I read his bio. I'm meeting him tomorrow. What's his scoop? Learn anything new?"

"Yeah," returned the older man, his voice scratchy from his two-pack-a-day habit. "I did some calling around Louisiana, asked people at bondage clubs if they'd ever heard of him, just to make sure he's legit. He checks out."

That was a relief—but it wasn't. Reggie had quickly become like a surrogate father to her, and she trusted him. But ignoring her curiosity about Master J would have been much easier if Reggie hadn't been able to vouch for him. If only she could have written him off as another crackpot who wanted to talk about sex on TV.

Morgan bit her lip . . . but her inquisitive nature won out. "What did everyone say about him?"

"A bunch. He's casual, not heavy into the lifestyle but fairly regular at a few clubs. Apparently, he has a way with women and a reputation to go with it. More than one person I talked to said that he could make Mother Teresa beg to be tied down and fucked. He definitely wants a woman submissive. Hey, you're not interested, are you?"

"What?" Morgan's heart skipped a handful of beats. "Me? No!" She scoffed. "Why would I want a bully who gets off on making a woman feel inferior?"

"You sure?" Reggie sounded skeptical.

"Do I seem like the type to get into this sort of stuff?" she countered.

Reggie said nothing. Distress coiled through Morgan.

A rattling of the lock at the front door had Morgan's head zooming in the other direction. She sighed with relief when her half brother Brandon shouldered his way inside.

"Gotta go," she told Reggie. "I'll call you after I've talked to this guy tomorrow."

"Hey, little sister," Brandon greeted as she hung up.

Shoving the conversation with Reggie out of her mind, she rose and stepped up on tiptoe to hug him. "Hi. Good day?"

His aristocratic mouth pursed into a frown. "Not exactly. I have to go to Iraq for the next three weeks."

Surprise, and if Morgan was honest, trepidation punched her in the stomach. "Iraq? I thought you sat behind a desk most of the time."

"Mostly, but there are exceptions."

"Oh, wow . . . Why Iraq?"

"Classified." He gave a bitter laugh. "You know the drill . . . I can't say where I'll be or what I'll be doing. I won't be near a phone or computer for most of the time. Morgan, I don't want to leave you. It's dangerous, and I know you're afraid."

She swallowed. Brandon had already done so much by taking her in, despite Daddy Dearest's ire, protecting her from the scum who stalked her. She was afraid, but she couldn't let Brandon feel guilty for doing his job.

"I'll be fine." She'd think of something—she had to. "I'm busy with work. It'll be fine."

"If anything happens, I think you should call Dad."

Morgan gaped at him, holding in a sarcastic scoff. "He may be your dad. He's my biological father—the one who's been denying I exist for the last twenty-five years."

Brandon sighed. "Morgan, you know how it is with politics, especially in the South. If people knew he'd had a fling with a barely legal volunteer while he had a wife and three little boys at home . . ."

"I know, it would ruin the senator from the great state of Texas."

"They're talking about a bid for the White House in 2012." Sympathy and regret tangled on his attractive face.

"Exactly why I can't call him. Not that he'd take my call, anyway."

"He would if you were in danger. Dad can protect you."

Morgan had her doubts but said nothing. "Too bad we can't just tell him I'm your fiancée. It's working with everyone else."

"Hmm. If our actual relationship ever came to light, we'd have to admit to incest or lying. Not fun choices."

"Let's hope it doesn't come to that. I don't think my sick stalker knows I've left L.A., so he has no idea where to find me."

Nodding, Brandon started to sift through the day's mail. When he came to a big manila envelope, he frowned. "Does anyone know you're here in Houston?"

Other than Master J, whom she'd met online all of fifteen minutes ago, Reggie, and a few close friends back home? "No."

Anxiety thundered across Brandon's face. "Someone here knows you. This was in the mailbox. No name, no postage. It was hand-delivered."

He held out the package to her, and Morgan took it with dread boiling in her stomach. She knew that handwriting.

Dear God, how had he found her here? And so quickly?

*No!*

Hands shaking, breath short, she opened the envelope and extracted the contents. As she did, red rose petals with moist centers and dead edges fluttered downward, skittering across the blond hardwood floor. They looked faintly like fat drops of blood splattered all around her.

Morgan gasped. *He* knew she was here. How had he found her?

Then her gaze fell to the photos. Pictures of her, one arriving at LAX the day she'd fled to Houston. The next of her in Brandon's backyard wearing thin sweatpants and a tank top, with nipples teased hard by a cool morning breeze. The last, a photo of her in her sage silk-and-lace shift with matching robe, kissing Brandon's cheek as they stood in the driveway before he left for work. Just this morning.

Fear biting at her belly, Morgan didn't protest when Brandon grabbed the photos from her numb fingers. He flipped through them with a snarled curse.

"These are from your stalker, aren't they? He's been here. Son of a bitch!" He raked a hand through his brown hair, ruffling the banker's cut. "I'm calling the police."

God, she wished it were that simple. "They can't do anything. The police in L.A. told me he was going to have to do something illegal before they could spend any energy finding him. Taking pictures isn't against the law."

"He's been on my property." Brandon held up the photo of her in the backyard of his rambling Houston home, his big fingers wrinkling the photo. "My backyard is private. The only way he could take this picture is by trespassing. There's a law broken."

He grabbed the nearest cordless phone and dialed 911. Morgan just shook her head.

While Brandon was right, she doubted the Houston police were going to be any more motivated to do something than the cops in L.A. Whoever this was hadn't stolen anything, vandalized anything. He hadn't hurt anyone—yet. Morgan could feel his anger building in the frequency of his contact, the fact that he'd followed her to Texas. And the police wouldn't care what her gut told her.

Brandon hung up the phone. "They'll be here soon."

Morgan just shrugged . . . and tried to calm the panic bubbling inside her.

With nothing to do but wait, she started to shove the pictures back in the envelope. When she encountered an obstruction, she realized something else lay inside. She stuck her hand between the layers of paper, perplexed. Usually the disturbed bastard only sent pictures—disconcerting, disturbingly private pictures, but nothing more.

Not today.

Out of the benign brownish envelope, she yanked a scrap of paper with a scrawl of ugly black writing.

*You belong to me. Only to me.*

Morgan swallowed a huge lump of fear. Now he was communicating with her. *To her.* Conveying his possessiveness, his fury that she might have another man in her life. This lunatic didn't know that Brandon was her half brother. He'd bought the cover story Brandon had concocted, as much to explain her presence at his house to others, as to warn off her overzealous psycho.

While the thought of being alone scared Morgan, part of her was glad Brandon had to leave tomorrow. If something happened to him, it wouldn't be because her stalker had decided to get the "competition" out of the way. In the three weeks Brandon would be gone, she'd figure something out, find somewhere else to go, so that when he returned, she didn't endanger the only one of Senator Ross's sons to give a rip about her.

Maybe, like Reggie suggested before she left L.A., she needed a bodyguard . . .

"You really have no idea who this creep is?" Brandon growled, staring over her shoulder at the note.

"None." She shook her head. "I wish I did. I have no disgruntled co-workers that I'm aware of. My ex-fiancé left me, not the other way around."

"Someone who's watched your show? A fan who doesn't know where to draw the line?"

Morgan shrugged. "Maybe. I've received odd fan mail before, but nothing this threatening or privacy-invading."

"I'm going to find someone to get to the bottom of this, kiddo. I'm not going to let anything happen to you," he vowed.

At times like this, Morgan wondered how she and Brandon were descended from the same loins as Senator Ross's other sons. They were nothing like the man and his other greedy, power-hungry offspring.

"Damn it," he cursed suddenly into the silence. "I wish like hell

I didn't have to go tomorrow. The car is picking me up at o-five hundred, and the timing couldn't be worse. Shit! Uncle Sam can be a demanding mistress."

Morgan didn't know exactly what Brandon did; he wasn't allowed to tell anyone. From things he'd said in the three years since he'd found the skeleton in their father's closet and tracked her down, she'd guessed he was in Intelligence. She had no idea who for.

"If you hate the job so much, and you want to run for office as badly as I know you do, why don't you just do it?"

For the first time she could remember, Brandon wouldn't meet her gaze. He turned away, fists clenching.

He unclenched them with obvious effort, then said, "I can't."

\* \* \*

THE following day, Morgan dropped down into a wrought-iron chair at a little sidewalk café in a quaint cluster of unique shops. The February afternoon hung thick, lazy, and surprisingly sultry all around. Fighting off exhaustion after a nearly sleepless night, she glanced at her watch. Three o'clock. She'd made good time on her drive from Houston. Master J should be here very soon.

Her stomach tightened at the thought.

That wasn't the only reason, though. She also felt eyes on her, watching, assessing, probing. The hairs on the back of her neck stood up. She looked around, scanned the crowd. Nothing.

Morgan took a deep breath, trying to quell her uneasiness. It wasn't hard to imagine that if a psycho would follow her from Los Angeles to Houston, he'd go the extra mile to trail her to Lafayette. She was probably safe sitting here in the middle of a sunny public square, but if he recognized her, he'd see her with Master J and make assumptions that would make him even angrier than the appearance that she was marrying Brandon. Then when night fell, and she was alone in Brandon's house . . .

No, she couldn't think that now. She would have to keep this all business, so that if her stalker identified her and watched this meeting, he wouldn't assume there was anything sexual between her and Master J.

She adjusted the scarf and hat to make sure they completely covered her hair and pushed the sunglasses up on her face. Maybe she was being paranoid. No one should be able to recognize her like this. Maybe after this interview, she would slip away to that cozy European-looking bed and breakfast she'd seen on her way into town and catch up on sleep so she could figure out how to shake this stalker.

A waiter came by with a wide smile, white teeth stark against his ebony skin. Morgan did her best to smile back as she ordered iced tea.

Once he'd gone, she tugged the boxy, lightweight coat she'd dragged out of Brandon's closet down over her hips and flipped up the collar. The waiter arrived with her tea. She checked her watch again. Five after three. She'd give Master J another few minutes. Sitting here in the open, vulnerable to the sick man who'd been following her . . . suddenly it struck her as very unwise.

"You must be Morgan."

The deep whisper came from behind her, delivered right in her ear. His warm breath cascaded down the side of her neck, and she gave an involuntary shiver.

She started, turned, stunned anyone had been able to sneak up on her, as jumpy as she was. But he'd been utterly silent.

And he was breathtakingly gorgeous.

Thick, dark hair teased his broad forehead. An angular jaw and cleft chin dusted with a five o'clock shadow shouted his masculinity with all the subtlety of a sonic boom. His wide mouth curled up with an expression that looked half smile, half challenge. But, oh, his eyes. They captured her. Accented by a sweep of black brows, those knowing eyes of his watched her, as if he could see deep inside her. As if he knew all her secrets.

Allowing her gaze to wander south didn't help tame her pulse, either. Master J stood about six feet tall, with broad shoulders and a body of well-honed muscle evident under a tight black T-shirt that made her think of a mountain with its solid, quiet permanence. No one could move a mountain. No one was going to move this man either, unless he wanted to be moved.

Just staring at him jolted her with attraction and a healthy dose of lust. Thank goodness their time alone would be limited to this one meeting in public. Otherwise, Morgan didn't think she could be responsible for her behavior.

She swallowed, trying to find her voice. "Yes, I'm Morgan."

When she stuck out her hand, he didn't just shake it. Too simple. Tangling his gaze with hers, he bent and brought her hand to his mouth, placing a kiss on her fingers.

*Oh, dear God . . .* Fire raced up her arm, turning her heartbeat into a staccato chug. He lingered, a hot breath caressing the back of her hand, his fingertips teasing the sensitive center of her palm. Tingles burst across her skin, up her arm.

His effect on her didn't end there. Instead, the impact of his presence, his touch, dove deep inside her, where an ache began to pulse gently between her legs. As if her clit needed to announce the fact that her libido wanted to get naked with this man.

*Business, business!* The demand chased itself in her head.

With a discreet tug, Morgan pulled her hand free. Master J smiled as he sat beside her—rather than across—and scooted his chair a few inches closer. She tried to ignore her awareness of his thigh brushing hers, the tingling under her skin.

"Thank you for meeting me here, Mr . . . what would you like me to call you, since I don't know your name?"

That grin seemed to taunt her with her own uncertainty and his wicked knowledge of their forthcoming sexual discussion. "For now, just call me sir."

"Okay. Yes, sir."

The moment the words were out of her mouth, Morgan realized how sexual they sounded. How sexual he'd intended they sound. Not just deferential, though they were that, too. But around Master J, she just couldn't seem to muster enough air to power her voice beyond a husky murmur.

*What would it be like to call him sir in private?*

Despite the dark sunglasses shielding her, his dark eyes seemed to dance with the knowledge of her every thought, every sinful feeling, as he held her gaze, as if he could read the desire all over her face.

Morgan used the untouched tea in front of her as an excuse to look away and scoured her brain for a safe, neutral topic.

Hard to do that when she'd invited him here to talk about sex.

"So, according to the bio I received about you, you're in the personal security business. A bodyguard?"

"Exactly." He shrugged those deliciously massive shoulders. "I guard a lot of politicians and their families, diplomats, an occasional athlete."

"You meet a lot of interesting people, I'm sure. Do you work with celebrities?" she asked.

A hint of humor curved his wide mouth to something nearing a smile. "Too flaky. Politicians are liars, but at least you know what to expect. You Hollywood types are either paranoid, self-absorbed, or as psycho as the people stalking you. No thanks."

Morgan couldn't decide if she was annoyed or amused. "I'm none of the above."

"Give it time." He winked.

Incorrigible described him perfectly. A hint of arrogance laced with a healthy dose of sex appeal and teasing humor. The mixture went down real smooth, thanks to his flirtation skills and a hint of Southern charm. No doubt, he was lethal to a woman's common sense. Morgan swallowed.

The waiter came by, and Master J ordered a cup of thick Louisiana chicory coffee. She shuddered when the waiter brought it to their table moments later.

"Tell me more about your show." His words should have been an invitation, but Morgan heard the subtle command in them. Not harsh, not driving. But his voice held a note of steel—one that made her stomach tighten . . . and her womb clench.

"*Turn Me On* combines interviews and facts to explore various facets of sexual life for both established couples and the newly dating, from the vanilla to the way out there. Last season, I did a show one week about sex etiquette on a first date, another about 'friends with benefits,' then followed it up with couples who had tattoo fantasies. This will be my second season, and I was thrilled to be renewed. Since the network provides cable programming geared toward women and couples, I think it's a perfect fit."

"Hmm. Tell me about this season's shows."

Again, another subtle command. "Well, we're still at the ideas stage, but we're definitely pursuing shows about boudoir photography, couples massage, erotic finger painting and—"

"And Dominance and submission."

Morgan swallowed. She'd been caught up in her enthusiasm for the show and almost forgotten they were going to discuss that topic. The topic that fueled her shameful late-night fantasies.

"Yes."

He quirked a dark brow at her expectantly, somehow managing to look sharp, displeased, and nonthreatening all at once.

Puzzled, Morgan stared. What did he want?

"Yes, sir," she ventured.

His smile dazzled, rewarded. "Very nice."

"I thought such forms of address were reserved for one's . . ."

"Submissive? Frequently, but you contacted me for a quick lesson or two. I thought it best to start with a hint of the dynamic and see how you do with it." He leaned forward, an elbow braced on the table. His gaze poured directly into her, molten and unrelenting. "Do you understand what it means to submit to a man? Completely surrender?"

Morgan tried to suck in a breath, stunned to find it ragged beyond her control. His eyes flared hot with approval.

"Th-this isn't about me," she argued breathlessly. "I just need to relate the concept to the—"

"How can you relate without a taste of it, *cher*? A little nibble ain't gonna hurt you." The smile he flashed her could only be termed pure sin. "You might even like it."

That's exactly what Morgan was afraid of.

She did her best to send him an expression that was all business. "It doesn't matter if I like it. After all, I managed to finish taping the show about couples' tattoo fantasies successfully without ever getting a tattoo myself. It's all about understanding why it's important to them."

"Paying someone to imprint a design on your skin while your significant other watches is a lot less personal than being blindfolded, naked, and bound for your master's pleasure."

With a gulp, Morgan realized he was right. Worse, that nibble he offered was starting to sound like a feast to her neglected sex drive.

No. This time around, Adam was offering the apple of temptation to Eve, and she was smart enough to know better. If she seemed interested, it was because he filled her head with suggestion. He was hard to ignore. She wasn't depraved, wasn't the kind of woman to get off on letting a bully chain her down and tell her what to do. The idea was just novel. She had a purely intellectual curiosity in the concept. Okay, mostly intellectual. That didn't mean she should indulge.

Even if Master J looked like the kind of man who could have invented the concept of pleasure.

"What are you afraid of?" he asked.

*Myself.*

She looked away from his intent gaze. "It's just not my thing."

That displeased brow snapped up again. His glare filled with impatient demand.

"Sir," she added, almost against her will.

His expression softened. "In the few minutes I've been sitting here, your skin has flushed, the heartbeat pulsing at your neck has accelerated, and your nipples have hardened. I know the scent of arousal. I can smell yours. I'm going to ask you again; what are you afraid of?"

Shock punched her gut. *Oh, my* . . . She'd been as easy to read as a book. Easier, even. Morgan closed her eyes, drew in a breath. Then another. Her mind raced.

"Don't think too hard," he cautioned. "Lying invokes punishment."

"Punishment? You have no right!" she returned in a heated whisper.

He stared for a long moment. "I told you yesterday online that a relationship of this sort requires a great deal of trust. I trusted that you were who you said you were. In order to earn a little of your trust, I allowed your production assistant access to some very personal information about me. That's right. No need to look surprised. I knew the minute he started calling around about me. If I hadn't advised my clubs in advance that they could give your guy information, no one would have even said good morning to Reggie, much less confirmed the details of my sex life."

He shifted in his seat, brushing his thigh against hers again, and then lifted her chin with his finger. Morgan melted—a combination of shock and arousal, topped with the delicious thrill of Master J's overwhelming sex appeal.

"Trust," he murmured. "I placed some in you. If we're going to work together, you need to have a bit in me. I'm not going to ravish you or force you or any other melodramatic scenario running through your head. If I'm going to help you understand the psychology of Dominance and submission, you have to have enough trust to be honest with me. And with yourself. Do you understand what I'm saying?"

"Y-yes, sir."

"Excellent. Now, for the last time, why are you afraid of the idea of submitting?"

A loaded question, one she didn't know how to answer. Rejection. Being ridiculed again. Shame. Fear of pain and degradation. A stronger fear that she'd love being mastered by someone like him and be unable to deal with the shame and guilt.

She couldn't admit that—not any of it. She might as well hand him her soul on a silver platter.

"Please," she whispered. "Please . . ."

Master J's jaw tightened, his eyes narrowed. For some crazy reason, she hated letting him down. She owed him nothing, damn it. Nothing at all. He was an interview subject, and he'd be compensated for his time and information. Period.

Fighting the dueling impulses of resisting until hell froze over and giving in, it took Morgan a few moments to realize that their waiter had returned to refill Master J's coffee. Then the young guy looked at her with a confounded sort of smile.

"Some dude paid me twenty bucks to give this to you."

He handed her a regular mailing envelope—with very familiar hand-writing.

The waiter departed.

Her heart started pounding. The speed of light had nothing on her as she opened the envelope to find a handful of red rose petals with soft centers and dead edges. They spilled through her fingers, and she gasped, feeling all blood drain from her face.

"No . . ." She looked around the sunny square with panic. "No!"

"Morgan?" Master J questioned, voice laced with concern.

She looked at him with wild eyes. "He's here. *Here.* Followed me. Oh, my . . . I have to go." She sucked in a scared breath and clenched trembling fists. "Hide. Now!"

Master J grabbed her by the shoulders. "Who is here and where are you going?"

Shrugging free of his touch, she looked around frantically for any face that might be dangerous or familiar. Most other chairs in the square sat empty, as did a few nearby windows and balconies. Shadowed storefronts held any number of people, but they all looked like natives. The little coffeehouse's other patrons either took little notice of her or cared even less. Like every other time her stalker had approached, he'd been as silent as smoke, as invisible as air. Panic ate at her gut.

"I can't stay. I'm sorry . . ."

He grabbed her again, looking determined to shake answers out of her. Instead, he froze, his gaze zeroed in on something across the street.

Morgan felt the energy burst through his body a second before he pushed her to the ground. "Down!"

He shoved her under a table and covered her body with his an instant before a gunshot erupted above her head.

# Chapter Two

JACK Cole curled his body protectively over Morgan's tiny female form and used the small iron table to shield her as another shot rang out. People around them screamed and scrambled away in the melee. He swore as she trembled violently beneath him.

Damn it! Revenge was *so* close, and now this? He couldn't fuck his enemy's woman until she screamed *his* name if she was dead.

Fury rattled through him, but the fact that someone was trying to thwart his revenge wasn't the only reason. Nope, he was downright pissed that some asshole had filled such a small but vibrant woman with complete terror.

Admittedly, he'd lured Morgan here to use her but never to physically hurt her. Just the opposite. He would find out what made her tick and fulfill every one of her fantasies until her body hummed with satisfaction.

Until she no longer had any interest in Brandon Ross and left the son of a bitch.

The jackoff currently at the other end of the gun, however, had other ideas, like planting a bullet between her eyes.

Another shudder went through Morgan. She held in a cry. Jack hugged her tighter, shoving her right against the iron table. Saving her was instinct. An occupational hazard. A necessity. Brandon Ross had earned this revenge three years ago, and Jack planned to deliver him humiliation in spades. He wasn't about to let Morgan die.

"I'll get you out of here safely." He whispered the vow in her ear.

His churning gut demanded he draw his .38 and return fire. But there were too many people around to take that risk. And he sensed it would scare the hell out of Morgan.

She was already terrified, damn it. She smiled pretty for the camera for a living, she didn't dodge bullets.

When the waiter had delivered the letter to their table and he'd seen the sweet flush drain from her face, leaving behind chalk-white shock as half-dead rose petals spilled into her hands, he'd smelled her fear. After catching a glint of gunmetal in the sunlight on a roof across the street . . . Jack'd had no doubt what would happen next.

He hated to be right about shit like this.

Glancing at the chair Morgan had occupied moments ago, he saw the discolored gouges left by unforgiving bullets. He swore again.

Beneath him, Morgan tried to sit up. Jack held her in place.

"Stay down!"

"I need to go. Run. H-hide."

A quick glance over the table at the rooftop across the street showed their shooter had fled. Either that or had come in for a closer shot during the chaos. That meant they were easy targets and he had to get Morgan out of this open area fast.

"*I'll* get you to safety," Jack emphasized, dragging Morgan to her feet. "Are you hurt?"

She shoved the hat back over her head and tightened the scarf beneath, which covered her hair. "No."

"Then let's run!"

He grabbed her small, cold hand in his. Engulfed it. Damn, she was tiny, much smaller than a powerful name like Morgan implied.

Taking off as fast as his legs would carry him, Jack tugged Morgan behind him, ducking behind upturned tables when the shots rang out again. He dragged her behind the cover of the café's coffee bar, then pulled her around the corner of the building, silently urging her to keep up. She did, clutching her hat against her head with her spare hand. Jack looked beyond Morgan with a frown. No way to tell if the shooter was following in this crowd, but he assumed so. Better safe than dead.

"Where are we going?"

Jack didn't answer; he was too busy improvising a plan in his head. In silence, he pulled her up streets, down alleys. More gunshots rang out. A bullet whizzed past his ear, and he swore. If this son of a bitch harmed a hair on Morgan's head, Jack was going to enjoy beating him senseless with his bare hands.

Ducking into a busy store, they narrowly avoided crashing into an elderly woman. Stepping aside so the scowling grandma and her walker could pass cost them precious seconds.

As soon as the path cleared, he took Morgan's small hand in his again and tugged, forcing her to run again. Out the back of the store, down a narrow walkway, into a darkening alley. Thank God he knew this town as well as the shape of his own face.

Another series of staccato blasts sounded again, this time in front of the store they'd just exited.

*Shit!*

"Run faster, *cher.*"

Panting, sweating, she merely nodded. And picked up the pace.

At the far end of an alley, they came to a metal door with scarred black paint and red lettering that read SEXY SIRENS. Even with the door closed, it vibrated with the pounding of raucous music and the rowdy crowd inside—despite the fact that it was barely three in the afternoon.

From experience, Jack knew the door would be locked. Raising a fist, he hammered on it with all his might, not caring if he left a dent. While he waited, he looked over both shoulders to see if they were being followed.

A blast of gunfire erupted, kicking out chunks of brick not six inches from Morgan's side.

With a quick scan of the alley, he cursed. It was rife with trash bins and overgrown with crawling vines, providing plenty of places for her shooter to hide.

"Son of a bitch!" He banged on the beat-up metal surface again. "Someone answer the damn door."

Finally, a familiar bleached blonde wrenched the door open. "Jesus, Jack. What the hell is wrong?"

He pushed Morgan inside, then followed her into the backroom cluttered with empty beer cans. "Shooter out there. I need your help."

A child's stick pony and a riding crop lay next to the stage entrance. Angelique had apparently just performed.

He slammed the door behind him and again scanned the darkened room, illuminated by a single red bulb and decorated with peeling black paint. One thin door separated this area from the main stage and the throbbing music in the club beyond.

"A shooter? Holy . . . Who have you pissed off now?"

"Alyssa, this is Morgan," he shouted over the music. "She's the hostess of a cable TV show—"

"You're Morgan O'Malley! I love *Turn Me On!*"

Morgan, who had doffed her sunglasses, extended her hand to Alyssa. Hmm. Blue eyes rimmed in red, a smattering of freckles, very fair skin—not Brandon's usual type. But times changed, he supposed.

Jack drawled, "Then I'm assuming you'd like to help me keep her alive long enough to do more shows. The shooter was aiming at her." Jack turned to the other woman. "Morgan, this is Alyssa Devereaux, owner of Sexy Sirens. The most famous—or infamous—gentleman's club in southern Louisiana, depending on your point of view."

Brandon's little woman flashed a weak smile, trying her damndest not to stare at Alyssa's inch-thick makeup, near-indecent skirt, and fuck-me boots. There was nothing subtle about Alyssa. She still dressed like a stripper, though she hadn't danced around a pole in years. She sucked a cock like a woman trying to ingest the brass off a doorknob. She had worse language than he did. But she also had a big, big heart.

Alyssa would use her wicked tongue to take the skin off his balls if she had any idea that Morgan wasn't a client but the means to achieve revenge. She might run an establishment where women took their clothes off for horny men, but she made sure *no one* crossed the line with any girl under her roof. Jack planned on crossing every line he could think of.

"Why would someone shoot at you?" Alyssa asked Morgan with a frown.

"That is a very good question," Jack answered, piercing Morgan with an unrelenting gaze, one he hoped like hell would persuade her to tell him the truth. He hadn't had the chance yet to establish more than the barest amount of authority. She had little reason to trust him. Damn it, another few hours, and he would have spent time in her bed, deep in her body, establishing his dominance. He would have had some assurance that she would accept his help. As it was now . . . he had nothing.

Not at all the way he'd planned his revenge.

"Jack?" she said his name experimentally, voice erratic, still shaking.

He wasn't pleased to hear the edge of fear and wariness in her voice. He much preferred a sultry "sir" coming from that pillowy mouth while she pretended indifference.

But they'd get back to that, just as soon as he got to the bottom of this shit.

"Morgan, tell me what's going on, *cher*."

Her skin still had all the color of a corpse, especially framed by the dark coat and the floppy hat, which was too large for her small body. She was terrified out of her mind, but still managed to nod. Jack breathed a sigh of relief.

"A-about three months ago, someone started sending me mail. Pictures of me in different places, mostly public. Weird, but not threatening. About five weeks ago, he started taking pictures of me in and around my house, through windows. O-one he took of me pulling out of my driveway while he was in my garage. I can tell he's angry. I don't know why.

"I came to Houston to be with a . . . friend and to escape him." She blew out a breath, forged ahead. "He followed me. I didn't know it until yesterday when this arrived."

She unzipped her boxy coat just enough to fish out a folded-over envelope from the oversized purse bisecting her chest. Morgan handed it to him with a shaking hand.

Tension gripping his gut, Jack ripped it open. Pictures spilled out. Morgan in an airport, dressed in low-rise jeans, a baggy T-shirt, and her hair shoved into a baseball cap. He only recognized her profile, her stubborn chin, the freckles across her nose that made him wonder how far they extended down her body. They gave him an insane urge to play connect the dots.

The next one was of her reading a magazine on a patio chair. The magazine covered her face. He saw only her hands, the cover of *People*, a splattering of delicate freckles on her arms—and sweet, unbound breasts with ripe cherry nipples that made his mouth water, nearly visible through a thin white tank top.

From the instant he'd heard whispers that she was his former pal Brandon's fiancée, he'd been intrigued. Talking to her online had only heightened his interest. Morgan in these pictures, in the flesh, engorged his cock. He couldn't wait to get her bound to his bed and begging to come—granting his revenge.

But there was something else about her . . . something pounded him with familiarity. He felt as if he should know her, like he'd seen her before and not just her picture on her show's Web site. Had he ever met her? No, he would have remembered a woman like Morgan. Still, there was something about her. He'd figure it out.

Swallowing a lump of rising lust, Jack flipped to the last picture and froze. The always-elegant Brandon Ross in a designer suit. He had his back to the camera as he leaned down to kiss Morgan. Jack could see only her half-bare legs covered by a bit of green silk and black lace, and the lightly freckled arms she curled around the Brandon's neck. The sight made his gut roll.

And the haphazard scrawl of the note at the bottom of the envelope, with its ominous, possessive tone, did nothing to ease his tension.

The last picture, the wife-to-be saying good-bye to her man before he left for a day at the office, also confirmed that Morgan O'Malley was Brandon Ross's woman. She was the means to pay his old buddy back for his stab in the back. He had to get Morgan out of here alive and undetected to do it.

"So this stalker followed you here from L.A.?" he asked.

"Yes." Her voice still shook.

Jack sighed. "Dedicated and sick. Not a good combination. Clearly, he's smart if he's able to take pictures of you without you knowing it or his identity. He knows his way around a gun. I don't think you can just walk out of here on your own unharmed, Morgan. You need help. I can give it to you."

She hesitated, then spoke in a surprisingly smoky voice. "You've gotten me out of the path of bullets that would have likely killed me. I can't ask you to risk—"

"You didn't ask; I'm offering." The asshole clearly knew his way to Brandon's house, and Morgan didn't look like the kind of girl with training in weapons and hand-to-hand combat. It was up to him to keep her alive. "Morgan, I'm a bodyguard. I won't watch you die when I can get you out of here in one piece."

"How much?"

Jesus, someone had been shooting at her and she wanted to barter? "On the house."

Surprise widened her mouth. "Why?"

He sent her a cool shrug. "If you're dead, there go my fifteen minutes of fame."

She lifted her red-rimmed blue eyes to him and shot him a cynical glare. "Seriously. It's clear you're not a fame monger."

So she had better sense than to fall for his line. But Jack still wanted to make her look at him with those innocent blue eyes while he force-fed her some logic. She couldn't be sane and deny that she needed help. But he understood why she'd try.

He was a relative stranger—but that wasn't her only hesitation. He'd bet every dime in his pocket on that. From their brief face time before the shooter arrived, he realized Morgan had some interest in him. And that she had curiosity about his sexual leanings. More curiosity than someone merely researching a TV show. Her reluctant arousal drew him like nothing had in years.

"That still doesn't change the fact you need me. The shooter knows you're in this building. You can't just walk out now. I can get you out of here."

Morgan set her jaw. Jack watched her fighting the urge to bite off a refusal. She didn't, proving once again that she was smart.

"How?"

"You'll dress as Alyssa. She'll fix you up with appropriately inappropriate clothes."

"She'll need help with makeup, too," Alyssa pointed out. "I don't have freckles, Jack."

A quick glance at Morgan proved she had a mere hint of cosmetics on her pale face. "Yeah, okay. Do it."

"No. This plan won't work," Morgan protested.

"You got a better idea, one that doesn't end with you in a pine box?"

Waiting for her to process the truth he couldn't afford to soften for her, Jack watched Morgan. Up close, he could see well-proportioned features, a full mouth, a nearly poreless complexion that was too fair to be caused by anything but fear, arched brows in some indiscernible color in this dim light. Without Dracula's complexion, the crappy hat and scarf, or the three-times-too-big coat, he suspected that, as an all-around package, she'd be gorgeous. Senator Ross's son wouldn't settle for less.

She sighed. "I don't have any other ideas."

"That's my point. Alyssa, take Morgan upstairs and put her in something scanty. You got any more of those wigs?"

"Yep." The bleached blonde nodded.

Morgan glared. "It still won't work."

"Because . . . ?"

"Alyssa and I, we're not the same . . . size."

Jack scanned the two of them. "She's taller. But you can wear her stiletto boots to give you some added height. What size shoe do you wear?"

She looked startled by the question. "Six and a half."

Jack sent Alyssa a questioning look.

"Hell, no," said the former stripper. "I wear an eight."

"We'll work around it," Jack said. "We'll shove toilet paper in the toes of the boots or something. It's temporary."

"That's not the biggest problem." Morgan's gaze drifted over Alyssa's surgically enhanced attributes, currently struggling to stay within the confines of a bikini top.

Jack let his gaze cascade over Morgan's small form again. He couldn't see much of her beneath the coat, but the pictures he'd seen told him that what she had under there was 100 percent natural and not on par with Alyssa's silicone D cups.

"Alyssa has a knack for picking out clothes that make any woman look bodacious enough to be a centerfold."

"Then what?" Morgan fidgeted nervously, her gaze darting to the door, as if expecting her unwanted admirer to burst through it at any second.

"We'll need to slip past this bastard and get you to safety."

"And then?"

"We'll cross that bridge once we've made our way out of here, okay? I'll get you to someplace safe until this mess can be sorted out."

Morgan bit one bee-stung lip, eyes anxious and wary. She wanted to agree but didn't trust him completely. Jack could see that on her face. Still, she hesitated, meeting his gaze squarely, as if taking his measure. Jack wondered how much, if any, Morgan knew about the past. Had Brandon ever mentioned him?

"This son of a bitch has been tenacious until now, I'm sure, but he's never dealt with me. I'm not going to let him come within a hundred yards of you, Morgan."

She hesitated an instant longer, then sent him a shaky nod. "You're the professional. We'll deal with what's next once we're away from here."

What was next would involve her naked and cuffed and open to the complete pleasure he was impatient to give her. Repressing a smile, he affixed his gaze to the puffed pout of her lower lip. Something about her, even in her awful getup, made the man in him take notice. Or was it the knowledge that she belonged to Brandon?

No, it was more. Under that ugly hat, scarf, and coat, he could tell Morgan was one damn pretty woman—somehow innocent and fresh, but also sexy, sassy, expressive. Corrupting her would be a treat. His desire chugged up another notch.

Who knew revenge would be so satisfying in every way?

\*   \*   \*

SURROUNDED by music pulsing so loudly that the walls shook, Morgan made her way up the club's narrow stairs, following Alyssa, the blonde who apparently owned Sexy Sirens. Morgan had no idea how anyone with decent vision would ever mistake her for the stripper, no matter how much makeup she slathered on. Alyssa had an ingrained sexuality that just about every woman wished for . . . and so few possessed.

Still, Morgan knew she had to try, put on her best act until she could escape Lafayette and the psycho hunting her. The only alternative was death.

Like it or not, that made Master J—whose real name was apparently Jack and a relative stranger—her only hope for salvation.

With a few glances and fewer words, Jack had made it clear he was no saint. Even now, she felt his gaze burn her back. Against her will, she peered over her shoulder. Jack stared up with an intent gaze, eyes looking nearly black, as he watched her ascend the stairs. A speculative smile creased the chiseled features of his strong-jawed face.

She knew absolutely nothing about the man, except that he had the kind of looks that made women do double takes and drool. Oh, and that he liked to dominate in bed. Hard to forget that. But his smile made her nervous. Why would anyone look happy in the aftermath of a shooting?

Finally, she and Alyssa reached the top of the landing. The blonde led her through the door at the end of the hall, into a small but surprisingly luxurious suite.

Alyssa shut the door behind them, blocking out the loudest of the music's throb. The floor beneath them still shook. The sexy tempo resonated around her, stark in its suggestion.

Morgan looked around the room. A large, rumpled bed lazed in the center, as a standing lamp cast muted golden light over the white sheets. Hardwood floors gleamed cherry beneath her feet. Soft beige walls accented flowing white sheers at the large window. Four black-and-white landscape photographs formed a grouping above the bed.

"You were expecting a red bedroom with a stripper pole in the middle?" Alyssa asked with a cocked brow.

Embarrassment stung Morgan. She had wondered . . . "I had no idea what to expect. This is lovely."

Some of the starch bled out of Alyssa. "It's peaceful. C'mon, let's get you out of that ugly rag."

Before she could ask for privacy and a bathrobe, Alyssa was unbuttoning Morgan's coat and prying it off her shoulders.

With a casual toss to the bed, the coat flew away. Like the mom of a toddler, Alyssa reached next for Morgan's purse and subdued floral-print T-shirt. Before she could sputter a protest, the stripper had them over her head and tossed them on the floor.

"If you'll point me to a bathroom, I can undress—"

Alyssa ignored her and plucked at the front clasp of her lacy white bra. With a drag and a tug, it was gone . . . and Morgan stood nude from the waist up before a total stranger.

Alyssa studied Morgan's breasts, lifting one in her hand to test its weight. "We can work with these."

Morgan tensed, resisting the urge to cover herself like a self-conscious seventh grader in a locker room. "What are you doing?"

"You don't have anything I ain't seen, honey. 34C." Another glance over the rest of her body, and Alyssa added, "You wear a size six. Right?"

"How did you know?"

She smiled. "It's my business. Strip out of everything else and hang tight."

Alyssa disappeared out the door, shutting it gently behind her. Morgan stared after her. Strip out of everything else? Like it was easy. Like she took her clothes off every day in front of people she'd never met. Well, Alyssa probably did, so it probably didn't faze her in the least. And Morgan realized that if she wanted to get out of here without a bullet in the head, she'd better get over her modesty quickly.

With a sigh, she took off her jeans and white cotton panties, folding them neatly and setting them on the edge of the bed. She looked around for a robe or spare blanket. A towel—anything to cover herself. Nothing. Morgan was not accustomed to prancing around without a stitch on. Clearly, that didn't trouble Alyssa.

The blonde returned with a black satin bra and a matching thong. With her teeth, she ripped the tags off, slipped a pair of gel inserts into the bra, and handed it all to Morgan.

Before Morgan could ask for privacy, Alyssa disappeared again, this time into the suite's adjoining bathroom. Grateful for the reprieve from the

woman's keen gaze, Morgan wriggled into the thong. Not comfortable—
who wanted a string up her ass?—but a perfect fit.

Alyssa emerged from the bathroom, carrying some very brief garments and her black high-heeled boots. In the doorway, the blonde
paused, waiting. Morgan pretended not to notice her. Instead, she frowned
at the gel inserts in the bra. The grown-up version of wadded-up tissues?

When Morgan winced, Alyssa laughed. "You gotta do what you gotta
do. They're like an instant boob job. With clothes on, no one will know
the difference."

Releasing the breath she'd been holding, Morgan realized that was
likely true. She had no business bemoaning the fact she wasn't a D cup.

Morgan began to don the bra, acutely aware of Alyssa watching her
every move. It was damn uncomfortable. She'd kill to have Alyssa's easy
attitude about nudity, but she just hadn't been raised that way. She had
been nearly twenty-one before she'd worked up the nerve to masturbate.
After all, with a born-again mother who'd sent her to an all-girls school,
she'd heard little about sex before turning eighteen. Until she'd gone to
college, Morgan hadn't really known the difference between her cuticles
and her clit.

Pushing away the thought, Morgan fastened the bra and lifted her
breasts into the cups—what there was of them. The bra was slung low on
wire-thin straps. A slash of black lace barely covered each of her nipples.
The gel inserts pushed the top swells of her breasts up and out on display.
Instant cleavage.

Alyssa whistled and shot her a saucy look. "I'll give you a piece of advice: Don't show Jack your tits unless you want to drive him insane with
lust."

The blonde turned away, heading back into the bathroom. Morgan
stared at the woman's slender back and silky blonde strands clinging to
her shoulders.

Centerfolds were less attractive than Alyssa. Though probably over
thirty, she was still very striking. Morgan knew for a fact, based on Reggie's
extensive research, that Jack wasn't gay. Given those facts, it seemed logical
that he and Alyssa were . . . involved. From the woman's offhanded comment, it sounded like Alyssa didn't care if she enticed Jack.

Lord, she'd left Los Angeles, where she'd always thought of life as being somewhat surreal, and landed in Cajun country, a place she began to suspect was the South's version of Oz.

"I don't plan to show Jack my breasts," she said, adjusting the bra, wishing for more cover.

"Maybe not, but ten bucks says he plans to see them."

Morgan frowned. "Based on what? I was interviewing Jack for my show. And then, when the shooting started, he offered to protect me—"

"And he will. He's the best. But Jack Cole is a breast man, and you've got a great rack."

As if she'd just announced something as mundane as night falling, Alyssa turned and lifted a makeup case off the counter. Setting the case aside, she studied Morgan's face with nothing more than a mild case of impatience.

"That doesn't bother you?" Morgan couldn't resist asking.

Her gaze strayed to the bedding, looking too rumpled to be caused by mere sleep. Morgan wondered if Jack had been here before meeting her—and why the thought bothered her.

"That Jack might fuck you?" She shrugged. "He's not mine."

Morgan frowned. *Too weird.* "Nothing's going to happen between us. I have no intention of getting involved with Jack."

"The road to hell is paved with good intentions," Alyssa shot back with a throaty laugh.

Before Morgan could wade through her confusion and reply, the blonde switched topics again. "Let's get your makeup on."

Alyssa lifted a slender hand and took the straw hat and scarf from Morgan's head.

A moment later, she began her cosmetics frenzy. A thick foundation coated Morgan's face. Concealer came next, and Morgan hoped it would cover the worst of the damage wrought from missing so much sleep. Next came the bright rosy blush, the siren-red lipstick painted on thickly with a brush. Dark eyeliner and eye shadow were applied in a quick blur. Black mascara followed, lifting and separating her lashes. An eyebrow pencil and brown mascara hid the fact that her brows were not the same pale brown as the other woman's.

When Alyssa stepped away and prodded her into the bathroom before the mirror, Morgan only recognized her blue eyes and the basic oval of her face.

"You look great. Hell, most everyone out there will probably be too drunk to notice whether you're me or not. But just in case they're not, the clothes I've picked out will ensure no man's gaze gets above your tits."

Morgan wanted to protest—the words lay on the tip of her tongue. She stilled them. If dressing like a stripper kept her alive, well . . . she could survive embarrassment much better than a bullet to the head.

"Whatever works," Morgan breathed.

"Let's get this hair pinned up and the wig on."

"I can manage." Morgan lifted her fingers to her head and rubbed.

"Wigs can be such a bitch. Sorry you'll have to wear one, but to pass for me, you have to look blonde."

Morgan shrugged. The discomfort was a small price to pay to stay safe.

"And make sure it's on good. Jack will want to inspect you before you leave. He won't let you set foot outside until he's convinced you can pass the test. He takes protecting clients seriously."

The idea of Jack inspecting her made her stomach jump. Jack was gorgeous, and the fact he was a dominant man only intrigued Morgan more, despite her wariness and fear.

Securing the long blonde wig in place, Morgan pushed the thought away. She was just tired. Lord knew she was stressed. She would not be having sex with Jack, so his sexual preferences made absolutely no difference to her.

Someone pounded on the door. Morgan started, her heart racing. Had the shooter managed to follow her here? She cut her gaze to the window, hoping it might prove to be an escape route.

Then the door opened. Jack entered, wearing a ratty T-shirt and faded jeans, a backward baseball cap, and a false moustache. Those few external changes made him look considerably different. But she still couldn't miss his pissed-off expression.

"Damn it, what are you two doing in here, having a slumber party?"

"Bite me, Jack. I worked as fast as I could since I need to get back to business," Alyssa said with a smile, then kissed his cheek. "And good luck to you," she threw back to Morgan.

Then she exited, leaving Morgan alone with Jack.

His gaze flew across the room and latched onto her. Black eyes scorched her, and a slow, sinful smile spread across his mouth. That look made her stomach clench. Quickly realizing she wore nothing but a revealing bra and thong, she glanced around for something—anything—to cover herself.

She darted across the room and reached for the white satin sheet draped over the bed. Jack ripped it out of her hand.

"No time for modesty, *cher,*" he whispered in her ear, his voice inflected with a lilt that was decidedly Cajun French.

His body buffeted her backside, legs glancing hers, chest brushing her shoulders. The heat he gave off warmed skin she hadn't realized was chilled. Despite his heat, goose bumps multiplied their way across her skin and a shiver ran down her spine. Her nipples made a sudden, unwelcome appearance.

She swallowed. He might be one of the good guys, but at the moment, his posture was pure predator.

"I don't need you in here while I get dressed."

"*Mais* yeah, too bad for you I plan to supervise. We aren't leaving here until I'm convinced you can pass for Alyssa."

"I've been putting on my own clothes since I was three. I think I can manage alone."

"True, but I use Alyssa as cover for cases. We walk around pretending we're drunk on hurricanes and sex. People are used to seeing me touch her. Often. But you . . ." He snaked a hand around her and laid a palm flat on her belly.

She jerked and gasped when his broad hand blanketed her bare midriff, his heat seeping under her skin, insidious, unstoppable.

"You," he murmured in her ear, "jump when I touch you. You do that in public, and people will know you're not Alyssa."

With every word, Jack made her more aware that he was male—all male—and she was female. He had the kind of personal power that drew her. Her stomach flipped when he spoke. Her breasts swelled. She felt jumpy, unsettled, when he stood too close. Morgan swallowed tension so thick she thought it might choke her and tried to ease away from him.

Jack didn't budge—or let her go.

Gnashing her teeth, she said, "There must be another way out of here besides you pawing me."

"I wouldn't take that bet. You wanna make it out in one piece, *cher*, without your stalker recognizing you through your disguise, you've got to act right. We've got to look real."

The hand on her stomach started inching slowly north.

Morgan's brain buzzed with the intimation in his words. He would touch her out in public, where complete strangers would see. Instantly, her breasts swelled again. Moisture gathered between her legs.

*This is impossible.* She wasn't into public displays. And Jack's caveman tendencies shouldn't be arousing her. Having such fantasies was one thing. Living them . . . that was completely different. Stupid to indulge, especially with a stranger.

Jack interrupted her thoughts by cradling her breast between his thumb and fingers—and continuing to inch up.

Until Morgan slapped her hand around his wrist to stop him. "I don't believe you. You don't need to touch me that intimately to get me out of here."

He stopped the upward progress of his hand. "Less than an hour with me and suddenly you're the security expert?"

"This isn't a game. It's my life!"

"Exactly," he growled into her ear. "Locals, not necessarily the trustworthy ones, will be out there tonight, seeing me with a woman they think is Alyssa. If you're gasping and fighting and pushing every time I put a hand on you, they'll know you're an imposter. And if the man chasing you offers them money for information about a suspicious female . . . you'll be an easy target to spot."

*And an easy one to kill.* Jack didn't say it, but he thought it. Just as Morgan did.

"Couldn't I leave here as a bag lady or a nun or something?"

"Your gun-toting friend is going to be waiting, watching. Don't you think the emergence of a nun from a strip club would send up a few red flags?"

He was right, damn it. She had to get a grip. If dressing like a stripper and letting a good-looking guy fondle her for a few minutes was all it took to keep her safe, she'd survive the embarrassment and the blow to her modesty.

There was just one problem: She reacted to Jack not like a decoy but like a woman. Her body heated for him with a few whispered words and a glance. Still, the embarrassment she felt for responding to him was short-lived, particularly compared to death. When this fiasco was over and she could find a new place to hide, she'd never have to see Jack Cole again or care that he knew he could arouse her.

Taking a deep breath, she let go of his wrist.

"Smart girl," he praised.

Morgan sensed him, his watchful gaze over her shoulder as he turned his wrist until her entire breast rested in his palm. She swallowed. God, her flesh felt heavy in his hot hand. He hovered there, breath scorching the back of her neck. Tension ramped up in her stomach . . . and lower, tightening with an ache she wanted to deny—and couldn't. Her nipples hardened impossibly under his hot gaze. Morgan squeezed her eyes shut.

Then he swiped a thumb over the taut tip. Electric pleasure shimmied down her spine.

Unable to resist, she arched, pushing her breast into his hand.

"Good girl," he muttered in her ear, then grazed the sensitive curve of her neck with his lips.

Arousal tightened again, pulsing low and hard. Her heart pounded away like a hoard of hammering carpenters. She squeezed her thighs together.

His left hand joined the right, taking possession of her other breast in a hot swarm of fingers. She didn't jump, but fought the need to squirm, as pleasure battered her senses with the double assault. It took biting her lip to hold in her groan.

Why did her body react this way to a man she didn't know and who practiced a sexual life she didn't participate in?

It ceased to matter when he pinched the hard pinpoints of her nipples between his fingers, rolling them slowly with erotic patience.

Need spiked in her belly, arrowing straight down between her legs.

"Jack . . ." she protested.

"Shh. You're doing fine, *cher*. As long as you don't act like I'm unfamiliar, we'll be all right."

All right? If he did that again, she'd be melting.

He didn't. Instead, his right hand left her breast to glide down her stomach, lower, lower, until his fingers edged underneath the damp black lace of her thong and unerringly found her swelling, hungry clit. She gasped and tightened her thighs against him. God, he'd feel how wet he made her. This was ridiculous. He wasn't going to touch her there in public.

"Don't do that," he warned, withdrawing his hand. "A tensing body and outraged gasps will give you away. Relax."

"This isn't necessary," she argued, her voice strained.

He snorted a cynical sound. "Spoken like a girl who's never run from a killer. He followed us here. Did you forget?"

"No, and I'm not a girl."

"*Non*? Then stop responding like one. It's going to take a damn convincing act to get out of here in one piece. I'm trying to save your life, not steal whatever virtue you might have."

"Wouldn't this kind of behavior simply draw attention?"

"New Orleans isn't the only place that celebrates Mardi Gras. The sun is going down now, and the party is about to start. Being too good would make us stand out in the crowd, *cher*."

He was probably right. She had to trust him. She had no reason not to, since he'd kept her alive so far. "Sorry."

Behind her, she felt him nod. "Spread your legs."

Oh, God. Why? What did he have planned?

Morgan froze in indecision. If one finger brushing her clit sent shock waves through her body, what might a whole hand do? Would he laugh if she orgasmed? As it was, she felt closer than she would have thought possible . . .

"If I need to tie you down to get you accustomed to my touch, don't think I won't."

At his warning growl, a fresh wave of moisture gushed from her, coating her already swollen flesh. Oh, how mortifying. If Jack realized she'd responded to that threat . . . She shivered.

With surprising force, Jack wedged a booted foot between her bare feet and pried them apart. "Put your hands on the wall above your head."

"What?"

Morgan struggled to close her legs, only to find Jack's hard thigh between them. Lord, would he feel her juices leaking through the thong and onto his jeans? Think her weak or easy?

"Last time I'm going to tell you," he swore. "Put your hands on the wall or things will get a whole lot more serious."

More serious? What was left, besides having sex? Her body jumped in anticipation at that thought.

"You're not listening . . . I guess you want to be tied down, Morgan."

"No," she snapped and put her hands on the wall high above her head.

But she wasn't sure she hadn't lied. The idea of bondage sounded primitive and tacky on the surface. Something only people who couldn't respond to "normal" sex did. But in a handful of minutes, Jack had forced her to face her own fantasy.

"That's better, but you've got to stop questioning what I say. I tell you, you do it. This isn't a negotiation."

That grated against her independent nature . . . even as it made the knot in her belly clench tighter.

"You're arrogant."

"And that isn't going to change. You better start following directions, little girl, or there will be consequences."

Morgan wanted to rail at him, deny that his power appealed to her. It would only start a fight they didn't have time to finish. If she wanted to get out of there with her pride intact, she needed to convince him she was ready to leave and fool her stalker. And she needed to convince the people they'd see that she was completely familiar and comfortable with Jack touching her.

"You got what you wanted. My hands are against the wall. I know you're going to grope me in public. I'll keep any surprise or discomfort to myself. Can we end this now?"

"You're not ready."

"I'll be fine."

"So, if I do this . . ."

His hand slid back inside her thong, fingers circling her clit before dropping down to her slick opening. He pushed two fingers deep inside her. His left hand traveled down her stomach, then covered her clit.

Unable to help it, she gasped.

"See, you're not ready," he said and began massaging her clit, while the fingers embedded inside her toyed with her until they encountered a bundle of nerves Morgan hadn't known she possessed. He rubbed there unmercifully, slow, insistent strokes ripping a scream of tingles deep inside her.

Orgasm raced toward her, like a car speeding through traffic lights to the edge of a cliff. Her channel clenched in weeping hunger around his fingers, her body begging for release. His teeth nipped at her neck again. Then he pressed himself against her backside, grinding an unmistakably large erection into the cleft of her ass.

At least she wasn't the only one affected, she thought as her head lolled back on his shoulder, perspiration breaking out all over her body as his fingers continued to fill her, toy with her clit. Her chest heaved with every breath. This was insane. Madness! The edge of pleasure was killing her. When had she ever been so aroused so quickly?

The feelings built, until she felt pleasure fill her up, nearly to the exploding point.

Then he withdrew his touch, easing his hands out of the thong and onto her hips. "No coming, not unless I say so."

Before she could stop it, a whimper escaped her throat.

Jack kissed her neck again, a brush of lips, a sting of teeth. "You'll thank me later."

Morgan couldn't imagine why he thought so. Her body was so tightly strung. He'd aroused her so thoroughly, she was tense, her mind racing. If he touched her in public, she'd probably climax so viciously, she'd black out.

His hands grazed up her abdomen again, to her breasts. He fondled them, rolled her aching nipples between his fingertips once more. She

arched into his hand, grinding her ass against the impressive erection behind her, biting her lip to hold in a groan.

He stepped away with a laugh. "Nice try."

"Jack . . ." She didn't want to beg. Really. But how was she supposed
to keep her wits around the bad guys when her body ached so badly?

"Are you going to question me again?"

The tone of his voice told her that would be a very bad idea. But leaving her wanting like this was no better. Still, a glance over her shoulder at
his suddenly forbidding face stilled the plea on her tongue.

"No."

"And if I"—he reached down into her thong once more and rubbed
her clit with his finger—"did this . . ."

Pleasure shot through her again, fresh and ferocious. She whimpered and thrust her hips into his touch. So, so close . . .

Again, he withdrew. "Excellent. Now you don't jerk away when I
touch you."

"You're going to leave me like this?"

"You inviting me to do something about it later?" His low voice rumbled like gravel in her ear.

Jack liked to tie women down and own them, body and soul. The
thought screamed through her mind. What the hell had she done?

Let him get away with anything, everything . . .

"Not a chance in hell." She stiffened, trying to draw away from him.

"That's too bad. I like little girls like you, all starch on the outside, all
creamy on the inside. The thought of hearing you scream your throat
raw while I fuck you turns me on."

Oh, God. Her, too. "You're the subject of an interview. That's all."

"You get that wet for everyone you talk to?" he mocked.

"Go to hell."

With a chuckle, he swatted her bare ass with his wide palm. "Get
dressed."

Morgan started to whirl on him, take him down for revving her up,
but then the sting in her ass turned to pure fire. Instead, she found herself
biting her lip to hold another groan inside.

*Just get your clothes on and get out of here. That will make all this go away.*

Stomping past Jack, Morgan shimmied into an indecently tight purple leather skirt. Next she put on a matching leather bustier that emphasized her small waist and shoved her cleavage so high, it was practically a shelf. All the while, she felt Jack's gaze boring into her back and the ache of the lust he'd created sizzling in her body.

Finally, she wriggled her feet into a pair of black thin-heeled boots with pointed toes. Shockingly, they were actually somewhat comfortable.

"Let's get this over with," she spat.

He eyed her. "You ready for what happens when we walk out this door?"

"We'd be arrested if we did more than we already have in public, so it appears I've lived through your worst."

He led her out the door with a smirk. "You think so?"

# Chapter Three

JACK made his way down the stairs, holding Morgan's hand. He barely refrained from using the other to adjust the length of his hard cock in his jeans. Damn, the woman about made him bust a zipper.

After their episode in Alyssa's bedroom, he knew several undeniable things about Morgan O'Malley: One, she had a body that called to him. The way she looked, felt, smelled—all of it reached him on a primitive level and urged him to chip away at her until she surrendered completely. Two, she'd be unbelievable to fuck. High breasts with sensitive nipples, a beautiful mouth, and an unexpected independent streak that told him she would be both a trial and a triumph to the man who could tame her. Three, she had a wide submissive streak . . . and didn't want to admit it. Her wet, nearly orgasmic reactions to his slightly—okay, way-over-the-top—demands that she become accustomed to his touch were very telling. Every time he'd threatened her with bondage, she'd gushed with fresh moisture. He'd needed a surprising amount of self-control to withhold her orgasm and keep from plunging himself deep inside her cunt while she had it.

He knew a few other things about Morgan: She didn't panic or surrender in the face of danger. She was scared, sure. Only an idiot wouldn't feel at least a twinge of fear knowing that a stalker who followed her across the country to end her life stood right outside the door. But Morgan had listened to his logic, pushed back when she disagreed with offered advice, and resisted his initial offers of assistance. Those facts told him a lot about her—and how to deal with her. Patience, persistence, a combination of tenderness and alpha demands.

Lastly, if Morgan was Brandon Ross's fiancée, she'd be wasted on the boring, uptight bastard. Brandon would ignore the needs he didn't understand and couldn't fulfill, fantasies Jack would bet his eyeteeth she had. Satisfying her fantasies required someone with more balls, tenderness, and self-control than Brandon ever thought of possessing. He almost felt sorry for Morgan. In fact, he might be doing her a favor in the long run . . .

But pity wasn't going to stop him from getting his overdue revenge against the asshole who'd fucked up his life.

First, though, he had to get Morgan out of the club alive.

As they hit the door at the back of the dark strip joint, he dragged her through a curtain that led to a backstage area. Abruptly, the pounding music stopped and wild clapping began. A slender brunette with large artificial breasts wriggled her hips at the crowd of men shoving bills in her miniscule G-string. Morgan stared, clearly uncomfortable with that much nudity and touching with complete strangers. *Good.* Despite the fact he'd been to dozens of places like this, he wanted a woman willing and eager only for him, not a whole room full of stiff dicks.

Looking away from the dancer, Jack scanned the crowd. He knew the mood of the clientele, the feel of revelers seeking hedonistic fun. Across the smoky room, a guy in jeans and a black sweater looked around, rather than at the stripper exiting the stage and giving the audience a prime view of her ass. A few feet from him, another man in a suit lurked in the corner, wearing a watchful scowl. He didn't fit in. The bulge inside his jacket hinted to Jack that the guy might have a shoulder holster full of weapon.

Either of these dudes—or neither—could be Morgan's would-be shooter. But Jack knew they couldn't afford to take chances.

As nonchalantly as possible, he turned Morgan to face him and covered their sudden stop in the crowd by pulling her against him and planting a series of kisses on her neck. She tensed.

*"Cher,"* he called.

Others near them would hear an endearment. Morgan's nod told him she took it as the warning he intended. She forced the tension from her shoulders.

"I see a couple of men who look suspicious," he whispered on the soft, soft skin of her neck. "Anyone look familiar?"

She hesitated, and Jack took advantage of her distraction and breathed in her sweet raspberry scent, brushed his lips against her soft-as-sin skin.

"I can't think with you doing that," she whispered harshly.

He dropped a hand down her spine, over the curve of her ass, more because he wanted to than because it was necessary. But it helped with the image that they were lovers who couldn't keep their hands to themselves.

"You can. You will."

Morgan breathed out a four-letter word, and Jack smiled. If her curse hadn't told him that he was getting to her, the pulse picking up speed at the base of her neck would. The scheming part of him loved knowing he affected her. So did his sexual side. Oh, he didn't forget that the shooter was probably somewhere near, but the asshole was too smart to shoot with so many able to see his face. And the sick jerk had no reason to believe that Morgan wasn't Alyssa.

"I can't see. It's smoky, and I'm too short."

True on both counts. *Damn!*

Curving both arms around her body, Jack anchored Morgan against his chest. The top of her head barely reached his shoulder, reminding him how small she was. With her big personality, her size was easy to forget.

Given her story, she'd been through a whole lot lately. He couldn't help but admire her grit to go on, her strength to fight.

"Let's get out of here, just in case one of them is your gun-happy nightmare."

Morgan nodded, but he felt her trembling. Jack eased back to look at her face. Under the thick makeup, her blue eyes clearly reflected the knowledge that she was being hunted. But equal parts fear and determination tightened her lush mouth. She wasn't giving up.

Neither was he.

"I'm not going to let anything happen to you," he assured her. "Take my hand. Smile. Good enough. Now, follow me out the door."

Slowly, Jack wended his way through the crowd, working the far side of the room as much as possible. He stopped to answer a greeting, endure some backslapping from frat boys he'd helped out of a scrape once, all of whom assumed fucking Alyssa would be every man's version of paradise.

The suspicious characters cast glances over them as they neared the door. The dude with the suit kept his gaze glued to Morgan. Jack covertly watched the man assess her, eyes narrow with speculation. Running would only alert the asshole if he was Morgan's stalker.

Instead, Jack whirled Morgan around and grabbed her. Her eyes went wide as he held her face between his palms and slanted his mouth over her own.

Right away, her softness assaulted him. After a gasp of protest, Jack sensed Morgan forcing herself to relax. To submit. At the press of his lips, she opened to him slowly, slowly, with shy hesitance that made him burn with need. A delicious uncertainty flavored her kiss, making him hard as a pike. But it wasn't enough—either to convince the assassin chasing her or to assuage the hunger that churned like a violent storm in his gut.

He couldn't wait for more.

A growl erupted from this throat as he dove into the kiss and urged her soft lips to part wider. He entered her mouth with a ravaging thrust of his tongue. And groaned as her wet, sugary heat and hot cinnamon-spice flavor exploded across his senses. Tangled with the taste of her fear.

Morgan began to kiss him tentatively. Unfurling to him, softening. Soon, she uttered a soft moan and matched his rhythm, her tongue seeking his when he retreated. She clasped his shoulders and clung, slanting her head until their mouths fit perfectly. Gripping her tightly, he sank deeper into her. The flavor of fear on her tongue receded. She trembled—but now her reaction didn't have a damn thing to do with fright.

Morgan gasped . . . then surrendered, opening completely.

Crushing his delight at her lush response, Jack promised himself there would be plenty of time to fuck her, screw Brandon out of a bride, and enjoy every moment of her soft, shy responses. Later.

Ending the kiss with a nip of his teeth on her plush lower lip, Jack opened his eyes in time to see the slick in the suit talking to some of the regulars around him. Jack made sure he blocked Morgan from the view of guys who hung out here at least once a week. He hoped like hell none of them would remember that they'd never seen him kiss Alyssa like that.

Mr. Suit listened, then nodded his thanks. Disappointment shadowed his face. The guy in the jeans and sweater had disappeared.

"I think we're good to go," he murmured to Morgan. "Let's get out of here."

Again, he took her hand. He led her right out the front door. The crowd on the street swallowed them up quickly, and Jack smiled.

Once the danger had passed, once he knew they hadn't been followed, he could concentrate on Morgan—and every delicious way he could think of to make her surrender.

*   *   *

WITHIN minutes, Jack led her to his truck, parked on a dark side street. Morgan hesitated. Brandon wouldn't be happy that she'd left his car behind, but what were her other options? She couldn't argue with Jack's logic that her stalker would be looking for it on the roads since he'd followed her here.

That settled, Jack tucked her into the passenger's seat of his sleek black truck. She'd have to be blind not to see his gaze lingering on the length of her exposed thigh and cleavage offered up by Alyssa's purple leather slut garb. The miles of skin it exposed made her want to find the nearest tent and throw it on quickly. Another part of her, though, heated at his look. The arrow of need that shot straight to her still-aching clit encouraged her to inch up her skirt a bit more and flash Jack a come-hither glance. She resisted the dangerous temptation.

The familiar dark desire, coupled with the stress and uncertainty, crashed in on her. How had her life gone downhill so quickly? How had she found herself at the mercy of a stranger who made her ache with a longing that shamed her?

"Don't leer," she snapped.

Jack looked away in his own good time. "Why not? You look good."

"I look like a whore."

Faster than lightning, he leaned across the cab and crowded her personal space. He smelled like midnight and elemental male. Like danger.

"You look available and willing. You don't look for sale."

"It's the same thing."

"*Non*, it is not."

Jack said nothing more for long moments. He eased away and started the truck, then pulled away from the tree-lined street and took off into the dusk. Then they headed southeast, toward the heart of the bayou.

With another hot glance at her, Jack finally explained, "When a woman looks for sale, a man checks his wallet before looking twice. Available and willing just makes a man hot. Available and willing for him alone makes a man boil with need. Right now, I'm hard as hell."

The night began closing around them finally, dark and absolute. Morgan swallowed. The way Jack looked at her through the inky closeness of the truck's cab gave her pause. And if she was honest, made her wet. Did he realize that she'd never dressed this provocatively for any man, for any reason, before?

"If you were my woman," he went on, his voice a sandpaper whisper, "you'd appear elegant in public. But in private . . ." He smiled, a flash of white teeth illuminated by the moonlight drifting into a smile that promised satisfaction. "In private, I'd dress you in less than you're wearing now. Much less. Without those useless lace panties you're wearing."

Morgan could barely catch her next breath. She didn't want to dress like this. It had to look cheap and easy.

Yet she could not deny it also made her feel aware of her body, of her feminine power. Sexy and wanted and desired. How was that possible?

"You're awfully direct."

"I'm honest," he admitted. "What's the point of lying?"

"Oh, I don't know. To be polite."

Jack simply snorted.

"And these panties aren't useless. They cover the essentials."

"Exactly. Why would I want those covered?"

She gaped. "I'm not about to flash everyone in the first good breeze that comes along."

"But if you were mine, what's under that skirt would be mine, not yours, to show or conceal as I saw fit."

His words burned her with shock—and terrible, unmistakable desire. She gasped.

"Shocked, *cher*? That's what submission is all about. Surrendering control utterly to someone else. Your privacy, your body, your pleasure."

He said nothing for long minutes, and Morgan lost herself in imagining. Would a dominant man really insist his partner show any—or all—of her body to anyone of his choosing? Anywhere? At any time? She squirmed in her seat at the thought. It was disturbing and exploitative. But some little part of her found his words reluctantly provocative. Forbidden. God, she'd gone insane.

But curiosity followed close behind. That, she allowed free rein. She was interviewing him about this very subject, after all. Journalistic integrity and all that.

"What you're saying . . . it sounds selfish and mean-spirited, to expose someone without regard for their feelings."

"It might look that way on the surface."

"What do you mean, on the surface?"

"Like I told you online, one of the jobs of a good dominant is to see inside the soul of his submissive and grant her every pleasure she desires. Many submissives aren't aware of their most secret desires." He turned to face her, his chocolate eyes piercing, direct. "Or find them shameful, so they refuse to admit to them."

He was talking to her. *About her.* With a hot glance, he made that clear. Her breathing shallowed, her heartbeat accelerated. She couldn't ignore the fact that her stomach—and her nipples—went achy and tight.

"And you force a woman to engage in acts you believe she secretly desires, even though she may not want to acknowledge them?"

"She has to accept them to find true satisfaction. My role is to help her."

"What's in it for you? I mean, if you're always trying to read her mind and persuade her to do new, unusual things . . . ?"

"New things that make her so hot, she's giving me total control and is begging me to fuck her however and wherever I want. I'm sure you see the obvious benefits."

Yeah, hard to miss that point. Was it possible to be so aroused that she would beg in such a way? A mental picture of Jack tying her down, feeling her up, as she writhed under his hands exploded across her brain. A blast of heat sizzled her belly . . . and lower. God knew his aggressive touch earlier today had flooded her with arousal so fast, she'd nearly been dizzy with it. And his kiss had obliterated most thoughts of fear and hesitation, the crowd, and her stalker.

She didn't doubt he could make a woman beg for anything, everything. If she wasn't careful, didn't keep her distance, she could quickly become another notch on his bedpost. Worse, he could open her psyche and expose all the hidden fantasies better left to the dark corners of her mind.

Time for a change of subject. "Thank you for getting me out of Lafayette. I would have panicked and run when the bullets started flying. On my own, I would never have been able to concoct this disguise and . . . distract him."

"That's my job, Morgan."

"You didn't have to do it." Then, recalling the way his hands roamed her body in Alyssa's bedroom, she shot him a suspicious look. "In fact, I think you did more than your job required."

"Think what you want." Jack's smile told Morgan that her assertion amused him.

"I usually do." She gritted her teeth, wishing she knew how to wipe that smile off his face. "Where are we going?"

"I've got a place. It's safe. We can hide you there until we figure something out."

The thought of being anywhere near Jack, even for just a few days, rattled her. "Maybe I should rent a car and drive back to Houston. I've already imposed—"

"He'll catch on quick and follow you, Morgan. This guy isn't stupid. Psycho, but not stupid. You want to be safe or dead? Besides, it'll be a good opportunity for you to learn about Dominance and submission. I can ensure you'll sound like an expert on your show."

"I think I get the picture."

"*Cher*, you haven't even scratched the surface."

"I don't need you touching me anymore."

His smile could have melted butter. "You may not think you need it, but I know better. You need it every bit as much as you want it."

Morgan's jaw dropped. "You are one arrogant bastard."

"You're submissive, and I'm arrogant. See how well we're getting to know each other already?"

His quip put her temper in a twist. "I am not—That's it! Take me back to Lafayette."

He sent her an amused glance. "Back to your friend's car, the one your stalker probably has his pretty rifle trained on as we speak?"

She bit her lip. Damn it. Why did he have to be right?

"Or maybe I should drop you off at the police station," he taunted. "They're always so much help in stalker cases."

Clenching her fists, Morgan said nothing, again knowing he spoke the truth.

"Or maybe you could hop a plane back to L.A. How long do you think it would be before he stopped shooting pictures and tried to shoot you between the eyes again? You got a death wish?"

"No." Her voice vibrated with the anger she felt coursing through her body. "You got an off button for your mouth?"

Jack just smiled. "You're too smart to want to face a killer more than your sexuality, Morgan. I'll ask you the same question I asked before your stalker started shooting: What are you afraid of?"

"I'm not having this conversation with you."

He shrugged, as if he didn't care about her response one way or the other. "Fine. It's your life. Am I taking you back to Lafayette or are you going to stay safe with me?"

God, she wanted to shock the bastard. Spit in his face and verbally cut off his balls by demanding he take her back to Brandon's car so she could zoom back to Houston, far away from his challenging words and his wicked touch.

But once again, damn it, he was right. Putting herself back in the path of a killer because Jack pushed a few of her sexual buttons was flat stupid. She had no safe place to go, and despite Brandon's suggestion, she was *not* calling Senator Ross. He wouldn't lift a finger to help her.

"I'll go with you," she said through clenched teeth.

"Good girl. We've got a few hours to travel, and it's getting late. Try getting some sleep."

Morgan wasn't sure she could. Being that vulnerable around a man like Jack, especially while she still had a stalker on her tail. "I'm fine."

"It wasn't a suggestion. We're not being followed. No one is on this road for miles." He gestured to the open road and fields around them, completely devoid of headlights. "You're safe, and you're going to need your strength later, *cher*, in case we haven't lost your stalker for good."

She sighed, then shot him a reluctant glance. Again, he was right.

Morgan crossed her arms over her chest and shifted her body toward the passenger window. But soon the rhythmic motion of the car lulled her. She closed her eyes and drifted off.

*     *     *

TWO hours later, Jack stopped the truck at the water's edge, in front of the boat waiting where he'd left it. After he scrambled aboard with a groggy Morgan, they cruised down the river for a while, Jack poling his way down the swamp with Morgan drifting in and out of sleep and shivering in the February air. He did his best to shelter her from the wind with his body. She unconsciously snuggled into him when he wrapped one arm around her.

That gave him a hard-on so stiff it hurt.

They reached their destination shortly before ten. Jack lifted a slumbering Morgan into his arms, settled her in his grasp, and headed for the dark cottage.

He'd expected to have to talk fast in Lafayette, to hustle and sweet-talk her to a hotel room to get his revenge. Having her here, in his domain, was better—and worse. Her stalker had helped him maneuver Morgan right where he wanted her and never dreamed he'd have her. He would have Morgan to himself, on his turf, where he could devote hours to her seduction and his revenge. Sweet, yes.

But Jack couldn't pretend her sick stalker didn't concern him. At least here, with him, he could protect her from the psycho who'd clearly decided that if he couldn't have Morgan, no one else would. He would keep her safe; he owed her that much. Particularly since it was clear Morgan could no longer fend for herself and was exhausted beyond her endurance.

But on a basic physical level, she trusted him. That trust shimmered through his body, both hardening his cock and softening his gut. Why fight it? He liked her, even if he hated her fiancé's guts. She was by turns feisty and vulnerable, sharp and gullible. And for some reason so damned familiar, as if he'd seen her somewhere before . . .

Shifting Morgan in his grasp, Jack shoved the key in the lock, then thrust open the door. Inside the little Craftsman cottage, clean lines and pine floors reminded him of his boyhood, of fishing with his *grand-père,* Brice. This place never failed to inspire great memories, even if the old family legends his grandfather told here made him laugh.

"Ah, so you made it."

Jack started—until he recognized the voice. "Holy shit, old man. You trying to scare me to death so you can have your fishing hole back?"

Brice waved him away. "You wish. I wouldn't have this place back for nothin'. Rat trap."

Jack knew better, but Brice was too old to live out here, so far away from a hospital.

"The place is stocked with food. The security cameras, they's all on, and the generator is running. Use it sparingly."

"Thanks. I knew I could count on you."

"This the girl you called about, the one runnin' for her life?" Brice gestured to Morgan, whom Jack still held.

"Yeah."

With narrowed eyes, Brice peered closer and stared at Morgan. "You sure he's not just out to bed her? She's one *jolie fille,* but she dresses like a whore, that one."

"It's a disguise, *Grand-père.*"

Brice frowned his gray head, disapproval still shadowing his strong features. Smiling to himself, Jack stepped around his grandfather and headed for the cottage's lone bedroom. He set Morgan down on the bed, then bent to remove her black boots. If his grandfather weren't watching, he'd pull off the rest of her clothes for the mere pleasure of looking at her . . . but Brice would both disapprove and get an eyeful that could damage his heart at eighty-two.

"You still been havin' them dreams?" his grandfather asked suddenly.

Jack rolled his eyes, ruing the day he'd said anything. "They don't mean anything."

"Boy, you been raised in the bayou, even if the army and big city spoiled you some. A curse is a curse. If you're dreaming about a redheaded woman over and over, you're about to meet her and she's your heart's mate."

*Here we go again with this bullshit,* Jack thought with a sigh. If Brice wanted to use the legend to justify his marrying an underage girl sixty years ago, goody for him. As it was, Jack refused to believe that some faceless woman he'd seen in his dreams with red hair glinting across bare shoulders in dawn's light was destined to be his one and only love. There was no such thing. The redhead was just a fantasy fuck his mind had conjured up.

"Well, I haven't met any redheads lately, so the whole point is moot. Dreams don't mean a thing."

"You keep tellin' yourself that, boy. She'll turn up. Won't be long now. Didn't you say you'd been having those dreams about five months?"

Six, but who was counting? Jack shrugged.

"She'll make a believer out of you," Brice contended.

"Whatever you say, *Grand-père*."

The old man grunted, knowing that Jack was blowing off the famous family legend he loved so much. The dreams . . . they had to be coincidence, a by-product of loneliness and the fact that he hadn't had a good lay in forever. Nothing else made sense.

"Well, this old man is taking his body home and going to bed. Need anything else, boy?"

"We'll be fine."

"Take care of *ta jolie fille.*"

Jack sighed. "She's not *my* pretty girl."

And for some damn reason, it annoyed him to admit that. Probably because she was wasted on an asshole like Brandon Ross.

Laughter cackling with both amusement and age, Brice left. Jack heard the slam of the cottage door and returned to the bedroom.

He turned on the kerosene lamp in the bedroom, which emitted a soft glow over Morgan. She looked uncomfortable. He watched her twist and mutter in her sleep.

He removed a pair of gaudy earrings he hadn't noticed before and lay them on the side table. The purple leather . . . it wasn't Morgan's style but would have to stay for now. Trying to take it off would surely wake her up. Shrugging, he realized he could only do one other thing to make her comfortable.

Gently, Jack reached under the sleek blonde wig and extracted a pin here and there. She sighed in sleepy appreciation when he lifted the wig away and tossed it on the table next to the earrings.

When Jack looked back, he frowned and lifted the lamp over Morgan. It couldn't be. It couldn't.

But with mellow golden light shining down on her, there was no mistaking the glint of her fiery red hair.

# Chapter Four

MORGAN woke to an unfamiliar room pervaded by shadows. Mosquito netting draped the warm, well-used bed. Beyond that, an old-fashioned kerosene lamp on a nightstand with mission-style lines dimly lit the room. Where was she?

Blinking, she sat up with a creak. She frowned when she saw purple leather stretched across her torso and hips. Purple leather? Her? It wasn't uncomfortable . . . but had to be discomfiting to be seen in. Why the hell was she wearing it?

Then she recalled. Her stalker shooting. Master J—no, Jack—to the rescue, his gaze eating up her flushed skin, his hands on her body.

Still, she had to thank Alyssa for the shocking getup. It, along with Jack and his outrageous behavior, had gotten her out of Lafayette alive.

A downy beige comforter warmed her legs. Black sheers floated at the room's lone window, made transparent by the silvery moonlight. A stout dresser of warm, old cherrywood sprawled against most of the wall beside the window.

Turning her head, Morgan skimmed the other half of the small bedroom. The open door led to beautiful hardwood floors, which gleamed in the dark, empty hallway.

And in the chair wedged between the door and an armoire sat Jack, shirtless and tousled, alert—and focused on her.

"Good morning, Morgan."

Morning? His stare touched her through the moonlit inkiness of the room, caressing her cheek, sweeping over her mouth, gliding down her neck to the rise of her breasts above the leather bustier. With just a glance, heat bloomed inside her. Even eight feet away, the potency of his sexuality broadcast in blaring waves. Everything they had done in Alyssa's bedroom came back to her in a rush . . . along with a tight, nagging ache between her legs.

She remembered everything—the way he'd touched her, his kiss, the way he took control. His mysterious scent, his growled words—they'd intrigued her. Even after a few hours' sleep, nothing had changed. Curiosity and desire gnawed at her as Jack stared, knowledge hot in his chocolate eyes. The ache knotting her body tightened.

She couldn't afford that, couldn't afford him. Morgan looked away, breaking their visual connection.

How he felt, how she felt—none of it mattered. She had to focus on staying safe and doing research for her show. Drooling over the heavy slabs of muscles covering Jack's shoulders and chest that screamed *virile* and contemplating all the ways he could use that power to pleasure her wasn't going to improve her show—or her chances of staying alive.

"How are you? Okay?" he asked.

"I'm fine," she said finally. "What time is it?"

He shrugged and glanced out the window. "About five in the morning. You can go back to sleep. I'll be here to watch over you."

Morgan stared back. The knowledge that Jack's eyes were on her was really going to induce her to roll over and sink into dreamland. *As if.* She could hardly breathe with Jack's gaze all over her. Sleep would be impossible.

What was it about this man? Sure, he was yummy, but she'd dated good-looking guys before. Something about the way he stared?

The truth finally hit her like a slap. No, it was his intensity, his self-possession, his air of controlled power. She'd always been a sucker for men of power. And unlike the other men in her past, Morgan knew Jack was the real deal.

He wielded one of the ultimate powers, a sexual one. He wouldn't just tie a woman down; he would dictate her response and his, be in complete control of her body, her orgasms, and in that moment, her very soul.

The thought appealed to Morgan far more than was wise.

Easing toward the edge of the bed to put distance between them, she said, "No, I'm awake. Do you want the bed to catch some sleep? I can get up."

"Stay."

The single syllable ricocheted through her body. It was a command, pure and simple. Every place it bounced around inside her, the heat intensified, confusing her. She didn't like being bossed around—by anyone. But Jack barking orders at her made her uncomfortably achy in all the wrong places.

Hell, maybe she was just horny in general, and it had nothing to do with Jack. After all, it had been nearly a year since she'd split up with Andrew.

"I've been sleeping in the chair," he clarified.

"That can't be comfortable."

He laughed. "*Cher*, go spend a few months in Afghanistan with the army. This chair will seem like the Ritz."

Morgan nodded, conceding the point.

"If you're awake, I want to ask you some questions. You need coffee first?"

She shuddered. "I don't drink the vile brew. Too bitter."

A flash of white teeth told Morgan that he smiled. "I wouldn't say that too loud around here. We're known for our thick chicory coffee. Not drinking that is sacrilege."

"I'm likely to burn in hell for some other things in my life, starting with painting my cousin's G.I. Joe's fingernails pink when I was five. I'll just add that to the list."

Jack laughed, a scratchy sandpaper sound. "Wow, that is vile. Satan's got a special place reserved just for you."

Morgan nodded. Then the room turned quiet. The momentary banter drifted away, leaving a tense silence in its place. Still, she felt Jack's gaze on her, lingering on her hair.

Self-consciously, she pushed the strands off her shoulders, behind her back. "You took off the wig. I . . . it's red," she stammered. "My hair, I mean."

He hesitated. "I didn't expect that."

His stare changed then, turned pensive. Morgan frowned. What had he expected? Why did the color matter? Maybe he only liked blondes. Maybe . . . but his stare said otherwise.

"And I see you took off the boots."

"They looked uncomfortable."

The idea of Jack touching her as she slept unaware raised the heat coiling in her body another notch. Had he touched anything more intimate than her head or feet while she slept?

That question ratcheted up her body heat again, now laser focused between her legs. Morgan squirmed, seeking relief. She didn't find it.

"What do you want to ask me?" she said. Conversation, yes. Much safer than staring.

Jack's slouched posture instantly gave way to a taut awareness. He leaned forward, balancing his elbows on his knees. "How about we start with anyone you can think of who might want to stalk and kill you?"

*Boom.* Direct. Morgan wasn't really surprised. That really was the heart of the matter, after all, and she suspected Jack would be a pretty bottom-line man.

"Honestly, I can't think of anyone. I've had weird fan mail, but not this weird."

"It seems as if this guy knows you pretty well, where you live, where your friends and family live, where you might run to." Jack's eyes narrowed. "Tell me about your relationships."

"What do you mean?"

"Previous lovers," Jack's raspy voice demanded as intriguing shadows played across the hard angles of his face and torso. She could stare at the man for hours and never be bored. Hot and bothered, yes. But never bored.

Damn it, she needed to keep her mind on her safety, her show, not her protector himself.

She shook her head. "The last one left me, not the other way around, so I doubt he'd suddenly demand that I belonged only to him."

"Before him?" he barked.

Morgan felt a flush creep up her neck. "I was involved with a pro football player a while ago, but when this started happening, he would have been on the road, so he couldn't be taking pictures and leaving them for me. I dated an ambassador briefly. He's currently abroad. So it's not him, either. I hooked up with a guy in college who's married with a daughter now."

"Who else?"

"Who else what?"

The line of his jaw hardened. "Who else have you let fuck you?"

The intensity of his voice—and the words—suggested that he asked for reasons that weren't strictly professional.

"You're getting awfully personal, not to mention crude."

"Just getting a full list of suspects and cutting to the chase, *cher*. Answer me."

His no-nonsense tone had returned, and she found it oddly difficult to argue. "No one else. Actually, I didn't even sleep with Ambassador Sweeny."

"Three past lovers?" Jack asked, curiosity ripe in his voice. "No more?"

She supposed that having only three lovers by the ripe age of twenty-five made her an anomaly. But she wasn't going to give him all the details about her sex life just to appease his curiosity. The point of this exchange might be to build a list of suspects, but the low-voiced probing in his tone had a sexual edge that shouted *warning*.

And he wouldn't stop staring. With every clinging gaze, he lashed Morgan with memories of his kiss, his touch, the way he took control. Her body kept warming like an oven on pre-heat.

"Why does it matter?" Morgan shot back, aware she was dodging the question. "Aren't the more important facts that this monster knows my habits, my friends, family, and the places I'm likely to go?"

He shrugged. "*Cher*, there isn't a man alive who isn't willing to kill to get a woman he's truly desperate for. But if she's running from him, thwarting both him and his lust . . . that man can get a hell of a lot more ruthless."

With a shiver, Morgan considered Jack's implication that that description could apply to more than just her stalker. Did he include himself in that group? Somehow, she didn't picture Jack needing a lot of excuses to get ruthless, but she also didn't picture a lot of women turning him down.

"He's especially dangerous if he's already had a taste of what he's missing. I need to know all the possibilities so I can check them out, run them down. Then we'll get to your other questions. Now, you've had just those three lovers?"

"Yes."

"I need names, vital statistics, ages, and last known addresses to start digging."

"This is embarrassing."

"This is critical. Start talking."

Morgan sighed, squirmed in her place, and looked down at her hands folded in her lap. "Sean Gardner is . . . about five-ten, maybe. Sandy hair, brown eyes. I think he's twenty-eight by now. Last I heard, he's living with his wife and kid in San Diego."

"And he was the first?"

She nodded. "When I was a sophomore in college, yes."

"When did you see him last?"

"About four years ago, just after he graduated. We only dated six months or so. It wasn't that serious."

"But you gave him your virginity?"

"I already said that."

"Why?"

"I'm not answering that. That goes beyond name and vital statistics."

"I need to establish motivation, *cher*. Maybe he still thinks of you as his little virgin and doesn't like the thought that you've shared the pretty pussy he considers his with other men."

Morgan held in a gasp. She wasn't used to those words, not with a born-again mother. She'd never dated a man like Jack, who used them so unapologetically. Her mother would have fainted dead away . . . even faster than she had after seeing the first installment of *Turn Me On*.

"Not likely. When we split up, he encouraged me to date his roommate, who was a major horn dog. Trust me, he was as over me as I was over him."

Jack shrugged, some of the tension leaving his shoulders. "Number two?"

"Brent Pherson."

"The Brent Pherson drafted by the Raiders a few years ago?"

"The same. If you want his vital stats, look them up on ESPN.com."

Jaw tight, he asked, "How'd you meet?"

"At a press party. He was doing a reality show about athletes during the off-season for the same parent company that airs *Turn Me On*. I doubt he's stalking me. We . . . it was just one night."

Jack scowled, looking decidedly unhappy about that. "Why did you let him fuck you?"

"Do you have to put it like that?"

"That's what happened, right? Why did you let him? Did you have feelings for him?"

Brent was built like the side of a mountain and had been the supposed leader of his football team. He'd been quiet and seemingly in control. That illusion had drawn her in, along with his good looks. A night had been all she needed to see how insecure and out of control he'd been.

"That's really none of your business."

Jack stood, approached the bed, towered over her. Morgan looked up, past the ridged abs and rippling shoulders that screamed power. Having him this near . . . it wasn't good for her mental health. He was part aphrodisiac, part beast. And she responded way more than she wanted to.

"If you want my help, I need to know your past. It's not uncommon for a previous lover to turn stalker, since he knows where you live, who you're close to, and may even know some of your friends and can get his information through them. You being modest and treating me like an auditory voyeur is only giving him more time to hunt you down. Do you have a death wish?"

"If I did, I would have just sat there in Lafayette and let him use me as target practice," Morgan grated out. "Do you think he followed us here? Did you see anyone follow us on the road?"

"No, I don't think he followed us. We're dead in the middle of a swamp, so he'll be hard-pressed to find us. But it's not impossible. You can't afford to underestimate someone like this."

Jack was right. Morgan's stomach quivered with that truth. "I know."

"Good, then cooperate. You holding back is tempting me to put you over my knee and spank your ass."

Morgan gaped. "You're not touching my ass!"

"Don't challenge me, *cher*. I'll make those pretty cheeks fire-hot in about three minutes."

A flame of desire burst to life between Morgan's legs. *Bad, bad, bad. Stop now!* She closed her eyes, blocking out the sensation, the longing. The rampant curiosity and the ache.

"You're a pushy bastard, you know that?"

"I'm a dominant man who's reached the end of my patience with your little-girl games. Now, have you spoken to Pherson since that night?"

Her temper fired up a notch. "A few times. He sent me flowers the week after I spent the night with him. He called every few weeks, whenever he was back in town. I just wasn't interested anymore. He finally got the picture and stopped calling."

"Nothing since?"

She shook her head. He let the subject of Brent drop.

"I'm still not ruling him out. And bachelor number three?"

"Andrew Cummings. He's about your height. Salt-and-pepper hair, gray eyes. He just turned thirty-nine. He was the producer for *Turn Me On* last year. We started dating shortly after the . . . incident with Brent. Within a month, he asked me to marry him."

"You said . . . ?" Jack inched forward, crowding her personal space.

"Yes. He was good-looking, cultured, connected, seemed intelligent and funny. Why not?"

He tensed—mouth, shoulders, abs. "When did it end?"

"About ten months ago."

"Because . . . ?"

Because Andrew's male ego had been frustrated by her difficulty climaxing in the bedroom. He'd seemed so worldly, like a beacon of inner calm in a stormy life, she'd been sure he would be the man to unlock that something inside her that would set her body and heart free. He'd tried often . . . succeeded rarely. Finally, he coaxed her into revealing her deepest desires, the ones that involved her being bound and dominated. Thinking it would help them, she'd bared her soul and even revealed her most secret fantasy: being taken by two men at once. Not that she'd really do any of the things that spun in the deep recesses of her mind. They were just fantasies . . . A fact lost on Andrew.

He'd called her depraved—and some other less flattering things that seared pain through her gut and fostered a shame that boiled her temper every time she thought about them.

She'd thrown his ring back at him. He'd taken it and quit the show. They hadn't spoken since.

And not for anything would she share a whisper of that with Jack.

"It just wasn't working out," she hedged.

"Why?"

"We . . . just didn't get along as well as we had thought."

"You're holding out on me," he growled, grabbing her wrist.

Morgan jerked away from the electric heat of his touch. "That's all you're going to get. He left me, and I was happy to have him gone. As I've said, I doubt very much that he suddenly wants me back."

"Until you tell me the truth, I can't comment." He crossed his arms over his chest.

"That's all the truth you need."

Jack's thundercloud of an expression told Morgan he disagreed. "Time will tell." He took a step back. "Who is your 'friend' in Houston?"

Knowing she hadn't heard the last of Jack's questions about her broken engagement with Andrew, Morgan took a bracing breath and answered, "His name is Brandon Ross."

Jack's jaw tightened. "Is he more than a friend?"

She hesitated. No one knew she and Brandon were related. Keeping the secret had been part of her mother's settlement with Senator Ross years ago. He would come after her with both barrels if she let the truth out. So she and Brandon had concocted the engagement hoax when she started staying with him. Maybe . . . maybe if she used it here, it would ease the temperature down between her and Jack.

"Yes. He's my fiancé. My . . . my current one."

Jack's mouth pressed into a grim line. "Where is he now?"

"Out of the country for a few weeks."

"While some off-kilter psycho is taking shots at your head. Sounds like a great guy."

"He didn't want to go," she defended. "His job—"

"Has anything else happened besides you receiving these pictures? Anyone break into your house?"

"Yes, and . . ." Morgan swallowed, then whispered, "He masturbated on my bed. That's when I got scared and left L.A."

Sudden tears scalded her eyes, her cheeks, surprising her. She'd thought she was more together than that. Tears weren't going to help this situation. But the reality of it all was hitting her hard.

Jack sat beside her in a heartbeat, all hint of anger gone. Gently, he eased her back and leaned over her, brushing a gentle hand across her cheek, wiping tears away.

Morgan stared at the man, the contradiction. Tenderness and compassion from a man who'd forced the truth from her, threw her arousal at his touch in her face? A man who bound his women?

"You did the right thing, leaving L.A. and agreeing to stay here. This guy is fixated and dangerous, no question."

Embarrassed by her tears and too conscious of Jack's closeness, Morgan looked away. "I hate being afraid and having my life turned upside down. The sooner we get this over with, the better."

"We'll fix it," he murmured. "Who knew where you went after you left L.A.?"

A furrow wrinkled her brow as she tried to recall. "Reggie, my production assistant. My neighbor, who's watching my cat. Sabrina, who does my makeup for the show. I can't remember. I left in a blur . . ."

"Having someone uninvited jack off on your bed would throw anyone for a loop."

Jack took her hand, sandwiched it between his strong, calloused palms as he hovered over her in the shadowed moonlight. Holy cow, he was so good-looking, he hurt her eyes. Strong jaw, chiseled mouth, two days' growth roughening what might have been an otherwise pretty face. Wide, muscle-capped shoulders topped off a hard, six-packed torso any woman would drool over.

Morgan wanted to be unmoved by him, his aura of power, his touch. It wasn't in the cards. His gaze roved over her, part reassuring, part hot remembrance. God, she couldn't forget either, his breath on her neck, his hands palming her breasts, his fingers buried inside her, nearly bringing her to orgasm. His mouth on hers.

Survival first, pleasure later. Much later. And not with Jack.

Yes, she wanted a self-possessed man, but this one . . . he was too much. Of everything that called to her, of everything she didn't need at this point in her life. She had no business thinking about him. Jack possessed lethal power, barely concealed by careful restraint. The primal male animal lurked just under the surface of his skin, leashed by his control and air of authority—and a thin façade of civility.

A woman didn't handle a man like Jack. He had all the subtlety of a steamroller, and if Morgan gave him the slightest hint that his brand of domination interested her, she knew he'd roll over her fairly inexperienced body and leave her flat. No thanks.

Now, if only her lust-saturated thoughts would catch on. He was a business contact and the man trying to protect her. Her response to him needed to stop there. She was focused on expanding her career, not the need moistening her vagina.

But she knew what Jack was and what he wanted from a woman.

Curiosity could be almost as powerful as desire. And none of her admonishments could douse the arousal that seeped through her blood.

Morgan took a deep breath. Okay, so he could bring her pleasure. Surely lots of other guys could, without all the domination and bondage. Without the frightening sense that he could control a woman's body with little more than a stare, a stern word, and a naughty smile. True, Morgan hadn't found such a man yet.

She sighed at her circular logic. Nothing mattered now except that Jack could keep her safe. She needed that so badly—assurances that she wasn't going to wind up dead in a ditch somewhere, that she could escape from the nightmare her life had become virtually overnight.

Jack squeezed her hand. "After dawn, I'll call a buddy of mine who has a lot of contacts inside the FBI and see if he can start a profile."

"Thank you." She hoped Jack and his pal would get to the bottom of this soon, so she could get on with her life and on with her show.

"Why don't you try to go back to sleep?"

Tension rose up like quicksand, threatening to drown her. "I'm done sleeping. Too worried. Too wired."

Jack leaned in and fondled a lock of her hair between his fingers and frowned. He turned dark-chocolate eyes on her. The air between them turned so thick, Morgan couldn't drag a lungful in. Heat radiated from him, warming her all the way to her bones. His scent hit her with the force of a battering ram—spice, sweat, swamp, and pure mystery.

Damn it, she was so aware of him as a man . . .

"Try. You've got to keep your strength up." He sent her a ghost of a smile. "You never know when you might need it."

\*   \*   \*

JACK escaped the cottage into the emerging dawn, spitting a curse.

Four lovers, two of them fiancés, including Brandon. Had the pansy-ass senator's son ever told Morgan about him? His guess: No.

As far as his revenge went, that was good news. Morgan had no idea who he was.

And through her entire confession, her blue eyes had eaten him up with hunger. Damn, he'd never gotten so hard from just a woman's glance.

He still wanted his pound of flesh, but revenge wasn't all he wanted anymore. The shitty fact was, Morgan aroused him unbearably. Being in the same room with her and not touching the pale silk of her skin or tasting the cinnamon spice of her kiss, the musky cream of her pussy, was making him hard enough to drill holes through steel. He barely restrained his impatience at being denied the opportunity to cuff her to his bed and coax her into submission. Need gnawed at him, demanding he clamp those pretty, pale nipples and toy with her clit until she begged for a hard ride. She nearly pushed him past sanity. He was dying to see just how submissive she was, taste her strength as he shoved his cock so far inside her, she'd never forget him.

Damn it, he had to get control. Feeling more than the need for revenge was stupid.

So why was he? The question plagued him like an annoying song he couldn't get out of his head. He'd never been particularly hot for redheads. Or short women. Or women already claimed by another man. So why her?

His grandfather's matter-of-fact voice echoed in his head, *If you're dreaming about a redheaded woman over and over, you're about to meet her and she's your heart's mate.* He'd always thought the family "curse" utter bullshit, propagated by the colorful loons and romantics in his family who believed it because they wanted to.

Now, it still didn't make sense. He still didn't believe it.

But he couldn't deny that he'd never responded to a woman this strongly.

Muttering an even uglier curse than the last, he headed around the left side of the cabin and began walking the perimeter, the marshy soil soggy beneath his boots.

He'd seduce Morgan, no question. Not even a blind man could miss the curiosity and awakening need in her eyes. He was far from blind. But he also sensed something holding her back. Latent affection for Brandon? Or a fear of being dominated, despite her curiosity and submissive nature? There was more to her past relationships than she was admitting, particularly her breakup with her former producer.

Her reason for denying her desire to submit didn't matter. He'd overcome it and have Morgan bound and hungrily accepting his every demand, gasping as he sank his cock into her mouth, her pussy, her ass. Give her things straightlaced Brandon Ross would never dream of.

Would that be enough to make her leave Brandon in the end?

Jack paused at the bedroom window and peered in. Empty. No Morgan in the bed or anywhere in the room. Damn it, she'd defied his good advice to rest. No doubt, she needed a strong man to heat up her ass to keep her in line.

His palm itched at the thought, but he shoved the tempting idea away. After the last thirty minutes—hell, the last few hours of watching her sleep—his pike-hard cock was finally getting the clue that he wasn't getting lucky. He welcomed a rest from having most of the blood in his body nowhere near his brain.

In fact, he needed to get her some clothes. Preferably made of flannel and three sizes too big. If he watched her parade around in tight purple leather and stiletto boots for too long, he'd be too distracted by wanting to fuck her to protect her in case the worst happened. The fucking would happen, he reminded himself, but not yet. Not until he was sure she was safe. Not until he'd earned a bit more of her trust and figured out how to get under her skin.

He'd need all that if he wanted her to completely surrender to him.

He walked on, pulling his cell phone from his belt clip, and dialed Brice. He'd get his grandfather to pick her up a few things. But after the sixth ring, he hung up with a curse. The old codger was probably having coffee with the "boys" at the local diner, playing *Bourée* and solving all the ills of the world. Too bad he couldn't convince Brice to buy an answering machine or a cell phone. He'd call back later . . . but that meant waiting to cover Morgan's tempting form.

At the back of the cabin, Jack paused, listening to the bayou, watching alligators slosh into the water and disappear beneath the murky surface. Cicadas sang the last of the night's song as dawn approached. Even in the February chill, moist air clung to everything.

This place had always represented peace to him. Not today. In the last few months since Brice had given the cabin to him, he'd made some modifications and upgrades—really made it his. It was the closest thing to a home he had. He rarely brought anyone here. He meant to . . . but in the end, he hid this place from submissives and all but his closest friends. So why had he brought Morgan here so readily?

Not looking too hard for the answer, Jack peered at the video equipment well hidden by the trees and the eaves. Looked good, functional, as it scanned the area behind the cottage. Then he continued on, trudging around the corner of the little house.

Flickering golden light emanated from the little window in the middle of the wall. Morgan was in the bathroom and had found the candles. What she hadn't done was completely close the shutters. She'd tried, but the broken one wouldn't extend over the window.

On quiet feet, Jack approached the small glass pane. He shouldn't look; he knew that. But he didn't have a lot of scruples where she was concerned.

Edging closer, Jack peered in, looking into the narrow bathroom. Steam rose from the claw-footed tub. Beside it, Morgan ran a hand under the water stream. Apparently satisfied with the temperature, she set the plug in the tub, then backed away.

Her hands settled on the first button of Alyssa's leather getup. At a push of her thumb, the button came loose. A second followed suit. The soft, rounded edges of her cleavage and a hint of the black bra he hadn't forgotten peeked out to torment him.

A sweat broke out across Jack's chest and back. His cock, which he'd just managed to get under control, rose up swiftly to full staff and saluted the view.

But the view only improved. A third button, centered around her navel, came loose from its mooring. As the fourth and final button came undone, so did Jack's ability to breathe.

Morgan peeled the garment off and laid it on the counter. He glued his gaze to her slender torso and high, round breasts as she reached behind her to unfasten the tight miniskirt.

With an alluring wriggle, a sexy shimmy, she peeled the garment down the sweet curve of her hips and past firm thighs.

When she stood again and set the skirt aside, the only thing stopping him from fully taking in the pale temptation of her body was a lacy bra that did nothing to hide her hard nipples, and a teeny-tiny thong.

Damn, was it possible to have a fatal heart attack at thirty-one?

He should walk away now. Focus on surveillance until he knew she was safe. Stop fixating on a woman he planned to fuck once . . . just so Brandon could appreciate the pain and rage a man felt when he knew his woman had surrendered willingly to another hard dick.

But walking away from Morgan was easier said than done. At this point, he couldn't find the will to try.

Drawing in a shaky breath, he watched as she reached behind her to unclasp the bra. The movement thrust her breasts forward, accentuating their round, firm shape and those pretty nipples he thirsted to suck into his mouth.

A moment later, they came into view. Plump, soft, blushing pink, and swollen, they beckoned like little bits of heaven topping the pale beauty of her breasts, which shimmered with dancing, golden candle-light. He grabbed the ledge outside the window and let out a ragged breath.

How the hell was he going to keep from fucking her into oblivion in the next ten minutes?

Before he could answer that question, she slid the little black thong off and tossed it away, revealing the last of her secrets to him. And boy, was it a doozie.

The tiny patch of hair covering Morgan's pussy was fiery red.

Now Jack knew how a bull felt when someone waved something red in its face: enflamed, ready to charge.

*Toro!*

He braced his hands against the side of the cabin to steady himself as Morgan stepped into the tub and sank into the steaming water, eyes closed.

Damn, he had to stop spying on her like some loser sicko who couldn't persuade a woman to undress for him. And he would . . . as soon as she stopped splashing water over her shoulders, on her breasts.

The water beaded up on her creamy skin, running in rivulets that dripped from succulent nipples. He'd love to lick her up with his tongue.

The sun edged up over the horizon behind Jack, making it harder to see inside the little bathroom. It was probably a sign that he should be noble and stop acting like a Peeping Tom.

Morgan dragged a thumb over one of her hard nipples, and her lips parted in a silent gasp.

Fuck nobility.

He stepped closer to the window to improve his view.

Her nipples responded to their wet state and the cool air, beading up even tighter, turning a shade darker. She lay against the back of the tub and sighed.

Then she lifted her hands from the water—to cup her breasts. A moment later, Morgan stunned him when she dragged her thumbs across the rigid peaks deliberately and moaned.

A fresh gallon of blood ran south to engorge his cock even more. God, he was going to go insane. He, who had never had even a hint of mental illness in his family, would be certifiable before Morgan finished her bath.

Jack held his breath as she pinched her lush nipples, rolling them between thumb and fingers, pulling at them harder than he would have imagined. First one, then the other, finally together, she worked them with her small fingers. She threw her head back, neck arched, moist lips parted. She looked like a sensual goddess, like the ultimate fuck.

In that moment, he would have charged into the house, plucked her damp, naked body from the water, and plunged his steel-hard cock right into her. But he wanted to know too damn bad just what she would do next.

As her nipples darkened and swelled from her fondling, she sank deeper into the tub, until only the twin peaks of her breasts rose from the water, wet and tempting. She lifted her right leg and rested her heel on the rim of the tub, then bent her left knee and spread her legs wide.

Jack couldn't see Morgan's pussy under the water, could only glimpse an occasional flash of red hair. But his imagination filled in the gaps. Fiery curls shielding swollen pink flesh, slick and pouting and ready.

If she were his, he'd keep her like that—naked and hot. Always wet. He'd spend mornings lapping at her nipples. While she ate breakfast, he'd eat her. They'd shower with her mouth around his cock, as she took him deep, all the way to the back of her throat. And then he'd get serious, push her to the limits of her body, her trust. He'd leave no part of her untouched. There would be nothing he wouldn't do with her, to her, to hear her scream her throat raw in pleasure.

Morgan jolted him out of his reverie when she trailed her hand from her breast, down her abdomen, and between her legs.

She began to stroke herself.

*Oh, shit* . . . If he hadn't yet lost his mind, it was going to go up in flames now—just like his body.

He shifted his aching cock in his jeans and edged closer to the window until his face was nearly pressed against it. Eyes closed, Morgan made lazy circles with the hand between her legs, while the other continued to pluck at her nipples, keeping them hard and ready.

Soon, the slow circles of her fingers gained speed. Water sloshed in the tub, dousing the ends of her silky hair, which hung wildly about her shoulders. Her hips began to lift to meet her fingers. Jack caught electrifying flashes of red, along with slick, spread flesh. Lust pooled in his belly, demanding relief, demanding her, as her chest rose and fell with quick, panting breaths. Morgan tightened the circle, moving faster than ever. Her lips, now a deep red, opened on a silent gasp. She squeezed her eyes tightly closed. Jack stepped closer still to the window for an even better view, clutching the window ledge with a white-knuckled grip, his own rapid breathing creating circles of damp heat against the glass.

Then her legs stiffened, her back bowed. She bit her lip to trap in a cry as orgasm washed over her in a long rush of shuddering sensation. Morgan rubbed at her clit furiously, extending her pleasure, extending Jack's hell.

She kept panting, teasing, bucking against her hand, stretching for the next orgasm. Moments later it came, crashing down on her like a tidal wave. She cried out, no longer able to hold in the sound. But the desperate pleasure in her voice stabbed Jack with a fresh bolt of lust.

God help her. God help them both. There was no power strong

enough on this earth to keep him out of her body right now. Fuck his plans. Fuck the consequences.

He was going to fuck her. Now.

As Morgan rose to the pinnacle of her peak, arching and flushed, her eyes flew open.

Her gaze connected with his.

# Chapter Five

OH *my God!*

Morgan leapt from the tub, grabbed a towel with shaking hands, and wrapped it around her, covering as much of herself as she could. He'd seen her—and everything she'd done!

She turned back to the window, eager to assure herself Jack had had the decency to leave and give her privacy, now that she'd caught him being a voyeur. But Jack still stood there unblinking, shirtless, his massive chest rising and falling with harsh, tightly controlled breaths. Worse, he watched her with a hot, predatory gaze. Completely sexual. Totally lacking in apology. His gaze told her that she aroused him. He wanted her. He meant to have her. Period.

The ache between her thighs that she'd tried to quench pulsed back to life. Morgan squeezed her eyes shut, struggling against the morass of feeling swirling inside her. Desire and fury galloped in her stomach. They raced neck in neck, mortification a close third.

But at the finish line, fury won.

Damn him! Jack might have saved her life, but that didn't entitle him to invade her privacy, to watch . . . whatever she did by herself—and arouse himself doing it. Arrogant. Rude! So like a man.

The famous O'Malley temper her mother had always talked about was rising hot and fast inside her, greedily lapping at propriety and calm.

Shooting him a venomous glare through the window, Morgan whirled and left the little bathroom, then stalked down the hall into the kitchen/living room area. She barreled toward the cabin's front door.

Before she reached it, the door opened. Jack stepped in, fierce and silent. And so taut she could probably bounce knives off him. He closed the door behind him with a quiet click that was nearly lost in the hard stamps of her wet feet across the gleaming wood floor.

"You son of a bitch!" she yelled, charging toward him until they stood a mere foot apart. "How dare you? Did you think I wouldn't notice or care? Or maybe you thought—"

"Enough." He didn't raise his voice, but it still lashed like the sting of a whip.

"Go to—"

"Morgan," he warned, jaw clenching.

She started, clutching her towel around her, her chest rising and falling with anger. His voice filled the room. A command burned in his eyes. *He* was angry with *her*? Unbelievable.

Before she could tell him to pound sand, he said, "I had no right to watch you, *cher*. I went outside to check the perimeter security. You left the shutters partially open, and I couldn't look away. I'm sorry."

An apology? That was it? No arguing, no defending himself?

Fury dissipated—much faster than she wanted it to. Hard to stay frothing furious at someone who'd offered an apology, damn it. Even harder to stay mad at a man who'd been transfixed because he liked the sight of her.

But she was an O'Malley and not nearly ready to give up the fight.

"You didn't have any right! I-I'm completely embarrassed."

He edged closer. "Of your body? Of being a woman with needs?"

"Of being watched! I can't believe you just stood there and looked at me like I was the star of some sort of freebie sex show."

"It's not good behavior for hosts, I agree. It's not a habit." His eyes sparked with truth—and a desire that wasn't going away. "Morgan, admit something, though: Knowing I watched you, that I couldn't look away, arouses you."

"No." She refused to give him the satisfaction, despite her awareness that moisture gushed between her legs at his words.

"Those sultry blue eyes say yes, *cher.*"

"You need glasses. Did you think I would be okay with you turning my bath into a peep fest? Did you think I'd say, 'Sure, I know we just met yesterday, but feel free to spy on the most intimate moments of my life'?"

"I was only aware of how beautiful you looked." He leaned in. "If you were mine, you'd have no reason to self-pleasure, *cher.*" He quirked a smile. "Of course, I'd love to see you stroke yourself now and then for the pure viewing fun."

Risking a glance down, she couldn't miss the outline of his rigid erection straining the front of his jeans. Morgan felt a flush rise to her skin and that ache tighten between her legs again. *No!* She needed her anger, all whipped into a nice, frothy fury.

Instead, she became all too aware of how close he stood. Of the fact that he was half dressed, while she was barely covered at all. Dangerous territory, especially with Jack looking at her with a dark flame of want blazing in his eyes. Especially with her body warming in response.

Morgan retreated a step.

"Stay there."

His quiet tone rang with command, vibrated through her. Morgan hesitated, mind racing. She didn't have to listen, didn't have to stand before him nearly naked and follow orders. In fact, it was much better if she didn't . . .

"Bite me. I'm not a two-year-old or a robot," she shot back and stepped away again.

Jack reached for her.

*Run!* she ordered herself. Instead, he encircled her wrist with a gentle grip, but she felt its steel beneath. And his heat.

*"Stay there."*

For some reason, something in his voice . . . She couldn't *not* listen to him.

Maybe that's because Jack embodied every sin she'd ever yearned to experience, ever masturbated to in her dark, lonely bed, only to have frustration douse her satisfaction when she realized none of it was real.

He released her slowly and began to pace around her with unhurried steps, brushing her shoulder with gentle fingertips as he stepped past. Her heartbeat accelerated. Goose bumps erupted across her arms. She didn't even want to think about what was happening to her nipples or how badly they ached.

He stopped behind her. Jack's hot breath tickled the sensitive spot between her neck and shoulders. His heat radiated along her back and legs. Morgan sucked in a breath. God, he was standing close. Too close to ignore. Too close to deny the effect he had on her.

The ache between her thighs zinged to new heights, as if she hadn't stroked her way to climax mere minutes ago.

She sent a cautious glance over her shoulder. Jack stood right there, waiting, as if he'd known what she would do. Their gazes connected, his full of fire and demand. He hovered a mere breath away, tall and towering.

He was going to touch her.

A zip of electric thrill raced through her, even as she called herself twenty kinds of stupid. She tore her gaze from his and stared at the front door again, clutching the towel around her body. He said nothing, but Morgan could feel his eyes on her, taking in her still-wet skin, her rapid, telling breaths.

Now what? This had gone from an ass-chewing to an ass-viewing in about two minutes. If she didn't want him doing anything else with her ass, she had to get away now.

"Tell me why you needed that orgasm," he murmured into her ear.

She couldn't. It would only confirm what he must know: That some deviant, out-of-control part of her wanted him, felt more than journalistic curiosity about what he could give her.

"It's really none of your business, Jack."

"Don't call me that, not when we're alone."

He wanted her to call him sir. Trembling, she stood still, thoughts and heart racing between uncertainty and forbidden thrill. She felt . . . claimed by Jack's words. His iron commands reached something inside her and called forth a barrage of need.

*What would it be like to surrender? To give in to that voice?*

Dangerous. Bad. Giving into everything Jack represented and

everything she shouldn't want. If she did, she'd only be forging a new path to hell.

"How about jackass, then? That's appropriate." She dug up her bravado and turned to face him. "Don't bully me."

She waited for his angry comeback, for a growled command of frustration. It didn't come.

Instead, he shuffled a heartbeat closer, until a mere whisper separated her from the raging heat of his body. "There is no reason to be embarrassed about your desires."

"I'm not. Call me repressed, but I am embarrassed about having an audience during orgasm," she snapped.

"That's not true," he said softly.

Swallowing, Morgan tried to tear her gaze from his knowing, sexual stare. His scent assailed her next, full of man and mystery, spicy as Cajun food and as hard to fathom as the swamp itself.

She inched back. "Do you think you know me now?"

"I know things about you. I know you're uneasy about your sexuality. You have desires you don't like to admit to. I see them all in your eyes. A craving to be bound and dominated—"

"You don't see a damn thing! I'm *not* depraved."

"No, you're not. Anyone who thinks you are is an idiot."

Jack reached for her again, determination all over the fierce masculine angles of his strong face. She didn't want to know exactly what he was determined to do. Panic flared, and she batted his hand away and leapt out of his reach. Her back hit the door.

And Jack kept coming for her with soft, slow steps. The pace of a hunter. She had to get away. Had to. Now.

Morgan lunged to her left to evade him. He blocked her way with a strong arm, then anchored it on the door, sealing off that avenue of escape. He used the same tactic on the right before she could make a move in that direction.

Then Jack leaned in, his hands on the door, just next to her head. She couldn't look at him, refused to. As if to get her attention, his body brushed hers, detonating ruthless sparks of desire that burned through her body. That brief contact was enough to light her up like a firecracker.

"Look at me." He leaned back to put a breath of air between them.

Something inside her wanted to obey. That smooth, rich voice, the hint of a French lilt combined with explicit command, tugged at her. The thought of surrendering made her stomach clench with anxiety . . . and desire gnaw at her clit. The man was a giant contradiction. An aggressive protector. A man who bound women was going out of his way to keep her safe.

It was confusing her. *He* was confusing her.

Finally, she raised her stormy gaze to clash with his. "What the hell do you want from me?"

"Honesty."

"No, you don't. You want me to give in, to spread my legs like a spineless airhead and give you . . . whatever it is you want."

A half smile curled up the side of his mouth. "You're half right. I do want you to give in, *cher*. I want you to spread your legs when I tell you to. Not because you're spineless, but because you're not." He moved in closer, brushing his body against hers again, all hint of a smile gone. "I want you to burn for me. I want all your fire and independence and sass underneath me. I want to show you what you secretly yearn for and try not to—and how good it can be."

Morgan swallowed, then opened her mouth to speak. How was she supposed to reply to that? What did a woman say to the man trying to spoon-feed her every sexual fantasy she'd ever denied?

"I don't think—"

"You think too much. Of all the reasons you shouldn't. Of all the reasons I scare you. Try thinking of the ways I could please you."

Oh, she'd thought of those.

One of his hands eased away from the door. He brushed the back of his fingers down her neck, over her collarbone . . . and kept delving down. He caressed down the terry cloth–covered slope of her breast, then brushed down over the erect nipple begging for his touch.

Even through the towel, she felt that touch all the way to her toes. A hot tingle sizzled her insides like bacon in hot grease. She gasped, felt her gaze locked in place by his dark stare.

He repeated the process again, then once more. Pleasure assailed Morgan from the aching points of her tight nipples, streaking through her tightly coiled body, straight to her vagina. She dropped her head back against the door, unable to hold in her moan.

"That's it." Jack feathered his lips down her throat as he moved in closer. His other hand joined the first in the soft torment of her nipples, with only the thin towel in between.

"I want to see those pretty nipples. I need to have them in my mouth, *cher*. Drop the towel."

Desire bubbled within her, at full boil, even as a last bit of sanity screamed somewhere in her head. The memory of his touch at the strip club and the jolting pleasure it suffused her with still haunted her. The lingering remembrances, coupled with his potent command, sent her self-control reeling.

Of all the men she could desire, why him? Of all times—while being chased by some whacked-out stalker—why did she have to want him now?

Gee, maybe it was because Jack was the embodiment of every midnight fantasy that had ever kept her awake. Maybe it was because he lowered his hand to the part in her towel and swirled his palm across her stomach, over the curve of her hip, then moved in to press an impressive erection against her. Certainly, he and all that testosterone . . . diverted her mind from the whacked-out stalker issues.

Her mother had always said, *You make your choices in life and live with them*. Could she live with herself if she walked away from the forbidden allure of Jack Cole without one taste?

He curved his hand over the rise of her ass and began to stroke his way down—fingertips lightly toying with the crease between her cheeks. A new rush of tingles filled her. Clever move, she acknowledged. If she arched into his touch, he had a handful of ass. If she arched away from it, she pushed herself right against his erection. How could he lose?

*How could you?* a little voice inside her head dared her.

In the next moment, his fingers stroked the cleft between her cheeks again, this time a little harder, deeper. A dark thrill zoomed up her spine. Without thought, she gasped and arched right into his hand.

"Good girl," he murmured into her ear, sending the shivers back down her spine.

His thumb toyed with her nipple, now so hard she could feel every brush of skin, every callous. She moaned again.

"*Cher,* drop the towel. *Montre-moi ton joli corps.*" His breath came hard and fast, his voice strained but still in control. "Show me your pretty body."

"You've already seen it, you Peeping Tom."

"Show me," he growled.

Oh, God. The command in his voice turned the ache between her legs into a throb. She wanted to obey . . . so bad. Sizzle coursed through her. Blood rushed everywhere, swelling her clit. Already wet from orgasm, she felt moisture pooling in her most intimate recesses, threatening to overflow. Jack's spicy, earthy scent was scattering rational thought. The parts of her body aching for his touch were in control.

*What's the worst that could happen if you gave in?* a voice inside her asked.

More disappointment and frustration. More rejection and ridicule.

Then again, it took her at least a dozen pairs of shoes to find the right fit. Were lovers the same way? Maybe three hadn't been enough.

Confusion spun in her head.

"Jack," she managed to murmur in between his wicked touches. "I talk to people about sex for a living. I don't need to have it to do the show."

"Forget the show. You need what I can give you. Stop denying yourself."

"I'm not denying myself anything." *Stupid!* Morgan bit her lip, sure that her flushed cheeks and hard nipples made her words an obvious lie.

He grabbed her jaw in one hand. "You lie to me again, and I'm going to spank you so hard you won't sit for a week. Tell me why you're resisting what you want."

"Don't touch me." She tried to jerk from his grasp.

Jack held firm. "*Cher,* I'm going to do more than touch you. Way more. And the longer you hold out on answering me, the more I'm going to make you beg."

Oh, God. His words alone made Morgan hot as she weighed them and the relentless demand in his eyes against her fears. He could do it; he could make her beg. And the thought raced a shiver down her spine. "Fine. If you have to know, I'm not some femme fatale. I don't respond much to sex."

Cajun charm softened pushy arrogance with a mere curl of his sin-inspiring lips. He placed hot kisses on her neck, nibbled at the curve of her shoulder. "You responded just fine to everything I threw your way in Lafayette."

Surprise. That's all it had been. She'd been too shocked to really react. To want, then bow to the pressure of self-doubt. Then clam up until, tense and frustrated, her body gave up. Besides, she might be curious about his . . . lifestyle, but participating committed her far more than simply wondering. And she had a bad feeling that one taste of Jack Cole would be as addicting as heroin to a junkie.

"We don't really know each other."

Jack's fingertips cascaded over her shoulder, leaving nothing but anticipation and a fresh crop of goose bumps in their wake. "I know enough to know how to make you scream. But that isn't what's stopping you."

He kissed her neck, her jawline, inched up toward her mouth. She melted under his mouth. God, that felt good. And his smell . . . Did it contain some ingredient that was like kryptonite for her restraint?

"We don't like each other much," she pointed out in a desperate gasp, evading his kiss—a kiss she wanted so badly, her gut clenched with desire.

Again, he smiled, a flash of white teeth visible in the room bathed with predawn light. "I'm liking you just fine right now, *cher*. I liked you the first time we talked online. I like that you're smart and gutsy and sexy as hell."

He whispered the words against her mouth, and Morgan felt her resolve fraying around the edges. Back in Lafayette, Jack had touched her breasts, stroked her clit, fondled deep inside her, yes. But his kiss lingered, haunted her. Like the smoothest wine, all wrapped in sin and velvet, with a kick of lust that promised pleasure. His kiss gave her a preview of his strength and self-control. Almost against her will, she leaned toward him.

For a wild moment, Morgan thought he would pull away. Tease her, enflame her with what might be. Instead, he grasped the sides of her face and kept her gaze locked to his dark one.

"The memory of you in my arms . . . it's been keeping me hard all night. Watching you sleep was torture. I kept thinking about lying next to you on the bed, peeling your clothes away and devouring everything underneath. I want to get my hands on you, *cher*. My mouth on you. Get inside you, drive deep and sure. I want you to scream my name when you come."

Morgan couldn't breathe. The impact of every word did more than rev up her libido; it struck her like body blows, every syllable battering her resolve with hot intent. He robbed her of air, of the will to resist. How would he feel? Taste? That terrible vise of desire clamped her clit with need. She almost whimpered with her need to come again. And he'd barely touched her.

What if she gave him free rein? What would it be like to let go and give herself to someone with his mastery, just this once?

She exhaled on a ragged sigh. Arousal flared like a forest fire under a harsh wind, burning her from the inside out. About to rage out of control.

Moisture threatened to trickle down her legs. She licked her dry lips, but when his gaze followed the motion, it only made her temperature spike hotter.

"You going to put that pretty pink tongue on me, *cher*? While I watched you sleep, I pictured you on your knees, my cock in your luscious little mouth."

Morgan knew next to nothing about oral sex from personal experience. Reading and talking about it to prepare for her show didn't make up for that fact. At this moment, with a mountain of a man like Jack in front of her, pressed against her, that seemed irrelevant. Jack inspired an urge to sample everything wicked, including his cock.

"Ah, I think you like the idea," he murmured, breath caressing her tingling lips. "Those blue eyes are turning darker. I wonder what else you like? I know you enjoy this . . ."

As he'd done before, Jack stroked her nipples, now painfully hard, through her towel, with brushes of knuckles and fingertips. She gasped and couldn't stop herself from arching toward him and seeking an end to the erotic torment of his touch.

"Sensitive nipples. I'll enjoy sucking them until I can feel them swell on my tongue."

Would he? The suggestion made her faint with pleasure.

"Don't presume. I didn't say yes," she pointed out, trying to hang onto sanity. But the croak in her voice made her protest a joke.

No, no, no! Jack might be thrilling her beyond belief—beyond bearing—but tomorrow . . . how messed up would her head and her life be tomorrow if she gave in now? Wasn't having a stalker enough? She'd agreed to meet him to facilitate an interview for *Turn Me On*, not to find a dominant looking for a plaything.

"Your body is saying it for you, *cher*. Breath chugging. Jackhammer pulse jumping. Your nipples are as hard as diamonds." Suddenly, he found the fold in her towel again, down near her abdomen, parted the halves of terry cloth, and planted his hot palm on her skin. He was so warm, it startled her. Stung. She jumped . . . closer to him. Now their chests brushed. His mouth was only a whisper away from hers as he dragged that hand over her hip, across her belly—then started heading down.

"You going to say no, *cher*?"

Morgan hesitated. If she was smart, she'd scream "no" now. She'd jerk away from him, march back to that claw-footed tub of his, fill it up with cold water, and dive in. But his fingertips whispered swirls and circles across her belly, over her thighs, brushing over her mound just enough to entice.

She clenched her thighs together, but it only magnified the ache. It climbed up into her belly, spread down her thighs. The fact that she wore nothing but a tiny green bath towel did not comfort her.

"Or are you going to say yes?" he whispered. "Are you going to let me fill you with my fingers and tongue? Are you going to let my cock ride you hard and deep?"

God, more of his wicked words that gave her lascivious ideas—and irresistible pictures to go along with them.

Morgan threw her head back against the door and closed her eyes. She wanted to say yes, yearned as she never had for the forbidden pleasure she knew Jack could give her.

*Once. Just once,* whispered a voice in her head. *What could it hurt?*

Soon, with any luck, this business with her stalker would be behind her, she'd be back in L.A. taping the next season of *Turn Me On*. Jack

Cole would be a hot memory she could drag out on a cold night when she needed to warm herself. That simple.

"Jack . . ."

"You want something?" His voice taunted her as his fingers glided like a ghost over her abdomen, her hip. Those dancing dark eyes, that playful mouth teased her without mercy.

She and her resistance were toast.

In answer to his question, she grabbed his hand and placed it right over her mound. He swiped a hot finger through the swollen folds and swirled around her clit once, twice. She gasped, assailed by an urge to spread her legs wider for him.

"If you want something, *cher,* drop the towel. I want all of you, and I want you bare."

Morgan refused to stop and think, to reconsider again. Plenty of time for that later. Instead, she tugged at the towel. It fell to the floor in a quiet rush, leaving her covered in goose bumps—and nothing else. She shivered—but not from the cold.

Jack looked his fill with hot eyes that promised mind-shattering pleasure. "I can't wait to get inside you, so deep you'll never forget it."

His mouth covered hers in a searing kiss. No, he did more than cover her mouth. He devoured, consumed, possessed. Morgan opened to him, accepting the hungry thrust of his tongue, which delivered the spice of his taste and the heat of his need in a devastating dance of seduction. Her knees weakened in seconds. His passion had the kick of cayenne pepper, balanced with the sweetness of honey, caged in control of steel. Unique. Intoxicating. She moaned into his mouth, and he swallowed the hungry sound.

Jack's hands fell to her hips and grasped her, fitting her right against his jeans-clad erection. He gave her a nudge in the right spot, and her need spiked. The ache in her sex built. He pressed against her again, compelling Morgan to lift her leg to wrap it around his waist, opening her body to him in a silent plea.

He accepted immediately, taking her thigh and anchoring it over his hip, bringing him in perfect contact with her clit. Morgan grasped his bare, steely shoulders, hanging on while she felt dizzy with need.

Had she ever been this aroused? No. Ever wanted so badly, she thought her blood would boil if he turned and walked away? No.

It was torture. It was bliss.

He continued to eat at her mouth, small nibbles of her lips, long swirls of his tongue against hers. Jack left no part of her mouth without his attention, his flavor. In desperation, she rubbed her breasts against the hot, hard wall of his chest, threw her arms around his neck, and pressed deeper into the kiss.

When he eased his lips away from hers, she clung to him in protest. He lifted her arms away from him and anchored them to the door with a warning stare.

Their gazes connected, his dark with broiling need, compelling her to accept whatever came next. Her body too ravenous, her mind too entangled in his spell, to refuse. The breath seesawing in and out of his chest was her only indication that he wasn't perfectly in control.

Pushing her flat against the door, Jack leaned in, his cock grinding against her clit again. But now he bent to add a totally new sensation to the mix: his mouth around her nipples.

Morgan arched up to Jack, not just eager to give him more, but aching to. He started with skillful suction, a teasing lick.

"Jack," she protested softly. "Jack."

"You know what to call me," he warned, thumbs and fingers pinching her sensitive nipples. "Until you come, I don't want to hear my name fall from your lips again, *cher.*"

"Yes, sir," she chanted. Anything to get her nipples back in his mouth.

He rewarded her with hot suction over the peaks of her breasts, first one, then the other. Back and forth. Over and over. Hot, swirling tongue, then tender bites that had her gasping and clawing.

For the first time ever, she could actually feel the blood filling her nipples, swelling them.

With a last lick, he pulled back to look at his handiwork. "Very pretty. I should keep them like this always, slightly tender, a rosy pink, standing up and waiting for just one more touch."

He closed thumbs and fingers around them again in a pinch that made her catch her breath. Then he twisted, just enough to make Morgan cry out—as the moisture gushed between her thighs in a fresh rush. Lord, she'd never been so sensitive, never felt as if she might actually orgasm just from having her nipples toyed with. She'd read it was possible but never believed it. Until now.

"Are you slick and hot for me?" he asked, his hot breath teasing her neck.

"Yes," she gasped.

"Yes, what?"

"Yes, sir."

Jack swiped a pair of fingers down the valley between her breasts, dragged them down her abdomen, her mound, then dove right into her wet heat. He grazed her clit, and she moaned against his mouth.

"Touch me," she moaned.

"You don't give the orders, *cher*. You take what I give you. No matter how I give it to you."

"But—"

Jack unwrapped her leg from around his waist and took a step back, ending all contact. Morgan stared, wide-eyed. Bastard.

"We either do this my way, or we don't do it at all. How is it going to be?"

"Damn it, you're arrogant," she said between gritted teeth as the ache and sizzle smoldered inside her.

"We've already established that. How is this going to go down, *cher*? Your choice."

In the end, Morgan was too far gone, too curious about the heights he could take her to, to consider saying anything except, "Your way . . . sir."

"Good girl. Spread those pretty thighs."

Leaning against the door, Morgan stepped wide. Jack trailed his fingers over her puffed, wet folds, toyed with the tip of her clit, trailed moisture down her thighs. Her breathing climbed higher, along with her heartbeat. Amazing. Jack knew just where to touch, when, and for how long to keep her on edge, to grow her want but never fulfill it.

Soon, she felt a flush suffuse her skin all over. She was one giant ache, whimpering, dying for him to fill her, conquer this monstrous need he'd created in her. Morgan ran greedy hands over his hard shoulders, the incredible lines of his pectorals, his ridged abdomen. He amazed her. Flesh so hard everywhere, but skin so silky soft.

He lured her close to the edge of restraint with talented fingers, an occasional nip at her breasts. His long, fevered kisses made her moan, arch, silently plead. He toyed with her, inciting her higher and higher until she became dizzy, delirious, willing to do most anything for him to end her torment.

In desperation, she trailed her hands down his stomach and grabbed the ridge of his cock through his jeans. Huge. Thick and like iron, he could give her what her body needed. So why wasn't he?

With a hiss, Jack grabbed her wrist and anchored it against the door, near her head.

"You didn't ask to touch me."

"I thought you'd like it," she panted.

"You thought you'd strip my self-control, Morgan, so you could get what you want. *Non*. You touch me when you're told, not before."

Restless, beyond needy, she shifted from one foot to the other. He kept her thighs spread with his feet between hers, so she couldn't clench them together. His fingers toyed again with her nipples, now slightly sore. And somehow that tiny hint of pain only made his every touch more vivid, shot every caress straight down to her clit.

"Please, sir . . ."

"Please what, *cher*?" He pinched her nipples and murmured the question against her lips. "You want me to fuck you?"

She'd never said those words to a man in her life. Never imagined saying them. But now, she couldn't imagine saying anything else. She needed Jack now—hard, fast, pounding.

"Yes," she whispered. "Fuck me."

He hesitated, dark brow raised expectantly.

"Sir," she added hastily, panting. "Fuck me, sir."

In reward, he slid a pair of fingers over her clit and rubbed tiny, torturous circles around the hard nubbin. Morgan had thought that, surely, her arousal could not climb any higher. She'd been dead wrong, she thought with a moan.

So close now, Morgan's every breath was audible. A drag in, a rush out, air filled her lungs but never made it to her head. There was only her heartbeat, drowning out everything except the need to feel him deep inside her.

"Unzip my pants."

Morgan didn't hesitate, didn't tease. She rushed to pull the zipper down and shove the hated jeans down his hips. He wore no underwear, so his cock sprang free into her waiting hands.

She rubbed him. Her technique was fast and inexpert, she was sure, driven totally by a need to touch him, feel the man who would soon be inside her. Fists wrapped around him, one on top of the other, she stroked his thick length and gloried.

Until he grabbed her wrists and took her hands away, shoving them against the door again.

"You're not following directions, *cher*. I said to unzip my pants, not to take them down, not to stroke my cock. Fail again, and you won't get this fucking."

She bit her lip, trying to find patience, and nodded. "I understand . . . sir."

Her clit pulsed just from saying those words. God, what was wrong with her? She was too far gone to care. Later . . .

In silence, he extracted a packet from his pocket and shoved his jeans down to his knees. Seconds later, he ripped open the foil square and sheathed the purple head of his cock, then rolled it down his long length. Slowly. Too damn slowly. Morgan resisted the urge to help him or hurry him up or tap her feet in impatience.

Suddenly, he bent, lifted her by her hips, and wedged her body between his and the door. "Put your legs around my waist."

She hesitated. Could people really have sex standing up? She'd never tried anything more exotic than woman on top.

"Do it." His voice was edged with steel.

Without another pause, Morgan lifted both of her legs and folded them around his hips. Moments later, he rewarded her with the feel of his cock probing at her entrance, all thick and ready. Breath held, she clung to his shoulders, on the razor's edge, waiting.

He eased his tip inside, and even that hard bit of him felt like heaven, like the magic elixir to cure the ache currently roasting her alive.

"Say it again," he demanded, voice strained. "Tell me what you want."

Morgan never considered holding back. "Fuck me. Now!"

With that, he pushed her hips down as he thrust up. Tissues unused to such invasion protested at first, unable to accommodate his girth. She cried out.

"Relax," he ground out. "Open to me, *cher*."

Morgan did her best to loosen her muscles—hard when she was dying a slow death by desire. Jack kept pushing his way inside, the blade of his flesh cutting through her like soft butter, probing past nerve endings with the wide head of his cock, awakening them, leaving tingles screaming in his wake. He made her need soar, and it seemed like forever until he was buried to the hilt. Oh, God, she needed to come.

She'd never taken a man this big, this deep. She could feel him in the back of her tonsils. The width of him stretched her until her flesh burned. But it wasn't enough.

That hint of pain fueled something inside her. Her blood raced, perspiration burst across her skin. The ache made her hyperaware of being alive, of the pleasure roiling beside the sting.

"More!" she demanded. "Please . . ."

Without warning, he withdrew nearly all the way, then eased back in, much gentler than before. The pain faded, but it had charged up the tissues in her sex as never before. She swore she could feel every inch, every vein of his cock rasping across suddenly sensitive flesh inside her.

Jack brought agonizing pleasure with every slow stroke, every rub of the swollen head of his cock right over the flesh inside that had her panting. Gasping, burning need took over. Everything else receded but the feel of him, her need for him.

"*Cher, tu sens si douce,*" he murmured in her ear as he thrust inside her again. "You feel so sweet."

She tried to hold on, hold out against the pleasure threatening to sweep away her sanity. But with those words and the next hard stroke of his cock, orgasm engulfed her like a raging hurricane—swift, strong, unlike anything she'd ever experienced.

"Jack!" she screamed, nails biting into his shoulders.

Morgan knew then that her first instinct was right; she was never going to be the same again.

*   *   *

WITH Morgan's scream ringing in his ears, Jack surged into the silken heaven of her pussy one more time and lost control of the orgasm he had held onto by a bare thread.

The explosion originated low in his belly, driving pleasure out through his cock. It burst out across his body, suffusing bliss everywhere. A wave of dizziness crashed over him. His toes tingled. The pulses of Morgan's second climax fluttered around him, milking him of every last drop of semen, leaving heavy satisfaction in their wake.

When had anything ever felt so good?

Struggling to catch his breath, he opened his eyes to her flushed face, her swollen mouth, the relaxed set of her shoulders.

*Did she look like this after a night in Brandon's bed?*

The thought slammed Jack from out of nowhere. Anger and denial sluiced through him in a shock, as if he'd jumped into an icy stream. He stilled.

Anger? Yes, that Brandon had touched her. That she belonged to the bastard.

*Ah, but you fucked her,* he reminded himself. *Revenge is sweet.*

True, but his gut, that gnawing spot that had festered like a wound in acid for three years because of Brandon's betrayal, wasn't whooping with elation. Instead, he fixated on the feel of Morgan around him, on her raspberry scent. He'd just come inside her and already he wanted to do it again.

*Not smart, Jack.*

He'd lured her in to fuck her as payback. First mission objective accomplished. End of story.

Jack forced himself to withdraw and set Morgan on her feet. She looked at him with wide eyes that simultaneously asked for reassurance and wondered what was next between them.

He couldn't answer either.

Stifling a curse, he turned away, tore off the condom, and tossed it in a nearby trash can. Why he should be pissed off all over again, he didn't know. Because he liked Morgan and she didn't deserve to be used? Maybe because he'd wanted to believe that she wouldn't betray the man she'd agreed to marry by spreading her legs for another.

Stupid him.

He zipped up his jeans and turned to Morgan again. Her lower lip quivered. Her posture had gone from satiated to guarded in seconds. Something deep in his gut wanted to reach out to her, reassure her. Another part was scared shitless at the magnitude of his reaction to her.

"Help yourself to anything in the kitchen," he tossed out, then turned away.

Jack strode to the back of the house, to his private domain. Fishing the keys from his pocket, he unlocked the door.

*Go in. Shut it. Don't look at her.*

Impossible.

Jack turned to face her. Across the length of his cottage, he could still see the shock on her face, along with the rosy marks of his whiskers on her bare skin, the swollen nipples so sweet and succulent they made his mouth water, and the fiery hair covering the slick utopia of her pussy.

His gut clenched. *Again. Cross the room, lay her out, fuck her again.*

Ignoring the voice, he slammed and locked the door, then stalked toward the computer desk in the corner. He plopped down in his chair and booted up his machine. But the thoughts and impulses pounding at him were unlike his mundane actions. His instinct told him he'd just made a big mistake by turning his back on her. If he'd been thinking beyond his desire to fuck her and the shock of his frenzied reaction to her, he'd have realized that if he wanted Morgan to leave Brandon, he had to keep her sated and enthralled. Constantly. Nothing else would ensure that she willingly walked away from his former pal. And if he had any sense, he'd get on his feet, march back in there, carry her to his bed, and tie her to it.

But Jack hesitated. Morgan had been like a match on the tinder of his control. He needed a breath to recover, to think. *She* and her feelings weren't important; only the fact that he'd achieved the first part of his revenge was. Deciding how to achieve the other half, the part where she left Brandon . . . that ranked up there.

Instead, dangerous fantasies of him laying her out on his bed and having a leisurely feast assailed him. He'd kill to work his mouth from the lush heat of her lips, down that silken throat, to the sweet treats of her berry nipples, over the sleek plain of her abdomen . . . all the way down to her wet, clenching little pussy, which he knew would be like ambrosia.

Damn it, he had to get his mind off his dick and remember that Morgan was the means to an end. She'd cheated on her fiancé—not the kind of woman to get tangled up with. Been there, done that. He had the scars to prove it.

To top it all off, she still had a stalker who wanted her dead. She was scared out of her mind, and he'd promised to protect her and get her some answers. It was the least he could do. Repayment for using her. He needed to focus on keeping her safe, not dwell on the feel of her around him. Not on how challenging she would be to truly tame.

He'd find some way to convince her to leave Brandon that didn't involve sinking his cock into her body over and over until they were both too sated to move.

A quick glance at his watch told Jack it wasn't quite seven in the morning. Too early to call Deke, his business partner, or anyone else. Deke had a million connections, from senators to janitors. He'd know someone who knew something about her stalker. But until then, all Jack had to focus on was Morgan or revenge.

Okay, revenge. He'd think about that, focus on how sweet it was going to be to pay Brandon back for his perfidy. He didn't feel elation, at least not yet. Likely, he wouldn't until Morgan left the bastard. But he'd known at the start there was a potential flaw in his plan: If Morgan didn't tell Brandon about her indiscretion, Jack had no way of ensuring Brandon found out. No way of proving it. And proving it—that was important. Everything, in fact.

Rising from his chair, Jack paced. How could he prove to Brandon that he'd gotten deep inside his woman and made her scream his name? He'd gotten irrevocable proof of Brandon's backstabbing via video but—

But . . . he might be able to provide Brandon the same.

Jack smiled. Paybacks were a bitch . . .

Ignoring the sting of his conscience, he raced back to his chair and fell into his seat, fingers on the keyboard. A few commands later, he found what he'd been looking for: the security footage inside the cabin from just a few minutes ago. Clicking into the file that started at 6 A.M., he watched it in double time until Morgan came out stomping and screaming in that little green towel.

Then he sat back to watch at normal speed and full sound. He didn't want to miss a second of this.

Hell, she was gorgeous, all that red hair hanging over her shoulders like a fiery flag of temptation. That creamy skin, lightly freckled and teasing his tongue. He got hard again just remembering the way she smelled, like fresh raspberries with a hint of cinnamon. Morgan was the kind of woman—strong, only bendable with effort—that he loved to dive into and eat. He hadn't found a woman like her in a long time. She was wasted on Brandon.

In his black-and-white video, he kissed her, touched her nipples. Watching her eyes slide shut, her skin flush, her back arch to him in offering aroused him all over again. Being there to experience her had been . . . beyond mind-blowing, but watching her this way was like having her again and savoring her every reaction.

She whispered something. He said something back, but the audio on the tape didn't pick it up. It hardly mattered when she dropped the towel. Though his body blocked most of the view of her body, he saw the plump curve of a breast, a flash of soft, pink folds guarded by fire-red hair. But he saw more. The lush line of her hip, the fluid shape of her thighs. The vulnerability on her face. She was taking a risk with him, and she knew it. And the reservation. She wasn't 100 percent committed to this. But the aching curiosity had finally overwhelmed her concern. She was dying for a dominant . . . and didn't want to accept it.

There had to be a reason why. He was way more interested in solving that mystery than he ought to be.

Jack swore again, torn between guilt, curiosity, and the hot flash of desire as he watched himself lift her up, brace her against the door, and fill her with a series of ramming thrusts. He remembered—so well it had him sweating—how tight she'd been, how she'd struggled to take him. But she never uttered a word, never complained. A wince of pain crossed her face, and Jack bunched his hands into fists. Damn it, why hadn't she said something? Hurting her had been the last thing on his mind. Next time—

*There may not be a next time,* he reminded himself. He had what he needed now that he'd found this video. Would the knowledge that she'd felt utter sensual devastation at the hands of a virtual stranger be enough to make her leave Brandon? Too early to tell, but he feared getting her to leave the senator's son wouldn't be that simple. He'd have to devise something . . .

As he watched her accept the entire length of his cock and her face suffuse with pleasure, he hoped like hell that one encounter wasn't enough, that she ached to submit to him again. And again. Why fight the truth? She called to him. Everything about her, her skin, her smell, her grit. She was an interesting mixture of naiveté and temptation. Shy and holding back one minute, opening wide and begging him to fuck her the next. He liked being a little off balance, and she gave that to him.

The video kept playing, second after second of their hard ride against the door. He could see the orgasm mounting within Morgan. Her sweet lips parted. She groaned and tightened her legs around him. He watched her gasp and could nearly feel her silken heat all over him, even now. Erasing the memory of her scent, her reactions—Morgan herself—wasn't going to be easy.

Jack shifted, adjusting himself in his pants. He grimaced. How often was he rock hard and ready to sink balls deep into a woman fifteen minutes after taking her? Rarely. How often had a woman lingered in his mind like this after one mere fucking? Never.

He exhaled. Why was she different? Then his grandfather's words hit him like a battering ram in the gut. *If you're dreaming about a redheaded woman over and over, you're about to meet her and she's your heart's mate.* Impossible. The woman in his mind, his dreams, was just a fantasy. It wasn't necessarily Morgan.

But she'd felt a whole lot like a fantasy come true.

On-screen, she clawed at his back. He could clearly hear her say, "Yes, more! So good!" She panted once, twice, before her lips feverishly brushed his neck. "Never better."

Jack shivered in remembrance. Yes, it had been good. Damn good. Spec-fucking-tacular, if he was honest. Damn it, he had no need to fuck her again. Now that he had proof they'd done the deed, this part of his revenge was complete. She'd served her purpose. And there was no such thing as a heart's mate.

"Jack!" He watched Morgan scream his name, bounce on him, taking pleasure, giving it.

Here in his chair, with his gaze fixed on her flushing body, his balls tightened, broiling with the need to come again. He gritted his teeth against the urge to stroke his cock through his jeans.

But he could also see her holding something back, keeping some part of her separate from him, removed from his touch. Something he hadn't picked up on with her tight, wet walls closing around his cock and his heartbeat drumming in his ears. He peered in, fixing his gaze on the grainy screen. It remained a mystery. What the hell was that about?

A few buttons later, he'd rewound the footage and played the last few moments again. Still, he couldn't discern what Morgan had kept inside. He only knew it pissed him off. Filled him with an odd sense of . . . betrayal. With the need to earn her full surrender.

Cursing, Jack finally spliced the video, just including the last minute, those few moments of Morgan saying she had never had it better, then shouting his name as she came. Maybe Brandon wouldn't notice that she was holding something back.

It was a thin maybe. Brandon was a son of a bitch but not stupid.

Still, this was the best footage he had. It would be more than enough to make his point with Brandon. He could deal with whatever Morgan was hiding later.

Before he could change his mind, Jack sent the snippet of video straight to Brandon via email, along with a friendly little note.

*How is that career in politics going, old friend?*
*Jack*

How long, he wondered, before his "pal" got an eyeful of his former Army Ranger squadron leader fucking his fiancée? And what would he do?

He didn't fight the cold smile of satisfaction.

But Morgan crept back into his thoughts. His smile slipped when he fantasized about having her spread out, tied up on his bed for his taking. Utterly at his mercy and utterly his. Wet. Begging. Willing and eager to have him fuck her in every way possible.

And he wondered what he'd have to do to persuade her not just to leave Brandon but to surrender that part of her she withheld.

He had to know. This urge wasn't going to go away, and he knew himself too well to believe otherwise. Screw everything else. For now, time was on his side. Morgan was safe at the moment. Her stalker likely had no idea where she was. It was hard for someone who wasn't Acadian to follow a son of the swamps into this untamed wilderness.

So Jack would seduce and coax Morgan into submission again. And again. She'd leave Brandon. And he would have that part of her she hadn't given him before. That part he suspected she'd never given to any man. Jack planned to make sure she gave it to him—whatever it took.

# Chapter Six

TWENTY minutes after Jack slammed the door in Morgan's face, she stood in front of the antique mirror hanging from the bedroom wall and studied her appearance. She looked remarkably calm for a woman whose knees were still shaking from orgasms so strong, seismic equipment had surely felt the tremors.

Scrubbed face, hair whisked back in a single, severe braid down her back. Nothing sexy . . . if she didn't include Alyssa's tight purple submissive-maiden leather getup in the picture. That, unfortunately, was hard to ignore.

She wasn't about to go prowling through Jack's closet for something else to wear. Too intimate. Chewing her lip, Morgan hesitated. She couldn't afford to have the bastard think the outfit was the closest thing to an engraved invitation for sex. Maybe if she gave off her best *get lost* vibes, he'd buy a clue. If not . . .

She could find herself screwed—literally—again.

And worse, she'd probably love it every bit as much as she had the first time.

Sighing, Morgan paced the room. What the hell was wrong with

Jack, anyway? They had fabulously mind-blowing sex and *he* ran away? Of course, if he hadn't beat her to it, she would have darted behind a door and slammed it between them in world-record time. But, still . . .

Jack was confusing the crap out of her. She should be the one freaked out. After all, she had a stalker after her. She'd just let a dominant man impale her against a door and drive her to two dizzying orgasms—after inspiring the two she'd given herself—all in about fifteen minutes' time.

Her desire to submit to him, to obey his raspy voice, thick with need in her ear, was so new—yet had felt so natural that she hadn't been able to resist. She'd responded to every whispered command as if he'd poured pure liquid desire all over her skin and let it seep into her blood. In those moments, Jack had made what they were doing feel . . . amazing. So perfectly normal. So right that she'd ached. She hadn't just been accepted as she was, but needed because of it. The sense of connection to Jack had swept common sense aside and made her cling to him like a life raft in a hurricane.

She'd barely been able to keep herself together while the pleasure Jack gave tore her barriers down. Something about him demanded the surrender of more than her body. She'd refused, clinging to her defenses by her fingernails—barely. He'd left her reeling and stunned. But not broken.

Then Jack had all but run from her, tearing off her rose-colored glasses. She was in the middle of who-knew-where with a man she'd only really met yesterday, wearing borrowed clothes, with no end to the nightmare in sight. Yet *he* ran away. Gee, she guessed that having sex with a client was a bodyguarding no-no.

The more she thought about his behavior, the more it pissed her off. And it hurt—way more than she wanted to admit.

With an impatient huff, she turned away from the mirror. Mr. Cajun Macho had another thing coming if he thought they were going to have sex again. So he had a touch that sizzled desire through her blood, intoxicating her like the most potent wine. She wasn't going to risk addiction with a repeat performance.

But just the thought of it had her body clamoring for more, turning soft and wet at the prospect of experiencing all his determined sexual fire and tightly controlled power again.

So damn stupid. Not only did Jack have *temporary* written all over him, the only message about him that was even more clear was the one that pronounced him a very bad boy.

Honestly, she didn't need this!

Down the hall, Morgan heard the click of a lock, the opening of the door. From the heavy footsteps, she knew he'd emerged into the hall. Maybe it was very thirteen-year-old of her, but she wasn't in the mood to face him. Not now. Not yet. Let him see how rejection felt.

Cringing, she dove onto the bed and quickly feigned sleep as Jack made his way down the hall. He paused at the bedroom door, but Morgan wasn't about to open her eyes. Seeing that too-sexy face taunting her with the carnal knowledge of her body or displaying annoyance—or both—was not her idea of a good time. Let Romeo eat breakfast alone. The thought of food right now held all the appeal of dog shit à la mode.

After a long moment, Jack's footsteps continued down the hall. She heard a series of electronic beeps, then a ringing. A speakerphone. Who was he calling at seven-thirty in the morning?

She rose and tiptoed across the bedroom to peek around the corner. Jack stood there, cup of coffee in one hand, making toast with the other. And standing by the cracked handset with an annoyed expression.

"Jesus, Jack!" rasped a scratchy, male voice. "Is sleeping in against your religion or did you just figure that if you're up, everyone else should be, too?"

Morgan couldn't help but overhear the conversation. It wasn't as if he was trying to be quiet. Who in the heck was Jack talking to and why? And she had to agree with the other guy; why had he called at this early hour?

"I didn't sleep at all last night, Deke. So whatever you got in the way of Z's is way more than I got. Quit whining."

"Have you turned vampire now?"

"Want to slit your wrists and make a donation to find out?"

"Oh, biting wit. You are cranky this morning. Get too little sex lately . . . or too much?"

Morgan felt the thick rush of embarrassment flood her skin. *Please, please don't let Jack have called some friend to do some locker-room bragging.* That would be the final insult to having her fantasies exposed and her common sense stripped away in a haze of desire, then being left naked, wet, and used against a virtual stranger's door.

Jack growled, "Stop being cute and try being a business partner. I'm out at the swamp cabin. I've got a woman with a stalker. I need you to do some research."

Morgan breathed a sigh of relief.

"No shit. A woman with a stalker?" said the man Jack had identified as Deke. "When did she become a client?"

"Yesterday, when he took a shot at her in broad daylight in a crowd. I was sitting less than two feet from her."

"Holy . . . What info do you have?"

Quickly, Jack ran down the information Morgan had given him at dawn. *All* the information—the minute details of her sexual history, thankfully excluding himself. Despite that small favor, the rush of mortification returned, along with foot-stomping fury. Gee, why not take out a billboard along the highway just to make sure everyone knew who she'd done the wild thing with in the past?

And now she had Jack to add to the list. What on earth had she done?

After offering to fax copies of the latest pictures her stalker had left, Jack hung up. He paced across the long, narrow room once, twice, then turned his gaze to the hallway, his face, barely visible through the crack in the door, alive with purpose.

Morgan leapt back onto the bed and feigned sleep again as his footsteps sounded his approach.

"*Merde,*" he snarled, then turned away.

She didn't know much French, but she knew enough to realize he'd said something that her mother would be happy to wash out his mouth with soap for saying.

Moments later, she heard the dial tone, the beeping and ringing again. Another call? Did he expect everyone to be awake at this hour?

\*   \*   \*

"*OUI?*"

"*Grand-père*, good morning."

"That it is, dear boy. How is *ta jolie fille*?"

"Her name is Morgan," he said with forced patience. "I told you before, she's not mine."

"Maybe. Maybe not. Time tells, yeah? She got red hair under that wig?"

Jack hesitated. Brice was going to make entirely too much of Morgan's hair color. It didn't mean anything.

*So what was that jolt of connection you felt to her when you were buried balls deep within her slick, wet heat? What was that sensation of wanting to crawl inside her and own her?*

Really good sex and the knowledge that she'd been holding something back he was determined to have? Had to be that . . . or insanity.

"I didn't call to discuss Morgan's hair."

"She does, doesn't she!" The old man crowed, then laughed.

"*Grand-père* . . ."

"I told you. Just yesterday, I told you. Those dreams, they mean something."

The old man was not going to give this up. "Okay, yes. Her hair is red. Happy?"

"*Très bon*," Brice said smugly. "She dressing any better today, *ta jolie fille*?"

"Actually, that's why I called you. Can you pick up a few things for her to wear in a size six and bring them out to the cabin?"

"This I can do. I'm having lunch with your aunt Cheré, then I'll be out."

"Fine. Warm, practical clothes, *Grand-père*. No surprises."

"Why you worried about surprises? I'll bring what you need."

\*      \*      \*

TIME dragged by. Morgan bathed again. Paced. She skipped breakfast.

Jack stayed in his locked room at the end of the hall, pacing with heavy footsteps she couldn't help but hear.

What did he have to be disturbed about? The stalker hadn't caught up to them yet, and Jack had gotten laid. From his angle, it had to look like a win-win situation.

Morgan hadn't been quite so lucky. She'd managed to hold a part of herself back from Jack—or thought she had—but as time passed she couldn't shake this damn yearning for him. It sank deeper, growing, urging her to touch him. Morgan feared she'd given Jack a chunk of her psyche. Not a good development.

As noon approached, she made herself a sandwich. The only drinks in Jack's refrigerator were bottles of water and beer. Normally, Morgan would opt for the water. Today, she gratefully took a beer and disappeared into the bedroom again, lying listlessly on the bed. She spent hours trying not to think about Jack, the way he'd touched her, the way his voice had crawled inside her head and her body, then seemed to challenge her, own her. Forgetting the pleasure that seared her was proving impossible, not when she could close her eyes and still feel the pull of his mouth at her nipple, the width of his cock stretching her. Not when she couldn't forget that demanding, compelling voice, those seducing dark eyes.

The thoughts brought on fresh desire. Thick, bubbling desire, swirling inside her to form an insistent throb. Her clit ached, and she could not believe how wet she was, how swollen her folds felt. She'd never been ruled by her hormones. Why now?

Morgan thought about self-pleasuring again, but refrained. She didn't want to be caught again. The mortification had nearly killed her once, but twice in one day . . . She grimaced. Still, she might have risked it if she had believed it would douse the fire raging inside her.

But the fire was one she feared only Jack could put out.

A knock at the cottage's front door startled Morgan. She whirled to the clock on the little cypress bedside table. Nearly four-thirty in the afternoon.

Jack tore open the door to his hiding place and streaked down the hall. On his way past, he cast a heated glance into the bedroom, right at her, a glance that said he remembered every kiss, every touch between them—and that as far as he was concerned, they weren't done. A quick glance down his muscled chest covered in a tight black T-shirt, past those six-pack abs . . . Oh, hell. He was hard. There was no mistaking that bulge.

Need slammed into her belly. Her gaze flew back to his.

"We'll talk later."

About sex. He didn't speak it, but the words hung in the air.

"I have nothing to say," she protested automatically.

Talking about sex would only make her want to have it with Jack again. Bad idea. Already, she was more fixated on him than was smart, more than she'd ever been on a man—even the one she'd agreed to marry once upon a time. She just needed to evade this stalker, figure out who it was, and get back to her job and the sanity of her life in L.A.

"We have plenty to discuss. Now come meet my grandfather."

Morgan crossed her arms over her chest, refusing to budge.

Any satisfaction she got out of watching Jack grind his teeth came to a halt when he stalked across the room, his intent to grab her and drag her to the door written all over his face. If he touched her, she would only want him more. The scalding desire inside her was already too hot, too dangerous. And it made her so angry she could spit.

"Don't touch me." She jerked away from him. "I can walk on my own."

"Then get your pretty ass moving before I paddle it."

Her eyes narrowed. "You wouldn't."

He snorted. "Wanna try me?"

No. No, she didn't. His hard determination to lift her purple skirt and spank her ass was etched into the dark challenge of his eyes, into the hard lines of his aggressive stance.

The thought outraged her. Unfortunately, it aroused her, too. More of the cream from her arousal soaked the little thong she wore, coating her sex thoroughly with every step she took. She prayed he couldn't tell.

"You're a bastard," she muttered as she walked past Jack and into the cottage's main room.

"If you were expecting Prince Charming, I'm sorry. He's with his boyfriend," Jack quipped as he sailed by her and pulled the front door open.

An old man entered, carrying two shopping bags in hand. Instantly, she saw what Jack would look like in fifty years. Tall, lean, with thick silver hair and dancing dark eyes, the man ambled into the cottage with a smile teasing the corners of his lips.

"Jack." He greeted him with a nod. "Your aunt Cheré sends her love and a loaf of homemade bread."

He reached into one of the sacks and retrieved a plastic container. Morgan smelled the yeast of the bread blend with the spice of the swamp's vegetation lazing in the temperate February day. It was unlike anything she'd ever smelled. Which fit. Nothing about being with Jack was like anything she'd ever experienced.

Before she could process the thought, the old man approached her, wearing a mischievous smile. "Morgan, I'm Brice Boudreaux, Jack's *grand-père* on his *maman*'s side."

He stuck out his hand, and she clasped his to shake it. Instead, he brought her hand to his lips and gave her a gallant kiss. Despite her discomfort in meeting an old man while wearing skimpy purple leather, Morgan couldn't help but smile. She'd bet that in his day he'd had a lot of luck with anything in a skirt.

"Morgan O'Malley."

His sharp brown gaze lifted to her hair. "A bonny Irish lass with fiery tresses. Jack loves red hair, don't you?"

She didn't dare look at Jack, not when she felt a flush climbing up her cheeks. Did he have a thing for redheads? That would explain the odd conversation she'd overheard earlier.

"*Grand-père . . .*" Jack warned. "Stop making mischief and give her the bag."

A glance at the bag told Morgan there were clothes inside it. She itched to get her hands around it, to wear something besides a getup that encouraged her recklessness and made her more aware of her sexuality than mere garments should.

Brice was in no hurry to hand the bag over.

"In due time. Can't an old man sit down for a minute and talk to a pretty girl?"

He cast Jack a challenging glance, then shuffled over to the sofa, making a big show of easing his weary bones down onto a cushion. Then he set the bag on the floor between his feet and patted the spot beside him.

"Come," he said to Morgan. "Sit next to an old man, yeah, and let him remember the days he could have asked such a *jolie fille* for a dance."

Morgan sliced her gaze to Jack for translation, brow raised in question.

"Pretty girl," he supplied in a long-suffering sigh. "And don't be suckered in by his old-man routine. He's sharp as a tack, that one."

Brice harrumphed. "Boy forgets I'm eighty-two."

"*Grand-père* forgets I'm no idiot," Jack said with a fond smile.

Morgan watched their byplay with an awareness of their love and affection for each other—and not without a bit of envy. Her biological father had never wanted anything to do with her, so she'd bet his parents knew nothing of her. And her mother's parents had disowned Mama when she'd become pregnant while unmarried. They'd died shortly before Morgan's tenth birthday, the rift unmended. She'd never had a grandparent, much less a character like Brice in her family.

The old man patted the sofa beside him again and sent her a hopeful glance. Unable to resist, Morgan gave in to the charmer.

Jack groaned. "He's a master fisherman. He just baited, hooked, and lured you in."

*Must run in the family,* she thought bitterly.

"Maybe I'm catching her just for you, yeah," Brice countered. "Thanks to the army, those nice manners your *maman* taught you ain't what they used to be. Without my help, I don't think Morgan would let you near her."

She froze, then forced a relaxing breath. The old man couldn't tell what had happened between her and Jack this morning. Thank God . . .

But one glance in Jack's direction, and Morgan knew she was in trouble. He sent her a hard, hot glance that forced her to remember and promised more, much more, until she drowned in pleasure. A ravenous ache resounded in her gut, echoed between her legs, and she felt her nipples swell again.

Morgan bit her lip to hold in a gasp. Too bad she couldn't contain the flush crawling up her cheeks.

Brice glanced away from Jack, over to her. A new smile danced at his mouth, moving the salt-and-pepper moustache above it. He looked mighty pleased. "Are you Catholic, Morgan?"

The question took her aback. "I—I was raised in the Church. Yes."

Jack groaned. "*Grand-père,* Morgan's religion is none of our business."

"Given enough time, it might be." He slapped his knee and rose to his feet in a surprisingly spry move and handed her the bag with a Cheshire-cat smile.

Wondering what the heck he meant by that comment, Morgan couldn't escape the feeling that the old man had pulled the wool over her eyes. He might be eighty-two, but he wasn't slow—mentally or physically. Jack had warned her . . .

"Put those to good use." Brice gestured to the bag with a jerk of his head and a wink.

Then, with a slap on Jack's shoulder, the old man practically skipped out the front door.

*     *     *

PUT *those to good use,* Jack's grandfather had said. Fingering the golden silk of the lace-edged camisole and matching thong, Morgan could take a wild guess at what Brice thought good use would entail. And it probably involved indulging in lascivious acts with Jack—acts she'd only vaguely heard about.

Cursing under her breath, Morgan stood in Jack's bedroom still wearing Alyssa's slut-in-purple costume and tried to decide what to change into. Brice had brought her three sets of undergarments, each sexier than the last. Nothing else.

"Damn it, Morgan!" Jack shouted through the door. "I called you to dinner ten minutes ago. How long does it take to get dressed?"

"Long enough to figure out how to cover all the essentials with the items your grandfather brought."

"What the hell?" Jack flung the door open and barged into the room. When he saw the garments all spread out on the bed, he stopped and stared.

His gaze roved over the golden lace-up camisole, drifted to the black corset with garter belts and thigh-high stockings, then settled on the burgundy bra trimmed in champagne lace—with cutouts so her nipples could poke through. It came with matching crotchless panties.

"Is this all he brought?"

"You got it."

"Son of a bitch." Jack's expression showed his inner war between annoyance and amusement.

"These aren't warm or practical," she pointed out, sharing his annoyance but none of the amusement.

With a turn of his head, Jack pinned his stare on her. Oh, sweet heaven . . . Heat infused the dark depths of his eyes, tempting as melted chocolate, alive like the rich earth. She knew in that moment he was doing his best to picture her in each set of undergarments.

Worse, Morgan could imagine herself wearing them for Jack. Imagine his reaction. If the hearty erection currently straining his jeans was any indication, he was more than a little interested. The thought aroused her far more than it should. Her vagina clenched, spasming with need. Beneath the leather, her nipples stabbed at her bra.

"They definitely aren't warm," he agreed. "Practical . . . well, that depends on the purpose."

"Since I'm not here to reenact a porn flick, they aren't practical for my purposes. Was this a joke or a mistake?"

"Neither."

"He wants us to . . ." Morgan's eyes widened even as shock raised her blood pressure.

"Fuck like rabbits? Absolutely. He's all for anything that might persuade me to remarry."

*Remarry?* Her first thought was that she'd only met Jack in person twenty-four hours ago, so leaping to the concept of marriage seemed extreme. Her second thought was that she never would have guessed he'd been married before.

"You've been married?"

Beside her, he straightened, tensed. "It was short. We divorced three years ago. End of conversation."

She frowned. That might be the end of the conversation, but that wasn't the end of the emotions for Jack. Clearly, his divorce still had the power to hurt or piss him off. But wisely, she let it go. Jack's personal life was none of her business. Digging into the man's past was only going to make her more curious about the man as a whole. Still, she couldn't help but wonder what had happened.

"Choose one of those getups," he snapped, gesturing to the lingerie on the bed. "I'll give you my robe and a pair of socks, then come eat. The food is getting cold."

Morgan wanted to say she'd just wear what she had on, but as the sun had fallen, the temperature had dropped too much for that. And it wasn't the best outfit to wear if she wanted to diffuse the awareness between herself and Jack. Not to mention, the thong she currently wore was uncomfortably wet and clinging to her swollen folds—a constant reminder of her arousal.

"Thank you," she murmured.

He grunted as he retrieved his robe and socks from a nearby wardrobe, tossed them her way, and left.

Morgan chose the items that seemed the least racy. She crossed the hall and let herself into the bathroom, golden cami and thong in hand, and set about changing.

The new thong was tiny. All lace as it wound around her hips, bisected the cheeks of her ass, and edged the legs of the garment. The fabric covering everything else . . . totally sheer. The mirror in the bathroom showed her the explicit way the outrageously feminine lace framed the red curls over the delta between her legs, showcasing the fiery color. It was designed to make a man's eyes latch onto a woman's mound immediately. Jack's eyes.

A hitch of both fear and arousal ticked in her belly.

*No, bad, bad reaction . . .*

Chastising herself, Morgan peeled off the bra Alyssa had given her. This camisole covered less than the bra, if that was possible. Again, trimmed in golden lace, it dipped low, half an inch above her nipples. It was formfitting and offered gentle support below her breasts but was cut low in between to reveal cleavage. Delicate lace decorated the top and bottom edges of the utterly sheer garment and served as the tie in the laces between her breasts, accentuating her tight nipples poking the thin fabric.

Morgan was pretty sure she'd never looked sexier in her life. Knowing that Jack could incite her to massive, broiling orgasms was surely making her feel hyperaware of herself as a woman. Imagining his reaction to this . . . outfit was arousing the hell out of her.

Her imagination needed to take a vacation.

But it was more than the orgasms, as much as she hated to admit it. With Jack, she'd felt a dizzying freedom unlike anything she'd ever known with a lover. A freedom to want whatever she desired. And utter acceptance of her longings. Despite her head telling her that her needs were wrong, her body ached. She didn't even fully comprehend what she craved, but Jack knew. Knowledge sizzled in his eyes, in the things he said to her. Jack could give her everything she'd ever fantasized about. All of that coupled with the feeling of security she had here with him, as if her stalker were a million miles away, encouraged her to explore her dark side with her infuriating, enigmatic protector.

She had to get a grip on herself. Fantasies weren't reality, and she didn't really want to perform all those acts that were springing deep from her imagination. Really, she didn't.

With shaking hands, Morgan grabbed Jack's robe. She belted the enormous thing around her waist, put on the sweat socks that were double the size of her feet, and marched to the eat-in kitchen's bleached wood table, hoping she looked frumpy.

When she reached the kitchen, she saw that Jack had laid out some thick soup that had an orangish base with lots of rice and chunks of meat, his aunt's homemade bread, and a slab of butter. A small salad sat in another bowl. A big glass of ice water sat above her silverware.

Jack, on the other hand, was fisting a bottle of whiskey and eyeing her as if she were a tempting treat, unable to completely shield the feral hunger in his eyes that told her he wanted to strip her, cram her full of himself, and make her scream. Apparently, he didn't see the robe as frumpy.

"I made chicken and sausage gumbo," he rasped as his gaze roved over her face, down her bare neck, to the hint of skin visible between her breasts. He shifted in his seat. "Ever eat gumbo?"

She shook her head, wondering—though she shouldn't—if he was still incredibly, mouthwateringly hard.

"It's thick and spicy."

Like the air between them. Like the flesh he'd filled her with this morning.

Trembling, Morgan looked away and stared into her gumbo. She had to stop thinking like this, with nothing but her hormones. But she couldn't eat, all too aware of Jack's stare fixed on her as he held the whiskey bottle in his hand.

Morgan swallowed, feeling her pulse accelerate. "You're staring at me."

He inclined his head. "I am, *cher*."

"All you can see is this overlarge bathrobe."

Jack set the whiskey aside. Suddenly, she felt her chair being dragged along the hardwood floor, closer to him. She looked down to find his foot hooked around the leg as he pulled it beside him, right next to his heat and spice.

"Yeah, I'm staring. First, I'm male, and you're a gorgeous woman. Second, I'm wondering which of those outfits of teasing torture you decided to put on beneath my robe. Third, I haven't forgotten exactly what you feel like pulsing around my cock."

Morgan sucked in air as desire slammed into her, leaving her short of breath. Clearly, any restraint exhibited here would be up to her.

Not good news, since she didn't have much.

He leaned down and nuzzled the sensitive skin below her ear. Morgan shivered as he said, "You were slick and tight, *cher*. So amazing to fuck. You responded to my commands like you were born to submit. Like it was so natural. I've thought about nothing all day long except tying you down and spending morning, noon, and night finding ways to make you come until you scream your throat raw, then beg for more."

Blunt. Graphic. Unapologetic. His words should have been a turnoff. The feminist in her thought she should be offended that he found her so purely sexual. She wasn't that lucky.

Jack was her mind's nightmare—arrogant, demanding, difficult. But he was her psyche's fantasy—hot, untamed, determined to have her and force her to experience every naughty fantasy her fevered mind had ever conjured up.

A fresh rush of moisture dampened her new thong, and her clit began to ache anew.

Morgan closed her eyes. This had to stop. *Had* to. Or she was going to give in. She wasn't sure she could live with the repercussions—or herself—if she did.

"Jack, I'm interviewing you for a TV show about your lifestyle, not inviting you to tell me every one of the thoughts lurking in the dark corners of your mind. If you can't keep it to yourself, you should take me back to my car. I—I'll return to Houston and—"

"And wait for your stalker to find you? Rape you? Shoot you? Kill you? We've been over this. You're in the middle of a swamp and much safer here, surrounded by sophisticated security systems and a bodyguard, than you are anywhere else. My buddy Deke is putting together a profile. Once we have it, we can figure out who your psycho is and nail him. Until then, I think you'd be wise to stay. Unless you're more afraid of sex than a stalker?"

Damn it, he'd picked the worst possible time to be logical. "Of course not. You're just making me uncomfortable."

"The truth is making you uncomfortable; I'm merely making you aware of it. I want you. You want me. It's pretty simple."

"It's oversimplified, big boy."

He grabbed the bottle of whiskey and took a long swallow. Morgan watched in fascination as his Adam's apple bobbed in his tight-muscled throat.

When it was empty, he set the bottle on the table. "You can't lie, *cher*. Your eyes, they tell me you want to be cuffed and clamped and fucked often. And you want me to be the one doing it."

Mind trying to outrace the desire searing her brain, she shook her head. "Look, we both had an itch this morning, and we scratched it. After, you ran as if I was diseased. You couldn't get away from me fast enough. If you hadn't, I would have. We're done with each other."

"You think, little girl? What we did, it was powerful, yeah," he said, those dark eyes boring into her, forcing her to listen, willing her to understand. "If I hadn't left, I would have carried you to the bed, tied you down, and not let you up until I'd fucked all of your perfect pink entrances and found each of your hidden sensitive spots and every way possible to drive your body insane."

Morgan gasped. That should *not* arouse her. The idea that he would have touched her anywhere he pleased, demanded a blow job and, if she look him literally, anal sex, absolutely shouldn't make any part of her leap with excitement. Curiosity and wicked fantasies were one thing. Actually indulging . . . No.

But there was no denying the desire that charged through her with the force of an invading army, pulsing need and heat into her clit, making her beaded nipples ache.

Just like there was no denying that if she tried to leave here and return to Houston, the person after her would very likely try to kill her again. And this time, he might succeed.

She let out a shaky breath. What a hell of a place to be, trapped by danger with a man capable of giving her amazing pleasure while making her submit to every wicked desire she'd ever denied. Damn it, she'd been fighting her wants since Andrew's rejection, warring against her dark side until she hurt. She couldn't just roll over and spread her legs for a dominant stranger—no matter how appealing her newly awakened body might find that notion.

"I grant you that I'm much safer here than in Houston or Los Angeles. I'm not stupid, and I know I can't fight a man I haven't seen and don't understand."

"But?"

"I want things platonic. I'm supposed to interview you. You're supposed to protect me. Nowhere in those job descriptions is the wild thing mentioned. We got *waaaaayyy* off track this morning."

Jack leaned closer, until she felt his breath on her mouth, smelling faintly of whiskey and something spicy. "Platonic?"

"You know, polite. Friendly." Morgan tried to scoot her chair away. "No sex."

He wasn't budging. "I know what it means, Morgan. Why do you think we shouldn't be having the most amazing sex of the year with each other?"

"I don't want what you want. I'm just not into your . . . scene."

She focused on her gumbo. It would be easier if she could tell him she thought his desires were twisted and wrong. Hurting him might make him go away faster. But having been on the receiving end of such slurs, she couldn't do it to him.

*You're not a talented liar, either,* a voice in her head whispered. She shut her eyes against it.

"And," she went on, "despite what happened earlier, I'm not a casual-sex person."

Jack said nothing for the longest minute. He simply stared, as if trying to decipher her every thought. He didn't touch her. He just stared—hard, hot, as if he was picturing and plotting to do every wicked thing to her she'd ever imagined. The explosive desire on his face ripped past her defenses, searing her clear to her unruly imagination, to her throbbing clit still so hungry for him, to the inexplicable draw she felt in her soul to him.

Damn it, she had to get away from him, now. Morgan wrapped the robe's lapels tightly around herself and started to rise.

He clamped a hand around her arm, holding her in place. "Those are the only reasons? You're not into casual and you're going to keep lying to yourself that you don't like the way I fuck you?"

"I want you to stop saying such outrageous crap and agree to keep our interaction professional."

"You want me to promise not to touch you?" His grip tightened on her arm.

"I've been saying that, yes."

Chin high, eyes declaring her resolve, Morgan hoped she looked convincing. She hoped Jack had no idea that inside, her heart threatened to beat out of her chest. That his nearness, scent, and touch just brought back the rush of pleasure and exhilaration she'd felt when he'd been deep inside her.

"You've been saying it; I just don't believe it." Jack laughed, an ironic chuckle, complete with a mocking smile. "What are you afraid of, *cher*? If I don't excite you, then, when I touch you, say no. If you're not interested, that shouldn't be too hard."

"I shouldn't have to!" Morgan gaped. "You're pissing me off. Can't you just be a gentleman and agree?"

"With chemistry like ours, no. Even if I wanted to keep my hands off you, which I don't, it would only be a matter of time before I was balls deep inside you, pounding away."

"Stop, damn it! That's not true. I don't say yes to every man who snaps his fingers."

He slid his palm up her arm to her shoulder, then diverted to her breast. His thumb encountered a hard nipple and flicked it, as if to make a point. She gasped, then bit her lip as she realized her huge error. Jack gave her a long, wicked smile—the kind that only made her more wet. Between that and his touch, he turned her on as easily as he flipped on a light switch. The hard pulse between her thighs was something she couldn't ignore.

"Sure it is. The street is going both ways, here. I can tell," he said. "As I see it, my job is keeping you safe. But I'm going to show you what your body craves and help you be honest with yourself. That," he caressed the hard point of her breast again, "is my pleasure."

Then he released her and rose, gumbo bowl in hand.

"Maybe you're lying to yourself about what I want," she blurted to his retreating back. "Did you ever think of that? Maybe you're totally off base."

Jack paused, turned, and pinned her with a blunt stare that made her heart stop. "If that was the case, you wouldn't be wet enough for me to smell, and I wouldn't know that you'd soaked two thongs in one day."

\*   \*   \*

HAZY morning. Sunlight slanted across the swamp in lazy golden rays to settle on his porch, illuminating the small figure of a woman and her fiery tresses as they cascaded down her narrow back, covered by a man's dark shirt. His shirt.

Contentment and yearning. Hope and need. And lust. It all hit him as she tilted her head. A corner of her mouth hinted at a smile. Happy. He wanted to see her happy, protected.

He'd never loved anyone so much in his life.

The woman, a mystery, was his. Jack knew that as well as he knew his own name.

Just once he wanted to see her face. After six months of futile dreaming and waking up hard with no relief in sight, of feeling this yearning for a woman he'd never seen, he needed to know who she was.

*Turn around!* he silently demanded.

Slowly, so damn slowly, she began to turn his way. A delicate ear, a graceful neck, a stubborn slope to her jaw, fair skin like porcelain. That was more than he'd ever seen of this woman, but the greedy part of him wanted more bared to his gaze. He wanted everything. She kept turning. A hint of apple in her cheek . . .

Jack jolted awake. Damn it! So close this time. So close . . . but he still couldn't see her face.

Stirring from a fitful sleep on the sofa, Jack opened his eyes and glanced at his watch. Just after midnight. Now what?

He laid back on the couch, breathing hard, gritting his teeth against a steel-inspired erection that always followed the dream. The fucking thing tormented him more frequently these days—nearly every night for the past two weeks. Why?

Certainly, his grandfather and the old man's crazy theories about soul mates and dreaming of destined lovers was all bullshit. It had to be. If there was any such thing as a woman destined to be his, he wouldn't torture himself with a dream. He'd simply find her and claim her. And prove she was just another woman he could walk away from. End of story.

Jack was perfectly happy with that explanation except . . . why did the woman in his dream have the same hair as Morgan if the dream was irrelevant? Why did Morgan feel like more than the means to his revenge when he touched her?

Shoving the stray thought aside, Jack blinked, trying to rid tired eyes of the grit of exhaustion. Last night, he hadn't slept even a handful of hours. Tonight was no different. Having these nocturnal visions haunting his sleep and Morgan under his roof wasn't helping him catch up on his beauty rest.

And judging from the erection throbbing inside his boxers like an insistent toothache, along with vestiges of the dream, he wasn't likely to get much more sleep tonight.

Rising with a stretch, Jack sighed and donned his jeans with a grimace. Immediately, his thoughts turned to Morgan.

Why couldn't he leave her alone? He'd tackled a big part of his revenge and emailed Brandon Ross the proof that he'd been as deep inside his enemy's woman as a man could get. Now, his revenge would be complete as soon as Morgan left the disloyal asshole she planned to marry.

But what if she didn't? Lots of women wanted to be married to one of the esteemed Senator Ross's sons. Money. Power. Connections. Good looks. Brandon had all that, but he'd never have a political career of his own. Jack had made damn sure of that.

Still, that didn't solve his problem. If Morgan and Brandon didn't part ways, revenge would be incomplete. That had to be why he didn't feel more victorious now.

Jack paced, spearing hands tense with frustration through his hair, too short to be ruffled by such a mauling.

Maybe he was looking at this all wrong. After viewing the little video he'd sent, sooner or later, jealousy would start eating Brandon's gut. No question about it. When a man had a woman like Morgan, he wanted to keep her safe and whole and so sated that the idea of sex with another man never crossed her mind. Once Brandon had time to gnaw on the visual evidence that Morgan had strayed—and with his enemy—the idiot's pride would demand he let her go.

Frowning, Jack realized a tactical error in that plan. Brandon dumping Morgan could cause her pain. The thought of her anguish made him want to flay himself with a whip of self-censure.

Not only would Brandon leaving Morgan hurt her, it wouldn't satisfy the writhing mass of hate he had in his gut for Brandon. In order for Jack to get closure, Morgan *must* realize that she deserved someone who understood her, a man who could give her what her mind and body craved. She had to acknowledge that Brandon couldn't satisfy her. And Jack figured it was his job to prove that very fact to her.

How could he tempt her to leave Brandon?

Pacing across the room, toward the cottage's lone bedroom, Jack pushed open the door.

Holy shit. Morgan had pushed off her covers, baring herself to the night. He wished she was bare to him. While that wasn't actually the case, it was close. She wore next to nothing, only the golden-lace camisole and thong. Moonlight spilling into the room bathed the sweet blush-pink nipples and fiery fringe of her pussy in a soft silver light. It called attention to things he loved about her body and made him want to howl at the moon, absolutely.

Coaxing his way into that bed, into her body again, was as necessary as drawing his next breath. It was the eye for an eye the vindictive part of him craved.

But his desire hardly stopped there. And he feared it was about more than revenge.

His cock gave a greedy leap at the thought of having Morgan again, in any way that would bring them both to screaming pleasure . . . The want was a blast of heat drilling straight through his erection and his brain. Damned odd, really. He didn't fixate like this. A willing woman was cause for a good mood and good times, always.

This was . . . more.

His body went wild at the thought of teaching Morgan about her sexuality, about the desires that haunted her to sweating resistance and whimpering wails of pleasure. He ached to show her how to take anything he dished out, give the burn back to him, and share in the mind-blowing mental and physical satisfaction.

The likelihood of that happening . . . Jack shook his head. She wasn't going to surrender easily or without a fight, and he wasn't out to break her. Just show her how much satisfaction she'd find in submission.

Stalking into the bedroom, Jack lit a few candles throughout the room, then dropped himself into the chair in the corner and stared, absently adjusting the unyielding length of his cock in his jeans.

How did he tempt her to take a walk on the wild side with him so he could prove to her she could be just as free and submissive as she yearned and still be okay with herself—all while convincing her to leave Brandon so he could achieve the vengeance he'd plotted for nearly three fucking years? How did he get her to give him that part of herself she'd held back from him before, the part he was sure she'd never given any man?

A mischievous smile lifted his lips as an idea occurred to him. Simple, direct, effective. Eager to put it in motion, he jogged back to his locked enclave and retrieved two pairs of heavy velvet ropes.

Let the games begin . . .

# Chapter Seven

MORGAN woke slowly, drifting on the haze of an erotic dream where she lay on the grass naked to the moonlight, arms tossed above her head in abandon as tender pulls at her nipples created a pool of sweet pleasure between her legs. She writhed. Silvery moonbeams worshipped her, caressing the undersides of her arms, her belly, the tops of her thighs with a feathery touch. She moaned.

Leaves fell from the trees above in a light summery breeze, drifting down to glide over bare breasts, sensitive nipples. Again and again the leaves dropped from their trees and found their way to her body, the gentle abrasion of their texture on her skin slowly awakening her sensual need.

One leaf had a sharp edge as it drifted across her body. A slight sting in the hard peak of her breast surprised her. She tried to dodge the leaf, but it was gone, replaced by a glide of heat, then a sudden well of desire between her legs. Another sharp leaf pinched at the other nipple. Another swelling of desire bloomed inside her. She arched to the gentle pain and was again rewarded with a fresh flood of heat and moisture.

The ache between her thighs became a throb, a drumbeat inside her body calling for release. Morgan moaned, shifted.

Beneath her, the grass seemed oddly smooth. She tried to sit up but was unable to move. Another leaf drifted over her left breast, smooth, silky, gently rousing. It was quickly followed by a sharp leaf that curled around her nipple and bit.

Pain faded an instant later, replaced by a merciless need in the tight tips of her breasts. She arched, seeking more, as another leaf drifted down her abdomen and brushed over the top of her mound.

Sensations mounted, one on top of the other, until her body demanded more. She struggled to move, to touch herself—only to find she couldn't. Another leaf clamped down on one nipple, this time harder than before. She cried out. Perspiration dampened the skin between her breasts and thick, liquid want converged into a unending ache between her legs.

Morgan opened her eyes and threw off the last vestiges of sleep.

And quickly discovered that her breasts weren't being tormented by leaves but by the smooth slide of Jack's tongue, followed by the erotic nibble of his teeth.

Before she even knew what she was doing, Morgan arched up, her body silently offering her sensitive nipples to a hot-eyed Jack, overruling anything her mind might have said.

"That's it. Good girl," he murmured hotly across her breasts.

Candlelight glowed softly as she looked down her body and realized that he'd unlaced the camisole and pulled it wide, completely exposing her twin mounds and their hard peaks.

As if in slow motion, Morgan watched him lower his mouth to her again. His wide, bare shoulders bulged, a pulse-raising shadow in the moonlit room, as he eclipsed everything else. She pulled at her arms and legs, desperate to embrace him. Instead, she found them bound firmly to the four posts of Jack's bed.

God, she was totally at his mercy. That realization jolted her with a rush of dark pleasure—and that scared the hell out of her.

A warning boomed in her belly like thunder. The hard clamp of desire plaguing her drowned it. The man made her want, so badly that dragging in a steady breath was difficult, so much that finishing a coherent thought was impossible.

What was it about Jack Cole and the way he touched her?

He ignored her writhing and peppered the full sides of her breasts with soft kisses, laved the nerve-heavy tips with a bold swipe of his tongue. The hard heat of his chest brushed over her belly, and her body fevered for more of the silky burn of his skin, his mouth. Her nipples tightened more, until they became pointed red nubs that begged him to continue with anything, everything, he wanted.

In response, Jack pinched her nipples, twisting slightly. A sharp mix of pain and pleasure had her crying out his name.

"I'm here, *cher*, to fulfill every forbidden fantasy swimming in your mind."

Desire jolted her body, making her buck under his tongue as he resumed the sensual torture on her nipples. She drew in another shuddering breath as his tongue curled around the throbbing tip. She whimpered. The man was twisting her inside out, turning her into a wanton stranger. Into a woman nearly willing to say yes to anything.

Jack didn't simply want to give her pleasure; he wanted to control her, addict her, turn her into the depraved wanton Andrew had been so contemptuous of. She'd never been any man's doormat. She wasn't starting now.

"No," she panted. "Stop. I didn't agree to this. I don't want this."

He raked a pair of fingers through the exposed slit of her sex. Morgan knew she was more than damp. She was embarrassingly wet, swollen. Aching. His touch only ramped up the pleasure, made thick moisture gush from her weeping opening again.

He sent her a low, sexy chuckle. His well-muscled torso rippled with every move and made the wicked part of her ache to put her hands all over his body and feel his vitality.

"Your mouth is saying the words, but your body is making a liar out of you." His whisper taunted, challenged. "Are you sure you don't want this?"

"Are you deaf? I said I didn't agree to this." She accused, "You still think I'm submissive."

"No, I don't."

Morgan arched a fiery brow, fighting all the sparks of pleasure leaping through her body, burning away her common sense. "Good. Finally getting smart?"

"*Cher*, I don't think you're submissive; I *know* it."

She gaped at him, then shut her mouth. Bastard! Fine. He was entitled to his opinion. She had her own, thank you very much.

He clamped his fingers around her nipples again and squeezed.

"Stop it. I didn't give you permission to touch me."

In an instant, his smile disappeared.

"I won't ask for permission, so stop playing this game. The brave woman who took a chance with me after being shot at, the woman gutsy enough to alter her appearance to disappear in a strange town with the help of a man she'd known for all of a few minutes—hell, the woman who talks about sex on TV . . . you are that woman, not the one who keeps running from herself."

His words smacked her between the eyes. She bucked again, struggling to break free. He'd called her a coward for trying to be sane! Unreal. "I'm not running from myself. I'm getting away from you! I wanted protection, not a mauling."

Sending her a sharp smile, Jack eased a hand down her rib cage, over her hip, a soft contrast to the unyielding bindings at her wrists and ankles. Damn him for being so warm and looking so scrumptious shirtless, so totally male and confusing the hell out of her. He could make her needy and angry at once. And angry because she felt needy. Damn! He was using his experience to crowd her, cloud her judgment, overpower her good sense.

And she had to stop her body from falling for it . . .

"That was me against the door this morning," she ground out. "I'm not running and I'm not playing a game. You're just expecting something that's not me."

"Yeah, that was you this morning, but it wasn't all of you. You're capable of deeper submission. You let me touch a part of what's inside you. But you held back. Yeah, I saw that; don't look surprised. The deep part, the dark one that wants to be dominated and fucked, that's the part you hid from me. That you deny exists. You have the guts to defy this sick asshole trying to stalk you, but not enough to take the pleasure I'm offering."

Morgan ignored the heat wave that flowed in with his words—and the sight of his thick erection pushing insistently at his jeans. She focused on her anger instead. "Maybe being around too many female doormats has made you assume all of us live to roll over and spread our legs for you on command."

"You want to submit because you're strong, because when you're fucking, you don't want responsibility. You want a man who can understand you and give you what you need—all without a word."

"Is that the kinky version of Dr. Phil?"

"Watch that mouth, *cher*. I own a ball gag. I know how to use it," he growled.

At his gravelly threat, Morgan's mouth snapped shut. Fury and desire both spiked inside her, threatening to boil up and up until it all exploded.

"I listened to you. I know you've been looking for a man strong enough to force your surrender in the bedroom. You've never explored your dark side, *cher*. I know you'll respond perfectly to what I want. I sense it in you, see it in you."

Male confidence and the physical power to back it up—all with that smooth control that wreaked havoc on her senses. Heaven help her. Jack looked so convinced of every word he said. Morgan trembled. For most of her life, she'd had . . . urges, curiosities. Fantasies. Didn't everyone? That didn't mean she wanted those fantasies to become reality.

She shook her head. "If you'd stop pushing your twisted needs on me, you'd figure out I'm just a normal girl."

His shoulders tensed, arms bunched. He looked ready to grind his teeth.

Then his expression smoothed, until no trace of anger, or any emotion, remained. He merely leaned over and worked at the knots at her left wrist, then her right. He repeated the process with her ankles, careful not to touch her anywhere. That quickly, she was unbound and free, no longer at his mercy.

An odd emotion slammed her, like she was . . . empty. Bereft. Morgan curled her knees up to her chest and watched Jack yank on his shirt. He didn't look at her—or avoid her, either. It was as if she was irrelevant.

She felt suddenly alone, even though he was in the room, gathering up the velvet ropes.

"Jack . . ." she blurted, without having any idea what she was going to say. Morgan only knew his indifference hurt.

"Yes?"

That expression. He could have been talking to anyone—a complete stranger, about nothing more vital than the weather.

The irony of his accusation fired her temper. "Talk about playing games! You don't get your way, so I get the cold shoulder?"

He ambled back to the bed and eased down on it, a good two feet away. No part of him touched her, and she ached for his hands on her. What the hell was the matter with her?

"If you're not willing to be who and what I know you are, I can only give you what you asked for: platonic and professional."

Morgan knew she ought to be rejoicing. She wasn't submissive at heart. A few scattered fantasies didn't make her any dom's dreamboat. She wasn't really wired like that.

So why did part of her yearn to call her words back, return to the moment she'd awakened and discovered his beautifully bare chest crowding her as he bent over to lap at her nipple with his blazing tongue?

*Yeah, and what would you do if you could, just spread your legs like a mindless twit?* Morgan honestly didn't know the answer. She just knew she couldn't let the conversation end with this chill between them.

"You're angry."

"Resigned," he corrected. "You're going to hide from yourself, and that's that. I'll leave you to go back to sleep."

Standing, he sent her a regretful glance, then turned his wide back on her.

Morgan stared at the solid breadth of his shoulders. Power, control, intelligence, patience. Everything she'd ever wanted in a man. And she was letting him walk away.

Did that make her a coward? Or had she just let Jack crawl into her head and confuse the hell out of her?

She bit her lip to keep her response inside, but the words scorched through her mind and were quickly out of her mouth. "Fine. I've had . . . thoughts about submitting. Nothing serious."

Jack paused and turned to look at her again, expression carefully blank.

"Go on."

Conscious of her near nudity, Morgan kept her arms tightly curled around her knees, covering her bare breasts. "I'd be lying if I said it had never crossed my mind. I just know me. And that's not me."

"Why do you think that?"

She frowned. "Why shouldn't I?"

"You've never been submissive to any of your previous lovers. How could you know something is not for you without trying it at least once? If you're having fantasies, the reality may be even more appealing."

Thoughts chased one another in Morgan's head. He couldn't be right. She only had to smell cooked cabbage to know she didn't like it, right?

Weak analogy. The fact was, she avoided submitting in part because of the shame Andrew had forced on her, because of the horror she knew her mother would express if Morgan gave in to such wicked urges.

The other reason . . . the idea tempted her more than anything had in her life. She feared addiction.

Jack leaned closer, making it hard for her to process her thoughts logically. He smelled amazing. Man and spice, cypress and leather and warm skin all rolled into one incredibly attractive package with abs so tight she could probably bounce a quarter off them. The man was temptation on two legs.

What if she tried submitting? To him. Just once.

If she liked it, Andrew would be right. She wasn't . . . abnormal, was she?

"I can almost hear the thoughts spinning in that pretty head of yours, *cher*. You're thinking too hard. It's simple."

"No, it's not! It's my body, my . . ." Morgan shook her head, trying to put it into words.

"Your life? The way you see yourself? I know. But would you rather tell yourself you were adventurous enough to try something once or have to admit that you were so scared you ran away before even dipping your toe in the water?"

Why the hell was he pushing so hard?

"Stop! This is about you. You just want to get laid."

He slanted her a self-deprecating smile—one that made her toes curl. "I want you, *mais* yeah. I've made no secret about that. But I also don't want to see you miserable when the truth could free you."

"I'm not miserable. I love my life!"

"I'm sure you love every part of your life . . . except sex. If you have the courage to find the truth, spend one night with me," he challenged. "Just one, but my way. Tomorrow if you didn't like it, no harm done. I'll never touch you again."

Lord, there it was—a challenge to find the truth, one that could be both simple and ugly.

Morgan sighed. Jack was right. She had never enjoyed sex, never explored the side of her psyche that wracked her with fevered dreams. Maybe . . . maybe those two facts were related. Maybe it was time to assuage her curiosity. She'd indulge her wicked fantasies once, and when they'd been fulfilled, she'd be over them.

And if Jack was just using her for sex . . . well, why couldn't she use him, too? A mad sex scientist in decadent bedroom experiment. He was absolutely no hardship to look at, and when he was buried inside her, the pleasure was intense enough to make her lose her mind. With his help, she could rid herself of the nagging desire to be dominated by a man when it came to sex. Then she could go back to a normal life and shake off Andrew's slurs and, someday, move into a new relationship with a clear head.

"I'm not a coward and I'm not a submissive. Mount up and I'll prove it."

He took her hand. "You need to find this out, once and for all."

Whatever. By tomorrow they'd both know the truth. He'd know he was wrong. She nodded.

"We need a safe word," Jack said.

"All right." She didn't pretend to misunderstand. She'd read enough to know what it meant. "If I say the word . . . *swamp*, you'll stop everything."

He nodded, dark hair skimming his wide forehead. "You say *swamp*, and we're done. But before you use the word, be certain you're in actual pain beyond your bearing. Mild discomfort isn't good enough. Either physical or mental. I'm going to challenge your traditional notions about sex. I will dare you to give more of yourself than you ever have. There's no place to hide here, Morgan. I want to be totally clear. Are you ready for that?"

*No.* "Ready to show you that you're wrong about me? Sure."

Jack fought a smile tugging at his mouth. "Good."

With that, he stood and tore off his shirt. His rippling shoulders straightened. Expression dissolved from his face. An air of authority, impenetrable and intimidating, surrounded him. As fast as lightning, as forceful as thunder.

Morgan shivered, even as she told herself to hang tough.

"You know the rules, Morgan. I'm master. Everything I say is absolute. You do what I tell you, when I tell you, how I tell you. You don't question. You simply do."

He clutched the velvet ropes in his hand, his thumb caressing the soft length of one. She tried to forget the feeling of those soft ropes at her wrists and ankles, holding her down tight, keeping her in place for him to do with her body as he pleased. Even the thought made her gut cramp with lust.

*No, no, no.* It wasn't sexy, just . . . weird.

A ghost of a smile graced his mouth when he caught her staring at the velvet bindings. "Very good."

A shiver went down her spine, and she looked away. But it was too late. He'd seen her gaze fixed on the ropes.

His voice, unusually gravelly, rumbled as he demanded, "Take off your thong."

\*   \*   \*

JACK watched Morgan tense, hesitate, her arms still wrapped around her knees, as she struggled mentally with his command. Normally, this sort of faltering would be a punishable offense. She was new to all this, her mind still pushing back from the mastery her body begged for. For now, he'd stay patient . . . as much as he could. But the reality that Morgan would soon be under him, spread wide, his to do with as he pleased, was driving him to the brink of control.

Swallowing down a lump of choking lust, he regarded her with a hard expression. "When I give a command, I expect it to be followed immediately. Take off your thong now or use the safe word."

She bit that lush lower lip. The sight made his cock throb inside his jeans. God, he wanted that mouth of hers around him, those bee-stung lips stretched wide to take him, pull him in deep, that little tongue darting over the head. *Patience*, he steeled himself.

"I thought . . . Don't we at least kiss or something first?"

Damn, she was naïve. She really had so much to learn if she was ever going to successfully submit. And he was dying to teach her everything.

Sometimes that meant playing hardball.

"You're questioning me," he warned. "If I thought now was the right time for a kiss, I would have demanded one. You're behaving like a *petite fille*, a little girl too scared to face her own wants. And you're wasting my time." Jack turned his back on her.

He took a step toward the door, then another, and began to wonder if this gamble was about to explode in his face.

"Wait! I'm scared. This is new for me," she said softly. "I . . . I don't want to like it."

Jack turned back to her. Finally, some honesty. That was a step in the right direction.

"What do you call me in the bedroom?" he challenged.

"Sir." The word trembled from her lips, and it seared him like a hot poker, shoving a slam of desire up his cock.

To reward her, he moved to her side and cupped her cheek in his palm. "You need to face yourself, *cher*. I'm not the enemy here. I can help you."

"I just can't stop thinking that—"

"You know the rules. Don't think. Just obey."

She sighed. "I've never been good at obedience, sir. Ask my mother."

Smiling, he promised, "I'll never ask you to clean your room or take out the trash. Obeying me will be a lot more pleasurable."

Morgan smiled back and sent him a shaky nod, innocence and need both shining from her blue eyes.

His heart turned over in his chest. Damn, she was so beautiful, so uncertain. Something about her made him want to fuck her in every way possible and reassure her of her perfection while he was doing it. Crazy notion . . .

Stepping away, he blanked the soft amusement from his face and crossed his arms over his chest. "One last chance. Take off the thong, Morgan."

She paused a mere instant before she released a deep breath and eased off the bed, exposing her lush, pale breasts, framed by the golden camisole. Her nipples still stood hard and rosy from his sucking.

Fresh lust kicked him in the gut, pulsed in his balls, as she sent him a hesitant glance, then hooked her thumbs in the lacy strips over her hips. Slowly, so damn slowly he tried not to hold his breath, she began pulling the thong down, displaying more pale-perfect skin dotted with tiny, faint freckles.

Then she exposed the fiery hair guarding her pussy. Jack clenched his jaw. He was dying to taste her. She was already slick. Totally wet and ready. Knowing that was killing him.

Finally, her thong made it to the floor. She straightened, casting him an uncertain glance, but played brave by throwing her shoulders back and holding her head high. Jack knew from the way she squirmed that she was fighting the urge to cover her breasts with the camisole hanging from her shoulders and place a hand over her mound. But she didn't. His respect for her courage climbed up a notch—as did his eagerness to have her completely at his mercy.

"Pick up the thong."

Morgan stared at him, a little frown crinkling between her brows as she looked for the logic in his request. He'd break her of that habit eventually.

"Don't make me repeat myself," he warned.

With an expression torn between confusion and resignation, she bent and picked up the thong, then held it against her bare breasts. Her fiery hair lay tousled across her shoulders. Her red mouth, which would do Angelina Jolie proud, looked moist, lips parted. A sweet flush spread across her cheeks.

Jack sucked in a breath. Damn it, she was so beautiful. And so wasted on Brandon Ross. The thought of showering her with pleasure until she screamed was clawing at his restraint. He was getting harder by the second. He had to retain some control here. Otherwise, he couldn't give her what she needed—what they both needed.

"Give me the thong, *cher*."

Swallowing, she reached out a hesitant hand full of golden lace and silk. Fear and eagerness to please warred on her face, clutched at his heart. He had to both soothe her and push her. Balance his responses. It was the only way to coax her into really letting go.

Jack took the thong from her and bunched it in his hand. It was damp. And even six inches from his nose, he could smell her arousal on the garment. The knot of lust in his gut wrenched so tight, he could hardly catch a breath.

"You're wet."

Morgan said nothing, just stared with wide blue eyes the color of the Caribbean Sea, dilating more with each second.

"Acknowledge my comment, Morgan. Yes or no."

"Yes," she breathed.

"Yes, what?" he prompted.

"Yes . . . sir."

It didn't roll off her tongue yet, but it would. He'd keep at her until it did. Softly and harshly. Alternating, keeping her off balance. Keeping her aroused and uncertain. It would be his pleasure.

"Good. I like that you're wet. I plan to keep you that way all night."

She absorbed his words, tensing slightly. Her eyes dilated further. Her areolas puckered tightly around the nubs of her nipples. She slicked her tongue over her full bottom lip. His cock jerked in impatience.

"Jack—"

"You don't call me that in the bedroom. If I have to remind you again, I'll paddle your pretty ass."

A mutinous frown furrowed her brow. Her jaw tensed. She wanted to snap some acid comment back at him. Instead, she swallowed it.

He kept his smile to himself. She was learning. Slowly, but surely . . .

"Yes, sir."

"Good. Take the camisole off."

Morgan complied almost without hesitation. Almost. Not perfection, but progress.

The gentle chastisement that rose to his mouth died as she exposed the lean line of her torso, a taut belly, graceful shoulders, the full curve of her breasts. Jack hadn't thought it possible, but his cock stiffened with a fresh surge of blood.

"Hand it to me," he demanded.

Again, a bare pause before she complied. Satisfied for now, he tossed the garments in the chair. When he turned back to Morgan, he saw her tongue swipe across her pillowy mouth again.

Damn it, the woman tested his patience and self-control. Now, this first time under his domination, he had to take total charge of Morgan. There could be no vacillation. He could show no weakness, no lack of control, only a reassurance that brooked no refusal.

Asserting his dominance was key to persuading her to listen to her body. It was the only way he could take her from that bastard Brandon. Then, after a hard fuck, after her complete surrender, after she admitted she needed a dominant man and left her backstabbing fiancé, he'd be satisfied.

"On your knees, *cher*."

Her gaze flew to his, her blue eyes filled with an interesting mixture of panic and lust. She was processing his request, trying to discern what he wanted . . . but she knew.

Just as he knew she might use the safe word rather than take him in her mouth. The thought chafed him. He wanted—needed—to feel her tongue caressing his cock, her lips stretching wide to take him. To see her bowing, submissive, accepting, aroused.

"Sir?"

"I didn't give you permission to speak. Either follow the directions or use the safe word."

A pinched mouth and the downward slant of fire-red brows told him without words that she was rebellious and frustrated. But her eyes, still sharp with desire, told him she was torn.

That expression encompassed everything he loved about looking at her, being with her. Her dichotomy—an innocent's experience with a wanton's needs—drove him to dangerous lust. A consuming desire he couldn't remember ever feeling before. This went beyond the psychological high of controlling, beyond the pure physical ease of a woman's body. In this moment, he wanted to own her, inside and out, rule her body and seize her soul.

Suddenly, Jack wondered if he'd be able to fuck Morgan enough to get her out of his system before he let her go.

Finally, she cast her gaze down—and dropped slowly to her knees.

She was so close, Jack could feel her exhalations on his jeans-covered cock. It took every ounce of self-control not to rip at his pants and toss them away so he could feel her breath, her mouth, on him. Lust throbbed even harder through his erection at the thought.

"Better. As a reward, you may speak. What is it, Morgan?"

"I don't know much about oral sex."

"How do you know that's what I want?"

"I assumed. If that is what you want, I think you should know, the one time I did it, he didn't . . ."

"Come in your mouth?"

A fresh flush stole up her cheeks. "No."

The information blasted Jack in the gut like a prizefighter's punch. So even straitlaced Brandon hadn't availed himself of this beauty's sin-inspiring mouth. He knew from this morning's encounter against the door that the idea excited her. He wanted Morgan to experience acts that aroused her. But the notion of being the first man to fill her tongue with his seed made his balls draw up even tighter, the lust crashing through him even more urgent. It was primitive and possessive and illogical, but something in him responded violently to the knowledge that no other man had ever taken her in such a way.

A glance down told him that Morgan wasn't repulsed by his demand, but uncertain. Her anxiety made her lapis eyes stand out in her pale face. She chewed her bottom lip nervously.

"My responsibility in dominating is not just to order you around. It's to pleasure you. To guide you. It starts with trust. You must place yours in me, *cher*. I will see you through, provide whatever you need. Do you understand?"

Morgan's gaze left his face, traveled down his torso, then rested on the insistent erection pushing against his jeans, right in front of her face. Her tongue peeked out to smooth over her bottom lip again.

Jack drew in a sharp breath, reeling back the thoughts that, soon, her pretty pink tongue could be laving the head of his cock. Lust twisted his gut, turning it into unbreakable knots of need. *Merde!* He was testing her as much as he was torturing himself.

"Yes . . . sir."

He barely managed to mumble a reply before he unsnapped his jeans and eased down the zipper. His cock sprang free, into his hand. He slowly stroked the length of it for her gaze. Morgan zeroed in on his hard flesh, her expression uncertain and hot. She wanted to touch him; her expression, like a kid with her face pressed against a candy store window, told him that. Fisting his cock, he waited, watching her greedy eyes follow his hand.

When a drop of moisture beaded on the head of his cock and she licked her lips at the sight, Jack eased his free hand around her head, anchoring it under her hair. The soft strands fell over his fingers like silk as he cupped her nape. He thumbed the soft skin at the side of her jaw and slowly urged her forward.

"Suck me, Morgan. Take me deep."

Closer, closer, her mouth came to his cock. Her gaze flew up to his, connecting, locking with his own as she edged in. Jack held his breath. God, he couldn't look away from her, couldn't stop watching those sensual red lips part to take him inside. Felt a fucking fever rage through him as he imagined how hot and silky her mouth would be.

Finally, she enveloped the swollen head, still seeping moisture. Her gaze never wavered as her lips closed around him and her tongue swept across his sensitive underside, sending a blinding jolt of pleasure screaming up his spine. He gritted his teeth to capture the moan threatening to spill.

She stilled, pulled back a fraction. He allowed it but tightened his hand at the back of her neck in warning. That pretty pink tongue laved the head of his cock, then wet her soft lips again. He watched it all, scorched by the sight, by her hot gaze drilling into him, innocence and wonder and the desire to experience everything finally overshadowing her fear and doubt.

At the sight, it took every bit of Jack's control not to start pumping wildly into her mouth. He drew in a sharp breath.

"Deeper, *cher*. All the way to your throat."

She nodded, her head bobbing, her tongue stroking the blood-engorged tip of his cock. Morgan opened wider, leaned in. The hot, slick heaven of her mouth enclosed half his length, cradled by her exploring tongue. He hissed. She shook her head, going down, trying to take more.

The feel of her all around him, the sight of her trying to fill her mouth with his flesh, combined to push him dangerously close to the edge. His fingers again tightened at her neck as he pushed another inch of his cock into the sweet depths of her mouth.

Morgan pulled back a fraction, then slid her lips even farther down his length—nearly to the back of her throat. She punctuated the motion with a moan. The sound vibrated inside him. Pleasure streamed up his dick, wrapped around his balls like a vise. It doubled when she raised her hand to his dangling testicles and cupped them with gentle fingers.

Damn, she had good instincts.

He tensed, again fighting the urge to unleash his lust, to fuck her mouth in a mindless pursuit of pleasure, let go of the come boiling in his scrotum. Her slow exploration was killing him, breaking him down. His toes curled against the hardwood floor. How the hell could he stay in control with those swollen lips and tight mouth slowly sucking out his sanity?

The head of his cock finally bumped the back of her throat, adding a new dimension to his pleasure. Unable to stop himself, he closed his eyes and groaned, an admission of his need.

"That's it, *cher*. That's right. Suck me deep."

Opening his eyes again, Jack found Morgan bowed over his cock, eyes closed. She was damn near reverent, the way she held him, took him so far inside. Then she eased back with a leisurely swipe of her tongue. Slow. So damn slow, he'd lose his mind, his control, before she fastened her mouth around his length again.

And he was leaking, fluids escaping his body in a desperate rush to orgasm. Every muscle in his body tense now, trembling, he shoved both hands into her hair and demanded more.

"Faster. Put that sweet tongue on me. There you go . . ."

With his prompting, Morgan established a more rapid rhythm but still slow enough that he swore he could feel every groove and bump on her tongue. Still slow enough to completely rob him of his ability to think, to remember his own damn name.

Not fucking her mouth was no longer an option. His hands fisted in her hair. He thrust past her wide, sleek lips, bumping the back of her throat each time.

"Swallow," he demanded, voice broken. "When I'm at the back of your throat, swallow on me."

Amazingly, she did. Every time he sank deep. Perfect rhythm, as if she were a fucking pro. Nothing had ever felt this amazing.

Hell, the woman was going to shatter him with this orgasm.

Sweat broke out at his temples, across his back, as he tried to resist the growing pressure in his balls. He couldn't deny the pleasure for long. The wave built into a dark, sharp ache, demanding he give in. He held it back, gritting his teeth every time her candy tongue danced over the flared purple head, every time her flushed cheeks hollowed as she sucked him in.

Jack wanted to stop the roaring rush toward the cliff, live in this honey-thick throb a bit longer. He withdrew from her mouth, fighting to get a breath without her scent on it, needing a moment that wasn't totally bombarded with the silk of her tongue bathing his cock.

When he left her mouth with a soft pop, she whimpered. Licked her lips. Turned a hot gaze up to him that pleaded and dared.

"Please, sir . . ." She fixed her hungry stare on his cock, mouth open wide.

He took his erection in his hand, swiped a thumb over the weeping head, then pushed the wet digit into her waiting mouth.

"You want more of that?"

Her breath came hard and she swiped the moisture from the pad of his thumb. Her eyes stood wide in her rosy-cheeked face. "Yes, sir."

"Tell me what you want."

"I want to suck you, sir."

"What part of me?" he barked, still torturing them both with long strokes of his hand up and down his length.

Her hungry little gaze was about to eat him alive.

"Your . . . cock, sir. Let me suck it."

"You haven't followed my instructions particularly well so far."

"I will, sir."

"I'll hold you to that, Morgan." He anchored his hand at her nape again. "Now suck me."

*Le ciel m'aident,* he thought as he gave in to the urge to thrust into Morgan's mouth again with a loud moan that should have shaken the cottage's rafters. *Heaven help me.*

Again, he couldn't resist the urge to fuck her mouth. His deep, insistent rhythm filled her, demanding she take and take. He watched her, lips swollen, cheeks rosy, eyes half-closed as if savoring him. Her nipples were harder than ever. The sight of her burned into his brain, shredded his control.

He stiffened again, the pressure in his balls nearly painful as he held in his breath and held back his climax. Delaying the earth-shattering inevitable.

Morgan's eyes opened, gaze lifting to him, asking and seducing at once. She wanted reassurance, sweetly begged him to let go, tempted him with the promise of ecstasy like he'd never known.

With that look, his control broke. The peak of rapture raced from the base of his spine, burned through his balls, up his cock, until he exploded. Pleasure ripped her name from his lips in a hoarse cry. It became a chant as he repeated it over and over while the sharp edge of bliss seemed to last forever, pounding his body with one relentless pulse of ecstasy after another.

Faintly, through the haze of his roaring heartbeat, he heard Morgan gurgling.

"Swallow," he rasped, rubbing one of his hands along her neck. "Swallow, *cher.*"

Sweetly submissive now—for the moment—she did. But Jack didn't kid himself. That smile breaking out across Morgan's face told him about her rush of excitement at breaking him down, stripping him of his iron defenses.

He pulled away from the sweet depths of her mouth and shucked his pants completely. Satiation lazed through him and control reasserted itself. Now, he could mow down her barricades and return the favor. Now, he could capture her surrender, strip her soul, and make sure that having sex with Brandon Ross would never be on her wish list again.

*       *       *

STILL panting, tired yet flying, Morgan stared at Jack as she rose to her feet. He tossed his pants aside and turned back to her with burning eyes. The short military cut of his hair only accentuated his angular face, his strong jaw dusted with a dark five o'clock shadow, his cleft chin. The gorgeous sights didn't stop there.

She let her gaze wander down the powerful bulk of his shoulders, the solid bulges of his pectorals, the tight abs that showed the delineation of every muscle . . . and made a treasure trail down to his groin.

Even soft, his penis was big. When hard . . . he'd put most men to shame.

And she had conquered him. Big, bad Jack had totally succumbed to her. Was that sense of being mighty and compelling the reason he liked to dominate?

Morgan licked her lips, high on power. Despite a personal first, she wasn't pausing to examine. Wouldn't ask if it was right or wrong—plenty of time for that later. Now . . .

She sent him a kittenish smile. She'd survived his challenge to submit with nary a scratch. It hadn't felt like being a mindless blow-up doll and taking orders; it had been more like following his clues until she learned exactly how to seize control and unravel him.

"You look happy with yourself."

Morgan tried to wipe away the smile, but she just couldn't suppress it. She didn't want to gloat; that would only spur him on. Instead, she just shrugged.

"You're thinking this is a game, Morgan. That you won, and I lost, and we can call it a night. You think we're done and that you can forget the fear that you might enjoy submitting to me."

His soft laugh gave her the first clue that she'd misjudged the situation. Her smile faltered.

"*Cher*, we're just starting. I promise, you'll give me complete control before we're done."

His whisper struck down to her gut, reawakening uncertainty. They weren't done? Every other guy she'd been with . . . well, as Andrew put it, after he came once, he needed eight hours of sleep and a bowl of Wheaties before he was ready to go again. He'd called himself a sprinter. Did that mean Jack was like a marathon runner?

The thought struck an uncomfortable chord of lust in her belly.

"Kneel on the bed." His voice startled her from her ruminations.

"Wh-why?"

Any hint of postorgasm softness or relaxation in his expression vanished. "Because I said. I dominate, you submit. If you ask me one more question or hesitate again, I *will* paddle your ass."

*Ticktock, ticktock.* Suddenly, Morgan could hear each impatient second between them lapse by. She glanced between the rumpled bed and Jack, whose even breaths and steady gaze told her he was completely serious.

She didn't want this; she didn't. But the ache between her legs had become a throb. The salty taste of him still lingered on her tongue, taunting her. Remembered pleasure from their fevered encounter against the door earlier bombarded her brain. She wanted that feeling again, of being taken, of experiencing an orgasm almost bigger than her body.

Worse, there was something about Jack himself. His commanding presence, alternating with his teasing smiles. He reassured her in the oddest way. She felt protected, which made sense. He'd helped her escape a shooter. The fact that he often seemed able to read her mind, as if he understood her, didn't fit. He was trying to cast her as a submissive. And she wasn't.

Jack's hands curled into fists, then relaxed. "Morgan . . ."

He took a menacing step toward her, shadows of a reprimand burning in his eyes.

In the end, her desire ripped the choice from her. She would submit. Just for tonight. Just as an experiment. Once couldn't hurt, right?

She scurried onto the bed and knelt, facing him.

"Turn around. Face the headboard."

In other words, turn her back to him. Knowing she only had seconds to decide, Morgan scrambled through her thoughts. What would he do? He wouldn't hurt her. Jack had protected her when her sicko had started shooting. He'd managed to sneak her out of Lafayette in one piece, but—

"My patience is wearing thin," he barked. "Turn around."

The demanding growl startled her. He meant it. Now.

With a last lingering glance at him, one she knew held all her uncertainty and anxiety, Morgan complied.

"Sit back on your heels." His voice drifted closer, punctuated by the military precision of his footsteps on the hardwood floor.

The stern note in Jack's voice was something Morgan couldn't overlook. She didn't dare ignore him or hesitate.

Once she'd sat back on her heels, Jack trailed a gentle fingertip over the slope of one shoulder, as if petting her in reward. She gasped. The feathery touch startled—and enflamed. A line of fire blazed behind that simple caress.

Then he flattened his palm between her shoulder blades. "Lean down until you're lying with your breasts over your knees. Arms above your head, palms flat on the bed."

Morgan processed his request, racing to picture it. Child's pose, if she'd been doing yoga. It was one she assumed nearly every time she attended a class. But doing it now meant leaving her ass and the line of her spine completely vulnerable to Jack.

His fingers between her shoulder blades began asserting pressure, gently but inexorably pushing her forward.

Finally, she went with it. She could always get out of it if Jack pushed her too far. She had a safe word.

With her cheek resting on the soft sheet, her arms stretched over her head while her legs remained tucked beneath her, Jack removed his hand from her back. She watched as he walked in measured footsteps to the head of the bed.

Her abdomen cramped with the unknown and her total fear of it. What was he doing? Planning?

"Sir . . . ?"

"Morgan, we've covered this. You don't speak unless you're given permission."

"I just want to know what you're going to do."

The air in the room seemed to stop. She sensed his stillness, the whiplash of displeasure that burst through him. Knowing she'd disappointed him incited a tart, unwelcome sensation. Morgan's abdomen churned again. Talking without permission was a no-no, as was asking questions. She wasn't sure why, but she knew without a doubt that she'd gone beyond a faux pas.

Suddenly, he spurred into action, grabbing her left wrist with one hand. Within moments, a velvet rope wrapped around her. A pull, another tug, and a yank later, he stepped away. Discreetly, Morgan tried to pull at her wrist.

It was securely bound.

Before she could do more than begin to reel with the implications of that, Jack made his way to the other side of the bed, captured her right wrist, and repeated the process.

Both of her arms were immobilized, tightly but not uncomfortably tethered to the posts of the headboard. She gave a gentle tug, then a not-so-gentle one. Nothing. The bonds didn't give so much as an inch. He must have been one hell of a Boy Scout, since those knots were perfect.

Panic rushed her like a wave from a tsunami. Oh, no. She was in over her head. Way over. Jack was . . . more. More man, more disciplined resolve, more iron control than she was ready for.

She struggled, pulling at her bonds with a frightened whimper. God, what had she been thinking? It was one thing to fantasize about giving a man utter control of her body. It was completely another to actually do it, even if she did trust him with her physical safety. How well did she actually know him?

But her bonds weren't budging.

When she cried out again, Jack gentled her with a soft touch, curling his palm around the back of her head.

"Morgan, take a deep breath." He waited until she did, then whispered in a quiet, hypnotic voice. "You're safe. You're fine. I've got you."

The calm in his voice reached deep inside her. His tone asked her to be reasonable, not to panic. For a reason her logical mind could not fathom, that soothed her. She heeded his voice and stilled.

In reward, he smoothed his palm down the exposed length of her back. "Submission is about trust, Morgan. You trusting me not only to keep you safe but to give you everything you want, every pleasure you imagine. I can grant you those things, but not without your help. The pleasure comes, in part, from giving up total control."

Suddenly, the caress at the small of her back was gone. Moments later, he replaced it with a sharp *thwack* on her ass.

Startled by his action, Morgan bucked against her bonds. "Ouch! Stop it."

No sooner were the words out of her mouth than a peculiar stinging began to prickle her skin. It created a fire that lingered where he'd spanked her.

"You're not in control, Morgan. Your body is mine to pleasure or punish as I see fit. Right now, you've more than earned a punishment."

She'd barely recovered from her surprise when he spanked her again, this time hitting the other cheek with an equal amount of force. Morgan bit her lip as the initial sting assailed her. Then, as before, the nip of pain gave way to the unexpected heat that spread across her ass.

"There are surprises. That's intended. I will do things you don't always understand or think you want. Or agree with. What's important is that you trust that I know your body and your limits, and that you comply. Because you have trust in me, in my ability to get past your mental barriers to give you the pleasure your body craves."

He smacked her again, a healthy slap for each cheek.

Morgan gasped. "Go to hell."

The rumble of Jack's laughter sounded behind her. "You're just digging yourself a deeper hole, *cher*."

He smoothed a calloused palm over the tingling flesh of her ass. The heat of his skin seeped in, mixing with the burn on her bottom, to create a fire that nearly had her moaning. How could she like it? Why should she? It made no sense.

"You can't experience what you want until you learn to give yourself over to me. Completely," he whispered in her ear.

Mentally, she railed against his words, even as she realized her vagina was completely wet.

*No, no, no!* He was spanking her like a wayward child. She didn't like it. Really.

But the pain . . . it was becoming pleasure, thick and throbbing and impossible to ignore.

Morgan shifted, trying to avoid his hand. No such luck. Two more smacks, one for each cheek, both with more vigor than the others. She managed a snarl of outrage, but that didn't stop the spread of fire from bursting across her skin.

Throbbing heat. Bone-deep want. *Oh my God* . . . Her flesh began to ache. Morgan felt blood dancing just under her skin, engorging her clit.

Fighting was useless.

"Do you understand?"

That voice, like a sexual drill instructor. Every word was wrapped in steel, but beneath that, she heard the taunting promise of what could be, the velvet promise of ecstasy.

Fresh heat crawled across her flesh, swelled her clit, strangled her protests. Her body demanded more.

"Yes, sir."

"Much better," he praised.

Only then did Morgan realize she was actually lifting her ass to his hand, anticipating the next blow. She became hyperaware of her empty sex and clawed at the sheet, aching for him to fill it.

The thrill of sensation took over then. Shivers chased one another down her spine. Her entire body felt hot, agitated. She'd been in-flamed by the feel and scent of Jack when she'd taken him in her mouth, but this position, his gently punishing touch, made her aware of the fact that she was a woman and under his control. Aware that she was in a position that bared the most secret parts of her body to him, and tied down as she was, he could touch her—or not—at any time he chose.

A scary, heady realization—one that gave her more pleasure than pushing him to lose control with her had.

He glided the flat of his palm down her back. Morgan curled her spine like a cat, seeking the tingling heat in his touch.

Immediately, he removed his hand. "You stay still unless I say otherwise."

His tone made it clear he expected a reply.

"Yes, sir."

"Excellent."

No, it wasn't. Morgan could feel her body temperature rising, her thoughts beginning to slide in a thick morass to a lust-choked swirl. Right and wrong were slowly being replaced with pleasure and pain, with the need to achieve orgasm. And oddly, with pleasing Jack.

He turned and walked out the door. Morgan glanced over her shoulder and watched him leave, his taut, bare ass inciting a fresh spark of need, even as his disappearance incited fear. Where was he going? He couldn't just leave her here like this! How long did he expect her to remain in this position, waiting?

Morgan turned her head and started watching the clock on the bedside table. It ticked away in the silence. The only other sound she heard was her own heartbeat.

Five minutes slid by. Then another five. Her legs began to turn numb. She noticed the slight chill in the room his absence allowed. But something told her not to move. Something told her this was a test.

She didn't intend to fail.

After another eight minutes, he returned with a smallish black box in hand and an erection that left her with no doubt of his ability to perform again. Without a word, he set the box on the bedside table, then glanced at her.

"You're still in position. Good. Very good."

He trailed a light finger from the small of her back down . . . down between the cheeks of her ass. She stiffened, gasped, tried to tighten against him. He hesitated, but when she made no further protest, he continued his quest down to her sex.

Then he was there, his fingertips gliding over the slick flesh pouting into his hand. Back and forth, all around the outer folds, spreading her moisture in a careless, unhurried pattern.

He was toying with her. Just toying! But she was too aroused for anger. Morgan thrust her hips back at his hand. *Do something!* her body screamed silently.

He merely used his other hand to smack her ass again.

"Stay still," he demanded.

He wrapped his fingers around her hip to stop the provocative wriggle of her hips. She tensed, trying so hard to do as he commanded. Her muscles trembled with effort, as pleasure streaked unmercifully inside her.

"Your sweet pussy is wet, Morgan. Even more wet than this morning. And swollen. You think you're ready to be fucked?"

Squeezing her eyes shut, Morgan tried to hold her answer in. If she said yes, he would only torment her. If she said no, he would torment her even more. But pretending indifference to the magical mastery of his fingers trailing through her juices, between her sensitive folds, just wasn't possible.

"Yes, sir," she finally croaked out.

She ached everywhere. The need beat at her. Everything between her knees and her navel screamed for his mouth, his cock. Anything! She needed him to do something.

Jack merely kept playing.

"There's too much fight in you. When you completely submit . . . then we'll see."

Oh, she wanted to argue that one. This was as damn submissive as she was going to get. He could either accept what she was willing to give or go jump off a—

*Oh my God!*

A pair of his fingers sliced through her moisture, through her slick folds—and plunged inside. A turn of his wrist, a flick of his fingers . . . He found her G-spot and began a firm but leisurely caress.

Almost immediately, the pleasure clamped around her thighs, pierced her clit, darted up her passage. Everything inside her body came alive as he continued an unmerciful press on that oh-so-sensitive spot.

She moaned, long, loud, then thrust her hips back at him in invitation once more. He declined, neither invading farther nor rubbing faster. He simply stayed the course.

Blood began to roar in Morgan's ears. She became aware of her heartbeat vibrating inside her. Her clit throbbed in time with the rhythm. Perspiration broke out between her aching breasts, at her temples and nape, between her rigid thighs.

Higher, higher the man was driving her. And God, she was almost there, almost to the edge of the cliff. This was going to be a free fall from unknown heights. Her body tensed, preparing. She panted, wailed, wanting it more than anything . . .

Suddenly, he withdrew.

"I didn't give you permission to come."

"What?" She could barely catch a breath.

"You don't come until I tell you to. Complete control, *cher*."

He disappeared around the other side of the bed for a moment and grabbed the black box. What the hell was he doing? She was dying here, dissolving into a puddle of need, and he was digging into a damn box?

She moaned, aching frustration wracking her body in shivers. Fine, if he wasn't going to help her, she'd help herself.

Morgan tried to wiggle back and forth to produce enough friction on her clit to send her over the edge. Moments later, Jack stilled her with a sharp slap to her ass. Then he anchored that palm on her hip, making it nearly impossible to move under the pressure of his grip.

"Bad girl. You'll come when I say so, under my hand, around my cock. Not because you wiggled your ass for it."

With that comment, Jack climbed onto the bed behind her. He plunged his fingers back into her. But rather than rubbing at that sweet spot inside her, he merely moved about, dousing his fingers.

"Spread your knees," he demanded, fitting his free hand between them, urging her thighs apart.

Morgan complied, breathless, mindless, so ready to fall into the swamp of desire pounding at her.

Jack removed his fingers from her passage, gave her clit a breath-stealing flick. She stilled, thoughts chasing. What would happen next? What would he—

A touch later, where she least expected it, he answered her question.

Before Morgan could even protest, one of his fingers, slick with her own juices, penetrated her ass, pushing past the tight ring of muscle. Tingles formed a shocking circle of pleasure around the invasion. She gasped.

"No . . ." she whispered.

"Yes," he asserted. "You have a beautiful ass. I'm not going to ignore it."

He invaded her anus with a second finger. Burning pressure. Something so foreign and forbidden. The pleasure zoomed sky-high. Morgan gasped, then bit her lip. How could she like such a thing?

Yet, suddenly, it was impossible not to crave more. "That's it, *cher*. Push back onto my fingers. I'm going to open you up and fuck you here soon."

Then Jack burned away anything she might have said and sent her closer to the edge, plunging his fingers into her body with a hypnotizing rhythm. *In, out, in, out* . . .

The sensations were so new, so unexpected. He'd awakened so many parts of her, and they all screamed with need now. Her nipples were taut nubs that rubbed against the sheets with each penetration. Her clit pulsed with her heartbeat. Her wet sex still danced from his touch.

And now his fingers drove her slowly mindless, awakening the senses in a part of her body she'd only considered erotic in her most forbidden midnight fantasies.

Then the pleasure was too strong for thought. She could only move with his touch, arching to meet his fingers, mewl at the shock of sensation, the thrill. Her entire body was tightening, focused on reaching the pinnacle that grew and swelled, towering above her, engulfing her.

Jack withdrew his fingers from her ass. Morgan whimpered in protest before she could stop herself, before she could even think about what she was doing.

"I'm not done, *cher*," he soothed.

A pop and a squishy sound later, Morgan felt something new, slightly cold, and definitely foreign, probing again at her back entrance. A vibrator. It shook as Jack teased a small circle around her sensitive opening.

Her pleasure was so focused there, so sharp, that Morgan couldn't imagine anything overtaking it. Especially when he pushed the vibrator in a fraction.

"Push down," he commanded softly.

Entranced, Morgan did. The vibrating probe quickly warmed in her body. She cried out in a sound of pure pleasure at the wicked desire it created. The vibe was about the same size as his fingers, but so smooth as he eased it in and out of her body. She arched to it, wanting more, feverish with lust. She cried out, grasping the sheet in her fists.

Jack moved directly behind her, covering her back with his body as he whispered in her ear, "You look so sexy with my vibe pleasuring your ass. A man could lose control just looking at you."

Morgan looked back over her shoulder at Jack. He knelt behind her, his chocolate eyes scorching her already overheated skin, his shoulders wide and bulging as he gripped her hips with large hands. The breath seesawed out of his wide, muscled chest, now slick with sweat.

He looked like a man hanging onto his control by a thread.

She had no time to rejoice when he thrust into her sex, all the way to the hilt in one sizzling stroke. Morgan gasped at the feel of him filling her completely, her passage made smaller by the vibe in her ass driving her out of her mind. She felt full, packed. The double penetration made her claw at the sheets again, grab them in desperate fists.

"Jack!"

"Yes, *cher*. You're like heaven," he groaned as he thrust inside her. "Fucking whipped cream and cinnamon-spiced perfection."

His rhythm quickly escalated to something fast and focused. The friction and vibrations had tingles screaming inside her tender openings. She felt her blood rushing south, flooding her sex, her ass. Morgan panted, screamed as the pleasure expanded faster than she could assimilate. Her knuckles turned white as she fisted the bedding. Dangerous need threatened to swallow her, steal her sanity, and never return it.

Jack was relentless. The climb to the peak came fast. Her teeth dug into her lip until she tasted blood. But nothing could hold the pleasure in.

Her cries became ear-splitting shouts. Morgan could feel herself tightening around his cock, gripping as if she would never let him go, rippling with the impending storm. He continued the smooth rhythm, fucking through the clamp of her sex with control and power.

With both passages penetrated, Morgan's fantasies burst free in her mind. The one she denied having in the cold light of day flooded her, the image haunting her. Two men, each filling her, working together to over-whelm her, own her, fuck her until—

"Come, Morgan. Come now!" he shouted hoarsely.

She let out a raw scream as orgasm blasted through her. Her body shuddered as she gripped him, milked him. And the pleasure . . . It spi-raled beyond anything she'd ever known, annihilating thought or con-trol, the ability to speak. All she knew was the devastating ecstasy that made black spots dance in her vision, made her body taut, weightless, as Jack hurtled her into the kind of pleasure she had only imagined.

His husky cry echoed hers as he came in a fevered rush.

They collapsed together onto the bed. He dislodged the vibe but kept himself buried deep inside her, slowly stroking her skin, as if he wanted to possess her beyond the orgasm. As if he found her not only acceptable, but wonderful.

As Jack curled around her, his panting breaths falling on her shoul-der, Morgan's body—worse, her heart—leapt in joy at those heady thoughts.

# Chapter Eight

EYES closed, Morgan rolled over and stretched in the warm, rumpled sheets. Her muscles felt deliciously heavy and relaxed, if a tad sore in some unusual places. But wow, such hard, dreamless slumber had rejuvenated her. She couldn't remember the last time she had felt this rested. Smiling, despite her lingering drowsiness, she drew in a deep breath. The scents of leather, male musk, midnight, swamp, and sex bombarded her.

Scents that belonged to Jack.

The events of the previous night rushed back. Every bit of it. In sudden, excruciating detail. Gasping, Morgan sat straight up in bed, gathering the sheet in her fists. Everything she'd done . . . not just done—reveled in. Lust boomed in her gut and her vagina clenched in fresh hunger as memories besieged her in vivid color.

Her mind shook with a mix of shock and disbelief. Dismay wasn't far behind.

And she was still naked. She, who never slept bare, still lay in the bed of the man who'd instigated her downfall into the most forbidden sin and had found a way to make her pant for it. And now, she lay in his bed like she was waiting for him to do it all again.

Frowning, Morgan remembered him sleeping beside her last night. No, not beside her; tangled with her. His solid warmth curled around her back, his hand splayed over her abdomen. The steady rhythm of his hard male breathing had drifted into her ear.

She hadn't slept well in weeks, not since the problems with her stalker had started in earnest. But even when she felt safe in her relatively secure apartment, she never slept that deeply. Next to Jack, she'd felt cherished, protected—totally able to fall into the black chasm of slumber.

She'd also felt claimed, especially when he awakened her deep in the night. He positioned her flat on her back and fitted his hips between her wide-spread thighs, gasping at the silken thrust of his cock into her swollen sex.

Despite being half-asleep, the euphoria of his slow, lazy strokes sent her into a red haze of need. Within minutes, she tried to claw at Jack's shoulders in silent plea—only to realize he'd tied her down again. And blindfolded her.

He'd released the ties at her ankles suddenly, she recalled, then shifted her close to the head of the bed. Keeping her wrists tethered, he sat her up and, with a grip of controlled fervor, guided her down on his cock . . .

"Ride me, *cher*. Squeeze me with that pretty pussy and ride me," he whispered in the midnight air.

With his hands clutching her hips, Jack dictated the speed and depth of his penetration. Never too deep, never too fast. Never enough to do anything but reduce her to a panting, pleading mass of tingles.

Morgan had whimpered for more. Perspiration dampened her belly, her back, as she strained toward a release he wouldn't give her. Instead, he merely drove her up, up, up to mindlessness with endlessly slow strokes.

"Jack . . ." she moaned.

"*Non.*" He sat up beneath her, then nipped at the tip of her breast with his teeth, even as one of his hands struck her bare ass.

The double pleasure-pain ricocheted through her body, spiraling sensations through her like hot lava. She gasped for air as Jack buried himself deep, deep inside her. He thrust up, but still in long, lazy strokes that multiplied the friction, exploded shivers of sensation within her.

"Wrong," he chastised, lifting her up, nearly off his cock. "What should you call me?"

Morgan hesitated, teetering on the knife's edge of need. Panting, her sex on fire, her bound hands preventing her from touching him, she cried out, "More. Please . . ."

"You'll get it when you address me properly."

"Sir." She managed to get the word out of her mouth in a rush. "Sir."

Jack rewarded her with a quick upthrust, his cock burrowing deep, filling her completely. Morgan cried out. The hand at her hip inched over until his thumb toyed with her clit. With a moan, she arched into his touch, seeking the edge of the cliff that was nearly in front of her. Almost . . .

With quick fingers, he untied her hands—and made it clear they would not stay idle. "Play with your nipples, Morgan. Show me how you like to have them touched."

She hesitated, apprehension tangling with a jolt of lust. *Put her hands on herself while he watched?* Oh, God, the idea excited her.

When she didn't comply, Jack stopped his slow, steady thrusts. Morgan whimpered.

"Touch them. Now," he demanded. "Or I will stop fucking you and spank that pretty little ass red again . . ."

Morgan didn't want to think about how much she'd liked his broad palm striking the cheeks of her butt. But she wanted his cock inside her more, as much as she wanted to please him. She brought her hands to her breasts and cupped them, wishing more than anything that she could see his face. Was he aroused by what she was doing? Repulsed?

"And your nipples. You don't ignore them when you make yourself come, do you?"

"No," she said breathlessly, squeezing them between her thumbs and fingers, then giving a slight twist. "No, sir."

A fresh rush of moisture surged from her passage, wetting her already-slick folds. Her body's gesture didn't go unnoticed.

"Yes, *cher*. I love you wet. You're so perfect to fuck, like you were made for my cock."

Jack lowered her on his erection again and poured into her with a heady, steady rhythm that made her head spin, her body burn. She met him, thrust for thrust, moan for moan, pinching her nipples on each downward stroke until they were so hard, so sensitive.

"Move your hands," he murmured against her skin.

It was almost with reluctance that she released the hard buds of her breasts. Difficult to admit that, but satisfaction was so close, she tasted it on her tongue. She whimpered for it. Her fingers pinching her nipples added to the pleasure Jack swarmed her with.

She didn't have to do without the delight for long. He took one of her stiff tips into his mouth, sucking so hard, pressing it against the roof of his mouth while his tongue teased the underside. His fingers tormented the other, putting so much sweet pressure, so much ache, around the sensitive crest that she nearly screamed.

"You're tightening on my cock, *cher*. You don't come until I tell you to," he reminded.

"I can't stop it, sir," she murmured, helpless against the rising tide of ecstasy threatening to overtake her.

"You can. You will. Just as you'll play with your clit for me." He lifted one of her hands to his mouth and sucked a finger into the shocking heat. "Lick your finger like this, get it all nice and wet, then stroke it over your clit for me."

She wanted to. Oh, God, she wanted to. The mere thought stabbed her with a fresh surge of need. But . . . "It will make me come."

He smacked her ass. "Address me properly."

Morgan swallowed against her need. "It will make me come, sir."

"Not until I say so," he warned. "Now take that finger into your mouth. Yes. Deep. Suck it. Beautiful, *cher*. Good."

He pistoned her up and down on his cock. Blood rushed in flowing rivers toward their joined bodies, flooding every nerve ending with need, swelling her folds until she felt the slick friction of every thrust inside, outside—everywhere. She squeezed her eyes shut, trying to focus, but she couldn't hold back much longer . . . Jack was driving her beyond her ability to endure.

Yet the last thing she wanted to do was use the safe word to stop him.

"Squeeze me with your pussy. Yes," he croaked. "Now put that finger on your clit and show me how you rub it."

Seared beyond modesty or shame by the flames of pleasure, Morgan did as he demanded, sliding her palm down her abdomen into the damp nest of her curls and circled her wet finger over her clit.

"Oh, yes!" She couldn't hold the sound in. Immediately, she realized that the hood had pulled back from her clit and every drag of her fingertip over the swollen little bud was like fire in her sex, burning down to the passage Jack filled with every thrust.

"Don't stop," he growled. "Show me how you play with your clit."

Actually, she couldn't have stopped for anything. Her saliva mingled with her own juices as she pressed a second finger onto her clit and began the motions she knew would rocket her straight into bliss.

Still, she strained to hold back her orgasm, waiting for Jack's approval. Somehow needing it. The pressure grew, mounted. She clenched every muscle, even as she felt compelled to drive herself higher. And Jack . . . He was now pounding into her, a moan punctuating his every stroke. Inside her, she could feel him thickening, swelling. He lengthened his strokes, the crest of his cock hitting her G-spot with every rapid-fire thrust.

And still Morgan held on, digging her nails into his hip with one hand, stroking the bundle of nerves between her legs with the other. Her thighs tightened around him. She cried out, trying desperately to wait for Jack's consent to release the gigantic explosion swirling inside her with the bright, shining promise of Nirvana.

"*Jouis pour moi,*" he demanded. "Come for me!"

Jack didn't even finish his sentence before it crashed over her, granting that dazzling dance with the stars as light and color flashed in her head. The beauty had a dark side, though, as it poured through her, swirling around her, then pulled her under, into a dark morass, like a riptide. It drowned her in violent pleasure, a place where only the white-hot sear of satisfaction lived. A ringing in her ears and a sting in her throat told her, over the roar of her pulsing heartbeat, that she was screaming. Jack's long groan of satisfaction joined her . . .

After that, she remembered nothing, just deep dreamless hours of heavenly sleep, cocooned in Jack's warmth.

Now the bed was empty, the bedroom door closed.

And the mere thought of him and their night together left her aching and wet again.

Morgan buried her face in her hands. God, what had she done?

Before Jack touched her, she'd worried that after one night with him, she would never be the same again. She'd been right to worry.

Worse, after arousing her into panting for everything she swore she'd never want, couldn't want, then satisfying her beyond her every erotic imagining, Jack had merely awakened at some point and left. No, she hadn't expected undying devotion or confessions of love. Crazy. Jack Cole didn't seem like the kind of man to bow to something as soft as emotion. The very notion made her laugh. Or would have, had she been in the mood to see the humor.

As it was, she saw only that she'd given herself—repeatedly—to someone who could turn her inside out, make her into something her mother would be horrified by, Andrew would scorn. A wanton she wasn't sure she could come to terms with. Then he would leave her.

It had to end . . . even if that reckless part of her craved more of Jack and the sweet insanity of the pleasure he gave her. Other than one night of sex, they didn't suit. Earthy, laid-back Jack didn't fit in her world. And she . . . didn't belong in his, a world of silken commands that came with velvet bonds and spankings and acts that both horrified and fascinated.

And why was she even contemplating anything she might share with Jack beyond last night?

He had challenged her to give herself to him for a night. Fine. She had. It wasn't going to happen again. Now they just had to divine the identity of this stalker, and she could get back to her life . . . and somehow forget Jack before she lost herself in him.

On the bright side, when it came time to film the episode of *Turn Me On* that dealt with domination, she'd be well prepared.

With a sour smile at her own bad humor, Morgan rose and fished around the room for something to hide her nakedness and ward off the morning's chill. A huge sweatshirt of Jack's that hung to mid-thigh and a pair of socks later, she finger-combed her hair to rid it of the worst of the tangles. Damn, she couldn't even find a pair of underwear. And the rest would have to wait. The way her stomach was rumbling, she needed food.

With a deep breath, Morgan opened the bedroom door and stepped into the hall.

The last thing she expected to see was another man standing in the middle of the living/kitchen area.

Built hard, with obviously Germanic ancestors, the man rose about three inches above Jack, who was no midget himself. Hair the color of rich caramel, cut military short, a square jaw, and shoulders a mile wide all screamed *male*! But it was the eyes, bright, razor-sharp, deep denim blue . . . slashing over Jack's shoulder to focus on her with cool assessment—and hot reaction—that startled Morgan.

This stranger could probably guess that she'd spent the night having sex with Jack. As if her own licentious behavior hadn't been bad enough, this new realization sent a fresh flush of mortification rising up her cheeks.

Jack turned to find her frozen in the hall. She probably had that deer-in-the-headlights look, she thought, forcing herself to take a deep breath and meet the stranger's gaze.

"Morgan," Jack called.

She cut her glance to him. My, he looked yummy in the morning. Just his voice, low, gravelly, with a hint of command, both reassured her and made her wet again. Bad, bad sign.

Her belly jumped, her cheeks flushing again when she remembered for the second time everything they'd done the night before.

His dark eyes burned with memories, even as he crossed his arms over his massive chest, jaw tense. His posture did not invite morning-after affection, even if she'd been so inclined. Was this remote man the same one who'd tangled his limbs with hers in a warm embrace of protection during the dark of the night?

"This is my business partner, Deke Trenton," he simply said.

Jack and this newcomer, they might look a bit like day and night, light and dark, but with iron bodies and hard eyes, they were cut from the same military cloth. She shivered. Too much testosterone in one room.

The big warrior stepped around Jack and extended his hand with a friendly smile that changed his whole face from forbidding to surprisingly approachable.

Haltingly, she held her hand out to him, and they shook. "Morgan O'Malley."

"Jack, you asshole. Hoarding the pretty girls again. I really ought to beat your ass for that."

Jack snorted. "Yeah, you try."

Deke grinned. "Later. Outside. You, me, and the gators." He turned to Morgan with a conspiratorial whisper. "Ask me, and I'll tell you who to place your money on. Better yet, maybe I can convince you to grant the winner a kiss. Then I promise it won't be any contest."

His gentle teasing set her at ease immediately. Despite the awkward situation, she felt herself relax and smile back.

"I'm not the human equivalent of a poker chip," Morgan teased with a roll of her eyes.

"Good girl," Jack praised. "And if my business partner doesn't stop messing where he hasn't been invited, he's going to find his face one bloody blob—uglier than it already is."

Deke laughed and sauntered back toward Jack, slapping him on the shoulder. "You're so damn subtle, Jack." He cast another heated look in her direction, gaze lingering on her bare legs and the outline of her unbound breasts through the sweatshirt. "And you're one lucky bastard."

Morgan bit her lip under his appraising gaze, at once discomfited. And shamefully intrigued. Deke looked like something out of a hardcore war film—not at all her type. Neither was Jack, for that matter. But . . . never mind; she wasn't going there.

"Did you come here for a reason? Or just to torment me?" Jack shot back acidly.

Morgan saw through the sarcasm immediately. It was clear he and Deke were great friends. Jack didn't trust many people, but she'd bet he trusted the big blond guy with his life. At this moment, however, Jack was tense, watchful, even a bit angry. He pretended to take Deke's teasing well—but he wasn't.

"Well, you know I never pass up the opportunity to torment you. Not that I need the practice."

"Nope, you've got it down to a fine art."

"Years of effort." Deke sighed. "But I did come here for a reason." He glanced back at Morgan, all business now. "You might want to hear this, too. It's about your stalker."

She sucked in a breath. In all her tangled emotions and the easy banter, she'd lost sight of the murderous lunatic. Silly her.

"Okay. Um, one minute. I can't face this without something to eat."

"And coffee, I'm sure," Deke added.

Morgan made a face. Jack laughed.

"She doesn't drink it," he told Deke.

He raised a tawny brow. "Is she human?"

Rolling her eyes, Morgan padded back to the bedroom. If she was going to face the testosterone inquisition, she needed something more than a flap of sweatshirt covering her ass. Once she'd retrieved Jack's oversized bathrobe, she padded to the bathroom and brushed her teeth and hair.

When she made her way down the hall again, Jack and Deke both sat at the round kitchen table, cups of strong coffee resting on the smooth pine surface. A piece of toast and a glass of orange juice waited for her.

She glanced at Jack in surprise. He merely guided her into a chair without comment.

He'd made dinner last night, and now this? The man who tied her up and told her exactly how to behave in the bedroom so he could send her straight to mindless orgasm did something as menial as cook for her? Like he was taking care of her?

"Thanks," she murmured, totally confused, as she settled into the chair across from Deke.

Jack sat on her left, then with a nod, turned to his business partner.

"Deke has some pals at the FBI who have studied copies of the photos the sick bastard has been leaving you and the pattern of his behavior."

Deke gripped his mug of coffee and leaned across the little table, a formidable presence even in the large, airy room. Morgan found herself holding her breath, hoping that he knew something, *anything*, to help catch her personal Norman Bates before he became a full-fledged Psycho.

"Your stalker is likely a man somewhere between the age of twenty and forty-five. He's someone you know. His behavior . . . he functions like an intimate-partner stalker, someone who is a little obsessed and can't let go."

"But if he's someone I know, wouldn't I know who? I mean, wouldn't he want me to be certain who he is?"

"The way he withholds his identity is unusual. Either he's purposely hiding it from you or he thinks it's so obvious that you must know who you 'belong to.' Judging from the bit of evidence we have, I think it's the latter. I don't think this person is into subterfuge for the sake of hiding. So that makes him delusional, too."

Morgan sighed, her stomach tightening with fear at Deke's every word. "Was there any question of that?"

"No, but the fact that he followed you to Houston when you went to stay with your fiancé tells us he's serious," Jack added.

Deke glanced back at her, surprise reflected in the raised arches of his brows.

*Fiancé?* Morgan searched her memory. Jack's tense jaw and black glower suddenly reminded her that she'd told him that she was engaged to Brandon. The lie hadn't kept him from moving in too close. But correcting Jack now would only give him a greener light than he already thought he had to pursue whatever sexual arrangement he might want from her. Nope. She was hanging on to her subterfuge and pleading extreme guilt in case he came sniffing around again. Next time, she'd have to remember she was supposedly an engaged woman.

"L.A. to Houston is a long way for a prank," she agreed.

"Exactly," Deke cut in. "But the way this character took shots at you suggests there's vengeance on his mind."

"He thinks you're his," said Jack. "But when he saw you having coffee with me, that's the first time he tried to shoot you . . . like he wanted to punish you and keep anyone from having you if he couldn't."

"That's twisted." Morgan grimaced.

"Stalkers aren't nice, normal guys." Deke shrugged.

She sighed. "I still have no idea who this is."

"I'm sure you know him, Morgan. This is someone you've been close with on some level, somewhere between conversationally and sexually. But in your interaction, he believed that you connected, that you were meant for him, which gives him the right to punish you for any 'bad' behavior you exhibit, like seeing another man. You've figured out that he's tenacious."

"Yeah, I know he's not going to call it a day anytime soon." The knot of apprehension in her belly tightened.

"Good," Deke praised. "You and Jack are doing everything you can. Stay here for now. At this point, don't try to be Miss Independent."

Getting away from Jack would be great for her self-respect—but terrible for her safety. Morgan sighed. "It chafes me to need a babysitter, but until I know who and what I'm dealing with, I feel better with backup."

"Good. Does he ever call your cell phone?" Deke questioned.

"No. About six months ago, I got a new number. Only three people have the number: my mother, Brandon, and my agent."

"Brandon?"

"Her fiancé."

Jack's rancor as he answered his business partner stunned her. He sounded very unhappy about the "fact" that she had a soon-to-be husband. Morgan frowned. He'd gotten what he wanted, right? He couldn't possibly be jealous.

"Oh, and my production assistant, Reggie, has the number."

Jack and Deke shot each other an oblique look.

"How much do you know about Reggie?"

They suspected Reggie, clearly. Morgan started to tell them they were being absurd. Reggie was a cross between a giant teddy bear and a father figure. But then she realized that anyone could be a suspect. Anyone at all, no matter how absurd it sounded.

"Reggie has been with me since the show started. He's somewhere around forty. Divorced. He doesn't seem like the type . . . but I guess no one gets 'stalker' tattooed across their forehead to make identification easy."

"Exactly. Do you talk with him about personal things?"

She shrugged. "Some, I guess. He let me cry on his shoulder a time or two after my big breakup with Andrew. After *Turn Me On* was renewed, most of the cast went out together to this trendy L.A. bar and put down a few too many. Reggie ended up telling me about his divorce and how his ex cheated on him before he ordered a pot of coffee and insisted on taking me home since I couldn't possibly drive."

"Did you have sex with him?" Jack prodded.

Morgan's jaw dropped. "No! I told you every bit of my personal past, which you shared with Deke."

"He was sketchy about the details at best," Deke said with mock regret. "You can feel free to provide details. Or use me to reenact anything particularly juicy."

Jack whipped around in his seat and burned a furious, quelling glare at Deke.

"Or not," said the blond giant.

Morgan's gaze bounced back and forth between the two of them. What in the heck was going on? Jack was acting almost . . . possessive. She held in a snort. Yeah, as if she mattered to a guy like Jack. To him, she'd just be a plaything.

"No chance you were too intoxicated to remember having sex with Reggie?" Jack asked.

"No. I woke up the next morning with my panty hose still on."

Jack relaxed a degree or two and looked at his pal. "Anything else, man?"

Deke's reply was suddenly very businesslike. "Not at the moment. I'll take the originals of the photos out for forensic analysis to see if this guy left behind any prints or other clues."

"That sounds unlikely," she said.

"It is," Deke admitted with a shrug. "But you never know. Maybe he had a careless moment, or never believed you'd try to have them analyzed. I won't know anything for a few days. But be patient. We'll get to the bottom of it." He patted her hand.

Suddenly, Jack stood. His chair scraped across the hardwood floors, ripping into the early morning quiet. His entire body was tense as he slapped Deke on the back.

"Let's go discuss business."

Deke hesitated, appearing to fight a grin. Morgan had the feeling he was completely amused by the demand.

"Okay." He turned to Morgan. "Nice to meet you."

When he extended his hand across the table, Morgan barely had time to shake it before Jack herded him down the hall to the door, unlocked it, and pushed him through. She watched them disappear with a frown. What in the hell was up with Jack?

*     *     *

JACK resisted the urge to slam the door behind them. He also resisted the urge to plow his fists into Deke's face—but that took a lot more effort.

*What in the hell is wrong with me?*

"Okay, whatever it is, spill it," Deke demanded, sitting in the chair beside the computer workstation.

Jack didn't pretend to misunderstand.

He sighed and plopped down into his own chair. Where should he start? The tangled tale only got more complicated with every minute that passed. Revenge, lust, attempted murder, sex that didn't just rock his world, but rocked his soul—all in the last two days.

But like every story, Jack figured he'd better start at the beginning.

"My ex-wife was having a fling with another man before she left."

"You mentioned that once after about your sixth hurricane that weekend in New Orleans."

"His name was Brandon Ross."

Deke frowned. "Brandon Ro— the Brandon that Morgan is engaged to?"

Jack rested his elbows on his knees and peered up at his friend. "The very same."

"I'd say it's a huge coincidence that you wound up with your enemy's woman under your protection and under your roof—and unless I'm totally off base here—in your bed. But I know you too well to believe in a coincidence that big."

"I planned it," Jack confirmed. "Everything to the last detail. I was going to seduce her, then fuck her, and rub that fact in Brandon's face, the way he rubbed it in mine."

Deke whistled. "Ballsy, man. Crappy but ballsy. So what happened?"

Jack stood, paced the small windowless room. When had it gotten so damn small in here? It had never bothered him before.

He turned his back on Deke. Sighed. Fisted his hands. *Merde,* he felt jumpy.

No, it was more than that. Anger—at Brandon for starting this shit, at himself for feeling the desire to get back at his former pal, and for being dangerously usurped by the desire to have Morgan under him again. Anger that Morgan had, all night long, cheated with perfect bliss on her fiancé and appeared not to care a single bit. Yet she'd still managed to hold back that . . . something inside her. Damn it, her body, her face, told him she still hadn't fully fucking submitted.

Then he'd had to endure Deke's teasing and flirtation with her. That just equaled wanting to rip the big blond giant's head off.

To top it all off, there was his desire . . . Jack swallowed against the need bubbling in his gut. He'd been inside Morgan less than four hours ago, and already he was like a starving man, panting, salivating. Ready to fight to taste her again. The need raged, like he had no control. It was unacceptable . . . and undeniable.

"I don't know," Jack said finally. "It just . . . It's not as simple as I thought."

"Did you become her stalker to get her where you wanted her?"

"You know me better than that. I wouldn't have called you to profile a pretend stalker. I'd just planned to lure Morgan to Lafayette for an afternoon. Nail her enough to persuade her that Brandon wasn't her one and only, then let her go. There's a real stalker, and when he shot at her in a crowd in broad daylight, she was fucking terrified. I brought her here."

"That makes sense, except this possessive thing. It's not like you. In the past, we've shared—"

"Don't even think it," Jack growled. "Morgan is very reserved. Besides, this is a woman running for her life, not some kitten one of us picked up in a sex club."

"None of that has stopped you from fucking her, though, has it?"

"Drop it, damn it. Now!"

"Okeydokey." Deke heeded his warning growl with a tilted smile and held up his hands in a show of surrender. "All lascivious thoughts of the luscious redhead in the next room are gone."

Jack rolled his shoulders, trying to release his tension. Damn, a night with Morgan had him completely tied up in knots and his head screwed on wrong. He wished he could banish his thoughts of her half as easily as Deke supposedly had. It wasn't happening. He wanted more of Morgan. And he wanted her now.

"My question is, why the jealous lover routine?" Deke skewered him with a piercing stare, as if he knew every damn thought screaming through his head. "Unless, of course, you really are jealous."

Damn! The sad reality was that the green gremlin was feasting on his gut. No question about it. He had shared a few women with Deke before. Good times were had by all. Repeating that with Morgan . . . the thought conflicted him. An instinct told him that she would love a ménage—if she could wrap her mind around it. But he felt oddly proprietary about her. Allowing his buddy/business partner to get in on the action made him want to spit nails.

There was something about Morgan that hit him squarely in the chest, so hard he couldn't breathe. Jack was too experienced to play the denial game. His burning want for Brandon's fiancée simply was, had little to do with revenge, and wishing otherwise wasn't going to change it.

It went deeper, though. Fucking Morgan for a whole night hadn't satisfied his libido or his desire to betray Brandon. Rather, something about her had been so perfect. Jack didn't remember ever . . . connecting with a woman so completely, as if he could see inside her, read her every desire. And he'd been physically inside her to the hilt, but that wasn't enough. He wanted more from Morgan: the right to give her whatever she needed, the freedom to hear everything she felt or yearned for.

Instead, she was holding back on him.

Damn it, he didn't want this. Aching for her wasn't a part of his plan. Fuck her, plant seeds of doubt, encourage her to leave Brandon. Walk away. Simple, right?

Not anymore. Jack didn't just want her to leave Brandon to make his revenge complete. Reckless desperation gnawed at him. He wasn't sure he could just let her go, walk away. Even though she'd cheated on Brandon. The knowledge didn't set well with Jack. He'd thought he could steer clear of two-timing women when he divorced Kayla, but Morgan was so much . . . more than his ex-wife had ever been.

The stupid, hormone-happy part of him wanted to earn Morgan's trust, make her his to command. His hard-on demanded he claim her.

There, he'd admitted it. Maybe owning up to it was the first step to recovering from his insanity and getting back to focusing on his revenge.

Darting across the room, Jack paced, mind flying as if his brain had short-circuited. Surely just too much sex on too little sleep.

But he knew himself too well. Something in his gut was shouting at him to abandon his revenge and grab the shimmering perfection of Morgan for himself. Treat her like a woman, teach her to respect her desires, care for her. Seize her and never let go.

That something in his gut also told him emailing Brandon the video of him taking Morgan against the door had been a mistake. A big one.

With a sigh, Jack sank into his desk chair. He shouldn't be troubled at the thought of Brandon seeing him fuck Morgan. But like a stupid schmuck, he was. Damn it, he wished he hadn't shared a single detail about their first time with anyone, much less a visual blow-by-blow.

His regret didn't make a damn lick of sense. Sending that video to Brandon had been half the point of his revenge! Despite that, Jack was uncomfortably aware that he'd sent something to Brandon that he wanted to keep between him and Morgan alone. What did that say about his feelings for her?

Worse, if she found out, Morgan wouldn't understand his revenge, just view his actions as a huge betrayal of her trust. One that could undermine any foundation he made with her. And if he wanted to touch her again, he was going to have to open up, take her into his care beyond the physical. He would have to show her that she mattered.

Fuck. He was going to have to choose between Morgan and revenge because their uninhibited night together had not been enough to sate him. Not nearly enough. She'd only dug herself deeper into his psyche.

How the hell could he just dismiss three years of fury, betrayal, hatred, and plotting?

How the hell could he just let a sweet, submissive firecracker like Morgan go?

"Oh." Deke laughed. "Morgan has you by the balls. You're strung out on this woman. Bad. Not that I blame you. She looks like one sweet little fu—"

"Shut up. Don't put Morgan in the same gutter as your mouth," Jack snarled.

As soon as the words left his mouth, he realized he'd done nothing but confirm every one of Deke's suspicions.

*Shit!*

Deke laughed.

Jack did his best to unclench his rigid jaw. "Let's talk shop."

His buddy held in a wide grin. "Sure. We can do that. Who among our suspects do you think is Morgan's stalker?"

"Could be anyone." Jack shrugged, struggling to relax. "I doubt it's the college boyfriend with the wife and kid. I tend to think she's right about Brent Pherson. A pro football player on the road can't be taking pictures of her at her house. So that leaves her former fiancé, her production assistant, or some random twisted fan."

"I suspect ol' Reggie has all the makings of a sicko."

"He's not as loyal as Morgan thinks. Hell, I paid him to get close to her, to pass my info and bio to her for the show. He took my money without asking questions and sent me her personal email address and IM info. But then he threatened me with everything short of castration if I so much as looked in her direction." Jack grimaced.

"So he sold her out, then turned on you. Nice." Deke sighed. "Was he more jealous boyfriend than protective father?"

"Hard to say over the phone. Could have been either."

"He bears watching. In digging yesterday, I found out he managed to avoid prison time for sexual assault due to a technicality."

Surprise ricocheted through Jack. "Really? Holy shit."

"Yep. I wonder if Morgan knows about Reggie's past."

"I doubt it. She says he's like a surrogate father to her. I don't think she'd feel that way if she knew he might have a hobby as a rapist. But we also need to see if we can rule out any creepy neighbors and fans, just in case, but—"

"My gut tells me this is someone Morgan knows, someone she trusts. That his identity is going to shock her to her toes."

As he gripped the arms of his chair, concern for Morgan gnawed at Jack's calm. This guy wasn't patient, and Jack was sure it would be a whole lot scarier before they finally caught the bastard and put a stop to his shit.

"Exactly."

"So you have to stay close to Morgan, watch her twenty-four/seven," Deke pointed out.

Wasn't that going to be a big help in unknotting his gut and getting his head screwed back on straight?

"Yeah."

With a toss of his head, Deke howled with laughter. "And you want her again so bad you can't see straight."

Jack sighed. He hated being a transparent as glass. "Yeah."

The question was, revenge or Morgan? Which should he choose?

\*　　\*　　\*

"TAKE care, Morgan." Deke paused at the cottage's front door late that afternoon.

"Thanks," she murmured.

From his lofty height, he looked down, his unusual blue eyes swirling with concern. He cupped her shoulder gently. "I'm going to have these original photos examined for any forensic evidence we can find. In the meantime, Jack will take care of you."

Morgan had liked Deke right away. His angular face softened up with a smile. He just seemed . . . nice. Definitely strong enough to protect. And he was easy to joke with. Probably easy to talk to, as well.

Unlike some people.

Morgan darted a glance to her right, at Jack. His gaze was fixed on Deke's palm caressing her shoulder. His glower couldn't be mistaken for anything else. *What was up with him?*

"If Jack doesn't take care of you, you walk over to that phone"— Deke pointed to the sleek black unit mounted on the wall—"and call me. I'm the second speed-dial button. I'll rush right out to give you whatever you need." He winked.

Morgan wagged a chastising finger at him, but she couldn't completely erase her smile. His teasing flirtation coaxed her. The man was a born flirt. He probably had women foaming at the mouth for his attention, but it was sweet of him to keep the mood light when both her safety and her sex life were weighing heavily on her mind.

Another glance at Jack told her that he was not amused. Not in the least.

"Thanks," she murmured. "I'll be eager to hear if you found any fingerprints on the photos. Or anything that might help."

With another caress of her shoulder, Deke waggled his brows at her. "I'll definitely keep in touch."

Again, she laughed. Then he waved at Jack and made his way out to the sunset-drenched swamp.

When the door shut, leaving her alone with Jack, sudden silence thrummed around her. Her smile died. In the distance, she heard Deke's boat splash away from the little dock. Inside, her heartbeat picked up its pace. Tension wrapped around her. Morgan had no idea why, but she didn't question the thick air.

"Thank you for asking him to help. I'm grateful to have any extra assistance that might identify this stalker so I can have my life back."

Jack paused a long time before answering. "Deke is smart and well connected. If there's any forensic evidence to be found on those photos, he'll turn it up."

"Good." She nodded.

Then the awkward silence fell. She couldn't read Jack's expression, but she felt his displeasure churning the air. Morgan frowned, completely confused. Did he think her flirtation with Deke meant something? Would he care if it had? Or was he just annoyed with her presence since she'd surrendered to his every whim last night? Maybe he just wished she'd go away.

"And Deke seemed nice," she murmured, hoping to lighten the tense atmosphere.

Jack snorted. "Deke is a lot of things. Thinking he's nice could be a costly mistake."

Morgan hesitated, brow furrowed with confusion. "He's your business partner. If he's not honest—"

"I didn't say he wasn't honest. He is, as the day is long. He's trustworthy and brave and smart, with a never-say-die attitude. He's everything the military wants in their elite forces. But where women are concerned, I wouldn't call him nice."

"It sounds like you're warning me away from him," she challenged. "Would it matter if I was interested?"

Jack shifted, shoulders tensing. "If you're having a hard time dealing with a few velvet ropes and silken commands, Deke would shatter your delicate sensibilities, *cher*. When it comes to sex, he plays seriously—but only if there are three people in the room."

Three people? "He likes to watch?"

The gravelly laugh Jack gave in response to her question took her aback. "Sex isn't a spectator sport for Deke."

*Wow.* The big German-descended warrior with the all-American smile actively engaged in the very French word *ménage*. Talk about a newsflash . . .

A vision of Jack on one side, Deke on the other, both pleasuring her helplessly bound body—it flashed through her mind, framed in white heat and red sin. Moisture pooled between her legs. In an instant, she went from damp to nearly dripping. Her clit ached without mercy.

Stunned, embarrassed, Morgan backed away. "Oh."

"Oh." Jack shot back with an acid grin as he followed her deeper into the cottage. "Next to him, I look like a choirboy."

Morgan nearly choked. "You've got to be kidding! You, a choirboy?"

"Hey, I was one until puberty. The choir director at Our Lady of Perpetual Hope told me I sang like an angel."

"And you've got a mind like the devil."

Jack merely smiled. "I've barely given you an introduction, *cher*. There's so much more I could show you . . ."

She believed him. Utterly. The very thought of the sensations and feelings he could introduce her to made Morgan shiver and ache. And not just for the stunning release he could give her. In his arms, his bed, she'd felt so liberated and alive. It frightened her to think that the only place she could fell completely free to be herself was bound to Jack's bed.

*God, no. Please no.*

"There won't be any more of that," she vowed. "You told me to give it a night. I did. I know enough now to do the show. That's all I need."

Jack sidled closer. "Are you going to tell me you didn't like it?"

Wouldn't it be nice if she could, and he'd believe it? Morgan knew better. "No. But that doesn't mean we need an encore."

"What's holding you back, your fiancé?"

Morgan gritted her teeth. Damn it, she'd kept up the pretense of a relationship with Brandon to keep Jack at arm's length, but her lie was doing a lousy job. In fact, his question seemed to taunt her for being every bit as naughty as he was.

"To some degree." Maybe pretending remorse would turn him off. "Yes. I feel terrible."

"You might, but it has nothing to do with cheating. Why weren't you wearing your ring when you came to meet me and talk about sex?"

"I-I don't have one yet. I want to pick it out myself."

Jack studied her with a tilt of his head and knowing dark eyes. "I think you're more afraid of your wants than cheating on your fiancé. Wanna prove me wrong?"

How could he know that? How could he just look at her and tell?

"Go to hell. I gave it a night, like I said I would. You're not taunting me into giving you another. No more domination. No more sex. And no more conversation about this."

With a determined shake of her head, Morgan turned away. She half expected Jack to grab her arm, stop her, growl something. She was nearly to the bedroom door when she started to wonder if she'd stunned him speechless. Started to feel both victory and crushing distress.

His voice stopped her cold . . . right before it made her blood boil.

"I can fulfill your fantasies, *cher*."

"Stop." Hand on the doorknob, Morgan paused. She drew in a ragged breath. "Damn you. Just . . . just stop."

"*Non.*" He stepped closer, closer, until he curved his hands around her waist, pressed his erection against her ass, and whispered in her ear. "Every last one of your fantasies. Starting right now."

# Chapter Nine

RUNNING into the bedroom seemed like a damn stupid idea for someone trying to avoid the torturous need to have sex with the man chasing her.

Holding in a wail of frustration, Morgan's mind raced. Where the hell else could she go in this three-room shack? The swamp was no place for a city girl, especially at night. She didn't much like alligators or crocs or whatever lurked out there with enormous teeth and a not-too-fussy palette.

The door, the one at the end of the hall. It had been locked earlier, but she didn't recall him locking it back up after Deke's visit. Maybe she could dart in and lock it behind her. Shut him out for a while and see how well that suited him. Make him find some way to cool down while staring at the bed they'd nearly combusted into flames with the blistering heat between them.

Spinning away, Morgan sprinted farther down the hall.

God, she couldn't believe she was running from him, and she'd berate herself for the stupidity of this tactic later. At the moment, she couldn't think of any other way to escape the steamy seduction of his voice luring her to her sanity's doom. He wanted her downfall, was playing hardball until she surrendered every ounce of her psyche and control to him.

No way in hell she was doing that.

With a crash of footsteps, she made it to the door with Jack in determined pursuit. Her hot, trembling fingers grasped the cold brass of the knob. He crowded in behind her, trapping her against the door. His hand clamped down around hers before she could twist the doorknob.

"Are you sure you want to go in there?" He breathed hard against her neck.

*Yes! The door has a lock.* If she could just get inside, put the door between them . . .

But as she fought the shivers brought on by his hot breath, his very nearness, Morgan suddenly realized he had the keys to open the door. Damn it!

"I don't think you do," he answered for her.

"Is this where you keep the dead bodies?" She sneered, hoping to piss him off.

Instead, he laughed, and his easy rumble vibrated clear through her body. Even now, he was determined to defy her understanding of both men in general and him in particular. Damn, the man could both infuriate and intrigue her.

"You'd probably like that better than the truth," he warned with a silky smile in his voice. "But keep going, and you'll find out."

He was yanking her chain. That's all. Trying to scare her, and she wasn't buying it for a minute.

Using all her body weight, Morgan lunged back, hoping to throw him off her so she could open the damn door and get on the other side of it.

With a rumble of laughter in his chest, Jack stepped back a mere fraction. "Go in. But don't say I didn't warn you."

Morgan hesitated. What if he wasn't just toying with her? What the hell could he be hiding here? And did she really want to dig herself in any deeper than she was?

Shaking her head, she decided it had to be a diversionary tactic. He'd

run after her too hard and stopped her too quickly not to have any interest in keeping her out.

"Bite me," she hissed. "And back off."

Jack just smiled as if he didn't have a care in the world and gestured
for her to step inside.

Refusing to admit any apprehension of what she might find, Morgan
yanked on the knob and shoved the door open.

And she frowned as she ambled in, somehow both relieved and totally disappointed at once. "This is it?"

Shrugging, Jack tried to pull off an innocent expression. Morgan
knew better. Jack was about as innocent as Lucifer at his hedonistic
worst.

"Just a little office space where I do paperwork and keep a computer."

She rounded on him. "Then why keep the damn door locked? There
are no dead bodies. Trying to keep me away from the precious porn on
your computer?"

"Why would I waste time looking at pictures of other people fucking
when I could be doing it myself?" He paced closer, sliding his finger
along the slope of her jaw, then deviating course to rub the lightly calloused pad over her bottom lip. "With you."

Morgan sucked in a breath, unable to look away from the scorching
heat melting his dark-chocolate eyes into something that epitomized sin.
She didn't tingle. His words didn't tighten the knot of need growing in
her belly by the second. *Damn it, no!* She didn't respond to a man who
wanted to subjugate her, to control her with orders and ropes and utter
submission of her will.

She wasn't depraved, as Andrew claimed when he'd hurled the slur at
her. She had always been a "good girl," as her mother had raised her to be.

"I'm not some blow-up doll here to do your bidding, oh arrogant
one. You're delusional." Her voice shook as she said the words.

"I'm determined," he corrected. "All that reluctant arousal and the
tender flush that lights up your body—it's nothing short of delicious.
You fight it, *cher*, but when you give in . . . you're like honey to sink into.
Thick and hot and so damn sweet. Those catchy little moans at the back
of your throat, the pretty way you finally ripple around my cock when

you're on the verge of orgasm . . . Even the thought of you like that is like fire licking through my balls."

"You just don't know when to shut up, do you?"

"Sure, I do. When you're shoved full of my cock and are about to come so hard you scream the walls down." He smiled, wicked, taunting—turning her legs to jelly.

Morgan drew in a steadying breath, determined to find some way—God, any way—to ignore him . . . and the wetness seeping out of her clenching vagina and drowning her thong.

"Dream on, sweetie. It's not happening."

"You mean, not again?" he clarified, crossing his arms over his chest.

It occurred to her then that Jack was blocking the exit. And his expression made it clear she wasn't getting away until they'd hashed this out. Damn the man!

"Fine. You've shown that you're an ass determined to get on my nerves and you have some little computer you like to lock up for reasons unknown. Now move so I can get out of here."

"Actually, I think I've shown I'm a dominant determined to make a submissive in denial admit that she likes to be tied and fucked until she can't see straight. As for what's in here . . ."

He cast his hot gaze across the room. It wasn't until then that Morgan noticed the door in the corner, hidden in shadow.

"Ah, you see the door now. There's more beyond this space." He didn't elaborate. On purpose, she knew. He was testing her. Tantalizing her with the truth. Trying to arouse her curiosity as easily as he did her body. He'd definitely succeeded on the former. Damn him! She refused to think for an instant about the latter.

"So the dead bodies are in there?" she asked tartly, with a bravado she didn't really feel.

"Something more sinful." Jack stalked closer, the intent to have her, to fuck her, blistering in his eyes.

She swallowed. "Stay where you are. Don't come closer!"

In typical Jack fashion, he just kept coming toward her. He didn't stop until he'd settled his hands on her hips, bent his knees, and pressed her wet, aching sex right against the ridge of his erection.

"Hmm. Your pussy is like summer in Louisiana, *cher*. Sultry. Intriguing. Inviting me to spend the day lazing inside."

Morgan tried to struggle away—before the hunger gnawing at her gobbled up her good sense. Already the things he'd done to her in his bed haunted her. She didn't dare give in again and make leaving him, when the time came, even more difficult. And she was no longer naïve enough to believe that being with Jack in his way would cure her of the forbidden midnight desires that made her sweat. She knew now he'd only make her wants sharper, more explicit. More urgent.

"Let go and leave me alone."

Jack took his sweet time responding, trailing the flat of his large palm over her ass, then lifting her thigh above his hip and leaning in to give her an electric nudge with his cock against her aching clit. Then slowly, he released her and stepped away.

By then, her body was thrumming with need, the desire so loud inside her, the front row of a heavy metal concert would be more sedate. She clasped her hands to stop their trembling.

"You don't give the orders, *cher*. I do. Especially when I've got you all spread out across my bed."

Digging into the pocket of his jeans, Jack pulled out a set of keys, strolled across the room, and unlocked the door. He flung the door wide and stepped inside long enough to flip a light switch.

Morgan tried to peer in discreetly, but the light inside was dim and red against black walls. She couldn't see much, just low light and shadows. Her gut tightened with apprehension . . . and devastating curiosity.

"Through that door, you'll find my playroom. In there, I have every means to restrain you, every tool to arouse you, every toy to fuck you. You take a nice, long look around, *cher*, so you can describe it on your show. I'll come back in fifteen minutes. If you're still here . . ." He smiled and shifted his weight, clearly displaying the huge bulge pressing against straining denim. "Let's say you'll get an up-close and personal tour."

Jack turned to leave.

"And if I'm gone in fifteen minutes?" she blurted.

He stopped. The glance he cast her over his shoulder could have melted steel. "You'll just be delaying the inevitable, *cher*. And it'll cost you."

*       *       *

MORGAN stood still, trembling. The door to Jack's most private room stood open not two feet away. She was curious about what he had in there. God knew she was.

Yet she hesitated.

Did she want to know those secrets? *Really* want to know? Having the knowledge would haunt her, change her. Would knowing exactly what he did within these four walls make him and the sexuality he could give her more objectionable?

Or more seductive?

Shaking away her thoughts, Morgan knew the clock was ticking. Jack would come back in less than fifteen minutes. If she was still standing in his lair . . . he'd take that as an unequivocal yes—to anything, everything. The only boundaries between them would be his own, coupled with the limits of his imagination.

In other words, there would be no limits.

Morgan swallowed against a flush of heat. Regardless of whether the room and its contents made her more afraid or less, she had to see, and not just out of curiosity. Labeling her emotions mere journalistic or feminine interest was too simple.

Morgan had to see that room because it would tell her about the alluring, mysterious conundrum named Jack.

Drawing in a shaky breath, she took a tentative step toward the red light in the corner that drew her like a siren.

*One foot forward. Yes. Then the other. Repeat the process.*

Sheer nerve kept her moving, coaching herself with each step. Finally, she stood at the door and opened her eyes. She hadn't even realized she'd closed them.

Air tumbled out of her as her jaw dropped. Shock pounded her as she stared.

The question wasn't what *did* Jack have in here. The question was what *didn't* he have. Just from the doorway, she first saw something that, with two horizontal bars about two feet apart, looked a bit like a standing towel rack. But given the wrist and ankle cuffs attached to each bar, those lowest to the ground fairly far apart, Morgan knew better. Had he stood a woman in that spot, restrained her with legs spread and . . . Finishing the picture disturbed Morgan too much.

She put herself in the picture instead. And instantly, fresh moisture seeped from her sex.

Did she honestly like the thought of being restrained and toyed with? Of being locked in place, helpless to do anything but take the pleasure or pain Jack gave her?

*Yes.*

"No," she whispered, squeezing her eyes shut against a moment's rush of desire.

But it was too late.

Turning away, Morgan spied another table positioned like the crown jewel right in the center of the room. Wide enough to accommodate someone supine, metal cuffs had been welded on each side at the top, center, and end. Most unexpectedly, another set of manacles faced outward like giant pinchers from the bottom of the table's legs, close to the ground. She didn't need a degree in aerodynamics to see the table was designed so he could lay a woman flat, immobile, and spread wide. Or bent over the table with legs and arms restrained. There were probably other positions, but that's as far as her imagination could take her.

No matter. She could picture Jack bending her naked body over the table, laying the heat of his broad chest on her as he clasped her wrists in the cuffs, then bent to secure her ankles, his lips trailing the backs of her thighs as he rose again to fit the broad head of his erection against her empty, weeping flesh.

Biting her lip, Morgan exhaled raggedly into the silence. Her heartbeat threatened to take over, consume her, it beat so hard. She had no doubt that she'd ruined another thong over a fantasy she prayed she wouldn't enjoy in real life.

Tearing her mind from the image, she whirled around to find shelves filled with neat plastic boxes, all clear. Vibrators and dildos, made out of rubber, plastic, glass, some thick, some reed-slim, some short, others that clearly intended to stretch the depth and width of a woman's passage. And Jack would know what to do with each of them. The thought staggered her, made her sex clench in hunger.

On the next shelf up, another organized row of containers held toys for anal play, she guessed. They tended to be shorter with ridges or beads, wide bases. One even looked to inflate with a small hand pump.

Flushing all over, Morgan remembered Jack filling her with one of these. Something slim and ridged and vibrating that had pushed her beyond her limits—right where she'd always dreamed she'd be.

Then he'd left her to deal with her shame and self-doubt the next day. The same shame and self-doubt that was still roiling in her gut.

Morgan spun away. The row of shelves now in front of her held all manner of blindfolds, lotions, cuffs, and clamps—all designed to heighten the senses.

Cinnamon and peppermint gel snared her attention. She wanted to sniff and taste, figure out what he did with that. She didn't dare. A feather sat next to a sumptuous silken blindfold, which she stroked with a tentative finger. Soft, like cream, like touching a cloud. Morgan shivered, imagining that next to her skin.

At least until a pair of clamps caught her attention. Tips encased in velvet, separated by a short length of chain, they could only belong on a woman's nipples. The tips of her breasts hardened at the thought of them pinching helpless, sensitive buds. With hesitant fingers, she reached out, ran a finger over the length of chain, only to realize the clamps lay in their original packaging, the seal unbroken.

She had an insane urge to take them—the one thing she knew he'd never used on another woman—and put them on, parade her breasts for him. He'd approve . . . and show it in ways she could barely fathom. Her fingers itched as a heavy ache throbbed in her breasts. Their tips stood hard, bursting against the lacy bra she wore.

*Just once*, a voice inside her whispered. *Just this one thing . . .*

*That's disgusting!* Andrew's voice invaded her head, replaying their last conversation. *Morgan, you're too smart and cultured to want some . . . caveman to order you around and tie you down. It's sordid and bizarre.*

*Can't we just have sex like normal people? You're not so depraved that you need pain and someone controlling you to get off, are you?*

"Three minutes," Jack called from the hall in warning.

Gasping, Morgan dragged her hand back from the clamps.

What was she still doing here? Worse, what was she thinking, imagining modeling a device designed to pinch a sensitive part of her body for him?

Stunned by her own thoughts, Morgan shook her head. She *could* have sex like a normal person, damn it. Being around Jack adversely affected her thinking. She had to get out of this room—now.

Stumbling back, Morgan charged for the door, leaving the hazy red light behind, racing past the office chair and computer in the corner.

Jack blocked the door to the hallway, arms across his chest, looking as movable as a mountain. "Leaving?"

His inscrutable expression told her nothing. His tone gave away even less. Yet Morgan sensed his frustration and disappointment. His reaction collided with her fear, the desire whipping through her, which she wanted so desperately to ignore, clashing with Andrew's slurs as they reverberated in her head.

Together, it tightened a vise on her heart, ripping a cry from her throat. "Let me go."

His biceps tightened, bulging with veined muscle. He clenched his jaw. And he stared so dead-on at her, Morgan didn't know what to do or say. Hurt flashed in his gaze, then disappeared.

Finally, he stepped aside.

Morgan approached with hesitant steps. When she stood beside him, his stare silently demanded that she meet it. She lifted her gaze to him, his searing-hot eyes filled with anger, disappointment, lust—and something else she couldn't identify. Her breath caught. Her belly clenched. The weight of her breasts, so achingly heavy, and her nipples, so painfully hard, screamed at her. God, he was tearing her in half. Making her want what she knew she shouldn't, what society, her mother, her friends would all scorn her for. What she wasn't sure she could live with herself for accepting.

"Go ahead and run, Morgan," he said, voice disquieting for its softness. "For now."

But the frightening truth lay between them: It wouldn't be long before she couldn't run anymore.

*     *     *

WHAT the hell possessed him to keep pursuing a woman determined to shut him out?

Lying flat on his back, staring at the gleaming wooden ceiling and waiting for the coming dawn, Jack grunted. *Possessed* had to be the operative word. He couldn't possibly be in his right mind to keep chasing Morgan. He'd already achieved the biggest chunk of his revenge, and she had told him with an odd combination of four-letter words, tears, and darting from his playroom like a child caught in a nightmare that she didn't want to spend any more nights in his bed, under his dominance.

But Morgan was lying to him—and to herself. Jack felt that down to the bottom of his toes. She'd had a taste of submission and responded so beautifully . . . except that little bit of herself she withheld. Still, the knowledge she'd given in at all would haunt her, drive a wedge between her and Brandon. But that wasn't enough anymore. It would be so easy to abandon revenge and focus on snaring Morgan for his own.

But with every cry of passion, every acceptance of his demands, she'd been cheating on a man she was about to vow to love until death parted them. And he wondered if she could ever belong to him.

Beyond Brandon, there was a reason she hadn't submitted herself totally, psyche, free will, and all to him. He had no idea what. That bothered Jack—a hell of a lot.

So why couldn't he just accept Morgan's actions? She'd cheated on her fiancé, and he'd proven to Brandon—with video—that he'd nailed his former pal's woman. Why couldn't he just walk away from her and let her relationship with Brandon fall apart on its own? Why get tangled up with another woman not willing to really submit, who was willing to break faith?

Cursing, something vile and sibilant, he scrubbed a hand across his tired face. The truth was, he wanted Morgan more than he hated the fact that she'd been cheating. He was determined to win her full surrender.

Which made him a stupid ass. And with every passing minute, he feared his yearning to possess her had to do with this strange instinctual urging to claim her as his own, not for revenge or even a great submissive fuck, but for emotions he didn't want to identify. That made him an even stupider ass.

He clenched his fists in silent frustration. It made no sense, but he needed to go beyond ending her engagement, beyond ruining her for Brandon's vanilla touch. He wasn't going to be content until she called him sir naturally and he'd used his body in every possible way to satisfy her. Denying that was self-delusional and pointless.

Was he going to have to hear her say that she was his to be satisfied?

Jack rubbed at gritty eyes as soft gray light eked into the cottage, heralding the encroaching dawn. Jackknifing up, he sat on the lumpy sofa where he'd spent the previous, mostly sleepless night and scowled. He wasn't sure if he or the sofa was older, but it didn't matter. No doubt, they both looked their ages this morning. He certainly felt his.

Except around Morgan. Anytime he got near her, he felt hornier than a teenager seeing his first naked woman.

He'd had dozens of women, most of them eager to please. Hell, he could find one in the next hour, if he wanted. So why would he keep after a woman who claimed she wasn't interested?

Sighing, Jack rose to his feet, ambled to the kitchen, and made a pot of coffee. A glance over his shoulder showed that the door to the bedroom was still closed. No surprise there. The only surprise was how badly he wanted Morgan to fling it open and invite him in.

He'd like to believe that the challenge she presented goaded him into pursuing her. An affront to his manly pride and all that. But he'd been turned down before, accepted it with a shrug, and moved on.

That didn't seem possible with her. Last night, as darkness fell, his cock rose and the raspberry-spice scent of Morgan flooded his senses— and strangled his restraint. If she hadn't already been soundly asleep by the time he barged into the bedroom and her tart refusals hadn't been ringing in his head, Jack wasn't sure what he would have done.

Where Morgan was concerned, he'd made an ass out of himself

during Deke's visit. No need to repeat his stupidity. He had to get control of himself before he approached her again.

Grasping his coffee cup in one hand, Jack shuffled outside, onto the cottage's wraparound porch. The sun peeked golden fingers over the shadowy domain of the cypress trees and Spanish moss. Sitting on a chair in the corner, he breathed in the heavy smell of vegetation, rich earth, water, and wildlife. And something spicy that epitomized Louisiana. That's why he loved it out here, why he'd bought the old place from Brice when his grandfather had gotten too old to see to its upkeep and to be so far from a hospital. But he knew his grandfather missed the silty swamp mornings, complete with beignets and bullshit.

The old man was a character, full of colorful stories. And of course the family legend.

Jack snorted. According to *Grand-père*, every male on his mother's side of the family dreamed of the woman meant to complete him, be his soul mate, before meeting her. Supposedly one of his long-dead ancestors made the mistake of marrying the wrong woman and found his true love too late. As the legend went, the man paid a voodoo priestess to "curse" all his male descendants.

Jack frowned. He'd been certain Brice had made the entire tale up to explain why, at twenty-four, he'd eloped with a girl of sixteen. Now, Jack didn't know what to think. His grandfather believed it. Once Brice had learned that Jack had not dreamed about Kayla before marrying her, his grandfather had never accepted her. Never treated her like family. Said she didn't suit him. Hell, he hadn't even attended his only grandson's wedding. A silent protest, Jack knew. The hell of it was, Brice had been right; he and Kayla hadn't been suited in the least.

But Brice seemed only too eager to throw Morgan at him . . .

Sighing, Jack shoved his thoughts away. It hardly mattered. The legend was ridiculous. It couldn't be anything but bullshit. It had no logic. He didn't do hocus-pocus.

Still . . . it would explain why he wanted Morgan for his own so badly his teeth hurt.

A noise to his left alerted him to the fact he was no longer alone.

Morgan emerged through the screen door into the hazy morning. Golden sunlight broke through the fog as she stepped into the morning breeze. The pure rays slanted in bright swaths across the swamp to settle on her as she strolled to the corner of the railing, clearly unaware that he watched her.

Soft sunlight lit up her fiery tresses as they tumbled over her shoulders and down her back. She wore a faded brown shirt. *His* shirt.

Jack frowned. He'd seen this scene before. It was oddly familiar, but how? The memories were vague, as if he'd seen this a long time ago or in a dream—

That was it, and it hadn't been just any dream. *The* dream. The one he'd been seeing nearly every night in his sleep for the last six months.

Holy hell.

As he sucked in a stunned breath, electric shock arced through Jack. Time stopped as he waited.

Morgan tilted her head and gazed out over the swamp . . . as the vision had in his dream.

Fierce lust, a heart-wrenching ache, pure apprehension, a need he couldn't explain. Everything tripped through him like a live wire, jolting him from fingertips to toes. What the hell was happening to him?

A lifted corner of Morgan's mouth seemed to hint at a smile. From his angle, the expression looked happy, and the need to see her like that—utterly, sublimely happy—kicked him in the teeth.

Damn. Her feelings shouldn't make a damn bit of difference to him. In a few days, a week at most, he and Deke would likely have solved her case and she'd be gone. If he did things right, her engagement to Brandon would be over, too.

But that wouldn't make Morgan his.

Jack gritted his teeth as he watched Morgan shift, lean over the nearest rail.

The veil of mystery that had always enshrouded the woman in his dreams suddenly fell away. He knew her face, her quick temper, the passion she tried to leash under misplaced modesty, her unexpected courage and sharp tongue. But he still wanted to see her.

*Turn around!* he silently demanded.

As if she were so attuned to him that she heard, she slowly began to turn his way. A delicate ear, a graceful neck, a stubborn slope to her jaw, her lush mouth twisted in an effort to hold back the tears drenching her stormy blue eyes.

And in that moment, Jack knew that he wanted Morgan more than anything else—revenge, riches, power. This woman had somehow zoomed to the top of his list.

Morgan gasped when she saw him. "I—I didn't know you . . ." Her breathing hitched. "Sorry."

She turned and darted for the cottage.

Jack bounded out of his seat, wrapped his arms around her, and turned her to face him.

*Mine!*

The instant he touched her, that feeling sang in his blood, settled deep into his bones.

At the moment, he couldn't fight it and didn't try.

*Mine!*

Everything in his gut told him not to let her get away.

Ever.

When she buried her chin in her chest, he hooked a finger under her chin and lifted her face to his. The pain there jabbed into his gut.

"*Cher,*" he whispered. "*Mon douce amour.*"

*My sweet love?* God, he was so far gone.

She pressed her lips together, blinking, valiantly stopping her tears. "I have no idea what you're saying. Probably that I'm an idiot." She let loose a sad, watery laugh. "Which fits. I am an idiot."

"No. Idiot in French doesn't sound much different. You'd be able to pick that up."

"Good to know," she choked, trying to break away. "I need to . . . Let me go."

An instinct screamed at Jack that that would be the worst thing he could do. He didn't fight that gut feeling. "*Jamais.*"

*Never.* The word echoed in his head.

He had to be out of his mind because he'd never reacted so strongly to a woman. Never wanted to hold her close for . . . well, forever. But he couldn't examine the feeling now, not when she was still trying to pull away, except to know it was nonnegotiable.

Instead, Jack anchored his palm on her nape and brought Morgan against him. "You're not an idiot. You're a challenge. You've got a saucy mouth that makes me crazy. I can't decide if I should spank you, laugh, or get you underneath me so all that fire can blister me as I sink deep into you."

"Jack . . ." Her voice held a pleading note. "I can't . . . I'm not made for what you have behind that locked door. I can't handle . . ."

Her stammering uncertainty shredded his composure and resolve. The way he'd rushed her into facing her sexuality had disturbed her, displaced her beliefs about herself. She was still trying to assimilate. He shouldn't rush her more. Not now. Or he'd risk losing her.

Not losing her was more important than his next breath. Definitely more important than revenge.

"Shh. We don't have to talk about the playroom now. I just want a kiss, *cher*. I missed holding you last night."

The tears in her eyes overflowed, spilling down her cheeks. The sight of it wrenched at Jack's gut as he wiped them away with his thumbs.

"Don't say that."

"I'm being honest," he whispered against her mouth. "Did you miss me, too?"

"It makes no sense," she confessed with a nod, then bit her lip as if to keep in the rest of her feelings. "I can't do—can't be—what you want."

Jack knew better. *Knew* it. And he'd prove it to her.

"I didn't know what half of that . . . equipment was," she added.

"And that, along with missing me, made you feel like an idiot?" He tried to smile softly, tried to reassure. Her answer sure elated the hell out of him. "*Tsk*. I'm a much bigger idiot than you. I didn't just miss you, I ached to hold you. I burned to touch you, in any way you'd let me. With or without toys."

That need inside him was rising, amplifying, drowning out all else, including good sense. His hand tightened around her neck, fingers tangling in her hair. Normally, his self-control was anywhere between stellar and legendary. With Morgan . . . resisting a woman he wanted this badly seemed not just pointless, but fucking impossible.

Slanting his mouth over the soft pillows of her lips, instinct charged through Jack. With a barely leashed passion, he alternately demanded and pleaded his way inside, coaxing her mouth open, relieved and revved when she let him in to steal both her objections and her breath.

He claimed her, pouring the need blazing through his gut and firing his soul into the kiss. Just touching her drugged him. Cradling her face in his hands, Jack was amazed anew by the silken warmth of her skin. The raspberry scent of her nearly drove him out of his head.

The sweet taste of her kiss hit him. Cinnamon sugar, hot silk, female want. Jack sank into her mouth, her essence. With every breath, he tasted her confused passion and reluctant need. Jack dove deeper still into her mouth, determined to lap up every bit of her doubt and warmth and uncertainty he could and give it back to her in reassurance and devotion. With purposeful sweeps through her mouth and soft nibbles on her lower lip, he fed her a taste of his greedy lust and declared his determination to get her close and keep her there.

In his arms, her breath caught. She clasped him tight, pressing her breasts against him. The tears drenching her cheeks moistened his own face, kick-starting his heart all over again.

Jack worked a hand through her silky tresses of fire and kissed a hot path across her jaw, working his way to her ear.

"I . . . Oh, Jack! I can't be what you want."

"You already are." He nibbled on her lobe. Beneath the onslaught of his lips, Morgan's breathing picked up speed. Her heartbeat pounded at the base of her neck, chugging with arousal. He covered the spot with his mouth, laving it with his tongue. She rewarded him with a moan, arching her throat to him in invitation.

Jack could smell the desire on her now, could tell she was wet. The realization made him hard as hell. So hard, it was as if he hadn't been balls deep in her in weeks or months.

Utterly, sublimely crazy.

Pulling her into the unyielding iron of his erection, Jack groaned. He'd intended to wait, woo her, cajole her. No. He had to get inside of her. Anything less wasn't an option. He needed to feel the hot grip of her sweet pussy closing around his cock as he swallowed her cries with his mouth. He had to see her submission in the softening of her body, the lowering of her gaze, the invitation of her creaming slit.

With a single yank, he ripped apart the tails of the shirt covering her, halfway down her belly. *Jackpot!* Her firm, pale breasts bathed in golden light beckoned him. Jack didn't fight it. Instead, he bent and captured one puckered nipple in his mouth, sucking hard and strong.

Morgan gasped. But she arched to him, silently encouraging him. She tangled her fingers in his hair to anchor him. No need; he wasn't going anywhere anytime soon. With his other hand, he squeezed the plump tip of her other breast, turning, plucking.

"Yes!"

He loved her responsive cry, but with a nip of his teeth across her sensitive flesh, he reminded her of her lapse.

"Yes, sir," she corrected.

*"Parfaite,"* he said, rewarding her by laving his tongue across the rapidly swelling nubs. "So fucking perfect."

Jack moved his fingers on her turgid little nipples. Damn, he was hungry for another taste of them. But the man, the dominant in him, craved something else even more. She smelled like heaven, got wet for him in a heartbeat. He'd bet money she tasted of pure wicked delight.

"Sit on the railing, Morgan."

With only a hint of reluctance, she hopped up on the wooden edge of the wraparound porch. Logic told him not to push her. But his need wouldn't allow him to back away.

He reached around with a light stinging slap to her ass. "Who do you obey?"

Confusion and yearning clashed in her tear-drenched blue eyes. Morgan was struggling to process the needs of her body, align them with her independent streak. She was overthinking things . . . but that was Morgan.

Using his other hand, he slapped the other cheek of her backside. "You, sir."

At least she hadn't denied it. If she had . . . Jack thought he might have gone out of his fucking mind. As it was, his control slipped as dangerous determination to drive Morgan to sweating, screaming orgasm slammed into him.

With a grunt, he tore the rest of the shirt Morgan wore apart, exposing every delicate, pale curve of her body. Excellent, no panties. The wet, pink folds of her sex were covered by a thin dusting of hair. But he wanted to see more. Needed to.

With one hand at her back to steady her, Jack spread her legs wide with the other. A quick glance down told him she was drenched in her cream. Yes! Her slick folds swelling and flushing pink with each passing moment. Gorgeous.

*Mine!* the instinctive beast in him snarled silently.

"Steady yourself," he ordered, placing her hands on the edge of the rail on either side of her hips.

"Sir?"

"You don't question, Morgan," he growled. "You take what I give you. You do what I say. You come when I tell you."

"We're outdoors. If anyone came by in a boat, they . . . they would see us." She eased her legs closed.

"We're in the middle of nowhere, but that's irrelevant. Your well-being is my concern. I will keep you safe. Put your trust and your body in my care. Can you do that?"

Morgan wanted to. Jack could see the need in her turbulent blue eyes conflicting with her modesty in her anxious expression. It wasn't lack of trust in him . . . but herself.

"Nothing bad will happen," he assured her. "Let me take over."

A ragged breath and a long pause later, she sent him an unsteady nod.

It was all he could do not to let out a whoop and devour her on the spot. She'd said yes, not because he'd surprised her or taunted her into it. She'd simply said yes. To him.

"Good. Steady yourself. Spread your legs for me."

With trembling hands, Morgan acceded to his demands, leaning back to brace her hands on the rail. Slowly, so damn slowly, she drew her thighs apart again.

Fucking beautiful. Perfect.

*Mine!*

Jack dropped to his knees and kissed the inside of each of her thighs. Her breath hitched, body tensed. With a smooth glide of his palms up her thighs, he held her still, anchored her hips to the railing. Then he just stared, breathing in the addicting musky-sweet scent of her. She was all blushing, slick flesh and trembling limbs.

It took every ounce of Jack's self-control not to dive into her like an all-you-can-eat buffet. He wanted to taste her everywhere, along the glistening folds hiding her deepest secrets, up high where her clit played hide-and-seek under its delicate hood, inside the hot, tight channel that held her cream.

"Show me where you like to be licked. Point for me," he demanded, already knowing and planning to save that destination for last.

"I . . . I don't know. Anywhere."

"No one has ever made you come this way." Jack didn't make it a question. He was pretty sure he knew the answer.

Morgan shook her head.

Amazing. Another intimate act he would be first to introduce Morgan to. The exhilarating thought went straight to his cock. Was every guy she'd dated a eunuch? He loved this, the intimate taste, the immediacy of knowing exactly which touch affected a woman most. No quicker way to make her putty, to make her beg.

To make her his.

Jack dropped his gaze to her swollen sex. Maybe . . . maybe he could coax her to connect him and pleasure together in her mind. That alone wouldn't be enough to keep her, but it would be a start. The rest he'd work out hour by hour, day by day, until she agreed not just to leave Brandon but to become his.

"You're going to come for me, Morgan. But not until I tell you to. Understood?"

"Yes, sir."

Her breathy, perfect reply made his cock tighten to the point of distraction. *Soon . . .*

"*Ma belle, si douce,*" he whispered over her clit. "Sweet, beautiful woman."

\*　\*　\*

MORGAN'S heart raced as she stared down her mostly naked body and saw Jack kneeling between her shaking thighs. The want coursing through her made her limbs feel heavy, her head feel light. Her sex clenched, ached. Something was different about Jack's touch, something between the two of them. God, what was happening to her? She swallowed against a whimper of need.

He gripped her thighs, pushing them wider, exposing her even more. Then, with his thumbs, opened her sex to his gaze.

Trembling, Morgan had never felt more vulnerable—or aroused. She dripped, arched to him, held her breath, waited. Jack could have no doubt that she responded to his demands, to the way he forced her legs apart, then stared at her sex as if he intended to eat it like a ripe peach.

Sanity—where was it? She was supposed to be engaged, for heaven's sake. She was not supposed to like his rough brand of domination. She wasn't the depraved woman Andrew had accused her of being. She didn't even know why a shameful part of her thrilled to Jack's orders.

The chilly morning breeze swept over her skin, but instead of wishing for cover, the contrast of the cool air on her heated body thrilled her.

"I love how wet you are for me. I feel your thighs tremble. I see all the folds of your cunt swelling, *cher.*"

She squeezed her eyes shut, unable to just let go and enjoy. "No."

In response, Jack merely dragged his thumb over her clit. It hardened into a pulsing knot of pure need.

A denial might have fallen from her lips, but her body was betraying her. Over and over. She'd never responded to anyone the way she did for Jack, flushing, aching, complying with whatever he wanted. Shaking with the need for more.

The knowledge of everything he kept in his playroom, items she'd only vaguely heard of and fantasized about, all just down the hall. All within the grasp of a man who surely knew how to use each with devastating skill.

"No what?" he taunted. "No, don't make you feel good? No, don't fuck you in every way I can think of, until you've come so many times your body is limp from the pleasure? Is that what you're saying no to?"

His words and the electrifying sexual images they conjured up bombarded her brain, denting her resistance like the hood of a car in a vicious hailstorm. But Morgan knew if she let go, Jack would just introduce her to one more touch to crave later, one more amazing sensation to heat up shameful midnight fantasies after they parted.

"Or are you telling yourself no?" he murmured, his lips brushing over the top of her cleft, so light yet charging her with a wicked zing that seemed to fist around her sex and squeeze. "Are you hoping to deny how good it will feel to have my tongue in your pleasure-soaked pussy?"

*Yes!* Damn, she had to be as transparent as plastic wrap for him to read her so easily. Forcing her eyes open, she gazed down at him—just in time to see his tongue dive between her folds. The sight of his calloused hands cradling the delicate flesh inside her thighs, his skin many times darker than her own, jolted her with a pure desire that sizzled up and down her spine and exploded in her belly.

God help her.

On that thought, the wet heat of his mouth covered her. Molten pleasure burst inside her as he licked from slit to clit, then swirled his tongue around her as if trying to lap up her cream.

"*Cher*, you're like a treat."

His voice sounded raspy and rough, half grunt and half groan. It dug past her defenses, scraping at what little resolve she had left.

He licked her in the same manner again, only this time hungrier. It wasn't an exploratory stroke of his tongue now; it was a veracious demand. With a growl, he drew her clit between his lips and sucked.

She gasped, once, twice—every time he pulled on the sensitive bud. The protests swimming in her head drowned in the face of her body's demands. The exquisite torture of his mouth drove her beyond her inbred decorum. Desperate for more of his touch, for him, she arched, clawing the smooth wooden railing and silently begging by spreading her legs even wider.

"Very pretty," he complimented, voice raspy and midnight raw. "And so sweet."

His tongue invaded her channel as his thumb pressed down on her clit. The pleasure converged so hard and fast between her legs, it was almost painful. She felt her own folds swelling with need, making her flesh sensitive to each dip and swirl of his tongue. The February breeze whipping over her diamond-hard nipples did nothing to cool her.

Jack continued his feast, his moans of appreciation ringing in her ears. The more he ate at her, the wetter she got.

Then he stopped.

"If you want me to go on, invite me to taste more." He nibbled at her thigh. "Tell me you want to come on my tongue."

Morgan pressed her lips together to hold the words in. But everything between her legs ached, throbbed in time with her runaway heartbeat. Every molecule in her body strained toward what Jack wanted to give her. Why the hell was she resisting such amazing pleasure? A little tainted modesty and the risk of a bit of humiliation seemed like a small price to pay for such stunning sensations.

Even more, the hot, eager expression on his face slammed her with the need to give in. It wasn't tender. He wasn't interested in hearts and flowers. The wild intensity of his dark eyes in the morning's golden light told her he wanted more. Wanted to possess her. On his face was his fierce desire to introduce her to every wanton sensation she'd ever pondered and force her to reserve her reactions exclusively for him.

The outrageous notion of belonging to him, of putting her body solely in his care and allowing him anything he wanted—they wanted—drove her past her limits.

As badly as a part of her mind pushed her to say no, everything else inside her yearned with exquisite pain to say yes.

"Taste me." Every whispered syllable trembled. "Sir."

Morgan knew she was taking a giant step that she couldn't take back.

She was agreeing to commit sins that would haunt her. Jack was replacing her scruples with pure, white-hot need she could no longer deny. Tantalizing her with the idea of being his to command.

A violent whip of blistering victory stormed across his face. "And?"

"I . . . I want to . . ." She swallowed, panted, tried to find the courage and the air necessary to go on.

Jack circled a finger around the small opening of her sex, scooped up drops of her cream, and massaged it over her clit. Fire shot straight inside her and burst in her belly.

God, she couldn't take more stimulation. Already on the razor's edge of sanity, of losing control of her body, Morgan gasped. Need tightened in her core. Blood raced. Thoughts vanished.

Jack reduced her down to her primal animal element. She'd always fantasized about such a state but believed it to be impossible. Not so. Before her knelt a sexy man who should have been a stranger. But he saw every hidden, sinful wish inside her. He not only understood them, but he could grant them—and make her feel perfectly wonderful both inside and out while doing it.

"I want to come on your tongue," she blurted.

"Perfect, *cher*." He rewarded her by lapping off the drops of fresh cream from her clit. "Such a good girl, with such a sweet pussy. I'm going to give you what you want."

# Chapter Ten

MORGAN looked nothing short of magnificent. The emerging morning sun splashed golden light across the pale purity of her skin, illuminating every one of her sexy cinnamon freckles. Intriguing shadows danced in the dips and swells of her luscious body, tantalizing him to lean in for an up-close look. For a personal taste.

Jack was all too happy to heed the call. Her trembling admission echoed in his head, spurring him to clutch her thighs, spread them even wider, and lick the glossy pink flesh in front of him.

God, she was like a drug. Every part of her had some new exotic scent or flavor. The crook of her neck smelled like ripe woman with a hint of raspberries. Her mouth soaked him with an addicting cinnamon sugar taste. But her pussy . . . Delicate, sweet, clean musk. Ah, she tasted like the want coursing inside her. Unique, enthralling. He could spend the morning here, lapping at her, and still be compelled to taste her again in an effort to figure out just what it was about her that so tempted his tongue.

Her ragged inhalation caught his attention. Morgan's thighs tensed in his grasp. He smiled against her sex, then worked his tongue about her vulva, laving her clit every now and then. No steady pressure . . . just enough to take her higher and higher. Then, as he worked in one finger and teased her inner walls, she trembled.

Fresh cream poured from her. A flush rose on her skin as she threw her head back, legs trembling. Her sex swelled even more. Morgan dug her short nails into the aging wood of the railing and moaned.

Idly, Jack wondered how long he could keep her here, right on the edge, feeling the sharp, sweet ache of impending climax . . . without letting her fall over. The idea of reducing her to incoherent begging held appeal. Not because he'd never heard a woman beg. He had—frequently. But Morgan and her inbred good-girl modesty lit him up like a match to kerosene. And when he drove her past her inhibitions, she took both of them up in the flames. Even now, the thick erection pressed uncomfortably against his jeans, growling for the attention of the syrupy, sugary flesh under his tongue.

"Jack," she panted. "Sir . . ."

Even her voice trembled, signaling that her orgasm was rising up hot and fast inside her. He smiled, easing back from the hard knot of her clit to focus on the swollen lips cupping his finger.

"*Cher?*" he returned lazily, swallowing against a lump of lust threatening to unravel him.

Before she could answer, he thrust a second digit inside her. Her open-mouthed gasp tore across the porch, across the open swamp.

Eyes squeezed tightly shut, Morgan said nothing. She focused on the pleasure—exactly like he wanted her to.

Jack began easing his fingers from her tight channel. She murmured a protest, but he knew she really meant it when her body did its best to clamp down on the digits, cling, and suck him back in. God, no wonder she shredded his control so fast when he had his cock inside her.

Shoving the observation aside, he withdrew his hand from the damp humidity of her sex. His fingers all but dripped with her cream. The sight and scent went straight to his head, like pure grain alcohol, kicking his libido into full gear. He tamped down the urge to shove his pants to his knees and thrust deep inside her.

Instead, he lifted his fingers over the rosy beads of her nipples and coated them with her own juice. The wind whipped across her body, tightening the tips of her breasts even more, until they stood long and thick and so damn tempting, he couldn't resist for another second tasting them.

Seizing her hips, Jack fit her against the ridge of his cock. He loved that for now, in this moment, she and every little gasp, blush, and moan were all his.

Slowly, he closed his mouth over one of those nipples that had him salivating with anticipation. *Hmm.* Raspberries and musk together. Velvet-soft skin over deliciously hard nubs begging to be sucked, nibbled, clamped.

He lapped at her, laving and biting, lavishing attention on her nipples until they swelled in his mouth. If her hitching breath hadn't indicated the truth, a quick caress from his free hand told Jack she was as wet as ever. The knowledge—the woman herself—called him like a siren. There was no resisting.

He forced a pair of fingers inside her sultry depths again, then swiped a thumb over her clit. Amazingly, she tightened on his fingers immediately, clamping down, beginning to ripple with the coming explosion.

Satisfaction swelled in Jack as he shifted his attention to her other nipple and enveloped it in the hot cavern of his mouth. He couldn't wait to feel the magnitude of this climax. And even better, he'd bet she was nearly willing to beg for it.

Taking one last sharp nip at her rock-hard nipple, Jack kissed his way up her chest to nuzzle her neck. His fingers played with that sensitive spot in her channel, just behind her clit, while his thumb strummed the hard little button in an unhurried rhythm. Though he wondered if he'd ever feel the blood in his fingers again, satisfaction poured through him when she tightened on his fingers once more.

"*Cher,*" he whispered in her ear. "What do you want?"

"Now," she panted as he rubbed the pads of his fingers right across that sweet spot inside her. "God, please. I need . . ."

"Me to stop?"

"No. No, sir!" Her voice came fast, hard, in between breathless sighs.

Color bloomed in her cheeks, and the sunshine rained down on her fair skin until she looked like she was glowing.

God help her, because Jack had every intention of taking her, not just to his bed but to his playroom, and driving her up and over so sweetly and so often that she would have no more qualms about pleading for what she wanted and turning to him when she needed it.

A savage bolt of lust lurched through his cock at the thought he could succeed, that she would surrender her body, her mind, and her will exclusively to him. The thought aroused him like nothing ever had.

"Tell me what you need," he murmured into her ear. "You remember what to say."

"I want to come on your tongue. Please, sir." She grasped his shoulders, nails digging into his flesh with the urgency of her need. *"Please."*

"You beg sweetly, *cher*. How can I resist?"

Her frantic fingers filtered into his hair and she gripped, little darts of pain exploding across his scalp. God help her when he finally got her under him. He was going to pound into her with the ferocity of a jackhammer, mercilessly plying that sweet pussy with his cock until she came over and over—and took him with her.

"Now!"

Her voice took on a panicked note. Her sex gripped his fingers so tightly he could hardly move them. She dangled at the edge of the cliff. And she'd been there awhile, long enough for her body to push past her mind.

"Demanding minx," he teased as he nipped at her earlobe and scratched at the sensitive point inside her clasping pussy. "I promised I'd give you what you want. Once I have, you're going to follow me into the playroom so I can bind, clamp, and fuck you any way I please, aren't you?"

"Yes." She sobbed. "Yes, sir!"

"Good girl. I'm going to bend you over my table and take your hot little pussy over and over. You'll learn to beg readily and come on command, *cher*. Then," he whispered against her skin as he began traveling down her body in a series of caresses and biting kisses, "I'm going to open that pretty ass of yours to my cock and settle in for a nice, long ride."

He whispered the words right against her clit. A strangled moan escaped her. The muscles of her thighs clenched, trembled. The slick heaven of her sex strangled his fingers. Her hands, still in his hair, tightened into desperate fists.

Perfect. Like a fantasy. Morgan responded to his touch, to his wicked, whispered suggestions exactly as he dreamed. Once he pushed her past her inhibitions, delved beyond her conscious mind into her untapped sexuality, a wealth of sweet, mind-blowing submission belonged to the man who could master her.

It was as if she'd been waiting just for him.

The thought charged through his cock like a live wire.

"Come for me," he demanded against her cream-drenched pussy.

Quickly, he extracted his fingers from her and raked them over her clit. In the next heartbeat, he shoved his tongue inside her rippling channel, reaching with the tip to manipulate the sensitive spot inside.

She exploded with a scream that echoed across the swamp. With the tight grip of her fists in his hair, she pushed his face against her, into her. Fresh cream gushed into his mouth, and he lapped at her greedily, triumph and a desperate urge to get inside her, command her, clawed at him. Need clamored.

*Take her. Claim her. She's yours.*

*Yeah, and what would Brandon say about that? What would Morgan herself say?* He hoped she would say yes, because for once in his life, he didn't want to just be someone's good fuck. He wanted every touch to mean something.

*Why her? Why now? What had happened to the drive for revenge that once glowed red hot, like fired metal, down in my gut?*

Jack frowned against the thought.

Long moments later, the clasping of her sex eased around his tongue. Her fists slowly uncurled. Jack took a last, longing lick of her, promising himself more later and rose to his feet. She looked dazed and flushed and shocked by her own response.

There was untouched sensuality inside her, ripe for a man strong enough to push past her barriers, caring enough to see to her safety and peace of mind. Morgan didn't know there was much more inside her.

Yet.

And damn, he wanted to be the man to show her.

"Good morning," he murmured.

He pressed a soft kiss to her trembling mouth, nudging her lips apart and sliding his tongue inside in a slow, coaxing glide. For a moment, she recoiled against the taste of herself on his lips. Jack grabbed her, cradling her head in his palms, and forced her to taste the sweet perfection of herself, all while deepening the swirl and dance of the kiss. Finally, she relaxed against him, opened her mouth to him, and drew his tongue and the taste of herself deep inside.

Respect of her quick acceptance surged inside him. No, it was flat-out pride—and that was both a joy and a warning. Morgan was sweet, and he could bend her, mold her into a submissive who could tempt him beyond his wildest fantasies. In time, he could help her accept that part of herself that she struggled so hard to deny. She would never be truly happy until she did.

But that feeling of pride . . . it was a step away from ownership. No dominant had pride in a sub he wasn't attached to, determined to make his. For years, he'd felt a distant respect for women he'd mastered who pushed past their boundaries to submit. Like a teacher to a pupil, he'd praised their progress, punished their setbacks, all while assuring them of their abilities.

With Morgan . . . it felt deeper, more personal. As if he *had* to help her. As if he had some personal stake in her blooming sexuality.

*As if she's mine.* The feeling confirmed everything inside him. This wasn't a phase or the heat of the moment. He wanted her. Period.

"Jack."

Morgan's shaky voice pushed into his consciousness, bringing him back. She shivered, and this time not from desire. Damn, it was cold out here. And yet, she'd endured. No, she'd excelled, outshining anything he'd imagined her capable of in that moment.

He wrapped his arms around her, doing his best to shelter her from the wind. "The air is brisk, huh, *cher*?"

And because he couldn't resist, he tucked her head beneath his chin and stroked her back with one hand. His other fit perfectly over her breast, his thumb lazily flicking the still-hard nipple.

She whimpered.

Any urgency to shepherd her into his playroom and hoard her in there for hours—days—that had left his body zinged back to life in that one sound.

He reached into his pocket to find his keys with every intent to command her to warm herself with a quick warm shower, then meet him in the playroom in fifteen minutes. Fuck breakfast. He'd rather fuck her.

"Bonjour," a faint, familiar voice rasped from just around the corner, near the front door.

Morgan gasped, stiffening in the circle of his arms. "Is that . . . your grandfather!"

*Yes. Who else has such impeccable timing?* Biting back a nasty curse, he eased Morgan away from his sheltering warmth, shoved the remnants of his shirt in her hands, and urged her inside the cottage through the side door.

"Go. Shower and dress. We'll finish later."

She hesitated, going wide-eyed at his words. Indecision spread across her flushed face. "Jack, I-I . . . Maybe we should talk about this."

"Bonjour?" Brice's voice sounded closer.

Time had run out.

Quickly, he pressed a hard kiss to her mouth, then spun her around, through the open door. With a sharp slap on her ass, he propelled her inside. "If you want. But we *will* finish this later."

Before she could sputter a reply, he shut the door between them.

Morgan's reluctance to continue what they'd started was both obvious and frustrating. Just when he thought he'd reached her . . . Granted, she wasn't saying no, but she hadn't given him the sweet little "yes" his body craved—and expected after her response this morning. Disappointment and anger gushed through him, confusing him, as he turned to face his *grand-père*.

Together all the urges concocted an astonishing brew of resolve not to accept another moment of Morgan's hesitation, no doubt equal in strength to her uncertainty. And he wanted to understand. What was hanging her up? It was something more than simple modesty or fear of the unknown.

Jack sighed. The question he should be asking was, what the hell was wrong with him that he was suddenly so determined to have this woman? Apparently, he'd lost his mind.

But it felt more like he was in danger of losing much more . . .

"Ah, there you are," Brice said, rounding the corner. He shuffled down the long stretch of the wraparound porch.

"Morning, *Grand-père*." Jack offered a seat on the chair in the corner with a wave of his hand. "Coffee?"

"*Non.* I came to check up on you and *ta jolie rousse.*"

His pretty redhead? Not at the moment. She might be one step closer now if it hadn't been for an untimely interruption. He bit back a curse.

"Morgan is fine," Jack muttered, sliding into the chair beside his grandfather.

He licked his lips and still tasted her sweetness there. That flavor—and the memories of her legs spread wide for him, her uninhibited moans echoing around him—wasn't doing anything to reduce his raging erection.

"Have you seen . . . more of her since my last visit?" Brice cackled and winked. "You were slow to answer my greeting and never noticed my knocking on the door, yeah."

"I didn't answer the door because I didn't hear it. I was out here. And it's early. I hardly expected company."

"What time it is?" Brice frowned.

Jack didn't buy his grandfather's innocent act for a minute. "What time *is* it?" he corrected. "It's way too early for social calls but early enough to catch us at something if we liked to start the day off right. Isn't that what you were thinking?"

"*Mon petit-fils*, you are suspicious."

"I think I have a right to be, since the 'warm and practical' clothing you brought Morgan looks like it came from the X-rated version of the Victoria's Secret catalog."

His grandfather's laughter made Jack roll his eyes.

"But you have enjoyed the . . . sights?"

"No comment. Why would you do such a thing? Wave an open invitation in my face to have sex with her. I know you want me to remarry, but you'd never met Morgan before that stunt."

The old man tapped on his chest. "Live long enough, yeah, and you know things. Them dreams, Jack, they mean something. Down through the generations, they've always meant love."

"Just because it did for you—"

"*Non*, not just me. My grandfather, too. He took a job in San Francisco for a few years. No more Acadian country for him, says he." Brice waved a dismissive hand at that. "He started having dreams, did he, about a *belle blonde*."

"Hell, I've had a fantasy or two about a gorgeous blonde in my lifetime."

"For months straight, *mon garçon*?"

Jack sighed, both because he hated being called anyone's boy and because reasoning with the old man was never an easy task.

"No," he finally answered.

"You see there, yeah. My *grand-père* had these dreams about a lady at a ball. He met her and discovered she was his boss's young bride. Since his love was already married, he believed the family legend was wrong. But he kept on dreaming of her. The dreams were hard on his heart.

"Two weeks after meeting *son amour*, the big earthquake struck San Francisco. Nineteen-oh-six. The lovely lady's husband, he died. And my grandfather married the pretty blonde a year later. Six *enfants* and over fifty years later, they were still in love."

Staring at the old man, Jack wondered if he was serious. Was it even possible, even a bit?

"And his grandfather before him," Brice went on, "was wounded in battle and captured by the Yanks at the end of the Civil War. His bride, she was a Union nurse in the field hospital. He kept a journal that said dreams of a faceless beauty kept him sane during months of battle, yeah. When he met her, it was a shock. They married three days after the war ended."

Three men of his blood all dreaming of faceless beauties. Jack had dreamed endlessly of one with sparkling red hair glowing in the sunlight. And just this morning, Morgan had manifested herself as his dream image. Did that explain his insane desire to lay claim to her, as if she wasn't taken, as if she was more than the instrument of his revenge? As if walking away from her wasn't possible?

Shock jolted a dizzying bolt through his system. Jack stroked his chin and tried to regain his balance. The concept of predestined mates and dreaming of them was so . . . otherworldly. So weird. Not that he hadn't grown up with the knowledge; he'd just never believed it.

"None of us want to believe that there's any truth to this *malédiction*. But facts is facts, yeah. It happens to every man in our line. And now, it's your turn, with Morgan."

"How did you know when it happened to you?" Jack asked, struggling to accept his grandfather's claim. "What made you sure, besides the dreams, that *Grand-mère* was the one?"

The old man smiled, deepening lines around his eyes and mouth, leaving no doubt the man had spent a lifetime smiling wide and often. "The moment I met her, I fought a crazy urge to grab her up tight and convince her to be mine. I never wanted to be away from her or see her blue. Most of all, *cher garçon*, I wanted her happy and I knew deep inside here"—he pointed to his heart—"that I could make her so. *Comprends-tu?*"

Oh, yeah. Jack understood all too well. Hadn't he been feeling the same way from nearly the instant he'd met Morgan? The insane desire to touch her, the willingness to do most anything to keep her safe, the snarling anger toward her stalker? He hated her dismay, but the key to her happiness lay in her caged sexuality.

"Listen to your gut, Jack. Follow your instincts."

"They don't make sense."

The smile lines bracketing Brice's mouth deepened. "They don't have to. The heart ain't meant to make sense. You ever feel this way about anyone else? About Kayla?"

The old man all but spit Jack's ex-wife's name.

Jack just shook his head. No. Never. Not even close. He'd married her because she was pregnant and he was very Catholic, even if she hadn't been. She'd miscarried in her fifth month. The marriage ended a few months later when he'd found a videotape of Brandon Ross fucking her, while she'd supposedly been grieving the loss of her baby too deeply to have sex with her own husband. Looking back, his divorce had been a guilty relief. And a bitter humiliation. Brice had been with him, expecting to see an episode of *CSI* Jack had promised to videotape for him. They'd viewed a whole different sort of action instead.

"You see now, yeah?" Brice murmured.

"It's complicated. Morgan belongs to . . . to someone else. They're engaged."

Jack couldn't tell his grandfather that Morgan belonged to the man who had been with Kayla in the videotape. Brice would know that he'd lured Morgan under his roof in the name of revenge. He'd have a pretty good idea of what Jack had done to her to obtain that revenge. And the old man would flay the skin off Jack's back with his old hunting knife and pour Tabasco in the wound.

Grimacing, Jack couldn't deny an unsettling sense of shame bubbling in his gut.

And if Morgan ever found out . . . Oh, God, she *would* find out. The minute she talked to Brandon. And stopping it was damn near impossible.

He let loose a vile curse. There was no way he could take back the email he'd already sent. Damn! He wished he'd heeded his instinct at that moment, which told him emailing the video was a mistake. And once Morgan and Brandon talked . . . he'd lose her for sure then. The thought filled him with a snarling, towering panic.

Unless he found some ironclad way to bind her to him before he told her the truth . . . Yes! He had to.

Brice shrugged. "Now, boy. Why worry? She and this man, they is not married. And why not? Maybe she knows this other man is not for her. Yeah? Maybe she gives you a kiss or two because her heart and her body know what her mind don't."

"That she doesn't love her fiancé?"

"*Exactement.*"

Was it really that simple? That Morgan was his . . . soul mate, and that she responded to him, had allowed him so much liberty over her body because somewhere deep inside her she knew he was meant for her? It seemed so . . . surreal. Fucking hocus-pocus.

Was it possible she wasn't a cheating sort of woman, just a confused one?

Just as confused as he was?

Jack sighed and held his head in his hands.

A slur of disgust rose from Brice's throat. "Ah, you young now. No sense of romance. Keep resisting. Make yourself miserable. Love will wear you down."

Love? The thought couldn't have been more alien if it was green and sported antennae.

"I want her. I don't love her."

"You know that, do you? You already know that you will always not love her?"

Jack slumped back in his chair. Damn the man and his questions. "No, I don't know that."

Brice sent him an all-knowing nod. "I brought some jeans and shirts for Morgan. You can fix me some mornin' grub, yeah. After that, you tell me if you want me to get them from the boat . . . or take 'em back with me."

Leaving Morgan in nothing but tempting lingerie.

Immediately, the memory of her in that golden camisole and thong bombarded his brain, engorging his cock. Oh, yeah, Morgan looked hot in that getup. But just the visual alone shouldn't fire him up to something between a boil and a blaze that quickly. Hell, he'd seen hundreds of naked women, especially hanging around Alyssa and her girls. They'd get a rise from him every so often, but this feeling scraping at his logic and peace of mind until he felt raw . . . Jack could only term it a caveman urge to claim. Like he *had* to know she was his and be secure in the knowledge that he would always keep her safe and happy. The thought of succeeding, of being able to convince her to be his in every way, jacked up his temperature another ten degrees.

*Holy shit.*

At this point, he couldn't think of a single argument that might prove his grandfather wrong.

In fact, if he wanted to have Morgan, and keep her, he was going to have to form a stronger bond between them right away. Something that might shake but wouldn't break when she learned why he'd agreed to be on her TV show—and that he'd bribed her buddy Reggie to make it happen.

That he'd done it all for revenge. And he'd tell her . . . but not yet. Not until they were solid.

First, he had to earn her trust on a visceral level, teach her body that he would always put her care first. The bedroom was a good place to start breaking down her barriers. Once she'd surrendered, then they could talk. The rest would fall into place.

Knowledge, rightness, and a plan clicked into place in that moment, like the pieces of a puzzle that had been hovering just out of reach.

Finally, he said, "I don't need time to think about it. Take her clothes with you, *Grand-père*. Don't bring them out here again."

Brice smiled wide, showing crooked white teeth against Cajun-dark skin. "*Laissez les bon temps rouler!*"

Oh, yeah. Let the good times roll . . .

# Chapter Eleven

W E will *finish this later*.

Jack's vow rang through Morgan's head as Brice charmed her through breakfast.

She chastised the older man for bringing her lingerie and nothing else. With dark eyes twinkling, he gave her a sanguine grin and a shrug but wasn't apologetic in the least.

But Jack . . . his gaze burned, telegraphing his earlier words. *We will finish this later.*

Morgan wished she could close off the memory, drown out the voice in her head. Over scrambled eggs, which both men doused with Tabasco, Jack stared at her as if she were a cross between a confounding puzzle and a tasty treat. And above all, something he coveted. Someone he meant to possess.

Damn it, why had she ever said yes to Jack and his playroom? Trying to say no after the exquisite pleasure he'd given her seemed nearly impossible.

But saying yes in that moment had been easy—imperative—with his mouth hovering over her and an enormous climax pending. Now that pleasure wasn't destroying her ability to breathe and think, Morgan wasn't sure that giving in, giving him everything he wanted, was a good idea. It would not only change everything between them but change *her* forever. Since being around Jack, her fantasies had become more urgent, more explicit. Impulses she'd always had now came with remembered sensations—and the memories also came complete with Jack's sigh-worthy face to haunt her.

On the other hand, she wanted him—and was beginning to crave having every wild pleasure he could give her. Something about giving in to the impulses he roused in her body made her feel more alive, more . . . complete. Did that even make sense?

*We* will *finish this later*. Given the weight of his stare right now, Morgan knew he still meant it.

Should she? Shouldn't she?

Like everything else about Jack, the promise he'd given her filled her with hot shame, even as it made her ache and shake with need. This morning, on the porch . . . God, she could still feel his mouth on her sex, forcing his tongue inside her, taking tender possession. Driving her out of her mind. He'd suffused every nerve in her body with speech-defying ecstasy, making it impossible to run away from the sensations he poured over her like sweet, warm honey.

But she was so damn curious—and excited—about whatever he did on those racks and tables with the cuffs and clamps . . . and other items she was too naïve to name. The more she tried to run away from her wants, the more insistent they grew, slowly overtaking her will like a clinging vine overtaking the garden.

What if she let him follow through on his threat to finish what they'd started? Would it be *so* terrible if she did? Just for now? No one but her and Jack would have to know.

Biting her lip, she watched Jack's taut posture grow more tense as Brice lingered for after-breakfast coffee. His dark eyes promised pleasure, prepared her for a hint of pain. His vow to totally possess her shone in his seductive gaze. She swallowed against a belly-tightening mix of fear and thrill and anticipation. Attraction layered over that, luring her directly to him, as if an invisible string lay between them, growing shorter and shorter with every hour.

It made no sense that she could want someone so desperately who brought out her very worst impulses. Someone who would take her places far beyond the norm, into a realm that would horrify her mother and sicken men like Andrew. If she let Jack, he would ruin her for every other man's touch. Worse, living with herself after he had molded her into a submissive wanton would be impossible. Doormat wasn't her style. She didn't take orders well, didn't like being told what to do. Her mother had started calling her an independent hoyden about the time she turned twelve.

But with Jack . . . Morgan sighed. His commands seeped inside her— not just her body, but her mind, her soul. The things he demanded of her never failed to shock her, and yet, he often ordered her to do exactly what she'd been secretly craving. Sometimes, she wondered how he could read her mind. It startled her. It shamed her. It made her ache for him beyond anything she'd imagined.

And she didn't think she had the will to keep fighting what they both wanted.

Maybe . . . just maybe she should embrace this time together, find out the truth about her desires. Jack wouldn't intentionally hurt her beyond a little erotic pain. Her mother's and Andrew's opinions wouldn't matter way out here, a world away from civilization. It could be her time, their secret time, before her stalker was caught and she returned to reality.

Just after noon, Brice rose to leave. Morgan knew Jack wanted to pick up where they'd left off earlier that morning. Like any nervous female, she wanted to look her best. Retreating to the bathroom when Jack walked Brice to the dock, she indulged in a decadent bath and spent extra time drying her hair. She lamented the fact that she had no makeup, which gave her absolutely no way to soften the smattering of freckles on her too-fair face. She licked her lips, pinched her cheeks, and shrugged. That was the best she could do.

A set of regimented footsteps started down the hall, pulling her out of her thoughts.

Jack. He'd be pounding on the door soon, demanding to pound at her. Her breath caught. Was she ready? Could she handle it? She released a shaky breath, torn between her rational mind and her demanding body. Her mind had always prevailed before, but since Jack . . . game, set, match to her body.

She was as prepared for a man like Jack as she'd ever be, considering she wore nothing more to shield her from his penetrating gaze than his bathrobe and bloodred undergarments with wicked cutouts designed not to cover the essentials.

Instead of being repulsed by the revealing exploitive lingerie, Morgan simply felt herself growing ever more wet at the thought of Jack seeing her in them.

"Morgan?" he barked through the thin barrier of the bathroom door. *Showtime.* "Jack?"

Anytime he looked at her, she felt sure those dark, knowing eyes could see every sinful secret in her soul. But today, her voice trembled merely because she spoke his name.

Before he could say or do anything, the phone rang. He uttered a ripe sibilant curse and stomped back down the hall. Morgan sagged with an odd mix of relief and disappointment . . . but she couldn't deny that the ache between her legs had ratcheted higher.

Taking a deep breath, she stepped into the hall and lingered in the shadows. And listened.

"What the hell do you want?" she heard Jack snap.

A rumbling laugh over the speakerphone in the cottage's front room echoed down the hall.

"I'll take three guesses as to why you're so crabby. And I don't need the last two."

Deke. She recognized his teasing voice, could picture the crinkles of laughter around those dancing denim-blue eyes . . . so seemingly at odds with that tall, hard body.

"Did you call just to annoy me?"

"Hell, no. You know I never go for anything easy. Where's the challenge in that?"

"So you called because . . . ?"

"I need to talk to Morgan."

Jack hesitated, his hands curling into fists. "Why?"

In that one syllable, he sounded somewhere between suspicious and downright pissed.

"Did that hard cock of yours make you forget all about the stalker trailing her sweet ass?"

"No, you SOB, I haven't forgotten. And you get your mind off her ass."

"It's not as if I've perfected the ability to reach my cock through the phone line and fuck her, Jack. It's a conversation. Lighten up."

Morgan frowned. Deke acted as if he thought Jack was jealous. The thought would have made her burst out laughing if she hadn't observed Jack's odd behavior around Deke before and he hadn't looked so . . . tense.

With a deep sigh, Jack uncurled his fists. "I'll get her."

"I'm here." Morgan took those few steps out of the shadow, into the light, then down the hall toward Jack.

He whirled to face her, his eyes grasping onto her like a vise. Morgan felt her nipples, bare from the cutouts in the bra, beat against the soft, thin jersey knit of his robe. Based on the way his eyes widened and his nostrils flared, she guessed he noticed.

"Morgan," Deke greeted over the speakerphone. "Hi, doll."

"Hi, Deke. Do you have news?"

"Yeah. We weren't able to lift any prints off the photos. I'm sorry. But we did learn some interesting information about them, so I have a few questions."

Disappointment trembled within her. When would this nightmare be over? And how would it ever end if Deke couldn't track this lunatic down? She wanted to feel normal again, return home and not worry that someone had breached her personal space and violated her bed with semen. She wanted her old life back. Clearly, she wasn't going to get it anytime soon.

To her surprise, Jack eased beside her and curled her suddenly cold hand into his larger, warmer one. Warm. Solid. Secure. He enveloped her in that simple embrace, and instantly Morgan felt stronger.

Until she realized that getting her old life back meant losing Jack. The disappointment that crashed in on her stunned her. She clung tighter to him. Why didn't the thought of getting away from him make her want to celebrate? She ought to be contemplating how many margaritas she could get out of her blender. Getting back to her old life would mean no more stalker, no more bondage, no more questioning herself. Instead, she latched onto Jack's hand and refused to let go.

"What do you want to know?" Morgan asked Deke.

"Anyone you know really into photography, like it's a big-time hobby?"

"Reggie, my production assistant. He mostly dabbles, but he's very good. He's had a few shows in the past." Morgan frowned. "You don't think Reggie would . . . ?"

He hesitated. "After my FBI buddies analyzed these pictures, we discovered they were taken by someone who knows his way around a camera. They weren't developed in a standard lab, like someone had taken them to a one-hour photo place. They weren't printed from a digital image to a photo printer. This is old-school, likely developed at home, using a pretty rare set of chemicals, and printed on photo paper that's made in Europe. This is someone who takes photography seriously. And while you may just feel threatened when you look at these, a couple of the psych profilers felt like he was trying to . . . make it art. He didn't just snap pictures. He looked for symmetry, lighting, interesting angles. There's no sloppy work here."

Reggie? Her *friend*, Reggie? No . . .

But she didn't know anyone else with a passion for photography, who thoroughly disdained the photo printers popular for digital cameras. Total crap, he called them. Not worth wasting an image on. She didn't know anyone else who had a darkroom in their apartment.

Morgan went numb. Breath rushed from her body. Reggie, who was like a father?

*No!*

Not many people knew her address in Los Angeles. Reggie did—along with her schedule. He could have snuck in and masturbated on her bed in her absence. Reggie was one of the few people who knew exactly when she'd gone to Houston and exactly where.

She rubbed her forehead against a sudden ache. Reggie? Could he have been in Texas to take pictures of her in Brandon's backyard a few days ago? She always talked to Reggie via cell phone . . . so she didn't know exactly where he was. Anything was possible. And if Reggie had come that far to stalk her, well, he alone had known she'd intended to go to Lafayette to meet Jack. Following her a bit farther wouldn't have been that difficult.

Had Reggie, the father she'd never had, taken secret, sexual pictures of her? Had Reggie stalked her, masturbated on her bed, tried to shoot her? No! But . . . who else could it be?

Just Reggie.

"Oh, God." Shock hummed through her body, buzzed in her brain. Morgan's knees buckled. She covered her mouth with a trembling hand to keep a scream in. "Wh . . . I don't . . . Why? I trusted Reggie. Completely."

As she staggered, Jack wound his arm around her waist.

"Steady," he murmured.

She stared at Jack in sudden horror. If she couldn't trust Reggie, a man she'd known for three years as the protective lout with a heart of gold, could she trust Jack, a man she'd only known for days?

"Morgan?" Deke's concern resounded through the phone wire.

She turned to look at Jack through wide eyes, pouring out uncertainty and panic. What did she know about him? Just what Reggie had told her . . . and that he'd tried to twist her sexuality into something she didn't want to accept.

She struggled to escape Jack's hold. Flee. Squirming and writhing, she tried to break free. Now. Go someplace where no one could find her.

"Steady." Jack used that patient but commanding voice Morgan knew so well.

Something deep inside her responded instantly, wanted to heed that voice. Another part of her feared . . . She didn't know what exactly. That virtually anyone could wish her harm, especially someone she trusted. Reggie only proved she couldn't judge the characters of those around her. What if she'd mistakenly trusted a stranger, not just with her safety, but with her body, her soul?

The stranger she only knew because Reggie had passed Jack's information her way.

An icy chill of fear blasted through Morgan. She kicked at Jack's shins, throwing an elbow into his stomach. He clasped her tighter and dodged her sharp jabs.

"I'll call you later," Jack growled into the phone. Then he slammed a finger on the button and ended the connection with Deke.

Jack picked her up around the waist. Morgan struggled harder, panic streaking through her belly, down her legs. He grunted when she managed to land a heel in his shin. Hope sprang inside that he'd let her go.

He held tighter.

Jack backed into the bedroom, dragging her with him. Morgan tried to grab the doorknob and use it as an anchor, but he was too fast, too strong.

"Damn you, put me down!" Morgan shouted. "Put me the hell down!"

"I know what you're thinking," he growled, ignoring her demand. "Stop it, now."

"You can't tell me what to think, asshole."

"Think logically, *cher*."

Moments later, she found herself tossed onto the rumpled bed, flat on her back. Faster than a flash of lightning, he covered her chilled, frantic body and pinned her to the mattress. His arms stretched out over hers, hot fingers clasped around her wrists in a gentle but unyielding vise. The weight of his longer legs secured her own against the soft sheets.

*No.* The word burned across Morgan's brain as she struggled, the need to escape and find an isolated hole to hide in overriding all else. Jack tightened above until he held her completely immobile. *No!*

"Relax." His dark stare slammed into her, penetrating her fear with a calm, commanding stare.

"Let me go!" Morgan tensed against him, arms, legs, doing her best to remain unyielding.

"I know what's running through that pretty head of yours, *cher*. Stop. I'm not going to hurt you."

"If Reggie is guilty, then . . . then anyone—you—could want me bleeding, dead . . ."

Her voice sounded breathy, trembling. Morgan hated the fact that her voice shook. On TV, she was the sexy bleached-blonde show hostess, professional with a hint of a wild streak. It worked. Out on the middle of the Louisiana swamp, under Jack's roof, she was a terrified natural redhead who hated this crappy, helpless feeling, hated being out of her element physically, mentally, environmentally . . . sexually.

Jack frowned, concern etching the furrow between his brows. "You're thinking with adrenaline, Morgan, not logic. Don't. We've been here alone for two days. At any time, I could have hurt you, if that was my intent."

Morgan paused, panting. Her mind raced. Jack'd had a million opportunities to rape or kill her—or both. He'd done neither. But coming down off the ledge wasn't that simple.

"How do I know you're not toying with me, waiting for me to lower my guard and completely trust you before you move in for the kill? What do I know about you at all?"

Jack paused, those endless chocolate eyes drilling into her, breathtaking in their stark sincerity and tight with frustration. "I am *not* your stalker. Nor am I in league with the scumbag. If you'd listen to your gut, you would know that."

"You never had any sort of plan to harm me?"

"Harm you?" He pinned her with a stare stripped of everything except resentment and honesty. "Who helped you escape the shooter? Who brought you to safety?"

She answered with a pregnant pause, her mind racing. Clearly, Jack hadn't harmed her, despite constant opportunities. He had saved her that day in Lafayette; she knew that. She just didn't understand why.

"Damn you, what have I done to earn your distrust?" he demanded. "Not one fucking thing except try to make you see who you really are and what you pretend not to want."

"Three days ago I'd barely heard your name," Morgan shouted into his tense face. "Now I'm supposed to place my sexuality and my entire life in your hands and think nothing of it? How many men would just . . . risk their lives to help a stranger?"

"That's what a soldier does every day, Morgan." He clutched at her wrists, holding her tight. "He puts his ass on the line to protect the citizens of his country, most of whom he'll never know. I was a soldier for too many years to change. Then I became a bodyguard. I wasn't going to stand there and watch you die."

The white haze of panic began to lift from her mind as Morgan processed his words. Jack had saved her because that's who he was. Maybe his behavior was part instinct, part chivalry. If he was working with Reggie to kill her, he was taking his sweet time. And that didn't seem Jack's style.

Okay, so it wasn't likely that he was Reggie's partner in some grand scheme, but something still niggled at her. Something didn't feel quite right.

"So helping me in Lafayette had nothing to do with being on TV?"

Braced on his elbows, which now framed her face, he shook his head. "I could give a shit about being on TV. Honestly, I saved you because I had to. That's my job. But I also did it because I wanted to touch you. The first time I talked to you online . . . something was there between us." He kissed his way down her jaw. "I sensed your innocence, your curiosity and uncertainty. That day we had coffee on the Square, the sight of you was like a punch to my gut. You and your aroused reluctance made me want you so bad I couldn't breathe. Within five seconds of meeting you, I was looking for ways to stretch out our meeting, to touch you. I want you still."

Her pulse leapt as if it had found a trampoline. Wow, he'd just . . . laid it all out on the table. Shock tumbled through her, causing words and thoughts to trip over one another. *Yes. No.* She wanted. She shouldn't. Instead, she swallowed, uncertain what she should say.

"You want me, too."

His pronouncement, stated like arrogant fact, startled her. But she couldn't deny it. Of course she wanted Jack. Even as he hovered over her and anchored her wrists to the bed again, a decidedly sexual question in his chocolate eyes, her nipples hardened. She felt herself getting wet once more.

He dropped a kiss on her forehead, another on her jaw. "You know I'm not going to hurt you, right?"

Slowly, she nodded. "You . . . You're right."

"And your friend Reggie. He might be guilty, yes. He might not. Until we know more, don't assume anything."

Morgan shook her head. "But he's totally into photography. No one else—"

"I understand. Just wait. Deke will keep digging. For now, I think it's important that you don't talk to Reggie, not until we know more. Had you planned to call him, check in?"

"I tried yesterday. I can't get a cell signal out here."

"No." Jack shook his head. "Most people can't. Will he raise some red flag if you don't call?"

"Not for a while; a few more days, probably."

"Hopefully, we'll have this sorted out by then. Until then, don't assume the worst. We have one fact that doesn't make things look good for Reggie, but nothing is absolute. And even if he is guilty, you know he can't find you here, right?"

Wherever here was . . . "Right."

"In the meantime, I'm here to protect you."

"Why?" Why would he go so far out on a limb for her? "You don't have to keep that promise."

"Yes, I do." He nuzzled her neck, teeth nipping at her lobe as his hot breath fanned in her ear. "Besides, with you, it's about more than protection."

Morgan shivered. She became aware of his fingers sliding up her arms to clamp around her wrists again, his legs pinning her own beneath him once more, the heat transferring between them, down the line of their bodies. And the stalk of his erection, thick, long, insistent.

"So much more," he whispered. "You amaze me. You are smart enough to stay one step ahead of a very determined psycho. Sweet enough to addict me. Stubborn enough to defy me. Strong enough to work to break into TV, which I know is a tough business."

The nicest compliment Andrew had ever paid her was to claim she was dazzling. Great, so she filled out a dress well. Whoopee. But Jack's words drizzled onto her one at a time, like hot fudge on a sundae, coating her fear with something soothing and wonderful.

A man out to hurt her wouldn't care if she was smart, sweet, stubborn, or strong. Even more, he'd paid attention to her. Her—the deepdown person she was.

Jack was getting to her, slowly making her melt. With a press of his hips against her sex, she melted a bit more. A flare of arousal ignited and spread through her body. With a sharp inhalation, she took the scent of him into her nose. He lingered there: leather, man, cypress, mystery. The urge—the ache—to press up and meet him gripped her.

"You puzzle me, too," he murmured against her skin, pretending not to notice how she tensed against him. "You took a big risk in digging beyond your own uncertainty and starting a TV show that encourages people to explore their sexuality, whatever it is. But you hesitate to explore your own. Why?"

"I explored. I'm just not sure I want to be . . . held down or restrained or—"

"Tied to my bed? You like being at my mercy."

"I don't want to work that way! It's not normal."

"It's perfectly normal not to want straight vanilla sex. You're not wired for that, *cher*."

"I've got to be. I want to be!"

Before Jack, she'd never had a man bring her to multiple orgasms. It didn't seem possible that he was only able to because he tied her down and filled her head with wicked suggestions of submission and other dirty deeds she had only fantasized about. That wasn't it. Any way he touched her would be mind-blowing because she found the man himself irresistible. The pleasure he gave her had nothing to do with his domination.

"I know you wish you were." He smoothed a tangle of wild, flamecolored hair back from her face. "But if you'd let me, I'd help you. I want to show you that your desires are not only perfectly normal but totally wonderful."

"You're out of your mind."

"You're burying your head in the sand and wasting yourself on what you want to be true, rather than what *is*," he growled, frustration tightening his mouth.

Morgan shook her head. *No. A thousand times no.*

But she feared he was right. Something deep inside her flowered at his words. Hope, need, yearning. It was all there, every bit she'd tried to push down, block from her conscious mind. A part of her—a big part—wanted to gobble up everything he had to offer.

"Why are you running from yourself?"

Andrew's ugly slurs replayed in Morgan's head, slashing deep at her self-confidence. *You're depraved. Only a whore wants that!*

As the tension ramped up in her body, so did Jack's grip on her wrists. He drew one hand from her own to slide against her naked cheek. The warmth of his palm against her cool skin brought her completely back to the present. Back to the fact that Jack lay on top of her, his big body taut and tense and spread out, completely covering her.

"Why are you the way you are?" she challenged. "Does there have to be a reason?"

"I can cuff you to this bed," he growled. "Order your sweet submission, fuck you half the night, and get you off half a dozen times."

Desire gouged her belly like a hot sword at his terrible, provocative words. Morgan closed her eyes, gritted her teeth, ignoring her dampening sex, and shook her head. "The only thing I want you to get is the hell off me."

She bucked beneath him, trying to throw him off her body. He didn't budge.

"I can feel your nipples stabbing my chest and your pussy getting all sweet and damp for me. I'm right, and you know it."

"I know you're pushy! Maybe I don't want to be ordered or bound or made to submit. Maybe I just want to be touched. Held. In the regular way."

He raised a dark brow. "You think you want vanilla sex?"

"Traditional," she corrected. "Absolutely."

Jack hesitated, his dark eyes scanning her face. The disbelief etched there played havoc with her composure.

"We have some . . . chemistry. I'm not denying that," she rattled. "I just think we'd find plenty of pleasure together without the ropes and commands."

Staring, Jack appeared to be sorting through the possibilities. Quickly, he came to a conclusion. And he smiled.

She didn't trust that wide, white-teethed Cajun grin for an instant.

"As you wish," he purred. "Vanilla it is, *cher*."

His capitulation was too easy. Now she really didn't trust him. "You mean that?"

"*Oui*. You'll get nothing but kisses, gentle fondling, and straight missionary penetration."

Jack made it sound dull, damn it, and it wasn't. It wouldn't be between them. Still, some weird stab of disappointment ached like a pain in her gut that he'd acquiesced so easily.

Gosh, did she ever sound contrary. She'd won her way. She ought to be thrilled.

"Thank you," Morgan whispered.

He shrugged and shot her an ironic smile. "I aim to please."

Ignoring the hitch of disquiet brewing inside her, she smiled back as Jack released her wrists, moved his legs to allow her own more freedom. The taut coil of his spine relaxed and he settled on top of her, elbows bracing him on either side of her head.

Jack glided gentle thumbs down her cheekbones and lowered his mouth to hers. Soft. Like a ghost, his lips whispered over her own, neither giving nor taking. Merely existing, soothing with a sweet press of lips, of breaths.

Morgan closed her eyes and tried to sink into the tender rhythm of the kiss that flowed and lulled and seduced.

Nice. Wonderful, even. But she wanted . . . more of it.

It took two to tango, so she could fix that. Reaching around Jack's head, she filtered her fingers through the soft spikes of his short hair and pressed his lips down on hers. He gave her more—pressure, access, passion. She moaned in the back of her throat.

The kiss was timeless, endless. The sweet exchange of sighs, the gentle slide of tongues, the total immersion of her senses in him as a man all filled her. Desire rose in lilting waves to wash a soothing sort of want over her. She couldn't wait to be closer, to touch him . . . but it wasn't exactly sexual.

Minutes slid by, one into the other. Still, Jack did nothing more than kiss her, sweep his palms across her cheek, her shoulder. The want inside her began to build to a soft crescendo. Something in her demanded more. Again, she took it.

Nudging Jack to her side, Morgan nipped her way down his jaw, then pulled away to tug at the belt of his knit robe. She parted the gray jersey material. It landed in a heap on the floor.

Beneath, she wore the naughty bloodred lingerie with cutouts that revealed both her nipples and sex. What would Jack think?

A mental image of his growl of lust fired her. She pictured his fierce need overtaking him, compelling him to pin her down, clutch her thighs, spread her open as he thrust his way deep inside her with a lot of passion and very little mercy . . .

No! No, they were here for traditional sex.

Shaken by her wayward thoughts, she sent him an uncertain glance. Jack sucked in a sharp breath and his eyes heated from a warm hearth fire to a toasty bonfire.

"You're beautiful, *cher*." He caressed the slope of her breast with the backs of his fingers, toying with the lace around the bra's cutouts, skirting around her nipple.

"Do you like it?"

"Very much." He leaned in to drop one sweet kiss on her shoulder.

Morgan frowned. "You're not touching me."

Jack knew what she wanted. He had to. The ability to read her body was one reason she found him virtually irresistible. Besides the fact that he was brave, could be charming, daring, funny, or tender. But he *always* knew just how to turn her on.

"How would you like me to touch you?"

"Don't play games," she bit out.

"Never. I want your happiness. I'm trying to make sure you get the experience you need."

"Just . . . touch me. Make love to me. You understand that."

He grinned. "My understanding and yours are different. I'm in somewhat unfamiliar territory. I haven't done . . . *traditional*," he said, using her word, "in years. And never with you. You'll have to help me out."

Morgan crossed her arms over her chest. "You're being uncooperative."

"I'm deferring to your wishes." Annoyance tinged his voice. "Tell me what you want, and I'll do my best."

"Touch my body, kiss me—anything you'd normally do without ropes or demands or pain."

Jack looked up at the ceiling, appearing to ponder her words. "That gives me a range of activities to choose from. I'll try."

Mollified by his seeming willingness, Morgan leaned forward and peeled off Jack's shirt, revealing the hard slabs of his pectorals and the firm ridges of his washboard abs sheathed in soft, golden-brown skin. Unable to resist, she sucked his flat male nipple into her mouth. She laved it with her tongue, pulled the point past her lips to nip at it with her teeth.

He sucked in a sudden breath, and she smiled to see the erection beneath his jeans take shape again. But as she backed away to gauge his reaction, he merely stared at her with a heated question.

"Doing something like that to me would be great," she said, trying to answer.

Nodding, Jack reached out and plucked her nipple with his thumb and finger. Gentle swirls of sensation made their way from her breast to her abdomen. When he repeated the process with her other breast, he garnered the same results.

Standing hard now, the nubs of her breasts demanded attention.

"Jack . . ." she entreated.

Without a word, he closed his mouth around one nipple, circled it with his tongue, sucked the bead past his lips . . . then released it. Again, he did the same to her other breast. Sensation began to tighten inside her. Yes, she wanted. Jack made her want—like crazy usually.

This wasn't usual. It was . . . slow. But slow was good. Long ramp-up to an excellent climax, right? A little delayed gratification.

Except it felt isolating since he wasn't talking to her.

Frowning, she placed more kisses down the line bisecting his amazing abs and headed straight for his fly. He made no sound, neither moan nor protest, when she eased his zipper down and slipped his jeans off his hips and onto the floor.

Morgan moaned. He looked unbelievable naked—a sex god come to life, just for her.

Once she'd divested him of his clothes, Jack did the same for her, easing the bra straps off her shoulders, then unclasping the garment at the back. He planted tiny, hungry kisses on her belly as he pulled her crotchless panties off her body and tossed them across the room.

Finally, they were both gloriously naked. Now the real pleasure would begin.

Jack kissed her once more, trailing his finger through her cleavage, then tracing her nipple. Sensation tingled its way through her breast. Morgan arched into his touch. It felt good, Jack's fingers on her flesh. She wanted . . . more.

Easing down her body, Jack captured the tip of her other breast in his mouth and gave it a loving lick as his palm smoothed its way across her abdomen. He stopped short of her sex, seemingly contented by fondling the curve of her waist and the slope of her hips.

He couldn't possibly be contented. Who would be? And the silence—it was really getting to her. She felt closed off from him, without any idea of what he wanted, what he was thinking, feeling afraid to communicate her needs to him in the midst of the hush.

Frustrated, Morgan reached down between them to grab his cock. Mostly hard, always thick, it filled her hand and then some. She gave a hard little tug on it, rubbing her thumb across the dry, sensitive head.

He closed his eyes and pressed into her fist. But said nothing else. Did nothing else.

So she pumped him, stroking her hand up and down the thick erection in her hand. He grew, hardened. Another pass of her thumb over the head of his penis proved he was still dry. Usually the slit in the head wept with need almost from the instant she touched him.

Biting the inside of her lip, Morgan came up with a plan to . . . engage him in the process.

She rolled him to his back. Leaving a trail of demanding kisses across Jack's skin, Morgan made her way from his nipples, sucking and nipping them again, down his abdomen, which tensed beneath her lips, all the way to his cock. She lifted the appendage with her hand, swiping her tongue across the purple tip, tracing the thick veins decorating the shaft with her fingers, then sliding her palm down to cup his balls.

Jack tensed, moaned almost silently, and closed his eyes.

What the heck was he thinking? What did he want? Given their lack of interaction, Morgan wondered if Jack would care if she left the bed and meandered into the kitchen.

"Does that feel good?" she whispered against his stiff sex.

"Hmmm." He nodded.

Then he answered again by stealing her nipple into his mouth and giving it a gentle tug with his lips. Pleasant . . . but not earth-shattering. Not what Jack usually did for her.

When Morgan would have cupped her hand behind his head to force more pressure into the embrace, Jack rolled her to her back and slid his fingers through her sex. She was damp, not dripping.

With gentle fingers, he administered a careful brush across her clit, then slipped slowly into her folds.

That was nice. No denying his touch made her melt. It just wasn't . . . mind-stealingly, toe-tinglingly wonderful, like usual. What was going on here?

His fingers played inside her, thumb manipulating that button of sensation at the top of her sex. Arousal climbed another sweet notch at the thought of Jack's hands on her pussy. He liked that word. And when he said it to her in bed, a part of her mind revolted against the crudity but . . . she always melted.

"Am I wet?" she asked.

"Yes."

"What part of me?" she asked coyly, wishing he would talk in that low rumble of a voice that held all the sexuality of a wild midnight coupling enshrouded in lust.

"Shhh."

Then he closed his eyes, shutting her out again. At least she felt that way, despite the fact that his fingers teased her inner walls with a slide of his fingertips and the caress of his thumb.

Under his stimulation, she grew wetter. Her body tingled in some great places. Usually, her very skin screamed for Jack—all of him to come to her, invade her, drive her up the mountain of need and pleasure until she fell off the cliff. Now, she wanted something—anything, damn it—more intense. Something that provided a deeper connection to him.

"Talk to me." She pouted.

"You look gorgeous, and you feel wonderful," he murmured.

"What do you want?"

"To please you." He rubbed her clit with his thumb again. "Does that feel good?"

Morgan didn't answer, didn't know what to say. It felt fine, just not as fine as Jack usually made her feel. In fact, it felt alarmingly like the times she'd had sex with Sean and Brent and Andrew. Good. . . . just not great.

He opened his eyes and sliced a stare of hot challenge at her. "Or did you need something else?"

The jerk was challenging her, as if he knew this wasn't rocking her world like he usually did. And she couldn't say that it wasn't because he wasn't trying. He'd stimulated her nipples and continued to plunge his fingers inside her sex, trail the pad of his thumb across her clit. Desire was building . . . but something was missing.

"You inside me," she whispered. "That's what I need."

"Always my favorite place to be."

With a smile, Jack sheathed himself with a condom from the nightstand, then rolled on top of her, a steamy kiss on his lips as he covered her mouth. A new swell of desire rolled in her belly as Jack probed at her entrance.

In one smooth stroke, Jack eased in, gliding all the way to the end of her channel, filling her completely. Morgan sucked in a breath as the length and girth of his erection caressed sensitive nerve endings inside her.

Slowly, he withdrew, easing out all the way to the tip, then stroked inside again in one smooth glide. Yes, that was nice. Heavenly. Desire inched up a notch.

Did he enjoy this? Was he feeling pleasure? Morgan wished he'd say something, moan—anything to let her know.

Silence.

In, out, in, out with soft, even slides of his cock. The ache built slowly, spiraling up. She clamped down on him as pressure built and need mounted. Morgan strained to meet Jack thrust for thrust.

Yummy . . . except, damn, she wished he'd say something. Usually she felt him swell inside her, saw him grapple to keep his control as his body tensed and sweat rolled down his temple. Today, just smooth strokes building to a soft peak.

Why wouldn't Jack say something? She'd had more interaction with the vibrator she'd reluctantly bought.

She shoved the thought out of her mind and clutched the hard bunch of muscles along his spine, pressing needy fingers into his damp back until she gripped his ass and pulled him in deeper, trying to make his flesh crash into hers with urgency and force.

Almost . . . almost there. But not quite. She let out a frustrated moan, which he swallowed with his kiss.

"Jack." She panted. "Jack."

"You need to come?"

"Please." She moaned, nails digging into the cheeks of his ass.

Bending his knees, he widened the part of her legs and pushed himself on his elbows, changing the angle of his thrust. The fat head of his cock rubbed against that sensitive spot on her inner wall.

Need spiked, closing into a ball of sensation centered behind her clit. Sweet with a sharp edge or two, it should have been enough to send her over. But still she couldn't come.

Jack reached for her nipples and fondled them with gentle fingers, adding to the downpour of sensations scattering over her. As his stiff sex continued to rub and press on that sensitive spot, her grip on him tightened. Pressure built inside her, her heartbeat began to echo in her head. *Now, now, now,* it demanded.

And still she couldn't come.

Then Jack said the magic words. "Come now, sweetheart."

She released, the ball of tension lifting, shimmering, then dissipating. It wasn't a burst or a rush of explosion. It was a soft cresting, a smooth dissolving of the buildup. Above her, he tensed and moaned gently in her ear.

As a climax, it felt . . . anticlimactic. Better than she'd achieved with any previous lover, yes. But not the amazing, bone-grinding, mindblowing starbursts of sensation Jack had never previously failed to give her.

Damn it, she felt like crying. Like stomping her hands and fists all over the rumpled bed until all the tension inside of her erupted and she spewed the lava of her lust and frustration. Until her mind and body felt weary and sated and beyond happy.

What the hell was wrong with her?

Jack withdrew from her, disposed of the condom, then lay down beside her again, taking her hand in his.

"You enjoy your traditional sex, *cher*?"

Too quickly for her liking, Morgan remembered Jack telling her that she wasn't wired for traditional. He'd only gone along with this now to prove his point. And she'd known that from the beginning, refusing to accept that maybe . . . just maybe, he'd been right.

"Did you?" he prodded.

Morgan sighed. It was time to make a decision: Either keep running, keep denying how much she craved and responded to Jack's domination or accept that, at least when she was with him, she needed more than traditional.

She drew in a ragged breath and brushed away the scald of her hot tears. His dark gaze was at once approachable, understanding—and blistering with explicit desire.

Everything inside Morgan leapt in response. Suddenly, she knew she had no choice. "Please take me to your playroom and fuck me as you see fit." She swallowed. "Sir."

# Chapter Twelve

JACK stilled, everything inside him froze. Shock, relief, jubilation, and something like warm, sweet honey spreading through his chest all tumbled over one another in a rush of emotion he wasn't accustomed to. Despite all that, he paused.

Morgan's eyes misted with tears. Her chin trembled.

Sighing, Jack restrained himself from snatching her into his arms and darting down the hall to lock her behind his playroom door. But not without great effort. He wasn't naïve enough to believe that one mediocre vanilla fuck had convinced Morgan she was a born submissive. She had layers and layers of guilt about something he didn't understand. And she wouldn't reach her full potential or full happiness until she got through it.

Since he planned to make her his—and would happily kill Brandon or any other son of a bitch who thought she belonged to him—Jack figured he'd better get to the bottom of Morgan's issues now. He hoped, right now, so she could begin to acknowledge him as her master, her lover, the man she could depend on to care for her in all ways.

Jack leaned in and kissed her forehead. "Why?"

She didn't answer for a long time. Instead, she sat up, drew her legs up to her naked chest, and set her head on her knees. He didn't prod, didn't touch, just waited.

Finally, she lifted her misty gaze to him again, proving she'd been shedding silent tears. "You said I wasn't wired for vanilla sex. I-I didn't want to believe it, but I think that just proved your point."

Damn. She'd just made two admissions he had to deal with—and he had to tread carefully. Easy first, with a slide into the more difficult.

"How did I prove my point?"

Those arched ginger brows of hers snapped together to form a scowl that questioned his sanity. "Did our sex just blow your socks off?"

He smiled, doing his best to keep the mood light while he could. "I'm not wearing any."

Morgan wasn't amused. "So you think this is funny now?"

"No, *cher*," he soothed. "It did not blow my socks off, but I didn't expect it to. I accepted long ago that I don't like vanilla anything, even ice cream. Tell me what it was like for you."

A subtle command. Morgan hesitated, grappled. Then she capitulated. "What we did . . . it was nice. Pleasant, like a picnic. I liked just being close to you more than I liked the actual sex." Tears pooled in her blue eyes, which reflected turmoil. "I didn't expect that. I kept wishing for . . . more. For a word or command—some indication of what you wanted, how you felt. Something that connected us. Something more intense."

The relief and jubilation rushed back over Jack. When he'd agreed to sex without domination, he'd hoped this would be Morgan's response . . . but he hadn't known for sure. She was turning out to be everything he'd believed, wanted to find for years. Still, he had to tread carefully.

"Your past vanilla experiences, were they satisfying?"

She cast him a vaguely guilty expression. "No. I . . . no."

Ah. There was a wealth of meaning there. He could have chastised her for imagining that she could enjoy simple sex, but she had to experience the difference for herself. One of the qualities he adored about her was that she had a strong mind and will, and she wanted to use them. Even if it made waiting for her to catch on to this discovery frustrating.

"Why did you think it would be different with me?"

Morgan lifted one shoulder in a halfhearted shrug. "You affect me more than anyone else. I just thought . . . it was you. That it would be different with you. Before, I rarely reached orgasm. If I hadn't been with you, you know, in the other way, I would have been elated by what just happened. But since I know how explosive we can be when . . ."

"I dominate you?" he prompted.

"Yes." She flushed. "I realized that it was about you, at least in part. Just being near you turns me on. It's also about the way you are with me: demanding, so knowledgeable about my mind and body. You manage to wrap my mind up around a million fantasies until I'm so hot . . ."

Jack forced himself to rein in the I-told-you-so smile threatening to break out across his face. Too early to smile. He had to make sure he'd really reached her. "Because you need your biggest sex organ, your brain, involved. Vanilla doesn't really do that. Dominance and submission can be a game or a way or life, depending on how seriously you play. But it absolutely keeps your mind engaged with your body. The promise of pleasure can be every bit as arousing as the pleasure itself—maybe more, as you found out from doing without a mind fuck tonight."

She hesitated, bit that lush, puffed lip that never failed to make the man in him notice. Then understanding brightened her sultry blue gaze. "Yeah. I kept missing the mental piece. Knowing what you were thinking, hearing your voice urging me on."

Now she was getting it. Jack smiled. "What does your current fiancé do for a living?"

Morgan frowned at the out-of-nowhere question. Hesitated. "He's an analyst for some organization in the government. I'm not supposed to know exactly who or what he studies."

Interesting information Jack filed away for later. "And sex with him . . . ?"

He had to grit his teeth to keep the snarl out of his voice. The thought of Brandon touching Morgan . . . Brandon might be taller than him, but in the army, Jack had never failed once to kick his ass at anything. He was tempted to remind his former pal of that fact again.

Morgan shook her head, fiery tresses spreading out across her pale shoulders. Her auburn lashes fluttered, hiding her expression. "We've never . . ."

*Never?* Jack exhaled in a shocked rush. He'd fucked Morgan before her own fiancé had? Sweet revenge had just gotten sweeter, yes. But the thrill rushing through Jack had nothing to do with revenge and everything to do with the knowledge that Brandon had never touched the woman he felt was his and his alone.

And she would be his . . . but first, he had to get through the hard part of the conversation.

"I don't think you really believed that vanilla would be better with me. You hoped. The question is, why? I know nothing about your college boyfriend, but your choices of a pro football player and a TV producer tell me you were, even unconsciously, seeking a man of some power and self-possession. Right?"

Her little gasp told Jack that he'd both guessed correctly and surprised her. "Yes."

"So you ended your engagement with the TV producer . . . when?"

"Andrew and I split up because . . ."

Her voice trembled. She looked away with a grimace. Definitely something here. After he'd brought Morgan here and questioned her on her sexual past, she'd refused to answer questions about Andrew or why it had ended.

"Because?"

She looked at him with tormented blue eyes, and Jack felt that look like a punch in the gut. Yes, he was going to finally get some answers. But it was going to cost Morgan to say this. He grabbed her hand and squeezed, hoping she'd understand his silent support.

"A lot of reasons. But sex . . . That wasn't going well between us. I couldn't orgasm with him." She faltered, shook her head. "I remember thinking that I enjoyed his sense of humor and his intelligence, but when he touched me, it was as if he thought I would break. It was always so soft and sweet. And silent. We didn't . . . connect. I didn't feel much of anything."

Jack cradled a hand behind her head and stroked the tangled silk of her fiery hair. He wanted to reassure her now, make her understand that not responding to soft and sweet and silent didn't make her wrong or a bad person. But he couldn't interrupt her. She had more to get out.

"Go on."

Morgan sighed. "He asked me what was wrong, how he could make it better. I trusted him. He seemed worldly and open-minded. So I told him some of my fantasies I'd never told anyone, fantasies of . . . you know, being manhandled and commanded. I told him I thought about—"

"Being bound and fucked and made to submit," Jack finished for her, even as his fists clenched at his sides. He'd bet everything he owned that he knew what Morgan would say next. "What was his response?"

This time she swallowed. Hard. And squeezed her eyes shut. A shimmering teardrop squeezed out of one corner. Jack wanted to hit something. No, someone—Andrew.

"He told me I was depraved. That only a dirty whore would want such things. He said he wouldn't stay in the relationship unless I got professional help and learned to drive those sorts of thoughts out of my head."

Professional help? Where was Andrew right now? Never mind hurting the asshole, Jack wanted to kill the bastard who'd made Morgan doubt herself and cry.

"I hope you called him every kind of a prick and told him to get fucked," he growled.

"Not in those words. I threw his ring back at him and told him to keep it." She bit her lip, and a hint of mischief lit her blue eyes. "I think I may have indicated that he needed to grow a real penis."

Jack's laughter was filled with relief. He brought her closer, tumbling her across his lap. "Good girl. There's nothing wrong with you, *cher*." He looked right into her eyes, hoping like hell she believed him. "Andrew is the one with problems, stupid jerkoff. He didn't like that you challenged his manhood, that you were stronger, that you wanted something he wasn't man enough to provide. You're not depraved. You need someone you can trust with your safety and pleasure, mind, body, and soul. I think that makes you wonderful and perfect."

Morgan's jaw tightened. She fought more tears. And he didn't want her to fight them. Time to get them out, once and for all. He hoped like hell she'd be too busy fucking later to succumb to more of them.

"Tell me," he coaxed. "It's okay."

"I just couldn't get his voice out of my head." She broke then, tears cresting from her eyes, down her cheeks, one crystal tear after another. She inhaled raggedly. "Over and over, I could hear his voice telling me how depraved I was. That I was abnormal and—and disturbed. That I was a whore."

If the little prick was standing here now, even God couldn't have saved him from Jack's rage. Andrew had nearly destroyed this beautiful woman's sexuality to preserve his own delusions about his adequacy. He'd be dealt with later. Jack would make sure of that. Morgan needed him now.

"You're nothing of the kind." He dried her tears with his thumbs, then kissed each damp cheek. "Did you like your pizza the same way he did?"

She frowned. "He didn't even like pizza."

"There was something definitely wrong with this guy."

Morgan laughed through her tears, and Jack kissed her sweet, swollen mouth.

"My point is, *cher*, not everyone has the same taste. Pizza may be oversimplified, but you understand. Don't let his voice play in your head for another moment."

Another command, a stern one. He didn't expect her to heed it completely right now. But if he could get his voice in her head to compete with asshole Andrew's, his own voice would eventually replace it.

"A-and my mother. Shortly after my engagement ended, she came to visit me, to console me. She found some of my . . . books. Erotic ones with bondage and—"

"*Cher*, mamas don't want to think about their daughters having sex, much less good sex."

Morgan looked at him with tear-drenched eyes and nodded. "It was terrible. I grew up in a religious house. Sex was dirty to her. Evil. To say she was shocked by my private library would be an understatement." She bit her lip as fresh tears threatened. "She shouted the same things as Andrew. Abnormal, d-depraved."

And hearing that from her own mother had hurt. Jack saw the pale torment all over her face.

"They're ignorant and misguided," he vowed. "Neither understands the deep bond of trust and understanding a dominant and his submissive forms. You do. You've been looking for it subconsciously for years. Now that you have it, you're too smart to let it get away, aren't you?"

A bare hesitation. A tiny one. She'd feel a not-so-gentle hand on the back of her ass for it later, not because he didn't understand her feelings or her need to think things through, but because she had to start associating her guilt with unpleasant consequences.

But she finally nodded in agreement.

"Are you ready to show yourself that you accept who and what you are?"

Morgan hesitated again. Swallowed. But she nodded once more. "Yes."

Jack eased off the bed and stood beside it, drilling her with a hot stare that demanded understanding and obedience before he bent to retrieve the lingerie they'd discarded earlier with the intriguing cutouts he was dying to explore. He thrust the garments into her hands.

Her wide, wet eyes were a blue beacon, drawing him to the vulnerability shining there. She looked so fucking young with bare, tearstained cheeks. Damn, he'd done his best to bring her out gently, break her just a bit. Now it was time to remake her, if she could just trust him.

Morgan reached out and grabbed his hand, squeezing as she tangled her fingers with his. As he reached out to stroke her cheek, Jack saw something new on her face. He saw resolve.

Now, he permitted himself the smile he'd held in earlier.

"Put these back on, along with the black stockings. Knock on the door of my playroom. Ten minutes. I'll be waiting."

\*      \*      \*

SQUARING her shoulders, Morgan lifted her hand to the closed black door and knocked. As the sound echoed down the shadowed hall. She pushed what she was, or rather wasn't, wearing out of her mind. No more thoughts of Andrew or her mother. Their opinions couldn't matter. She wouldn't let them.

Jack had opened her eyes.

Her mother had been a shriveled woman, bitter toward all men, thanks to Senator John Morgan Ross breaking her young heart. And her former fiancé, she realized, focused his energy on frustration. Andrew had elevated angst to an art form. He didn't want to be happy or fulfilled. Their relationship had always been an emotional roller-coaster ride, towering highs and crashing lows all in one day—one hour, if Andrew could swing it. People on the *Turn Me On* set had called him a drama king. He'd been threatened by any show of strength on her part, any strong opinion she expressed. Rejecting her sexuality had been his way of creating the next calamity and making her every bit as frustrated as he'd been.

Yes, she could still hear their voices, their slurs, in her head. She just wasn't going to give either of them the power to make her miserable anymore. If she was still not completely comfortable with her sexuality, Morgan suspected time and another man like Jack—he wasn't hers to keep—would turn around her reluctance.

She pushed aside a sharp pang at the thought of no longer having Jack.

Instead, she concentrated on her body, the cool air on her exposed nipples, the bra lifting up her breasts like a proud offering. She focused on the crotchless panties that didn't quite cover her ass or stop the gush of moisture rushing from her vagina to coat her inner thighs. She felt the thigh-high stockings hugging her in every way, emphasizing the small square of cloth covering her damp curls.

Nervous, yes. But far more aroused. And determined not to examine what she and Jack did or judge their actions. If it aroused her and felt good, she'd just do it.

That all sounded good, but without any idea what Jack might want—demand—from her, Morgan waited, aware of the ache of erotic fear and need building inside her.

Jack opened the door wearing black leather pants—and nothing else.

His gaze walked all over her, starting at the swollen mouth she'd been chewing on for the past ten minutes, down the pale slope of her breasts, gliding over the flat of her bared tummy, then zooming in right between her thighs, framed by lace, silk, and fishnet.

She watched his face. The heat raced to his eyes. The firm lines of his jaw grew tight. Her gaze skipped down past the bunched golden muscles of his wide chest and shoulders, down farther to the thick erection that grew at record speed.

Despite her nerves, Morgan smiled.

"I wouldn't be too happy yet. I'm going to make your earn my cock and your orgasms tonight."

Her smile faltered. If he noticed it, Jack said nothing.

"Come in and sit on the table."

"But—"

"No speaking unless I give you permission. Is that clear? Either nod or shake your head."

Stern, intense, beautiful. Morgan supposed she should have been furious with his high-handed attitude. Instead, she was curious and wet and wanting. And filled with an electric thrill.

She nodded and made her way into the room.

Jack swung the door wider to accommodate her, and it felt symbolic. A door opening. She would just embrace this part of her without judging it, without dwelling on what others would say.

"Sit," he barked. "I won't repeat myself again."

Morgan snapped to attention and brought herself back to the present. There would be time for thinking later. The time for obeying was now. With quick steps, she made her way to the center of the room and perched her ass on the table, scooting back until she was fully seated. She crossed her legs, clenching her thighs together to relieve the ache, and waited.

With a hot challenge lighting his eyes, Jack placed a hand on each knee and pried her thighs apart, then wide. "Don't cross your legs to me. When we're alone, they're open wide, signaling your availability and showing me your sweet, wet pussy. Understood?"

She wanted to be angry that he was going to tell her how to sit now. It was damn demanding. Overbearing. And arousing as his stare made its way down to the wet flesh he exposed, and he caressed her with his gaze. A fresh ache tightened behind her clit, gently pulsing in time with her heartbeat.

And she understood. This was why she thrilled to Jack's domination. He was so focused on her, so concentrated on taking her in with each sense, in every way he could. He enveloped her mind in the sexual experience so thoroughly, she couldn't possibly think, much less think about anything else. Soon, she would have all his power, testosterone, and self-control directed at her pleasure. At the thought, she felt flushed, faint.

And Jack hadn't really even touched her.

"Do you understand?" Jack asked between gritted teeth.

Morgan answered him with a nod.

He turned away to open a few boxes on the counter behind him. He stuffed something she couldn't see in the pocket of his pants, then turned back to her with something long and sparkling and golden. When he held it up for her, she saw it was a thick gold chain with a dangling ruby-studded heart. It was beautiful. Stunning. Too big to be a bracelet, certainly. Too short to fit around her neck and have the pendant dangle between her breasts. What did he intend?

"If you agree to wear this, you agree to be mine. Only mine. Sexually, you do what I say, when I say, how I say, and where I say. If you put this on, the word *no* leaves your vocabulary. You answer me with a polite 'Yes, sir.'"

He stroked the ruby pendant across one exposed nipple, then the other. The cold of the gems, the riot of sensations, forced her to draw in a trembling breath.

"You may speak. Ask me questions before you answer."

Be his? For tonight? That had to be what he meant. No way was the man talking forever.

Morgan licked her dry lips, aroused, oh-so-needy. "I have no questions, sir. I want to be yours."

The pulse jumped at the base of his neck. He swallowed. His Adam's apple bobbed. This meant something to him, and the fact that he couldn't quite conceal it touched her heart. But her eyes didn't stop their visual dessert. Her stare moved onto the veins roping his heavy forearms, bulging as he formed fists. His flat belly taut, as if he was poised to spring into action. And his cock. She hadn't thought it possible but he seemed to lengthen another inch.

"I want that, too, *cher*." His stare seduced and revered her at once.

Palms sweating, Morgan longed to press her thighs together to relieve the fresh, heavy ache he'd created . . . but she didn't dare.

"You understand that once I put this on you, you are mine to tease, punish, torment, and fuck at will?"

*Yes. Fine. Hurry*. The waiting was killing her. Quickly, she nodded.

"You know that your entire body will belong to me?"

Again, she nodded.

"That any time I indicate I want to make use of your mouth, your cunt, or your ass, you assume the position I request, no matter what?"

Morgan hesitated for a moment, then nodded. The unknown, anal sex, and anything else he could dream up, wouldn't worry her. She had to trust Jack to make everything good. God knew his words alone were reaching into her deepest fantasies, pushing her past caution, past her inhibitions.

She shot a deferential gaze up to him, her nipples hard as diamonds. "Yes, sir."

"I will take care of you. Trust me to know when and how you need my cock. Trust me to understand your fantasies and make each of them come true. Trust me to know when you need a good spanking and when you just need me to wrap my arms around you."

Wrap his arms around her? As if he would, what? Support her? Love her? He talked like he meant this to be beyond tonight. Like he did mean it to be forever . . .

"Understand?" His voice was soft but no less demanding.

Not really. But she was too impatient to ask. "Yes, sir."

Without another word, he stepped behind her and clasped the jeweled pendant around her neck. It clung to her like a choker, snug but not restrictive. The pendant of rubies pooled in the hollow at the base of her throat, rapidly warming to her skin. He walked around the table again for a peek.

"It looks perfect on you." With a gentle finger skimming her skin, Jack outlined the pendant.

His gaze never left hers. Never wavered. A world of promise and sinful mastery lay in his eyes. Morgan had seen Jack a lot of ways in the past few days: angry, asleep, protective, aroused. But never like this: possessive and totally determined.

Morgan exhaled a ragged, aroused breath.

"Perfect," he murmured. "Lie back and keep your legs spread so I can see that sweet pussy."

She only hesitated long enough to remind herself that she'd come here to be with Jack, to experience the ways he could make her feel. To embrace her sexuality.

Dark, hungry, his gaze roamed over Morgan, heating her up from the inside out. He looked so big, so . . . male standing over her, the hard ridges of his torso taut, defined, rippling with every breath. Her mouth went dry.

Now all she had to do was trust him with her pleasure.

Slowly, Morgan did as he commanded and laid back on the table, legs parted. She wanted to ask what he had planned for her, for them. But she knew that wasn't allowed. She had to trust him. So far she had—with her life. And she was still alive.

Maybe for the first time, totally alive.

For a long moment, he did nothing but gaze at her, his dark stare penetrating her body, her mind. She couldn't have looked away, even if she had wanted to. But breaking the connection between them was the last thing she desired. The jolt of it was like a live wire, stunning her, shaking her to her core. Breathless. Suspended. Tormented with anticipation. She waited.

"Close your eyes."

Oh, what did he have planned? Not seeing what he was doing . . . Morgan wasn't sure she could handle it. But the weight of the choker around her neck reminded her of all she'd agreed to. The twin slashes of Jack's black brows warned her against further hesitation.

Stomach jumping, heart pumping, Morgan allowed her lids to flutter shut, concealing Jack and anything he might do from her view.

A moment later, a scrap of something soft and silky fell over her face. Jack adjusted it over her eyes, then tied it off at the back of her head. A blindfold. She gulped. God, he meant for her to go into this totally blind and give him complete trust.

Morgan took a calming breath. She was up for this. She could do it, even if she had to disregard the wild thump of her pulse to believe it.

Jack leaned closer. She could feel his heat, scent his heavenly musk as he approached. It soothed her, as it made her even more aware of herself as a woman, even more wet.

His lips settled over hers like a whisper. A brush of heaven, a slide of hot taste, a forbidden brush of his tongue. "Thank you for your trust."

She relaxed into the table and arched her neck to receive more of his kisses.

Instead, she felt the grip of his fingers around her right wrist. He lifted her hand, easing it a few inches to her right. She felt cold metal around it a click later. Not tight . . . but not giving either. There was no way she was moving this arm. He repeated the process with her other wrist. Then he bound her ankles in the same way he had her wrists, locking them on either side of the table, knees bent, thighs wide.

"In time," he murmured, "and, I'm sure, after your fair share of punishments, you'll learn to trust me as you should."

The soft note of censure reverberated through her belly like a warning. Without being told, she knew she had punishment coming now.

Still, the sharp rap of his fingers slapping the mound of her pussy shocked Morgan. The sensation vibrated through her, down her nether lips. Then the ache centered right under her clit—but it wasn't pain. Pushing past the alarm and desire flooding her mind at once, a ferocious need seized her body, concentrated between her legs.

Jack repeated the process, this time just a fraction harder. The ferocious ache became monstrous, gripping her in its clutches with an unavoidable grasp. Morgan bit her lip to hold in her moan.

Then once more, the flat of his hand struck the pad of her pussy, with more force. Sensation zinged through her, ricocheting through her vagina. Equal parts pain and pleasure. The vise of need tightened until it strangled her thoughts. The moan lodged in her throat broke past her resistance and filled the silence between them.

"One more like that, and the pain will outweigh the pleasure. I'll reserve that . . . unless you hesitate again. Understood? Shake your head or nod."

The rumble of his voice dug down inside her, inciting a fresh wave of want. He'd already reduced her entire existence to her beating heart, her pounding pussy, and that line that seemed to run between them with some link she didn't understand.

Finally, she realized that Jack was waiting for an answer. She nodded.

"Good. Tonight, I'd rather pleasure you than punish you."

Footsteps across the hardwood floor told her he'd turned away, crossed the room. Was he leaving? No! She'd pushed away her inhibitions, resolved to embrace what he wanted to share with her. Dismay stole over her, and she tried to fight the cuffs at her wrists and ankles.

Then the footsteps announced his return, measured in a precise military-like cadence.

"You aren't going anywhere. Neither am I," he vowed and placed his palm in the center of her stomach. His skin was like a hot brand, promising more, swearing to make her completely his.

Morgan stilled, more relieved than she would have thought possible.

The wet slide of Jack's tongue brushed across the swell of her breast. His finger trailed a gentle path down the inside, then around, tracing the naughty cutout in her bra, so close to her sensitive areola. She arched in invitation.

He ignored her.

"Your nipples are the palest blushing pink," he whispered, his hot breath fanning right against one of the tight beads. "They turn a sweet, pale rose when you're aroused."

Even as he teased her with the possibility of his mouth over her breast, his finger was on the move again, drawing in a seemingly random pattern across her chest, down her abdomen, then back up. "Your freckles are fascinating to trace, and one day, I'll spend hours finding each and every one and licking them until you beg me to fuck you. But not now."

God, his words were like throwing gas on a bonfire. The ache he'd started between her thighs still gripped her in its unyielding clutch, so strong, sweat broke out on her forehead. Her toes curled against the need. And now her breasts were tight, screaming for him to do something— anything—to ease the unforgiving pleasure demanding release inside her.

And she'd barely been here five minutes.

"Tonight, my mission is to see how dark I can make those sweet pink nipples."

Before Morgan could even ponder what that meant, Jack's tongue slid over a hard point, once, twice. He primed it with unhurried strokes, sending her heart rate into turmoil. Certain he meant to slowly kill her. Morgan moaned.

Jack sucked the peak without mercy, as if he could inhale her at once. The clasp of his teeth both above and below her nipple anchored her in place for the hot suction of his mouth. Equal parts pleasure and pain exploded sensation through her breasts, darting out in all directions through her body until, like a flash, it burst between her legs.

She gasped. In response, he bit harder, sucked more strongly in seemingly endless draws. Fresh pain bombarded her like icy pinpricks, drawing her nipples tighter. She whimpered.

"Take the pain, *cher*. Take it for me. You can."

Disappointing him was not an option for some reason. Nodding, Morgan pressed her lips together.

Jack swept the same nipple back in his mouth, clamping down tightly with his teeth again as he drew on her breast with remorseless suction. The pain shot through her system again. This time, a thick slice of pleasure followed, shocking and scrumptious. The whimper that had escaped her once before became a moan.

Her nipples would be sore tomorrow—and she didn't care. What he was doing made her body ache yet soar, made her tremble with erotic fear and sexual need all at once.

This was everything she'd ever dreamed in her deep, dark midnight desires.

A moment later, Morgan felt the grip of his fingers tormenting her other nipple in a tight press. He twisted the hard bud, wrenching another moan out of her. A tight pinch coincided with an erotic bite on her other nipple.

She gasped.

"That's it," he coaxed, easing away. "Pretty."

He teased the wet nipple with the soft pad of his thumb. Pleasure, pain, pleasure again. The lines blurred. All she knew was how much she wanted Jack to cover her, fill her, make her come.

Make her his, God help her, for more than tonight.

Lifting her hips, Morgan wriggled them, enticing him, silently pleading.

Laughter rumbled from his chest. "Oh, I'm tempted. But not yet, *cher*. Not for a long while."

She sounded a fresh moan of protest—until something sharp with little metal teeth bit into her damp nipple. A gasp tore past her moan and shoved its way past her throat.

"Oh, God!" she breathed against the pain.

"I know. Take a deep breath. I have a feeling you'll come to appreciate the bite of the clamp . . . sooner rather than later."

No. It was horrendously painful, bordering on cruel. She took a deep breath. It didn't help. Another breath.

Jack lowered his mouth to the other nipple, the one his fingers had toyed with previously. A soft suck, a gentle lave. The contrasts between sensations sent her soaring. Pain balanced with pleasure. The ache behind her clit tightened again, so intense. Her vagina clenched, so achingly empty. Morgan arched up. Her hips moved restlessly. What was happening to her?

She had never been so aroused in her life.

The pain biting into her clamped nipple began to ease as she grew accustomed to the sensation. The sting turned to a pressurized numbness. And Jack's attention to the hard little point in his mouth grew rougher.

"Jack!" she cried out, her fingers digging into the table's black leather and the padding beneath.

For a split second, his mouth left her breast. He slapped the flat of his fingers across her mound again. Sensation ratchetted through her body. A crescendo of tingles rose in her body like a scream. A pending climax bubbled between her legs, and she raised her hips in offering again.

"That's not what you call me," he growled.

"Sir." She panted. "Sir, please . . ."

"I'll fuck you, but not until I'm ready. Not until *you're* ready. Now be quiet before I turn you over and spank your ass."

His words dashed her hopes for relief. She sank her teeth deep into her lip, trying to hold in a groan of protest. It was soon forgotten as Jack returned his teeth to her nipple, nipped down, sucked hard, and groaned.

His voice vibrated deep inside her, shooting all the way to her clit. She was on a torture rack of pleasure. Amazing sensations piled one on top of the other, smothering anything that resembled thought or dissent. She ached beyond anything she'd ever dreamed, anything she thought possible. And he had yet to even touch her vagina, much less penetrate it.

Then another clamp bit into her other nipple, digging into skin, dredging up even more response. A fireball of pleasure darted straight from her breasts, down between her legs, adding to the conflagration already burning. If Jack touched her there, even once, she feared she would launch like a rocket, no matter how much he demanded she hold it back. The orgasm was huge, so enormous it would swallow her whole. Morgan fought against it, shaking her head in desperation. Sweat poured off her. She gripped the table tighter.

The ache just kept building and building. When would it crest?

"And now those nipples are a deep, demanding red. Beautiful," he murmured.

Every breath was between a pant and a moan when Jack uncuffed her wrists and ankles. He helped her rubbery legs to the floor. In passing, she wondered what he had planned, but realized it didn't matter. He would give her amazing pleasure. And sooner or later, he would detonate this awesome ache roiling inside her.

Willingly, she folded herself into his arms. He dipped her head back and dove into her mouth, devouring. It was a kiss of hunger, a kiss of possession. Morgan responded, meeting him halfway, tangling her tongue with his.

"You challenge my self-control, *cher*, just by being so fucking beautiful and submissive. No one has ever pushed me so hard, so fast," he rasped against her throat, then moved up to nip at her lobe. "I can't wait to get deep inside you and open you up to all new pleasures."

Restlessly, Morgan shifted her weight from one foot to the other. She could hardly wait for Jack to get deep inside of her, too. She hoped now. Right now.

He spun her around and grabbed the strappy edges of her crotchless panties. The moisture pooling inside her and drenching the delicate fabric gushed out, spreading wetness down the insides of her thighs.

"You're so juicy, like a sweet ripe peach," he praised as he bent her over the table.

She whimpered as her clamped nipples made contact with the surface of the table and a fresh jolt of pleasure-pain screamed down her spine, into her drenched channel. She tensed, wanting to fight, wanting to reach her own hand between her legs and give her clit a furious rub until she exploded. Instinct told her such an action would bring down enormous punishment. With another moan, she managed to refrain.

"Such a good girl. So beautifully submissive, *cher*. Do you want me to fuck you?"

Morgan didn't even care what she said anymore as long as Jack made the ache go away. "Yes," she gasped. "Yes, sir. Please . . ."

With her feet flat on the floor, Jack removed her thong, peeling the damp fabric from her flesh. Then he cuffed one ankle at the corner of the table and licked his way up her thigh. Closer, closer he strayed to the heart of her ache. She burned, yearned, moaned as his mouth neared her pussy.

He only laughed and bent to cuff her other ankle, then laved off the juice coating that thigh—still providing no relief to her weeping vagina. Instead, he stepped away for a moment, his footsteps alerting her to his retreat. Movement, the soft clash of plastic on plastic, the opening of a drawer. God, why wouldn't he hurry?

"Ah, yes," he muttered, seemingly satisfied. Then he turned back to her. "You've earned a reward."

*Yes!* Thrill and need and longing all twined together at his words, wrapping around her clit, spreading a new warmth to her heart. She was absurdly glad that she'd pleased him, and insanely proud of herself for submitting so totally. And she absolutely wanted that reward.

The rustle of clothes came next, brushing against her anticipation. Naked. He had to be naked. She wriggled her ass, praying it would entice him.

"The minute I praise you, you turn naughty." His mock chastisement came accompanied with a playful swat to her backside.

The laughter in his voice had her gritting her teeth.

"I'm losing my patience, and I've already lost my sense of humor," she bitched, knowing it would piss him off. But she couldn't stop herself. He'd pushed her too far.

Jack said nothing, merely stepped up behind her and blanketed her backside. An inferno of male muscle and musky skin enveloped her. The strong, thick column of his cock nudged its way between her cheeks. Morgan clawed at the padded table.

Only to have Jack grab her wrists and cuff them again.

Before the echo of the last click finished resounding in the room, the sound of his hearty smack on her ass took its place.

Fire heated her cheek, then seeped down toward her needy pussy. He was going to tease her some more? Damn it, she'd had enough.

"Jack. Sir . . ." she corrected. "I—I can't take it anymore. Please, fuck me."

"In my time, in my way," he growled, then punctuated the statement with another smack to her ass.

Fresh heat bloomed inside her, pushing past her sudden rush of temper.

Suddenly, she felt his fingers probing her ass, wriggling between her cheeks, bringing something cold and liquid with them.

*Lube? Oh, God.*

Her heartbeat revved up like an Indy 500 winner's engine. He'd said just this morning that he intended to bury himself in her ass and settle in for a nice long ride. Did he—?

The press of two lubricated fingers inside her ass cut off the rest of the question. The stretching and burning of tight, virgin flesh hit her first. The pressure followed, along with a sense of fullness. And when he manipulated the fingers in and out of her body with a slow drag, then, oh hell, the pleasure completely shut her brain down.

"That's it." He gripped her hip with his free hand and encouraged her hips back, down onto his invading fingers.

She moaned.

"You like that?"

Almost without thought, almost against her will, she gasped, "Yes."

His fingers stilled. "Yes . . . ?"

"Yes, sir."

"Excellent. Let's find out just how wet you are."

Jack lifted his hand from her hip and brought it around Morgan's body . . . right onto the swollen, hard knot of her clit.

She shouted as tingles tore through her belly with his first touch.

Fingers pumping in her ass, swirling on her clit. Sensation overload threatened. She felt the blood surging between her legs, along with the dangerous ramping up of pleasure. She clamped down, trying to stop, but it was no use. She felt the first flutters of orgasm begin.

So did Jack.

"No coming yet," he commanded, withdrawing his fingers from her clit, her ass.

"Sir, please. Please!"

"You beg so sweetly, how can I refuse?" he purred in her ear. "But I must . . ."

He retreated a moment, and she mourned the loss of his spiced flesh over hers, his body heat seeping into her skin. A tear, a snap. A condom, she realized. Thank God!

But she had only a moment to celebrate before he pried the cheeks of her ass open and she felt the broad tip of his lubricated cock pressing against her anus.

"Push down and take me inside you. I'll make you come so hard you'll scream the walls down."

*Yes. Please, yes!*

Morgan tilted her hips back and pushed with her muscles. The fat head of his cock slid in, pressing, burning. The pain. Oh, God . . . It wouldn't work, wouldn't fit. Every time he moved, even breathed, the pain rushed over her. In desperation, she clawed at the table again, moaning.

Then he glided past the tight ring of muscle and tunneled his way inside, slowly. So slowly. Morgan gasped as he forged each new inch into her body, deeper, deeper, in a seemingly endless, pleasure pain–filled slide.

When she stood on her tiptoes, certain she couldn't take a centimeter more of his cock, she felt the gentle slap of his balls against her. He was in to the hilt.

"You're so fucking tight," he groaned. "You're going to rip at my composure every time you breathe."

Morgan certainly hoped so. That pending orgasm still bubbled just under the surface of her skin, waiting for one more touch to her clit, one long stroke of his cock.

Instead, Jack gripped her hips with insistent fingers, drew in a harsh breath, then another.

"I'm not going to last long," he croaked. "Neither are you."

With that, he pulled back, almost to the point of withdrawal, then sank all the way inside the depths of her ass again. The wicked, burning pressure had Morgan pounding a fist on the table. Pleasure and pain. Forbidden and fabulous. Oh, she could lose herself in sensation like this. Close. So damn close . . .

He ripped off the blindfold then. She blinked, trying to get accustomed to the haze of red light overhead. Being able to see again didn't blunt her sense of touch or smell at all. Instead, she could see a mirror beside the door, and the strain apparent in Jack's reflection as he held back, all corded muscles in his shoulders, the stress of restraint in his neck. Veins bulged in his forearms as white-knuckled fingers gripped her hips.

"Watch us," he commanded. "Watch me fuck your tight virgin ass."

Morgan watched, helpless to do anything else as he pushed in, pulled out, in long, strong glides, filling her with mind-numbing pleasure so hot, so huge, she could barely take it in. She whimpered, transfixed by the sight, by the feel of him inside her.

"One last thing and I'll let you come, *cher*."

Morgan licked dry lips. "Yes. Anything, sir."

"In the fantasies you told Andrew, did you mention being tied down?"

"Yes, sir."

"Did you tell him you wanted to have your nipples clamped?"

"No."

"Do you like it?" He reached up and gave a gentle tug on the chain between the clamps.

Great swells of pain and ecstasy tumbled through her nipples, spun through her body, swelling her clit again. "Yes."

"Did you tell him you wanted him to fuck your ass?"

"Yes, sir."

And Jack did, two more bittersweet, slow, strong thrusts into her, all the way to the hilt. Morgan gasped, moaned. She couldn't take any more.

"Please, sir!"

"Almost . . ." he promised. "What else did you tell him you wanted?"

*No.* If she told him that . . . No. What would he think?

"Th-that's all," she lied.

He smacked her ass and plunged into her with a series of quick, harsh strokes. Morgan cried out. More heat thrown onto the ever-burning fire between her legs. Damn, why couldn't she come? The climax burning inside her was bigger than anything she'd ever felt. She should have tumbled over long ago.

Had her body already learned to wait for his command?

"Lie to me again and I'll stroke myself, come at your feet, and leave you to ache all night."

Morgan swallowed, never doubting he'd do it. "Please don't make me say it, sir."

"Last chance," he grated out, stilling his thrusts completely. "Or I'm leaving."

She squeezed her eyes shut, grappling helplessly between her body's needs and her fears. Would he judge her harshly? Would he think she was a depraved whore, too?

"Tell me," he cajoled.

With a gentle pinch, Jack removed the clamps from her nipples. Blood rushed back into them, swelling them with a burst of need. Yes! Then the sensation rocketed down to her clit.

Just as it hit her there, he reached beneath her again, fingers hovering so close to her aching bundle of nerves, she could feel the heat of his hand. But still, he didn't touch her clit. Morgan moaned. All she had to do was be honest about one itty-bitty secret and he'd give her the best orgasm of her life.

This was Jack. He understood her fantasies. Clearly, he had some of his own. He'd given her everything her body secretly desired, so far. He would help her deal with this, too. She had to believe he would. Had to have trust . . .

"Two men," she blurted as she opened her eyes to find Jack's gaze in the mirror by the door.

Instead, she found Deke standing in the portal, watching them.

Her eyes widened. She bucked under Jack, trying to get away. But cuffed at the wrist and ankle, she wasn't going anywhere.

Neither was Deke. He stood and stared as Jack tunneled into her ass. The heat of brutal arousal on his face, doubled with the thick spike of cock in his pants, burned into her. Deke's blue eyes locked with hers, and pristine, pure need burst through her body.

She tore her gaze away, found Jack's in the mirror to Deke's right. Her gaze connected with his dark one. Locked in place.

"What?" Jack barked.

"I want two men." The words tumbled out of her.

Jack grabbed her hips with renewed urgency and shoved his way inside again. "Fucking you at once?"

"Yes," she managed to squeeze out on a pleasured moan.

A curse slipped out under Deke's breath as he adjusted the very tight fly of his jeans. Morgan's heart beat so hard, she barely heard it over the roaring.

"Look at him!" Jack roared, reaching around her to lift her chin, forcing her to meet Deke's gaze.

And he stared back, his denim-blue stare pouring over her bare flesh like hot acid, scorching her, as Jack tunneled with relentless, measured strokes in her sensitive back channel. She felt each hard inch and every vein of his cock, the heavy swell of his glans scraping past all her nerve endings as he shoved his way home, propelling her teeth-grittingly close to orgasm.

"You'd want Deke's cock in your pussy while I'm deep in your ass?" he rasped in her ear.

Even the words cranked her need up so tight it neared pain.

"Yes, sir." She sobbed, clawing at the table. The idea turned the burn between her legs into an inferno that was about to explode into a conflagration beyond her imagining. "God, yes!"

"Jack, get your fingers on her clit before the poor girl dies. She needs to come," Deke pointed out, his voice calm and even, despite the arousal flaming from him.

"Don't tell me how to fuck my woman," Jack growled.

"You're pushing her too far, too fast. She's not used to this. You're about to break her."

Behind her, Jack snarled something distinctly unpleasant to Deke. But he took his friend's suggestion. For that, Morgan thanked God.

The second Jack's fingers touched her clit, the massive ache between her legs converged into a hard, dark ball of fire licking at her restraint, tormenting her very skin.

"Come!" he shouted.

The sensations concentrated, blurred with pain, burned from the inside out as she burst like a thousand suns.

Morgan screamed as she convulsed around Jack, clamping down on his cock. The sharp crest of the orgasm slammed into her, and her surroundings disappeared until all she knew was Jack and pleasure and a release so sublime, so perfect, she lost all sense of hearing, the need to breathe. Vision blurred. Her heart threatened to burst from her chest.

But she felt Jack's hands tighten on her, felt his teeth in her neck, then the hardening of his erection deep inside her. A long, harsh groan tore from his chest.

He slowed. Stopped. Morgan slumped on the table, beyond exhausted. Still, she was conscious of Deke's gaze hot on her body.

Worse, she felt every bit of Jack's tension behind her.

Suddenly, he withdrew from her body, tore off the condom, and tossed it in the trash can in the corner. "Son of a bitch!"

Jack threw Deke a filthy look as he padded to the door completely naked.

What . . . ? Morgan watched Jack through stunned eyes. Where was he going?

Once he reached the threshold, Jack turned to her with a fierce, furious stare, as if she'd betrayed him somehow. His pain and anger singed her in that one glance.

Then he slammed out the door.

# Chapter Thirteen

THE silence in the wake of Jack's exit deafened Morgan. Down the hall, he slammed the door to the bathroom. Despite being strapped to the table, she flinched.

With a long sigh, Deke shoved away from the wall. Morgan watched him watch her as he drew closer, really understanding the feeling of a deer in headlights. What must the man think of her, after she'd admitted she wanted him buried inside her clinging sex while Jack pumped her ass full of his cock? She was better off not knowing. Yes, according to Jack, Deke was into *ménage*, but still, what a thing to confess out loud. At least Deke seemed incredibly unruffled by everything . . .

Unlike Jack.

Her worst nightmare had come true; she'd given in to Jack and the submissive nature he swore she had, then told him her fantasy. And he'd freaked. Not like Andrew had. Jack hadn't called her a depraved whore and suggested she get professional help. But he'd been blazingly pissed. He couldn't have made that any more clear if he'd drawn her a picture.

God, she'd ruined everything! What the hell was wrong with her? If her ultimate fantasy shocked even Jack, she must be totally, terribly wicked.

Morgan resisted the urge to close her eyes and cry. She'd done that once before, after Andrew slammed her. Tears didn't do any damn good. Shedding them over this particular fantasy and all the associated problems wasn't happening again.

Jack himself had been swearing to her that her wants were perfectly normal and nothing to be ashamed of or embarrassed about. *Liar*, she wanted to shout. She saved her breath.

So much for all his assurances.

Damn it, these fantasies kept screwing up her life, wracking her with guilt, chasing men off. She had to move past them, get them out of her head. Somehow.

Deke rounded the table, and Morgan watched his progress, craning her gaze over her shoulder as he settled behind her without a word. He could see . . . everything. The long line of her spine. The wet heat of her sex swollen by Jack's touch. The bare globes of her ass. A fresh wave of mortification rolled over her, along with something else she didn't want to name. She closed her eyes.

Clamped at wrists and ankles, Morgan could do nothing but let him look and absorb his heat as he stood directly behind her. In exactly the same spot Jack had occupied mere minutes ago. Her breath hitched.

In silence, Deke leaned over her, blanketing her cooling skin. The soft cotton of his shirt and the hard muscles of his chest covered her bare back. Hard as iron, his jeans-covered cock burned hot between the cheeks of her ass. A spark of shocking heat, too strong to ignore, blended with her humiliation.

That alone had to prove how twisted she was. Why couldn't she just . . . turn it off?

His hot palm fell to her waist, settling in the curve with warm fingers that soon dipped down the swell of her naked hip. He nuzzled his face in her neck, and Morgan drew in another shaky breath. Oh God, what was he going to do? She was already stripped, bound—defenseless. The only things keeping him from violating her was a button, a zipper, and his conscience.

Jack's warning that Deke wasn't a nice guy rang in her head. Morgan panicked.

This huge blond stranger was going to touch her, seduce her. Fuck her. She couldn't do a damn thing to stop him. Fantasies of *ménage* aside, she didn't want it or him—not without Jack.

She tensed against her trembling limbs and warned, "Deke . . ."

Behind her, his cock only got harder. "Now I know why Jack is so crazy for you. You smell fantastic."

His voice was like a caress feathering its way down her spine in a sensual vibration. She shivered. Broad fingers clamped harder at her hip to keep her still.

"Damn it, get me out of here!" she demanded.

"Shh," he whispered into her hair, the pad of his thumb caressing down her hip a fraction. "Patience, doll."

"Screw patience! Being used and abandoned doesn't bring out my best virtues. I just want the hell out of here."

Deke sighed. His free hand caught the latch at her right wrist. He repeated the process on her left. Then he eased back, withdrawing the solid heat of his body away from her back. He knelt and unlatched her ankles.

"Can you stand?" His gaze, which shone with both mischief and concern, snagged hers.

He'd let her go? Just like that? Relief fell out of her in a shaky breath. Morgan stood straight up and zipped her gaze over her shoulder to find Deke adjusting his fly.

"You're gorgeous, and I'm still a guy." A smile flirted with the corners of his wide mouth. "I'd never fuck you without Jack. Scout's honor." He held up three fingers in the Scouting symbol.

But he'd fuck her *with* Jack? Morgan shook her head at the ridiculous question. After Jack's reaction to that very suggestion . . . She had a better chance of being nominated for sainthood. And her body leaping at the prospect . . . damned annoying and totally irrelevant.

She turned to face Deke, crossing her arms over her chest to cover her exposed nipples through the cutouts in the indecent bra. Deke hadn't touched her . . . but she still wasn't the sort of siren who stood basically bare-assed naked in front of virtual strangers.

"Um, thanks, but you don't look much like a Boy Scout."

"I wasn't," he admitted. "I just meant general principle and all. Besides, you've had enough for the night."

In a flash, the evening replayed in her head. Jack coming. Jack cursing. Jack leaving.

Damn him! Granted, it wasn't Deke's fault—Jack should be taking all the blame—but he wasn't here. Deke was the nearest testosterone-based mammal, so he'd have to do as her temper's whipping boy.

"You think?" she shot back sarcastically as she stepped away from the table.

Her legs collapsed out from under her. If Deke hadn't been quick to reach out and grab her, she would have fallen in an ignominious heap to the cold cement floor.

With a curse, he lifted her into his arms, up against the hard heat of his chest. "You have every right to be pissed at Jack."

Morgan covered her swollen nipples with her arms and glanced up into the unreadable angles of Deke's strong-boned face. "You're not going to take Jack's side?"

He glanced down at her with a scowl. "Hell, no."

Spoken as if that should be obvious. Didn't guys usually have each other's backs, purely for principle?

With footsteps that barely registered on the hardwood floor, he carried her down the hall, past that closed bathroom door, to the bedroom, and set her on the rumpled bed. Gently, he drew the sheet up to her shoulders, covering her exposed nipples.

"Hang tight. I'll be back."

Frowning, she watched him turn and leave the room with a sort of military precision that shouted of his years in the army. He was a soldier. A warrior. Big and ready to fight. Ready to protect. Ready to fuck. So like Jack. But Deke seemed easier to talk to. Why did she want enigmatic Jack so much more?

Morgan sighed. Apparently, Jack flipped her switch because she needed more challenges in her life. She scoffed in the silence. Yeah, that was it exactly . . .

On those same, mostly silent footsteps, Deke returned with a small tube in his hands. He sank down on the edge of the bed and brushed the hair back from her forehead.

"I know you're upset. Jack broke your trust. He made you a promise to care for you and your pleasure. Tonight, he didn't do a great job. There are reasons. Jack will have to share those with you. Not my place to do it." He shrugged and set the tube aside. "I can't do much about how you feel inside, but I can help the outside. Sit up."

Dazed as she sorted through all of Deke's words, Morgan complied, holding the sheet above her breasts. Jack had reasons? What the hell reasons could he possibly have for hurtling her high into the sphere of pleasure, then tossing her into the pit of despair? For making her feel like a freak yet again?

Before she could sort anything out, Deke reached around her back with one hand. With a single pinch of his fingers, her bra with the handy cutouts came unhooked. As Morgan gasped, the straps fell down her arms. He ignored her and set a gentle hand on her shoulder to lay her back, then drew the sheet down to her waist.

Morgan swallowed hard and raised her hands to cover herself. Deke anticipated her and grabbed her wrists, forcing them back to her sides.

"Let go," she snapped.

He leaned over her and heaved a long-suffering sigh. The clasp of his fingers around her wrists was surprisingly gentle. "Look, I just watched you come hard enough to cause an earthquake while my best friend fucked your ass. Do you think we could drop the modest virgin routine? I'm trying to take care of you so I can go knock some sense into our mutual pal."

Hmm. Put like that, Deke had a really good point.

With a sigh, Morgan stopped fighting and relaxed into the mattress.

Shaking his head, Deke reached for the tube he'd set beside her. After a quick turn of the cap, he pulled it off and, with nimble fingers, squeezed the bottle. A puddle of clear oil collected in his palm. Deke rubbed his big palms together.

Then he put one on each of her breasts.

Morgan gasped, tensing, and zipped her gaze up to his face. Deke ignored her and focused on his task.

The oil, warmed by his skin, permeated her breasts, coated her sore nipples. Until he soothed them with the liquid balm, Morgan hadn't realized how raw they actually were.

But as he rubbed his palms directly over the aching points, friction sent a zing of reaction straight through her body. Morgan closed her eyes, partly in shame. The other part of her reaction she didn't want to think about. What the hell was wrong with her?

Then he changed the stroke, concentrating the oil just above and below the angry red tips, rolling them gently between thumbs and forefingers, massaging in a slow, hypnotic rhythm. And with every roll, pull, caress, the sensation built into something uncomfortably but undeniably like arousal.

"Morgan." His voice was deeper, husky now.

She tried to ignore the pull of his voice. But it echoed in her head, throbbing in time with his tender strokes across her sore nipples.

Surrendering the losing battle, she opened her eyes and shot him a warning. Red flags of color dusted his cheekbones. His eyes now burned a deep midnight blue. Yet he removed his hands from her breasts, arched a brow, and flashed her a self-deprecating smile.

"Now I know exactly why Jack is so over the moon for you. Sizzle and submission all in one soft sigh." He drew in a rough breath. "Roll over."

"Over the moon for me?" She tossed her hands in the air. "You saw the same man I did, right? The one who cursed at me and stomped out of the room for telling him . . . Well, I should have kept that to myself. But his kind of behavior doesn't say anything except *get lost*."

"Doll, I've known Jack nearly ten years. We went to Basic together. We've fucked women together, and the idea has never bothered him in the least. Until you."

Jack had participated in a *ménage* before? With Deke? Shock punched her in the stomach, stealing her breath. Her mind raced back over the conversation she and Jack had once had about Deke's . . . preferences. It made sense that Jack knew about Deke's sex life because he'd been part of it at some point. Even if the idea seared her with jealousy.

But if he'd participated in the past, why did he suddenly find the idea so objectionable?

"If *ménage* is your fantasy, Jack needed to hear that," Deke assured.

"But—"

"He seemed pissed? Yeah, it's his issue, not yours." He sighed. "Roll over."

She hesitated, but Deke didn't notice. He rose from the bed and disappeared from the room. With a frown, she stared at his retreating back.

Odd man. Gentle, despite getting quite the floor show tonight. Seemingly calm and rational and normal, despite having three in his bed all the time. He was clearly aroused and doing nothing more than taking care of the marks another man had left on her body. He never pressed her for more, despite her own reaction to him, when most men would have viewed the first blush of her arousal as a green light.

Then he tried to soothe her feelings, assure her she was meaningful to Jack. While Morgan knew he had that part all wrong, she appreciated him trying to make her feel better.

Rolling to her stomach, Morgan lay her head on the pillow with a weary sigh. A ragged inhalation later . . . and she smelled Jack. Musk, leather, mystery, man. His scent never failed to work through her bloodstream like heady wine and drug her with desire. Only this time, it came with a pang of loss.

Upon hearing her deepest fantasy, Jack had left her. He probably didn't want her back. And that damn urge to cry now tightening her throat was really pissing her off.

Footsteps sounded on the hardwood floor. Morgan tensed until she recognized the cadence of Deke's footfalls, longer and slower than Jack's, a bit more silent. She relaxed, somehow relieved and disappointed at once.

With brisk hands, he covered the globes of her ass and parted them. Morgan clenched against him and opened her mouth to ask what the hell he thought he was doing. But the warm comfort of a hot washcloth covered her back entrance, and he rubbed gently, wiping away the excess lube.

"If you're sore later, a warm bath will help, but you should be okay," he murmured, easing her onto her back again. "Sleep now."

Morgan nodded, watching with wide eyes as he leaned in. Was he going to . . . ? Yes, he was.

A moment later, Deke laid his mouth over hers. The sweet press of lips lasted through one breath, two. Dry, almost chaste. Still somehow, he managed to convey caring, comfort, a bare hint of want. Then, with a light brush of his lips over hers, he drew back.

"Yeah, now I know exactly why Jack is wild for you," he said with a bittersweet curl to his mouth as he rose to his feet.

"Wait!" She grabbed at his hand. "How did you come to terms with it? How did you learn to be okay with . . ."

"*Ménage?*" He guessed it right on the first try and shrugged. "At seventeen, the first time I heard a woman scream in ecstasy under double penetration. There's nothing like knowing the perfect way to drive a woman absolutely wild."

"But it's not exactly what normal, everyday people next door do."

Deke crossed his arms over his chest. "Luc and I have neighbors. I doubt they know we share women, but I don't give a shit if they do."

"Luc?"

"My cousin. It's his place. I crash there now that I've been discharged. He's made it all warm and cozy and is just waiting on the right woman to come play house with us."

Morgan doubted a deaf woman would have missed the mockery in Deke's voice. "You don't think it's possible to find someone?"

She felt sad for him. The regret in his eyes told her how badly he wanted just that.

"What woman in her right mind wants to live with a temperamental chef and a former drill sergeant? Alone, either of us would drive a woman to drink. Together . . ." He shrugged. "It works for a night or two. It's enough."

Deke was lying. To her. To himself. His wants had cost him a chance at happiness, too.

"And right now, it's irrelevant." He busted in on her thoughts. "We were talking about you and Jack . . ."

Clearly, Deke didn't want to talk about himself any more than she wanted to talk about herself.

"You'll have to accept your own desires to be happy. And you shouldn't settle for less. Jack will come around, and he'll help you. I can't tell you when or how it will happen or what will make you okay with your needs. I just know you'll manage."

Morgan tried to rein in her frustration. Why did everyone keep insisting that the answer was inside her, was as simple as accepting herself? Clearly, if Jack was going to curse her and tear out of a room as if the hounds of hell were at his back, it wasn't that simple.

Damn it, she'd been feeling so good about her choice to come to Jack's playroom. The way he'd touched her, the pleasure in his touch, the praise in every caress, made her feel so accepted, like everything transpiring in his playroom between them was right. And then . . . then, he'd disparaged her wants. That had to mean there *was* something wrong with her, right?

Damn, had she ever been more confused?

For Deke's sake, she just nodded. "I . . . Thanks."

A mere word of appreciation seemed inadequate, given that he'd seen to her physical comfort, treated her without lust . . . but still like a woman. Tried to answer her question, but bared his soul instead. His gentle attention made her feel feminine and cared for, and was a balm to Jack's rejection.

Smiling, Morgan sat up on her knees and reached for the broad planes of his cheeks. "It's not much, but thank you."

Then she settled her mouth over his, a light dusting of feminine sighs, warm lips, and thanks before pulling away. It was odd, really, this . . . bond of understanding sprinkled with a light dusting of desire. Morgan didn't understand it any more than she understood him. But suddenly she was grateful for both.

"You're welcome." He stepped away, smoothing a broad palm down the cascade of her fiery hair. "Try resting now. You should be able to with some assurances, by the way. Hard to believe after everything that's happened, but I came out here because no one answered the phone. I wanted to tell you two that your stalker appears to have left Louisiana. Tell Jack, because I'll be too busy beating his ass, that the creep trashed your fiancé's house three days ago and tried to set fire to your house in L.A. yesterday."

"Oh, my . . ." Poor Brandon. He was so proud of that house and hadn't asked for any trouble. He'd merely been trying to help. And her own house . . . "Damn it!"

"I know," Deke soothed. "It sucks, but the good news is, with anger like his, if the bastard knew where you were right now, he'd be out here hunting you down, not hopping all over the country trying to draw you out by destroying property."

Deke had a point, and it seemed to solidify the rationale that Reggie was her stalker. She hadn't called him in days, and he'd been one of the few people who knew she'd made it as far as Louisiana. And he'd never had a good temper on the best of days. Was he disturbed? Obsessed? Probably both of the above. She sighed.

Until now, she'd been safe because she'd been staying with Jack. But today, everything had changed. Given Jack's rejection—yet another man who had snubbed her after hearing her fantasies—and Deke's information, she was ready to take action.

If Reggie had made his move, maybe . . . maybe it was time to make hers.

* * *

JACK had predicted Deke would make his way onto the wraparound porch, where night was settling over the swamp and the cold February air twisted over his bare skin. After a long shower, he'd wrapped himself in the robe Morgan had left on the back of the bathroom door. Damn thing smelled like her and gave him another fucking hard-on.

Trying to blot out both the feel of her tight ass around his cock and the stark pain on her face as he'd stomped out of the playroom, Jack gripped his bottle of beer and turned to his friend for the verbal ass-whipping he knew he deserved.

"You don't have to say it," Jack assured him, taking a long swallow of his brew.

"Oh, but I want to." Deke settled into the chair beside his and glared. "You behaved like a stupid prick."

"You're right. Morgan just . . . shocked the hell out of me. I had no idea she was harboring fantasies about *ménage*. She can barely wrap her mind around the idea of submitting to me. That she's thought of servicing two men . . ." He shrugged. "It blew me away. I reacted before I thought."

"You betrayed her trust and made promises you didn't fucking keep."

"You're right again." Jack scrubbed a hand across his tired face. "Shit. It was bad enough that I turned my back on her. I damn near punished her for having the fantasy. She probably feels wretched and rejected."

"You don't want to share her."

"No, I don't," Jack admitted, imbibing another long swallow of his beer. Absently, he wondered how long it would take him to get drunk and if he could forget about behaving like such an ass if he did.

"Because of Kayla?"

Nothing like getting right to the heart of the matter. His ex-wife's betrayal of their marriage vows with one of his closest friends had carved a pit of fury in his gut that had just kept filling up with ire and hate over the years. Now it was thinly lined with a scar that enraged him at the thought of another man touching Morgan. Hell, he hadn't cared much about Kayla, and knowing she'd fucked around on him had nearly driven him to a killing rage.

He cared about Morgan much more.

"When it comes to Morgan, I want to be a selfish bastard and keep all her sass and submission and sweet smiles to myself. I want to be the only man who wraps his hands in that gorgeous flame-colored hair and watches while she takes me deep in her mouth. I want to be the only man who tastes her pussy, feels the bite of her tight ass on my cock." He blew out a long breath. "But that's not what she wants."

"You love this girl?"

Jack squeezed his eyes shut and gripped the cold bottle in his hand so tightly, he wondered if it might break. How could he answer that when he'd never experienced love before? If feeling euphoric at her happiness and somber at her sadness, being willing to kill anyone who threatened her, and kicking himself in the ass for cursing her desires and crushing her burgeoning sexuality, then . . .

"Yeah. I'm pretty sure that's the case. From the beginning, it's just been . . . so different with her." He barked with bitter laughter. "Hell,

I even dreamed about her *before* I knew her. Her body, her smell, the way she makes me feel. From the first, I felt like she had me by the balls, but I'm thinking maybe what she's holding is a bit farther north."

"You've got to make this right for her."

"I just don't . . ." He heaved a long sigh and started over. "I intend to claim her, and I know it's my responsibility to see to her every desire. But I honestly don't know if I could see someone else—you—fuck her and not want to rip your balls off."

"If you love her and you want to see her happy, you've got to give her what she needs. Or she's never going to be whole. And what you have is going to be a lie."

So calm, so rational. So perfectly correct. Damn Deke!

"Not only that," Deke went on, "but whatever it is she's holding back from you is something she'll never give if you're not fulfilling her."

"Holding back?" Jack paused. A sick knot twisted his gut with apprehension. He still hadn't reached her, not totally. He'd hoped . . . But no. So apparently, he'd hoped in vain. How could he make her his if she wouldn't surrender completely?

But then, Deke's words reminded him that she was only part of the recipe. The other part had to come from him.

"C'mon, Jack. You know what I'm talking about. Don't you? You've seen it? Felt it?"

"Do you take some perverse pleasure in being right and throwing that in my face?" Jack sighed and took another long swallow of his cold beer. "Where is Morgan?"

"I tucked her into bed, safe and sound, and I'm hoping she's asleep. She looked worn-out."

"Did you cop a cheap feel?"

Deke smiled at Jack's growl. "I might have. She's a hard woman not to want."

Jack knew that too damn well. While he didn't like Deke touching her, he had no one to blame but himself for running out on her. So he let it go . . . this time.

"Morgan is like a soft stroke to the cock and a kick in the teeth all at once," Jack muttered.

"You're not the only man who loves her. She's got a fiancé back in Houston, right?"

Brandon. Son of a bitch! As if he needed the complication of that pansy-assed bastard.

"Yes."

"What are you going to do about him? With him in the picture, she's not yours to keep."

"Thanks for the reminder," he shot back sarcastically.

Taking Morgan from Brandon would be the best revenge of all, way better than simply emailing video footage of them fucking to her esteemed fiancé. But that wasn't the reason Jack was determined to win her. Not even close.

He just wanted her all to himself. Today, tomorrow, every morning, every night. His.

Deke rose with a quirk of a smile. "What are friends for?"

*Indeed*, he thought, watching Deke amble down the steps, get into his boat, and push away from the dock.

For endless moments, he sat there. And damn it, he couldn't even manage to get drunk. Instead, he tried to sort through the tangle of shit swirling in his gut: fear, anger, possessiveness, jealousy, determination, concern, need . . . love.

When his feet finally turned to ice, his stomach started growling, and he thought Morgan might have rested sufficiently to talk, he stalked into the house, threw his empty beer bottle away, and headed for the bedroom.

Only he didn't find Morgan.

Her scent lingering in the room told him she hadn't been gone long. The ruby pendant he'd given her lay abandoned on his pillow and told him more effectively than words that she'd left.

He'd lost her before he had her.

And if he didn't find her fucking fast, he could lose her to a stalker's jealous rage for good.

# Chapter Fourteen

"YOU can stop hiding now," Deke said, laughter lilting his voice.

Morgan stiffened under the tarp on the floor of the little boat. Deke was talking to her. Crap! How on earth had he known she was here?

His rhythmic paddling ceased, and now the boat sat stationary, the thick waters of the swamp splattering against the sides of his small metal vessel. Had they arrived at the little dock outside Lafayette?

"I know you're there, Morgan," Deke said as he lifted the tarp off of her.

The night's cold breeze suddenly swept across her half-dressed form as she looked up—way, way up—at Deke. The silvery moon backlit his towering frame, shadowing his angled cheekbones and strong, square chin. Amusement played across his grayed features.

"How did you know?"

"I had to step over you to get into the boat." He laughed. "The tarp hid you, but the displacement of the boat made it obvious someone was on board . . . and not a big someone. That left you as my only suspect."

Damn it, she'd tried so hard to get away from Jack, from the tangled morass her life had become, without anyone knowing.

With a chuckle, Deke bent down and helped her to her feet. "You look adorably frustrated, doll. Don't feel bad. We Special Forces types pay attention to the small details. You never know when it will keep you alive." He shrugged. "Jack would have heard you sneaking out the bedroom window if he hadn't been sitting on the porch and drowning his thoughts in beer."

The wind whipped around her again, and Morgan shivered. A pair of Jack's overlarge sweatpants, a cotton shirt with the tails tied at her belly, and a thin pair of socks were no match for the cold slice of the humid breeze in forty-degree temperatures.

"I'm not going back."

"You don't have to."

Morgan wrapped her arms around herself, trying to ward off both the cold and a suspicion that Deke's answer was intended to mislead.

"Good. I just want to get my purse, find my car, and get as far away from here as possible."

"You mean as far away from Jack?"

"You're going to blab to him, aren't you?"

He shrugged. "Only if he's too drunk to figure it out himself. As it is, I expect to hear from him shortly, so I won't have to say a word."

"Drunk or sober, he's not coming after me."

"Give him an hour, two tops." He glanced at his watch. "My guess is more like forty-five minutes."

That didn't seem possible. Was Deke blind? Stupid? "The man walked out on me after I shocked the hell out of him."

"*You* shock *him*?" Deke laughed. "That's funny, but not possible. You surprised him. He just walked out to think. If I believed for a second that he wouldn't come for you, I would have left you with him in the swamp."

Deke honestly believed that Jack was coming back for her. Tonight. Was he delusional? Convincing himself so that he didn't have to babysit her?

It didn't matter. She had to get out of here, away from the swamps and Lafayette, and from Jack, before she did anything else she'd end up regretting.

"Why? I want to get away. Why would you leave me with a man who doesn't want me?"

A fresh rush of February wind cut through the thin clothing, chilling her to her bones. Morgan huddled further into her arms.

"Doesn't want you?" Deke asked incredulously as he ripped his sweatshirt off over his head. "Woman, you know shit about men. When he comes, ask Jack why he came after you. It won't be long now."

Morgan tried to follow the train of his words and not swallow her tongue. Every sculpted inch of Deke's torso was blessedly, achingly bare. She took in the angled dips and hard swells of his body. The man was enormous! Those shoulders . . . they had to be damn near three feet wide. Holy cow, it was a good thing she already knew Deke wasn't going to hurt her. Otherwise . . . she'd be terrified to meet the man in a dark alley.

"Arms up," he commanded.

"You're going to get cold."

He shook his head. "I've got a spare in my Hummer. Arms up."

This time, she complied. The allure of warmth was too strong to resist. The sweatshirt settled over her body like a soft, warm cloud that extended at least six inches past her fingertips and nearly down to her knees.

Deke laughed. "You're a little thing, doll. My sweatshirt makes you look like someone's six-year-old sister."

Torn between laughing and screaming, Morgan stomped out of the boat and onto the decaying wooden dock. Deke tied the boat off and followed her.

"If we're done laughing at my expense, can you drop me off at Sexy Sirens so I can get my purse and blow this taco stand?"

Deke raised a tawny brow. "You know that's the first place Jack will look for you."

"Well, then let's hurry so I can be gone by the time he decides to chase after me." *If he does.*

"Your chariot, my lady." He gestured to a gleaming black Hummer H3 sitting in the dirt-and-gravel lot ten feet ahead, perched up on monster truck tires nearly taller than her.

Morgan snorted. As if a guy that tall and huge needed such an intimidating vehicle to make a statement. Talk about overkill.

Once he unlocked the doors with the press of a button on his key fob, he opened the one on the passenger's side and lifted her into the vehicle. She couldn't call it a car. It was more like a tank with leather seats and satellite radio.

Settling into the seat and shutting the door, she was grateful for the fact that it blocked that terrible, cold wind.

Behind her, a rear door opened and closed. A few moments later, Deke climbed into the driver's seat wearing a West Point sweatshirt and a smile.

On the road to Sexy Sirens, Morgan asked him to drop her at the back door. The last thing she needed was to crawl through the crowd wearing Jack's too-big sweatpants and Deke's even bigger sweatshirt, sans bra and shoes. She probably looked like a refugee from an all-night frat party.

"As if I was going to drop you off at the front door." Deke's voice dripped sarcasm. "I think your stalker friend is in California. I don't *know* it. Until I know where the bastard is, we lay low."

Morgan couldn't argue with that logic. Better safe than sorry. She wanted to believe Reggie was still in California stewing that she'd given him the slip, but who knew . . .

Deke parked the Hummer in the alley behind the club, then helped her down. He stopped before the back door and pounded his fist on the cracking paint. A new blast of arctic wind cut down the narrow lane of the alley. Morgan's teeth chattered. Her thin L.A. blood really couldn't take this.

With a curse, Deke moved his body to block the brunt of the wind and he wrapped his arms around her.

Alyssa opened the door and stared at them with a surprised gaze that quickly turned jaundiced. "Well, if it isn't He-Man."

The sexy club owner was dressed tonight in a black leather corset just shy of illegal and a matching skirt a breath away from indecent that emphasized long legs encased in sheer, thigh-high stockings. She stepped back on black stilettos to let them enter. A wall of throbbing music made the little back room vibrate, despite the doors closing them off from the club's main stage. It was hard to miss the heavy suggestion of the song, some 1980s tune about naughty girls needing love, too.

They stepped inside and Deke shut the door behind him. "It's my favorite pole dancer. How the hell are you?"

Alyssa tossed back a curtain of platinum hair and regarded Deke with disdain. "Smart enough to avoid you and your tag-teaming cousin. The last woman the two of you finished with didn't walk for a week."

"You're in no danger. We're looking for a *lady*."

The former stripper stiffened. "Fuck you."

Deke gave an easy shrug. "I would, but you're not Luc's type. Thanks, anyway."

"I wasn't offering," she spit out. "Next time you feel the need to be here, send your cousin instead. He's got charm."

Meaning Deke didn't. What was the problem with these two? Morgan watched their byplay with a frown. Alyssa and Deke disliked each other. Intensely.

"I hate to interrupt," Morgan blurted, lying through her teeth, "but can I get my purse, Alyssa?"

The woman looked at her. "Morgan? Oh, shit. I'm sorry. I didn't recognize you with red hair and . . . What the hell are you wearing?"

"Jack's sweatpants and He-Man's sweatshirt."

Alyssa's expression turned ripe with X-rated questions.

Morgan flushed with both embarrassment and anger. "It's not what you're thinking, but don't ask. I just want to get my purse and get out of here."

"Did Jack find your stalker and put him out of his misery?"

"No, but we think he's gone to California looking for me since he set fire to my house there yesterday."

Alyssa grabbed her hand. "I'm not so sure, hon. Come with me. You, too, steroid boy."

Morgan followed her into a narrow hallway that bloomed into an office. Deke trailed behind, grumbling that he'd never used steroids. She barely paid attention. Alyssa knew something about her stalker that she didn't?

The woman shut the door to the small, cubiclelike office. Ah, soundproofed. Very nice.

Hustling behind her desk in a surprisingly long, confident stride, despite her staggeringly high stilettos, Alyssa produced a big envelope. A familiar manila-style envelope. One without postage marks.

Morgan's heart took a nosedive.

"These arrived this morning. Apparently, some homeless woman said a man paid her to deliver it by hand. I would have called Jack to tell him, but I was in New Orleans today. I just got back and found them."

With shaking hands, Morgan opened the envelope and extracted the pictures. There were only two, both taken near Sexy Siren's main stage the day Jack had brought her here to transform and hide her. Had that been a mere three days ago? So much had happened since then, it felt like a lifetime.

The first picture showed Jack in disguise, his fingers curled around her hip, his palm resting on the curve of her ass. His mouth hovered above her ear. Morgan shivered as she remembered his hypnotic voice and five o'clock shadow rasping against her senses.

She swallowed down a tangle of grief and yearning as she flipped to the next picture. This one knocked the breath from her body.

Jack seizing her, holding her still for the onslaught of his mouth. Eyes closed, he devoured her. The still picture captured aggression, possession in the clutch of his fingers on her neck, the thrust of his shoulders, as if he was determined to get as close as possible. His wide mouth utterly devoured hers. Morgan couldn't avoid looking at the picture, her arms around Jack's neck, her breasts pressed against him, her lips parted in eager readiness to taste every bit of his kiss. Not just accepting, but craving it. She tingled just looking at it.

Deke whistled. "That's one hell of a kiss."

"Yep, I've never known Jack to be so intent on anything that didn't involve handcuffs," Alyssa commented baldly.

Morgan cut a pained glance at her. Of course Alyssa had slept with Jack. Probably more than once. What red-blooded woman wouldn't, given the opportunity? Still, looking at the exotic creature in black leather with a waterfall of platinum hair wrapped in easy sexuality, Morgan felt like the ugly duckling—all baggy clothes, freckles, and repression.

God, she had to get far away from here. If she stayed long enough to watch Jack touch this woman or any other . . . the sight would crush her. No question. She'd trusted him, opened up to reveal herself to Jack in a way she never had with any man. She cared. More than cared. She didn't even want to think about how much more.

Twelve kinds of stupid, that's what she'd been.

"If handcuffs is all it takes to interest you, I'm sure I can scrounge up a pair or two," Deke baited Alyssa.

The blonde scoffed. "You wish."

This conversation was crawling on her last nerve. She had no idea why Deke was trying so hard to get a rise out of Alyssa's temper and she didn't care.

"Did you call Jack already?" Morgan demanded.

Alyssa frowned at the sharp tone. "No. I was getting ready to."

Morgan shook her head. "Wait until I leave. I want to be good and gone before he shows up."

"Doll, you can't leave with this guy running around. He could be near."

She tried not to wince at that possibility. "I have to go. I'm exhausted and I want space, some sleep. Tomorrow—"

"Tomorrow could be too late. You have to wait for Jack, tell him about these pictures. Let him protect you."

"I'll be fine for one night. I'll call around and hire someone to protect me bright and early in the morning." She turned to Alyssa. "Can I just have my purse, please? I need my driver's license, my keys, my money . . ."

"What about the note?" the blonde asked.

"Note?"

Alyssa grabbed the envelope from Morgan's hands and dug to the bottom until she retrieved a folded piece of paper. "Note."

Trepidation battered Morgan's nerves as she took the white paper in hand and unfolded it.

*You belong to me. Only me. I will kill you before another man touches you again.*

The brevity and resolution in those words chilled her. Reggie meant it. Morgan covered her mouth with her hand and felt her knees weakening under her.

Deke caught her in his strong grasp before her legs gave out. Alyssa moved into her line of vision, concern and confusion written all over her face.

"Let me call Jack. He's going to want to hear about this."

"No, he's not." Morgan looked away, fighting the sting of tears that was suddenly like an ice pick in the back of her eyes.

Alyssa closed the space between them and lifted her chin in a surprisingly strong grip, despite her long French-tipped claws. "Okay, now I'm really going to call him and ream him out. How the hell did he break your heart in three damn days?"

"I don't think it's one-sided," Deke offered.

He was delusional, Morgan decided. And she'd heard enough from both of them.

Tearing herself away from both Deke and Alyssa, Morgan made for the door. She was exhausted and sore. She wanted a shower, wanted the solace of deep sleep. Until she got out of here, she wasn't getting any of it.

If Reggie had arranged for the delivery of this envelope to Alyssa, it meant he was still determined and unhinged. He was probably back in the area. He knew who she'd left the club with and when. All the more reason not to stay with Jack, to find a new bodyguard.

For every reason she could think of, she had to get out of here. Now.

"Give me my damn purse!" she shouted. "I'm leaving."

Alyssa tossed up her hands in a gesture of surrender and walked back behind her desk. She lifted her super-short black skirt and revealed a set of black garters holding up her thigh-high stockings. A small ribbon tied a little desk key to one of the garters. Alyssa plucked on the red satin ribbon, and the key fell into her hand.

With a taunting glance at Deke's riveted gaze, Alyssa palmed the key, then straightened her skirt and unlocked her desk. An open drawer later, she handed Morgan her purse.

"Let me call Jack before you go."

"I'll be fine. Deke can walk me to my car to help me retrieve my things safely. I'll figure out what to do from there."

Morgan didn't wait around for either of them to answer. She whirled away and headed for the alley exit. It was dark. She could stay in the alley's shadows.

A few moments later, she heard Deke's footsteps behind her.

"I'll stay with you tonight, until you can find a new bodyguard."

And let him call Jack to come and get her and probably spank her ass for running off in the first place? "Just drop me off at my car. I'll grab my stuff and call a cab, just to be on the safe side. Your responsibility ends there."

"If I do, Jack is going to kill me," he muttered.

"If you don't, I'm going to kill you first, slowly, and string you up by the balls."

Though Morgan was painfully aware that she couldn't make good on that threat, she was relieved when Deke just shook his head and sighed.

He drove her straight to Brandon's car, stopping beside it. He leaned over the steering wheel.

"What Jack did was shitty, Morgan. I won't deny it. He knows it. But this asshole stalking you is dangerous. And it's possible he hopped a plane back here. Let me call Jack. He can keep you safe until—"

"Damn it. What part of *no* don't you understand?"

"What if this sick freak finds you? He's tried to kill you once. He'll try again. You saw that note."

"I'm a grown woman with a brain. I can manage to hide myself for one night. Then tomorrow, I'll make other arrangements. Jack is not the only person who can keep me safe."

"He's the man who cares about you most. He would do anything to keep you safe, give his life for yours."

"All bodyguards take that risk."

Deke nodded. "The difference is, on the job, we risk our lives because we're paid to do it. I have no doubt Jack would simply lay his down to save yours."

"No, that's . . ." Morgan shook her head, disturbed by the soaring joy and terror inside her. "He'd have to love me to—"

"He does."

Morgan swallowed. It wasn't possible. Logically, she'd known Jack three days. He wasn't the kind of man to give his heart easily, if at all.

*Was it possible?* a voice in her head whispered. An agreement to an interview had led to an agreement to protect her, which had led to . . . so much more. Visions of Jack bombarded her: shielding her from bullets, impaling her against his front door, teasing his grandfather, encouraging her to accept his domination, cursing at her fantasy.

Leaving her.

Jack didn't love her. Deke must have thought saying otherwise would persuade her to wait for him. Well, Deke thought wrong.

She stripped off Deke's sweatshirt, handed it back to him, and gathered up her purse. "I'll be fine."

"I don't think that taking this car is safe. Who knows what the weird-ass did to it. Why don't you let me drop you somewhere until we can get the car checked out?"

So he could tell Jack where she'd gone the minute his Hummer door shut behind her? "Thanks for the offer, but I'll call a cab."

With a long sigh of defeat, Deke put his Hummer into park. "At least let me help you down and make sure this bastard hasn't tampered with your car."

As much as she wanted to, Morgan couldn't argue with that request. She nodded.

Deke hopped down and walked around to open her door. He grabbed her around the waist and lifted her out of the vehicle. His hands lingered. "Are you sure?"

"Yes." She still had a stalker to contend with, but she could hire someone big and mean and ugly to watch over her, return home, and start filming the new episodes of *Turn Me On*.

A new batch of ice picks seemed to stab at the back of her eyes. "I can't stay."

Morgan fished the keys from her overstuffed little purse, cursing as Deke bumped her and half the contents spilled out onto the dark street. God, couldn't anything go right?

"Sorry. I tripped." Deke bent and gathered her brush, her wallet, her hand lotion, then put it all back in her purse. "Be safe."

Deke checked the vehicle inside and out, then shook his head. With a soft curse, he called her a cab.

"Thanks." She couldn't seem to make her voice any bigger than a whisper.

"I hope I see you again."

Sincere. His words weren't cute. Weren't a come-on. A fresh wave of dejection swarmed her.

Morgan nodded and watched him drive away with hot tears scalding her cheeks as the truth hit her: She'd never see Deke again. Worse, she'd never see Jack again. She'd known him mere days and leaving him felt like she was leaving behind a part of herself, like she'd dismembered her heart from her body.

Perfect. How like her. The minute she had to leave Jack was the moment she realized she loved him.

The taxi blessedly arrived moments later and whisked her away.

*    *    *

NEARLY groaning with every step, Morgan checked into a quaint European-style bed and breakfast on the edge of town with a small overnight bag in one hand and her laptop in the other. She took the renovated carriage house out back, which wasn't visible from the road and came complete with a Jacuzzi tub and a back door for a quick exit. The whole place sat alone, the yard surrounded by guard fences. The owner swore they'd never had so much as a flower disturbed in the twenty years he'd been running the place. And that sounded like heaven to Morgan. She wanted to lie down and sleep for a week, and after tonight, she just might.

But she had to take care of a few things first.

Dragging her laptop out, Morgan hunkered down in the plush king-sized bed and dashed off an email to Brandon. She explained about the damage to his house and promised to return to Houston and get the repairs started. She told him she was alive and safe, that Jack had been watching over her. She sent him the name of her hotel tonight in case he could contact her—and not much more. How could she possibly explain to ultraresponsible Brandon that she had fallen for a stranger in a handful of days? Then, after beseeching him to stay safe in Iraq, she grabbed her phone. She'd read on the Internet that sometimes confronting your stalker with a firm "No" could make them go away. Maybe that tactic would work with Reggie. But one glance at her phone told her there'd be no calling Reggie tonight. Her phone was deader than dead. Damn!

Resigned that everything would wait until tomorrow, she headed for the blissful steam of a shower.

Twenty minutes and two travel-sized bottles of shampoo later, Morgan emerged from the charming pedestal-sinked bathroom.

Only she wasn't alone anymore.

# Chapter Fifteen

"J-JACK?" Her stomach clenched into a tight ball, then fell to her knees.

He stood just outside the bathroom door, big and broad and tense with fight, completely blocking her in and covering both her exits. Morgan licked suddenly dry lips. Most people might mistake that expression on his face for flat. Uh-huh, she knew better. And she shivered.

"How did you . . . ?"

She glanced at the clock visible on the wall just above his shoulder. Deke had told her Jack would probably catch up with her in forty-five minutes. He'd done it in thirty-seven.

All while maintaining tight control over his anger—barely. The clenching fists, the thick veins roping his forearms, his taut jaw, the inky slashes of his brows over reproving dark eyes, she could hardly miss all that.

Nor could she miss the raging erection pushing against the front of his jeans. But it was in her best interest to try like hell.

Jack reached for her purse, dumped it upside down, scattering the contents all over a little round table. He extracted a black one-by-one-inch plastic device. The little gray letters GPS on the back told her everything she needed to know.

Damn! Deke had slipped that into her purse, probably when she'd dumped its contents everywhere after he'd "accidentally" bumped her and he'd "helped" pick it all back up. Morgan made a mental note to slap him silly when— No, she wouldn't see him again.

"He gave you the means to hunt me down," she spat.

"I would have found you, no matter how long it took. No matter what I had to do. Deke just made it easier. I wasn't far behind you, anyway."

Morgan muttered an impossible wish under her breath.

"No, I won't leave you the hell alone. In fact, I have a question: Are you out of your fucking mind?"

"For wanting to get away from you after your mortifying exit earlier this evening? Gee, I must be."

He flinched. Oh, it was subtle, but she knew Jack well enough to catch it.

"Fuck!" He raked a hand through dark hair and stalked closer. "Alyssa called me when you left the club and told me about the pictures and the note. Deke confirmed. What the hell were you thinking? Or were you hoping your dangerous admirer would just pack it up and go home?"

"He couldn't have any way to follow me here. I'm safe for a night or two. After that . . ." She shrugged. "You're not the only person on the planet capable of helping me stay safe."

Apparently not liking that answer, Jack stepped closer, looking big and dominant and worried as hell under all that anger.

"Know someone else who's a qualified bodyguard? Who you gonna let protect you?"

"I don't think it's any of your business anymore."

"Why, because I behaved like an ass earlier tonight? Don't look shocked. I was wrong and I'm saying so. I'm sorry."

Jack apologizing, just like that? No. It was too simple. There had to be a catch . . . "You're only willing to apologize so I'll be a good little girl, come back, and let you tear me down again."

"I'm willing to apologize so I don't lose you. But whether you forgive me or not, I'm not letting this sick bastard anywhere near you."

Morgan gestured around the otherwise uninhabited room. "As you can see, all's clear. No psychos here ready to kill me. You can go now."

A muscle in his jaw ticked. "I'm not going anywhere. It's possible this asshole followed you here from Alyssa's. He could have been watching the club, just waiting for you. You don't know."

She hated to admit that he could be right . . . but in this case, he could be. Damn it, she had to start thinking smart, with the brain God gave her, not with her weeping heart.

"And you may think we're done," Jack went on, advancing closer, closer, larger and more insistent with every step. "Think again. I don't want to lose you to this stalker; that's a given. But I don't want to lose you. Period."

Morgan rolled her eyes. "Lose me, how? As a . . . little fuck toy. That's all I am to you. You enjoyed every minute of tearing away all my misconceptions about myself. Congratulations for convincing me I'm submissive. Now get the hell out of my life." She whirled away.

Jack snagged her around the waist and hauled her back against his chest. It didn't take more than a second to feel the steel-inspired cock prodding the small of her back. The knowledge shouldn't matter, shouldn't make her sex clench with need, shouldn't make her ache to latch onto him, to surrender everything to him.

Shouldn'ts weren't her reality. Morgan did want him, with a desperate craving that made her body tight and achy, a condition she feared only he could ease.

"A fuck toy?" he growled in her ear. "No. A fuck toy I could have put back in a box and forgotten. I could have sent one of those away without another thought. A fuck toy wouldn't have me hard every time I hear your voice, or worried when I see you cry. Or feeling ready to hand you my heart on a platter every time you do nothing more than fucking smile."

Morgan's breath caught. He didn't mean it. Impossible after the way he'd treated her tonight. "Let go."

Her demand fell on deaf ears. Instead, he growled in her ear, "When I put that collar around your neck tonight, that meant something. That dangling heart represented something. I know you get it. The symbolism can't be lost on you."

His heart? No . . . "It meant so much that you cursed at me and stormed out. You're the one pushing, pushing, encouraging me to open up, let loose, promising me that it's okay. Yeah, it's okay as long as it's some fantasy you've been harboring, but when I—"

"My ex-wife cheated on me," Jack cut in, panting in her ear, once, twice. "I learned she was fucking my then–best friend when I found their homemade video."

Gasping, Morgan's jaw dropped. Her tirade stuck in her throat. He'd actually *seen* his wife and his best friend together? Not just heard gossip about them. Not just listened to their confession. He'd witnessed it in a way he could replay over and over.

To a strong, proud man like Jack that would be the ultimate slap in the face.

Morgan risked a glance over her shoulder. Defenses stripped, Jack's gaze seethed anger and begged her forgiveness all at once. "We weren't . . . close. I tried to give her what she needed—money, health insurance, time, and space after she miscarried. I was faithful, but . . ."

It wasn't enough. He hadn't known what else to do. His burning eyes and painful silence told her that.

Jack turned her to face him and released her. "Knowing that she let another man fuck her ate me alive. She *begged* him to touch her." He swallowed. "She could barely stand to be in the same room with me. And then she left me. For him."

The rest of the message shone clear in his tortured gaze. Morgan mattered, and he wasn't letting her go. He wasn't hiding his intention to have her again.

And she'd staggered him with the fact that she'd fantasized about having two hungry cocks command and possess her at once. He fought the knowledge that she ached for Jack to share her.

Another man screwing his ex-wife had pissed him off, hurt his pride. The hot drill of his stare told Morgan that another man touching her had the power to turn Jack into a red-hazed, full-fledged postal maniac. She could bring him to his knees.

*Oh, God.* He hadn't stormed out of the playroom because he was shocked; he'd done it because he was scared. Of losing her.

Because he cared.

"I kept wondering what my ex needed that I didn't give her." His voice cracked. He cleared his throat, closed his eyes. Looked away. "In ten months of marriage, she never told me she loved me. On that video, she told him three times in eight minutes. Ever since, I've wondered if maybe . . . maybe I don't have that something a woman needs in order to be happy."

The way his intense gaze gripped hers made her breath catch. In those dark eyes lurked the fear that she could never love him. Of all the things she'd expected, this would have been dead last on the list.

Warm, gooey feelings exploded in Morgan's chest. She cupped his stubble-rough cheek in her hand, thumb caressing the hard thrust of his cheekbone. His vulnerable frown tore at her heart as he kissed the inside of her palm and watched her with a gaze scraped raw by need.

"Have you ever told anybody else about your ex-wife?"

"No." His tight voice sounded somewhere between a whisper and a mutter, then he cracked a pained smile. "Well, I told Deke after one too many hurricanes."

This proud, dominant man had just laid bare his fear and pain. For her. To help her understand why he'd walked out.

"You have everything necessary to make a woman love you." Her voice shook. "After all, I've been fighting the dangerous urge to fall in love with you for three days."

Jack's eyes widened, heated. He stalked closer, against her, greedy fingers curling into her hair, hungry gaze eating her up. "Did you succeed?"

Morgan hesitated. Answering this question gave him so much power . . . Yet, intertwined with a ragged catch of emotion, she heard that subtle command in this voice, the one that never failed to rouse both her body and her instinct to submit. She saw apprehension tighten his bold features. And couldn't stay silent.

"Not well enough for my peace of mind."

A smile broke across his face, white teeth flashing in Cajun-dark skin. Chocolate eyes melted. That expression . . . so brilliant, so happy. "Good. I shouldn't be in this alone."

Then he covered her mouth with his, a soft urge for entry with a hint of demand beneath. Tender control. Silken mastery. Her cold lips warmed under his touch, quick as a whip's lash. Her body melted, heated, ached. The brush of his lips, the sensual dance of his tongue, and suddenly her head swam with everything Jack—his scent, the hard breadth of his chest, the flavor of his mouth, the way he held her, as if she was . . . everything.

Breathing harsh, he pressed a light kiss to the corner of her lips and backed away. "This fantasy of yours, it's important to you, isn't it?"

She could do without it, couldn't she? It wasn't that important. After all, she'd been doing without it for years. Why pursue it if it was going to cause him more distress? Why risk hurting him, a man who'd already known pain?

"The truth, Morgan. Not what you think I want to hear."

If she lied, even for the sake of his feelings, there would be hell to pay. That message wouldn't have been any more obvious if he'd paid to put it on a neon billboard.

Morgan crossed her arms over her chest. How important was it? Blowing out a breath, she tried to sort out the tangle.

Well, she'd had nothing but miserable relationships since she discovered men. And Jack had known why by looking at her the first time they met: She hadn't been listening to her needs, giving her psyche what it required to unlock the key to her pleasure. No denying she'd sacrificed her wants, burying her desires, for the greater good of those lousy relationships. Instead, ignoring her submissive nature had killed those relationships.

Big admission for her, and she had Jack to thank. He'd taught her not to hide, forced her to face the fact it was impossible to build happiness on a lie.

And the truth was, of all her wicked midnight fantasies, the idea of two men taking her, at once, had been the most explosive. And yes, she might be able to renounce it now, for a while. But how long before denying her desire caught up with them?

"I—I wish I could just make it go away. But I'm afraid I'll never feel truly . . . settled and satisfied until I have it, at least once."

He frowned, nodded, turned, and paced to the other side of the room.

A silent implication that she wanted more than he was willing to provide. The truth hurt, ripped her insides like an industrial paper shredder. But she'd done what she had to do. Lying wouldn't work. Ultimately, the fallout would only be more painful. She'd be doing them both a disservice. Being engaged to Andrew without being honest for too long had proven that.

Besides, better that they crossed this bridge now, rather than later, after she convinced herself to stay and lie . . . and surely only grown more attached to him.

Would she ever be able to move past Jack? Looking at the tense set of his shoulders, his clenching fists, remembering the feel of that inky hair in her hands and that broad Cajun smile . . . Probably not.

Morgan sighed. "I'm sorry."

She watched those broad shoulders lift in a shrug. "I wouldn't want you to lie to me." He turned and paced toward her again. "Don't ever lie."

But his eyes raged, as if the pain was nearly beyond his bearing. Morgan ached for him.

"I understand why you can't—"

"Shh," he whispered against her mouth. "You're exhausted, and I just want to feel you, know you're okay."

Jack eased her down to the bed and removed the plush robe the inn had provided to reveal her clean, bare skin. He removed all his clothes and slid onto the mattress behind her. He lifted her breasts into his hands, thumbing her nipples. He settled his hard cock against the curves of her ass. But he made no demands. After tonight, she doubted he would.

"Sleep," his whisper encouraged.

Was he out of his mind? She pushed back tears, trying to relax, trying not to make him feel worse for what he wasn't able to give her.

"I'll take care of you." Jack kissed her shoulder and nuzzled his face into the curve of her neck.

He felt good against her. With him, she felt warm, protected, aroused. Even accepted. It was all Morgan could do not to turn and tell the man she loved him, that she could do without that one fantasy. But with a lie between them, they had no future.

"Jack—"

"We'll deal with it tomorrow. That's a promise."

*     *     *

JACK flipped his phone shut just as Morgan emerged from the old-fashioned bathroom wearing a towel and an awkward smile. His gut clenched at the sight of her.

She looked so tempting with an emerald green towel shielding her fair skin and curves from his eyes. Knowing those blushing pink nipples were bare under the scrap of terry cloth didn't exactly calm his libido. With a dash of black mascara, her blue eyes looked vivid and huge in her uncertain face. A swipe of some amber-colored gloss over her lips emphasized their pillowy softness. That flame hair fell in a silken curtain halfway down her back, framing alabaster skin with little cinnamon freckles. She glowed.

And Jack wanted her so damn bad, he could barely take a single breath without thinking about having her bound and open for him, taking him in every way his twisted mind could conjure.

Had he made the right choice?

Too late now. What would happen, would happen.

"Feel better after your shower?"

She nodded, then looked around the room, bed with sumptuous jewel-toned comforter rumpled from nothing but sleep, hardwood floors gleaming, little area uncluttered. "They came to take the breakfast dishes away?"

"While you were in the shower."

"Good." She chewed on her lower lip.

"I just talked to Deke. He's friends with local police." He reached for her hand, hoping it would help steady her. "Your pal, Reggie, was arrested at about three this morning for trying to accost Alyssa in her club. Deke's been to see her. From what he said, according to Alyssa, Reggie demanded to know where you were and was getting pretty physical about it."

Morgan gasped. If it was possible, more color slid out of her face, leaving behind those blue, blue eyes wide with fear, disappointment, anger, relief.

"So I'm not in danger anymore."

"Maybe. Maybe not. He won't be in jail long, a day or two. And we don't know for sure that he's your stalker."

"He has to be. No one else knew that much about where I lived, where I'd be. Photography is his passion. If he could make a living at it, I think he'd quit *Turn Me On* tomorrow. He has a volatile temper sometimes. I've heard whispers that he has a record . . . I've never known him to be violent or anything, but there's no one else in my life with the ability to follow me here and take all those pictures in quite that way."

It was possible she was right, Jack mused. Probable even. But he wasn't about to take chances, especially not with her safety. He drew her closer, placed a soft kiss on her bare shoulder.

"I'll know more later. I have an appointment to chat with him this afternoon. I'm hoping to wring a confession out of him, if he's our guilty party."

Her shoulders drooped. "I'm grateful to know that I have a few hours of peace in order to plan my next move, but it pains me to lose someone I thought was a friend. And . . ." She stepped out of his embrace. "I guess I'll be leaving here, get out of your way. I—I . . . Thank you for last night, for keeping me safe again."

Leaving? Not if he could help it. Not ever. "You're welcome."

Jack waited. She had something more to say. Her pensive gaze told him it weighed on her mind. Was she going to ask more questions about Kayla? Recant her fantasy? Tell him to get lost? Impatience gnawed on his composure like a rabid dog with a juicy bone. But he waited.

"Thank you for telling me about your ex-wife. I know it wasn't easy. I appreciate you explaining . . . It was a relief to know you didn't leave the playroom because the idea of a *ménage* was too shocking for you."

He regretted her thinking that for an instant. Regretted it like hell. And he planned to make it up to her.

"*Cher.*" He crossed the room and took her shoulders in his grasp. "Nothing you say or do can shock me. Or make me stop wanting you."

She lifted her face to his with a sad smile, one that told him she was holding back tears. And he, the man with control whispered about in hushed tones among D/s circles all over Louisiana, couldn't wait another second to touch her.

Thrusting his hands into her hair, he anchored her underneath him and captured her mouth in a blistering kiss. He possessed, unable to stop himself, unable to temper his thirst to ravage her lips, make her melt and moan . . . and give in. Hell, he didn't even try to stop.

*Seize, devour, dominate.* It was like a chant in his brain, over and over, as he slanted his mouth over hers. Sinking deeper into the heaven of her, he allowed his tongue to find hers and intertwine in an urgent dance of need.

Beneath him, Morgan moaned, the sound vibrating into his body. When had he not wanted her? When had he ever looked at her and not wanted to call her his?

And last night . . . he'd dreamed of her again. Not as he'd seen her on the wraparound porch of his little swamp cottage with the sun glinting on her hair. No. He'd dreamed of tomorrow, of her in his bed, wearing his pendant, submitting to the burn of his demands, accepting his heart the way he cherished hers.

"*Cher,*" he whispered against her lips. "*Je suis fou d'te caresser.*"

*I'm desperate to touch you.* He'd never said anything more true.

"Jack, we shouldn't . . ."

He heard the catch in her voice, the regret. Damn, he had to change that. Erase it. Replace it with the sharp edge of joy, the raging burn of pleasure. With complete submission.

"This morning," he murmured against the sweet curves of her swollen lips. "Give me this morning. We'll sort everything else out later."

Morgan looked up at him, her blue eyes so clear, like a bright December day. And just now, they telegraphed her uncertainty tangled with her need to give in. But that overthinking mind of hers made her hesitate.

"Morgan." He dropped his voice an octave, leaned in, pressed his advantage. "Don't say no."

Closing her eyes, the long lashes fluttered down to pale cheeks ripe with a hint of a rosy flush. A self-recriminating smile twisted her full lips. "I've never been able to say no to you."

Jack hoped to erase that word from her vocabulary, starting today. But first . . . they had to face her ultimate fantasy.

His ultimate nightmare.

Tension raked at him, scraping at his insides until he felt pissed and . . . what was the right word? Vulnerable. Yeah. His gut clenched. And he started to sweat.

Despite all that, he had to know, once and for all, if he and Morgan could make it.

In the back of Jack's head lurked one haunting fact: Morgan's total submission to him would hand him his ultimate revenge on a fucking silver platter—to have Brandon's fiancée begging him to master her. Telling him that she loved him while clawing at his back and coming all over his cock. Sweet . . . but the idea of revenge now sat sour in his gut. Nothing about the way he wanted Morgan, about the need that turned him inside out and focused with unerring demand on this woman, had a damn thing to do with retribution. Morgan. Just Morgan.

She'd come to mean everything to him.

And if Morgan returned to Brandon after today, well . . . then his former buddy would leave his heart gutted and have the last laugh—again.

Damn, he wished he could avoid telling her the truth for just a bit, until he had time to assure Morgan of his feelings, of their rightness. She was still skittish, but he had to move fast or he was going to lose her.

"Stand in the middle of the room," he commanded into the soft morning air.

Morgan bit into that plump bottom lip with her little white teeth. Her sweet pink tongue swiped across the surface next, and Jack imagined watching her drag it across the head of his cock. He engorged, biting back a curse at the way this woman got to him.

"Jack . . ."

No backing down now. He raised a sharp black brow at her, knowing she'd get his displeasure without a word.

"Sir," she corrected.

"Give me this morning."

With an obedient nod, she turned and made her way to the center of the room, near the end of the bed. She faced the disheveled bedding.

"Good girl," he murmured as he moved toward her, until he stood before her, facing the door. Their gazes locked, making his cock jerk with impatience. "Give me your wrists."

For once, she complied without pause. And he couldn't stop a smile from creasing his face. She'd come so damn far in just a few days. Not just admitting her nature, but giving into it. Morgan knew he intended to bind her, and she just . . . complied. With perfect obedience. With trust so pure, it sent a bolt of pride, along with a stab of hot need, straight through him.

"Very sweet."

He kissed the soft spot where her neck and shoulder joined and enjoyed watching her shiver. Kissing his way down her arm, he nipped at the tender flesh in the crook of her arm. Her breath caught, and he smiled against her wrist, feeling her pulse accelerate against his lips.

Withdrawing a pair of leather hasp-style cuffs from the bag by his feet, which he'd placed there earlier, he attached one to each wrist. She didn't say a word.

With a smooth glide of his palm under her towel, he teased her inner thigh with whispered fingertips, hovering oh-so-close to her damp heat, that sweet honey spot he couldn't wait to taste. The starch began to leave Morgan's posture, and when he tapped the tender flesh just below her pussy in silent demand, she parted her legs. He knelt to her and slipped on the matching thigh cuffs, buckling each in place.

Jack felt Morgan's eyes on him, sharper than before, but he didn't raise his gaze to her, not yet. He didn't want to give anything away, and as aroused as he was now . . . no telling what she'd read in his expression. Instead, he fished into the bag at his feet again and withdrew two velvet cords and set them on the hardwood floor between them.

Let her wonder.

Then . . . he unwrapped the thick green towel from her body, unveiling her lush curves—and sucked in a harsh breath of need. He left her completely bare, sunlight shafting giant golden rays through the room, making her fiery hair the color of a living flame and illuminating the alabaster skin of her shoulders, translucent breasts, and soft belly. And her ripe pink nipples.

She didn't flinch, didn't protest, being suddenly naked. The only re-action he saw was an adorable rosy flush spreading across the pale cream of her skin. So damn beautiful, naked and submissive and surprisingly self-assured. The sight of her made his cock swell more, jerk. He felt strangled by his jeans, by his need for her touch . . .

"Sir, where did that bag come from?"

And all the equipment. That's what she wanted to know. He smiled. She shouldn't be asking, but he'd indulge her this once.

"When I realized you were gone last night, I threw together a few things to make sure that, when I found you, you couldn't get away again."

"Oh." Her voice fluttered.

Hell, he could hear the arousal in her voice. That quivering note, ripe with curiosity yet a breath away from a needy whimper, just about turned him inside out.

Jack swallowed against a harsh blast of lust. "Are you ready for what-ever I give you?"

She met his gaze squarely. "Yes, sir."

Not testing her wasn't an option. He dug into his bag again and pro-duced a pair of padlocks. With them, he attached her wrists to the cuffs around her thighs. The locks clicked into place, loud in the room so silent, except for the harsh clip of her breathing and the pounding of his heart in his ears.

He stood, intentionally crowding her and forcing her gaze to his. "You're ready for everything I'm going to give you?"

"Yes, sir."

So far so good . . . but did she mean it? He found a set of ankle cuffs in his bag. The super-soft black leather whispered over his fingers, thrilling him with the idea they'd soon be wrapped around her even softer skin, keeping her in place for anything . . . everything he wanted. He lifted the velvet cords from the floor and tied each on the O ring at the front of the cuffs that now hugged her trim ankles.

"Be very sure," he demanded.

Morgan hesitated, her soft gaze pointed down, seeking his. Yes, she wanted to know what was different, what awaited her. But she didn't ask, just stared.

"I'm sure," she whispered. And the confidence on her face told him she meant it. "Sir."

"You're amazing, *cher*."

The sight of those blue eyes, filled with lust and trust was a kick to his self-control. It was a fucking wonder he didn't tear off his clothes and ram himself inside her sweet body in two seconds or less.

Instead, Jack urged her legs farther apart. Morgan complied without a word. Then he wrapped the cord attached to her cuffs around the base of the bed's solid cherry posts, down low. He secured them tight.

She wasn't going anywhere now. And she looked gorgeous, such fairness outlined in black leather, the red velvet cords serving to anchor her in place and keep her legs deliciously spread. He'd never seen anything so fucking sexy.

Jack stood, fighting off a shiver of desire searing him and threatening to strip his control.

Eager—hell, shaking—with the need to touch her, Jack smoothed his palms down her sides, dipping in with the slight curve of her waist, as he dusted kisses down Morgan's skin. She swallowed a gasp as his touch drifted down the flare of her hips and his mouth found a sensitive spot where hip and thigh met.

Was there anything more perfect than her offering of such fair skin, more tempting than palming the firm length of her legs, kneeling so close to the heaven of her pussy? Not in his mind. This . . . Morgan and everything she offered was everything he'd looked for.

He prayed to hell today proved they both had what it took to fulfill one another, be the lover the other needed.

Reaching around, he trailed his fingers down the slope of her buttocks, gripped the back of her thighs. Was she soft everywhere? Yeah, and it just tore him up. He, who'd killed in battle, taken a bullet, sustained scars from more than one knife fight, learned to tell his enemy to fuck off in eight languages, touched Morgan and her seemingly untouched skin. He glided his way down clear to her ankles, his mouth following the same hot path until she was clenching her thighs, until her legs tensed beneath his hands and mouth.

"Are you wet?" he asked.

"Yes," she gasped, watching his every move with wide eyes. Not stunned or shocked. Aroused. Dilated. Hungry.

"Morgan?" he growled in warning.

"Yes, I'm wet, sir."

"Better," he said, nibbling at the creamy flesh of her inner thigh before gliding his tongue up her hip.

The sound of her moan resonated in his ears. Damn, how the hell was he going to last, without rising to his feet, tearing off his pants, and taking what they both needed?

With gentle tugs on all her bindings, Jack assured himself they were secure. Just one more . . .

Reaching to his bag again, he pulled out a thick red silk scarf. *Perfect*, he thought, folding the crimson scrap of cloth and settling it over her eyes. Morgan could touch and taste and hear—and through those senses experience everything she needed. But she could not move or see, which allowed him the control he wanted and might need . . . just in case.

For a mere instant, Morgan tensed. But she forced herself to exhale, to relax. Proud of her calm, dazzled by her show of absolute trust, he kissed her mouth lightly, savoring the flavor of her hot tension and bee-stung berry lips.

Fists clenched, he eased back and stepped past her. A deep breath, a little prayer. Then he forced himself to uncurl his fingers, cross the room and open the hotel room door.

# Chapter Sixteen

MORGAN felt Jack walk past her. Behind her, the door opened. A draft of February air breezed a chill across her skin. Then footsteps.

She tamped down her panic. He wasn't going anywhere. He couldn't be. The raw tenderness in his eyes and the unrelenting grip of his hands on her convinced Morgan of that. So what the hell was he up to?

He cupped his hand around her shoulder and settled against her, whispering in her ear, "The safe word is still *swamp*."

Even blindfolded, his tension couldn't have been clearer if he drew her a picture. "Okay, but I won't need it."

Jack exhaled. Warm breath on her cheek, then the soft skate of his fingertips down the slope of her breast, followed by the hard pull of his mouth on her nipple.

Instantly, a path of fire zinged between her breasts and her clit. Moisture rushed between her folds. The pleasure was so bright, Morgan even felt a curious warmth at her back. She couldn't squeeze her legs together for relief, since Jack had tied them so far apart. With her wrists attached to her thighs, she couldn't raise her arms to clasp him closer when he shifted to the other breast, making the second nipple as hard as the first. A moan slipped free from her throat.

Caressing a hand down her belly, Jack rewarded her with a soft touch. His fingers made teasing circles across her thighs. His knuckles swept over the fringe of her pubic hair.

His hand shook.

Morgan held her breath, waiting, wondering . . . What was going on?

Slowly, he knelt between her feet. His hot breath hit her right— Oh, yes!—there, as he parted her slick flesh with his thumbs and exposed her every secret, stripping her bare of uncertainty and inhibitions, ripping out any concept of wrong or taboo, and replacing it with need. Morgan simply *felt* his eyes devouring her most secret flesh, hungry, singleminded.

Blood rushed through her body. A rush of tingles scraping across her skin made her feel so totally alive. Cool air against her breasts contrasted with a blast of heat at her back . . . and the rasp of Jack's hot tongue dragging across her clit.

Her head fell back on a gasp.

"That's it," he murmured. He laved her again. "Cream for me."

He followed the gentle nibble with a firm swipe of his thumb right there, where she needed it. Once, twice, punctuated by his seeking tongue again. And again. Then his mouth covered her, his tongue lashing her clit, toying, stroking, inflaming.

The rise of pleasure was sharp, beyond fighting—even if she'd wanted to. But resisting was the last thing on her mind. Thick desire stormed her . . . along with a bittersweet curl of emotion. How was she going to exist without Jack after he'd finished with her?

Shoving the thought aside, Morgan focused on the here and now. Desire. She dug her fingernails into her thighs. In the face of her spiraling need, a brief sting was the only sensation she could spare. Everything else was focused on Jack and his mouth. And when he worked a pair of fingers into her, she gasped, hanging on the edge by a thread.

"You can't come yet, Morgan."

She whimpered. "Please . . ."

"Tell me again, do you want everything I can give you?"

"Yes! Yes, sir. Now."

A hesitation, brief, bare. Then Jack sucked her clit into his mouth. An ache bit into her belly with unmerciful ruthlessness and pushed her closer to the abyss of pleasure. She whimpered as the hot swell of need rushed up on her, pushing her close, so close to the edges of her restraint. Every muscle in her body tensed under the lash of Jack's lazy, insistent tongue.

"Good," he murmured against her wet, swollen sex. "Then come for us."

"Us?"

Shock pinged through her. Had she heard him correctly?

As the word fell out of her mouth, the hot press of a huge naked chest enveloped her back. And Jack still knelt between her feet, her clit captive of the slow swipes of his tongue, two of his fingers pressed deep inside her.

From behind her, a pair of broad hands reached, cupping her breasts, squeezing her nipples in a tight grip just short of pain.

The stranger dropped a tentative kiss just behind her ear, as if testing his welcome. "Hi, doll."

Scratchy, slightly short of breath, yes, but that voice . . . Deke.

*Oh, my . . . Was this really happening?*

As she gasped, he swept a burning palm from her breast, down her belly, delving straight into her damp curls. The rough skin of his finger-tips brushed over her clit, while Jack's fingers were lodged tight inside her. Two insistent men, both strumming parts of her body that made her scream. The friction and pressure just about killed her, obliterating everything but the ability to ache with pent-up need. She couldn't breathe, couldn't think. She couldn't do anything but revel in the electric sensation arcing through her body.

"Come for us," Deke demanded in her ear, pressing in on her swollen bud as Jack scraped the inflamed nerves inside her channel.

"Now!" Jack demanded.

A flood of blood and need crashed in on her pussy and burst, exploding out with pleasure and a scream of shocked ecstasy. Her body clamped Jack's fingers in a vise grip. Deke groaned as she all but drenched his hand with her cream.

Slowly, they brought her down. Gentle touches, so easy. They worked in perfect tandem, in silence, both reading the cues of her body perfectly.

Stunned, awed, Morgan felt tears prick the back of her eyes. The reality of what had just happened roused a fresh ache deep inside her.

Jack slipped his digits from her channel's grip and removed the blindfold. She blinked against the sudden rush of sunlight as each of the men rounded her shoulder and came to stand in front of her.

Brown eyes and denim blue, both piercing, questioning, scorching. Morgan shivered, and they pressed closer, their wide, muscled chests covered in fever-hot skin and nearly eclipsing her. She didn't have to look down to know she'd see two hungry cocks intent on giving and taking satisfaction.

Morgan drew in a shocked breath. Oh, unreal. She and Jack and Deke, mostly naked and in a hotel room . . . This was actually happening. Trepidation, forbidden thrill, a flare of arousal—the feelings bombarded her so quickly, Morgan could barely sort one from the other.

Except amazement. Just last night, Jack had poured out his guts, his heart, his pain, his fear. He'd been afraid that sharing her meant losing her. What had changed?

Deke thrust his finger in his mouth, sampling the juice of her arousal with a wicked smile. At the sight, a fresh flush swept through her, and Morgan cursed her fair skin. He just laughed.

Jack's gaze was more serious. "Deke and I are here to grant your fantasy, *cher.*"

"We won't hurt you, just give you the good kind of pain," Deke promised with a wink.

"Why?" Her questioning gaze fell to Jack, and the whisper fell out of her mouth.

He cupped her face in his hands and stepped closer. "I realized that, if I want to claim you as mine, I have to have the balls to give you everything you need. Otherwise, I can't truly be your master and I'm no better than that jackoff Andrew. Tell me this is what you want, and you'll have it now. We're both ready to devote today to your pleasure."

*Claim me as his? As in beyond today?* Her heart picked up speed at the scary, wonderful thought of having Jack in her life forever.

She stood, unmoving, struck mute, mind racing. "Oh . . . wow."

"I'm more than ready." A thread of ironic laughter wove its way through Deke's voice.

"Do you really want this?" Jack murmured.

Those words pounded a heavy drumbeat of desire between her legs . . . where both of their fingers had possessed her and pushed her to a searing realm of pleasure.

Sensation overload aside, this was a moment of truth: Did she want both of them? Could she handle a *ménage*? Could she take receiving what she'd told Jack she'd always wanted?

An image of Jack and Deke both filling her, fucking her, nearly had her moaning. Her breasts ached, her clit already throbbed for attention again. And her heart swelled as she realized that Jack had put aside his fear and given her his trust so that she could experience her fantasy.

He clenched his jaw, fingers tightening on her cheeks. He needed her answer. She searched his familiar dark eyes, now like a vise on her own gaze. He needed her. The fact he was willing to do this to keep her stunned her utterly. Joy burst through her chest.

"Are *you* sure?" Her voice trembled.

"Watching you flush and swell in the sunlight, feeling you writhe on my fingers, seeing you smile, yeah." Jack sounded like he'd swallowed a truckload of gravel. "Yeah."

A beautiful answer, but still . . . she had to ask the hard question. "You're not going to turn into Destructor on steroids, watching Deke touch me? This isn't going to upset you?"

Cupping her cheek, he sighed. "If I don't give this to you, I'll lose you anyway. And I believe we belong together, *cher*. We have to trust each other to have any tomorrows." A reluctant smile tugged at his wide mouth. "Besides, you looked hot as hell coming for both of us."

"Jack and I talked about it early this morning. His head is in the right place, doll."

"So it's up to you." Jack swallowed. "All it takes is one word, and we'll fuck you beyond your every dream. You just have to accept your needs. Yes or no."

The moment stunned her . . . humbled her. Simply amazing. Seemingly implacable Jack was willing to put aside his every misgiving to grant her wish. A ballsy move, one that proved he really didn't want to let her go. Because he cared.

Thank God, because her every attempt to shut him out of her body and heart had failed miserably.

Now, all she had to do to fulfill her fantasy was be brave enough to accept her wants, the pleasure, their demand.

A few short days ago, she couldn't have accepted this offer. Oh, she would have wanted to. Ached and yearned to, in fact. Jack's words alone would have set her on fire. But shame and worry and fear would have doused it in the end.

Now ... no embarrassment, no apprehension. Just a whole, open acceptance of who she was and what she wanted.

Jack had set her free. For that alone, she loved him.

Fresh tears pooled in her eyes as she looked at Jack. "I'd hug you, if I could."

She wiggled her hands beneath her wrists bound to her thighs as dual tones of male laughter filled the room.

"Is that a yes?"

"Yes." She pressed her body against his. "Please, yes."

"*Cher*, it will be our pleasure."

He sealed the deal with a kiss, slanting his hungry mouth over hers and urging her lips apart for him. Immediately, he filled her mouth with his unique flavor, something dark, spiced with Cajun coffee, whiskey, and mystery. She'd know the addictive taste of Jack anywhere. She also tasted just a hint of her own juices. But the gentle note of his kiss was new, infused with not just desire, but hope and promise. Morgan melted.

Deke wasn't content to be idle, though. He pressed his hot mouth to the sensitive curve between her neck and shoulder, skimming his fingers up her body, from hip to navel, up again to swirl around her taut nipple begging for attention.

His thumb brushed across it once. Just once. She gasped into Jack's mouth. Then she moaned when her sexy Cajun hottie pinched its mate.

The two of them together were going to be pure combustion.

A rush of hot desire blasted her, and her knees damn near turned liquid as Jack pressed kisses down her jaw, her shoulder, working his way straight to the nipple he still gripped between his thumb and forefinger.

Deke apparently took that as a sign because he curled huge palms around her cheeks and lifted her face to his, eyes burning. All traces of the teasing big guy who called her "doll" had been replaced by one hard, hungry man. A fresh bolt of lust crashed in her belly.

That need resonated in his moan as he took her mouth and pushed his way inside. Deft, seductive, his clever tongue danced around hers, flirting, tasting, then backing away. He taunted, giving her a brief taste of his rich flavor, tinged with something minty.

She was drowning in a sea of need. The feel of Deke's mouth over hers as Jack toyed with her nipple was making for one hell of a riptide.

Her ability to tread the waters of heavy desire didn't improve any when Deke nipped his way down to her other nipple and both men each worked at a sensitive nub. If she hadn't already been incredibly wet, the sight of two male heads, one like tawny light, the other like silken midnight, would have had her juices running like a leaky faucet. Blood rushed through her body. Desire burned achy and tight just under her skin, pooling between her legs, creating a sea of need.

The tugs of their mouths, different times, different pressures, produced a unified result: arousal that had her sweating. Sensations darted from her nipples to her clit in a rapid-fire sequence her body could barely process.

"Feel good?" Jack lifted his head, lips wet and red and so damn kissable.

She whimpered in answer.

"I think that's a yes," Deke whispered beside him.

Standing at her side now, Jack urged her toward the bed. Deke helped, one hand guiding her by the shoulder, the other palming her ass. She waited for them to help her onto it.

They didn't.

When her thighs bumped the mattress, they bent her over the rumpled bed, then disappeared behind her. Morgan closed her eyes, aware of being naked and vulnerable and exposed. And of two sets of eyes devouring her.

Zippers rasped, clothes rustled. Someone dipped a hand into that little bag of tricks near her feet. Foil ripped. Her heart picked up speed. What were they doing? No anxiety in the request, just dying-to-know curiosity. A million forbidden images flooded her brain, each sexier than the last. And all because Jack wanted to fulfill her so he could claim her.

She'd barely recovered from the thought when Deke eased around the side of the bed again, this time completely naked. She'd seen the hard muscles that slabbed his chest and rippled across his abdomen. Even more solid, lean flesh roped his thighs and framed a thick, heavily veined cock. Her gaze flew from it to his face, and he shot her a wry smile as he climbed on the bed.

Behind her, Jack grabbed her hips and leaned over her back, the hair dusting his chest rasping over sensitive skin. She shivered.

"I'm the director here, Morgan. What I say goes. Are you clear?"

She swallowed, nodded. "Yes, sir."

"Good. Deke . . ." Jack lifted one of the hands from her hips, just for a moment, apparently giving the other man some sort of signal.

Clearly, Deke understood it, because he sidled closer as Jack edged her away from the bed just enough for his friend to ease in front of her.

Morgan's heart began to pound double time. Deke's body was so close, she could smell the heady musk rising from his slightly parted legs, see the individual hairs dusting his thighs, see every vein bulging under the soft skin of his rigid cock.

Jack urged her closer to it, grasped her hips in his greedy hands and pressed the swollen head of his erection to her weeping entrance. He eased in a fraction, but only enough to tease her.

His flared flesh burned against hers. She moaned, writhed, doing her best to tempt him. She ached to feel him impale her, stretch her. A jolt of need nearly had her screaming. Morgan bit her lip, wriggled her hips. Jack merely kept her in place, stretched out on a torturous rack of denial.

"You want me to fuck you?" he demanded.

"Yes, sir."

"I will," he whispered in her ear. "When you suck his cock."

His words lashed her like a whip of desire, stinging across her senses. Morgan tossed a wide-eyed stare over her shoulder.

"I want to watch your mouth on him while I fuck you. Do it now."

A heavy craving gnawed at her, pulsing low in her belly. She wanted to. And she wanted Jack to watch—and get hot as hell.

Turning back to Deke, Morgan focused on his erection. He was definitely in proportion with the rest of his gargantuan body. There was no way she was going to be able to take him all in her mouth. Ever.

But it could be damn fun trying, knowing that with every swipe of her tongue, she'd be driving not just Deke out of his head with lust, but Jack, too.

"Yes, sir."

Before she'd even finished speaking, Deke took her nape in a gentle grip with one calloused hand and wrapped a ruthless fist around his cock with the other. Then he led her head down.

As she dragged her tongue across the swollen head, Deke groaned. Jack issued an echo.

Morgan did it again, laving more of Deke's flared crest with the flat of her tongue. Watching his thighs go taut, she swirled around the ridge of his cock, then swiped her way across the surface again, gratified at his growl in her ear and the salty-musky taste of him leaking across her tongue.

"Jesus, Jack," Deke moaned. "She's torture."

"She's just getting started. Aren't you, *cher*?"

He eased the hot head of his cock out of her aching vagina, and she moaned in protest, right against the purple crest of Deke's engorged erection.

"Suck him," Jack demanded. "Don't toy with him."

But damn it, Jack was toying with her.

Casting a glance up at Deke's face, taut lines of strain bracketed his mouth. His blue eyes flared with demand and a fiery hunger that tightened the screws of lust inside her, until the power of her need obliterated all but her hunger.

He gritted his teeth, but still managed to joke, "Can you hurry, doll? You'd really be helping me out here."

Looking back down, she watched with helpless fever as Deke stroked the stalk of his flesh ruthlessly, his grip so tight and rough, it shocked her. Thrilled her.

The heavy knot of desire pulsed between her legs and swelled at the sight of him. It jabbed her with hot impatience as Jack fed her two scant inches of his cock and stopped. Sweat broke out across her back, and she licked her lips, her brain unable to keep up with the needs of her body. The torment was almost too much.

Deke's fingers tightened on the back of her head, pushing her down again. Yes, she wanted this. To taste him. To know that Jack watched in approval and arousal.

Morgan opened her mouth and sucked in as much of Deke's hard length as she could, coating his hot, dry skin with her saliva. The moisture eased her way as she drew back, then pushed down his cock again, taking him to the back of her mouth.

He sat heavy on her tongue, salty, so damn hot and spicy. His taste ratcheted up her arousal. So did knowing Jack watched her every move.

"Good girl," Jack praised as he plunged his cock deep into her channel, up against the mouth of her womb, where he pressed against a spot that made her moan and squirm and writhe. "As long as you're sucking him good, I'll fuck you good. You stop, I stop. You come before he does . . . I'll give you hell."

A fresh bolt of lust hit her like lightning, white-hot and electric. Jack wasn't just getting three people in a room for a fuckfest. No. Just like he understood the thoughts that made up her darkest needs, he dominated her, ordering her to participate, freeing her from any reins her morality might have put on her.

Nodding her assent, Morgan bobbed her head, her tongue rasping against Deke's cock. The big blond giant hissed in appreciation, and his fingers tugged on her hair, sending delicious pinpoints of pain across her scalp.

God, she was burning up. Jack's firm strokes rasping against her wet flesh were short-circuiting her brain. His every push sent her bobbing over Deke's cock, and she swirled her tongue all over him, moistening, laving, teasing him with every stroke, loving the feel of him heavy on her tongue—and Jack's stare hot on her back.

Between the two of them . . . The torture rack of pleasure stretched her further. She was on fire, seared with lust that agonized. Her nipples ached, her clit screamed for attention. She imagined pushing Jack and Deke into climax at the same time. The thought made her insane with need.

Morgan tightened around Jack, clamping down on him, as she dragged her tongue up the slick length of Deke's cock. Both men groaned, long and guttural. One of Jack's hands tightened on her hip, the other delved past her damp curls and press-rubbed her clit until she cried out. Deke upped the pleasure by pinching her nipples until the bite of pain, the shocking hedonism of their demands, nearly thrust her over the edge and sent her plummeting into hot satisfaction.

"Not yet," Jack warned, voice strained nearly beyond recognition.

He eased back on his long, grinding strokes deep inside her.

"No!" she protested, tearing her mouth away from Deke. Damn it, how could Jack do this to her? She throbbed. They'd tied her in knots of need. And wasn't this her fantasy?

"Jack!"

"That's sir to you," he reminded her with a growl—and a firm whack to her ass and a gentle pinch of her clit. "Now suck him, make him come. Then you'll get yours."

With no mercy whatsoever, Deke watched her with raw hunger as he filtered his hands through her hair again and tugged her down to his cock.

Morgan closed her eyes. She ought to be pissed. Flamingly furious at the way they demanded and controlled and withheld. But no. She was more aroused than she'd ever been in her life.

"Suck me hard."

Deke's voice was like sandpaper on steel wool. The sound of it made heat flare like a furnace running full throttle, made her pussy clench with need.

She sucked Deke into her mouth and gave a demanding pull on him. He stiffened even more against her tongue and gripped her hair in harsh fists. In reward, Jack plunged into her, prodding at her swollen clit with his fingers, now coated with her juice. She cried out.

God, it was so much. Too much. And even though Jack had backed off the hot pace of his strokes, she still felt the inferno of desire raging, climbing, threatening to lick at her until her body exploded into a thousand pleasure-rent pieces and sanity fled.

As if sensing how close she was, Jack eased away again. Morgan whimpered. She had to come. *Soon, damn it. Now!*

She rededicated her efforts to Deke's cock, laving from root to tip, lingering on the hidden spot just beneath the flared head, wrapping her tongue around the thick root. Then she took him in her mouth, deep, back to her throat and sucked hard. Her cheeks hollowed. Beneath her, Deke got even harder. And he groaned, urging her on.

"Oh, that's it. Holy shit, doll, you've got a mouth . . . That's it. So hot, so good. Suck my cock."

He thrust up into her, fucking her mouth once, twice. Again, he swelled against her tongue, bulging so that she felt every ridge, every vein, the pulse of semen beneath the skin.

"Jesus, Jack." He panted. "I'm not going to last."

"Good girl," Jack panted in her ears as he covered her back with sweat-slick flesh and finally began to piston in and out of her aching pussy. "Swallow him. Every drop."

Morgan bobbed her head in understanding, frantic now with arousal. She clawed her thighs as desire ballooned inside her. Her belly cramped with need as Deke engorged again. He pulsed on her tongue—hard. Then he cried out, the guttural sound ripped from his chest as if the plea- sure was pure agony. His hot seed filled her mouth, salty, milky. She barely had time to swallow before Jack stiffened behind her, gripping her hips ruthlessly, and fucked her with every ounce of power he possessed.

Up, up, up—she didn't climb the ladder of arousal. She rocketed straight to the top with the feel of Jack's cock stretching her, rasping against her every nerve ending. The beginnings of climax fluttered inside her, and Morgan whimpered, so ready to let go.

"Don't come," Jack commanded. "I didn't give you permission."

*Who the hell was he kidding?* Frantically, Morgan shook her head. She couldn't stop it. Couldn't.

Jack smacked her ass, and Morgan instinctively jumped to obey. Why, damn it? She wanted to come.

But she wanted to please him more. So Morgan tensed, trying to push out sensation, to stop her body's headlong rush to satisfaction.

"Hold on, doll," Deke encouraged.

She raised her eyes to his, pleading, needing. He just shook his head, those blue eyes promising more—much more . . . later.

She railed, whimpered. God, the erotic edge of pleasure-pain had never been so overpowering.

Behind her, Jack gripped her hips as he pounded into her with jackhammer strokes that had her weak-kneed and mewling. The drumbeat of desire pulsed in her clit as he continued to ramp her up and up.

Then he swelled, stiffened. And with a savage shout and a last brutal thrust, Jack came, long and hard and powerfully.

Morgan didn't. Though denying herself had her tense as hell and crying out. God, she'd almost rather tear the top off of her head and pour acid inside. The ache was eating her up. So hot. So damn achy. Tears stung her eyes. This couldn't go on . . .

Jack withdrew from her body and tore off his condom with a satisfied smile. Bastard! He just left her here to burn alive.

She glared, making plans to skewer him alive, string him up by his balls. This was her fantasy, and nowhere in it did she go without orgasm!

"Wow," Deke commented.

"Fiery, isn't she?"

"Stop talking about me as if I'm not here! You two put me in this . . . state."

"We'll fix you," Jack assured.

"When? Next month isn't good enough. Even five minutes from now is too long to wait."

Morgan jerked against her bonds, frustration eating at her. But she couldn't do anything, especially touch her own clit. Having two pairs of hot male eyes devouring her was only making her hotter, expanding the never-ending need.

"Get on the bed."

Jack's deep voice pinged in the air, telling her he wouldn't tolerate any more of her outbursts. It was on the tip of her tongue to tell him to fuck himself . . . but ultimately, she couldn't disobey. Not when he spoke like that. Not knowing the way she longed to please him. The submissive in her relented, needing to bow to his stronger presence and give herself into his care.

She trusted that he would give her what she needed.

Morgan approached the bed, uncertain exactly how he wanted her.

Jack didn't let her flounder, but helped her onto her knees—straddling Deke as he lay back with a grin. His searing blue gaze was fixed on the wet curls between her legs, and already his cock stood like a stone column against his belly.

Please, please don't let them want her to fuck Deke without coming.

On her knees, Jack urged her up Deke's body, past his thighs and to his hips. But he didn't stop. He kept pushing her up and up, past Deke's abs and chest. Then the blond hulk himself lifted her, settling her knees on either side of his head.

"I've got to get my mouth on this pussy." He groaned.

He dove into her like a man possessed, tongue spearing at her drenched channel, then lashing at her clit. Morgan gasped at the shocking burst of sensation. Any cooldown she'd achieved in the last three minutes evaporated at the first touch of Deke's mouth. She squirmed, trying to find relief from the sweet torture of his teeth gently nibbling her. He wasn't about to allow that. Instead, he wrapped his arms around her thighs anchoring her in place.

Morgan might be on top, but Deke was completely in control.

"You look so damn sexy," Jack rumbled in her ear from behind her, his voice thick with desire. "I can't wait until we're both fucking you and you wash us in your cream as you come."

Both fucking her? God, yes. Jack understood what she craved. And he'd give it to her. She hoped before she expired from unfulfilled need.

Jack fiddled with the locks at her sides, and suddenly her wrists were free—just in time for Deke to suck her clit into his mouth and nearly send her rocketing into the stratosphere. Nearly. But he didn't let her go yet.

"Can I come?" She turned pleading eyes on Jack as he bent to retrieve new items from his bag of tricks. "Please."

"Not yet. I'll tell you, *cher*."

"I can't stop . . ." She panted, gasping for her next breath. "It's too . . ."

"You can. You will," Jack demanded.

A fresh coat of perspiration glazed her skin. A new jab of lust sizzled inside her pussy. The same whimper that failed to move Jack before failed to move him now.

Damn him! She was barely hanging on here . . . Her folds felt swollen to four times the normal size, and still Deke kept bringing the heat, the pleasure, leaving her just on the threshold of an atomic orgasm. And Jack just kept watching the show, idly toying with her nipples, like he had all day to enjoy.

"Lean forward and brace yourself on your hands," Jack commanded.

Morgan complied, hoping that they'd let her come and end the maelstrom of lust driving her out of her mind. The orgasm brewing just grew and grew, expanding into something larger than she'd ever imagined. When this peak hit, it was going to kill her.

A moment later, Jack wedged a pair of fingers deep in her pussy. He wriggled, reawakening nerves his cock had stroked to life. But he didn't stay. No, those fingers of his dragged her juices to the smaller hole in back.

He was going to fuck her there again. And once he did, there was no way she could stop the orgasm bubbling in her gut from completely overtaking her.

"Jack! Sir . . ."

"Your skin is so flushed and pretty," he murmured against her back as one finger toyed with the puckered rosette.

"Her taste is fucking addicting, too," Deke muttered against her pussy before he dove back in, sucking her clit into his mouth.

The dark ache of desire throbbed harder. The edge rushed closer, looming huge and unavoidable in its burning grip. God, the heat blistered her. She couldn't hold back much longer. Her inner walls fluttered. Her clit throbbed against Deke's tongue. Just one more sensation, and denying her climax would no longer be possible.

Jack seemed oblivious to her sensual distress, taking his sweet time dragging her cream from her weeping entrance to the forbidden hole in back. Morgan found herself pushing back toward his fingers, whimpering, pleading.

"Are you mine?" he whispered right in her ear, so she alone could hear.

"Yes."

"Completely?"

"Yes. God, yes."

"You'll stay with me? Be mine? Wear my collar?"

"Yes, yes, yes," she chanted.

He positioned a finger against her back entrance, and every nerve ending jumped as he began to press in.

"Oh, yes!" She could barely get the words out, barely find a breath to say them. Dizzy, hot, aching tight under her skin, Morgan babbled with mindless appreciation.

Jack thrust his finger deep in her ass at the moment Deke scraped her clit with this teeth.

"Come!" Jack shouted.

But she'd already started. Nothing could stop her from flying apart, exploding into a million sizzling pieces, burning under the pressure of Jack's invading finger, aching at the adroit ministrations of Deke's insistent tongue.

She didn't moan or cry out. She screamed, long and loud, gripping the bed sheets with her hands as the pulses went on and on and on. The climax shattered her, hitting so hard she lost her breath. Her gut cramped. Dizziness assailed her as her heartbeat pounded in her ears like a staccato drum.

God, she was dying. Right here in this little cottage room, bursting into so many flaming little pieces of herself, she'd never be able to put them all back together. And she didn't care.

Deke eased her down his body and reached for something near his hip. A condom, she realized a moment later, as she watched him tear open the foil with his teeth, roll it on, and grab her hips in world-record time.

Again? Oh . . . She had all the muscle control of a rag doll right now, had just taken what felt like the first ragged breath of air in hours, and they wanted to fuck her into orgasm again?

Before Deke thrust home, Jack withdrew his finger from her ass and replaced it with the searing width of his lubricated cock.

"Jack . . . Sir," she began to protest.

"Take me," he demanded on a groan. "Take us."

And he slid in, dark, ruthless, demanding that she open wide and accept every inch of him in her ass right now. Moaning at the feel of him stretching her so completely, Morgan pushed down until he'd sheathed his entire cock inside and his balls slapped at her pussy.

And there he stayed, completely unmoving.

Shockingly, the feeling of him tunneling inside her dark, forbidden passage roused her all over again. She tried to wriggle and whimper. Deke's hands stayed her hips. Her previous scream had stolen most of her voice. The new jolt of demand scorching through her body took the rest.

They were killing her. Honest to goodness killing her.

Before she could find a way to recover, to cope, Deke positioned his thick cock at the weeping entrance of her pussy and thrust inside, driving his way in quickly, pushing past resistance, shoving in inch after inch after ruthlessly hard inch inside her.

*Oh. My. God.* Stretched so full, packed tight. The burn of their cocks put her senses on overload, sent her reeling straight back to the kind of sharp arousal that had her holding her breath, calling Jack's name, gripping Deke's shoulders to stay grounded in reality in the midst of this mind-blowing fantasy.

And then they began to move, like a well-timed dance designed for maximum devastation to her senses. Jack withdrew, Deke thrust in. Jack thrust in, Deke withdrew. And friction, oh, God . . . The heat overwhelmed her. She'd never had so many nerve endings screaming all at once, and Deke only made it worse when he pressed a thumb to her clit.

"Jesus, she's tight," he ground out.

"And she has a thin membrane between her ass and her pussy. I feel the head of your cock dragging over me. Damn!"

"Yeah." Deke's face twisted into a mask of concentration. "She's killing my control."

"What control?" Jack growled. "*Cher*, come when you can, as much as you can."

That was all the invitation Morgan needed. At the feel of Deke's cock pressing right against her cervix and the slick pad of his thumb dragging across her swollen clit, she exploded, seeing light and stars behind her eyes. Hell, she wouldn't be surprised if someone told her the heavens had parted.

The explosion was Jack's to command, and sharp as a machete. The two men tore her apart with thick, sublime, unearthly pleasure.

Jack rewarded her by reaching around her and lifting her breast to

Deke's mouth. He took the nipple between his lips hungrily, drawing hard, nipping with his teeth. Sensation zinged from her breast to her belly, straight down to where Deke impaled her with the wicked length of his cock . . . and lower, to the forbidden thrill of Jack lodged deep inside her.

Together, they scraped her raw, shoving her up impossibly higher, right into something huge and irresistible. Indescribable.

She'd barely caught her breath when she felt Jack's flesh push into her, dragging across all her tingling nerves while he exhaled on her neck and whispered, "You're mine. I love you."

Something cracked in Morgan at his words, deep inside. The last of her resistance broke free. She sent a helpless glance over her shoulder at him, knowing her total submission showed in her eyes, and she climaxed again, zooming higher than ever in shuddering surrender.

Clamping down on the pair of cocks so hard, both were trapped deep inside her as the orgasm rolled over her, wave after wave erupting, bringing utter submission with it.

Tears rolled down her cheeks. In that moment, Morgan wasn't herself. She didn't worry about whether this choice was right or what others would think or if she could live with herself later. As they came with her, groaning and gasping, she was at peace. Perfect blessed peace in perfect rushing pleasure for the first time in her life.

"Yes!" she cried out, her voice a screech of pain, need, love, and completion.

"I love you," he panted in her ear. "Tell me . . ."

"Yes! Yes, I love you."

As the pleasure subsided, Jack wrapped his arms around her tight, so tight it seemed he'd never let go. That was just the way Morgan wanted it.

*       *       *

NOON slanted through the windows of the bed and breakfast's quaint cottage, illuminating Morgan's fiery hair and bare, pale skin as she curled up next to him in slumber, her head pillowed on his shoulder. Deke lay behind her, his hand lax in sleep as he draped it around her waist. They looked so peaceful.

And he was in hell.

Not because Deke touched her. Surprisingly, he'd known almost from the moment they laid their hands on Morgan just a short few hours ago that she might appreciate Deke's touch, but her heart wasn't involved. After that, Jack had simply enjoyed the fireworks her fantasy had inspired.

As he'd hoped, Morgan had surrendered utterly, totally, given him every bit of herself, her body, her passion. He'd wrung from her the sort of abiding submission he'd been seeking since the moment he'd first seen her.

She'd told him that she loved him.

So how the fuck was he going to tell her now that he'd arranged their meeting and plotted to fuck her, strictly to get revenge against her fiancé? Ex-fiancé. There was no way he was giving her up to Brandon Ross after today.

Problem was, what if she wanted to go back to the pansy-ass bastard?

He was going to have to come clean, explain how and why he'd arranged their meeting, and swear on his life that his every intent had changed, virtually from the moment he'd touched her.

Hell, he should have done this a long time ago. Jack sighed, clenched his fists. When revenge had taken a backseat to winning Morgan for himself, he should have been honest, laid his cards out on the table. Dreaming up ways to win her trust, only to confess that he'd lied, had been the stupidest freakin' idea ever.

Shoving down the gut-tightening fear that he was going to lose her, Jack kissed her awake.

Please God, don't let this be the last time she let him touch her.

Slowly, her eyes fluttered open. Her languid blue gaze, sated smile, and catlike stretch all jabbed at his heart. She wasn't just beautiful to him, but perfect for him. He loved her like . . . he'd never loved any woman. And if he didn't play his cards right, she could walk out the door forever.

He held in a biting curse.

"Morgan. *Cher* . . ." he whispered.

Now what? Where were his suave words. How the hell could he phrase this?

"I have to tell you something," he murmured.

Her ginger brows sloped down in a tired frown. She yawned, covering her mouth with the back of her hand in a gesture both womanly and childlike at once.

Tenderness jerked his heart, as anxiety kicked him in the teeth. God, he'd almost rather cut his balls off with a dull rusty knife than shatter the bond between them.

"Hmm." She moaned. Her eyes drifted half-closed as she sent him a sleepy smile.

Behind her, Deke shifted, his hand lowering, curling around her hip. Then he let out a snore. Morgan giggled.

Ignoring Deke, Jack took hold of her face, gaze delving down into hers. "I love you, *cher*. I have to know something. You and Brandon . . ."

That brought her eyes open. Wide open.

She gasped. "Jack, I—"

"Do you love him?" he demanded.

Morgan hesitated, clearly searching for words. Pain stomped his gut. Damn it, this was going to rip his fucking heart out to hear that she did.

"Yes, but not the way you think. He—"

Something—someone—pounded on the door. A moment later, wood splintered in a deafening sound. The door crashed open, slamming against the wall.

Jack scrambled in front of Morgan and faced the threat that stood in their doorway.

Brandon Ross wearing a business suit and a snarl from hell.

"Get your fucking filthy hands off her, Cole." Brandon raised a mean-looking Browning Hi-Power and pointed it at Jack. "Now!"

# Chapter Seventeen

"BRANDON!" Morgan cried, peering around Jack's shoulder.

Her half brother's thin, elegant frame filled the doorway. Fury morphed into shock when he realized she was in bed with two men. Mortification blasted open a pit of dark dread in Morgan's stomach. Too bad she couldn't crawl into it and disappear, she thought as she scrambled to cover herself with a sheet.

"Put the gun down!" she demanded.

He ignored her, instead scowling at Jack as if the fires of hell lurked in his eyes.

On her left, Deke had awakened and leaped in front of her, beside Jack, to protect her.

"This isn't the way it looks, Brandon," Jack assured.

"Yes, it's *exactly* the way it looks."

Morgan couldn't mistake her brother's growl, but it barely registered. Besides that unnerving gun, she was stuck on one fact . . .

"You two know each other?"

"Oh, shit," Deke muttered and eased off the bed to put on his jeans. "Here we go . . ."

Even Deke knew what was going on? Morgan frowned and shot Jack a questioning glance, scrambling mentally to understand. Jack's face tightened with anger, regret. And unmistakable guilt. What the . . . ? She was having as much success deciphering this situation as she would watching a soap opera in Swedish.

"You didn't tell her?" Brandon said incredulously. "No, of course you didn't. That would have made getting your revenge much harder. But this way, not only did you get to fuck her and get back at me, you obviously shared her with your GI Joe buddy here for payback with interest, since it beats the hell out of anything I did to you."

*Revenge?* "What is going on?" Morgan demanded, frowning.

She couldn't follow the conversation . . . but what she did understand seemed damn ugly. Jack had taken her to bed to get back at Brandon? For . . . ?

"Let me explain." Jack turned and took her shoulders in his hands. "This is going to look bad and sound worse, but I swear—"

"He's a sneaky son of a bitch looking for any way to stab me in the back," Brandon spat. "Get away from him, Morgan. Don't listen."

"I told you how I felt, *cher,*" Jack vowed in a whisper. "Whatever you hear today, my feelings are real. I didn't lie about that."

Until this moment, she hadn't doubted it. Now, dismay infected every breath Morgan took. She knew, just *knew*, something was really wrong. And that she wasn't going to like it.

"But you lied about something else?"

"I told you to get your hands off her!" Brandon waved the gun at Jack again.

"Take it easy, man." Jack eased off the bed and slowly reached for his jeans. "Let's have a calm conversation about this situation and—"

"No, let's tell Morgan the truth and see if she feels like having a calm conversation."

"You don't know the truth!" Jack snarled, tendons standing out in his neck, fists clenched. "You know what this looks like, but you don't know shit."

"So you didn't pursue Morgan and bribe her production assistant, Reggie, to forward your name and IM to her for supposed use on the show?"

Morgan looked to Jack for a denial. He said nothing.

"Why would you do that?" she asked.

A muscle ticked in his jaw. "I . . ."

"Because he wanted to meet you. No, that's not right. He wanted to lure you to his side, fuck you, then make sure I knew about it so he could get his pound of flesh. Literally. Isn't that right, Jack?"

Thick horror slid through Morgan. She turned her gaze to Jack, hoping, praying for his denial. He closed his eyes and bowed his head. The guilt on his face came raging back, digging into his furrowed brow.

*Oh, God.* Brandon was telling the truth. Morgan's stomach lurched as betrayal stung her heart. Shock blanched her blood. "You did . . . all this to me? For revenge? How could you?"

Jack opened dark eyes swimming in shame. "The way I planned things . . . that isn't the way it ended up happening."

The pleading on Jack's face, the seeming sincerity, tore at her. But she'd believed him before. And he'd apparently lied.

"Sure it is." Brandon kept digging up ugliness. "The video footage you emailed me of you fucking Morgan certainly drove your point home. Thanks for that. I clearly saw her back against the door, her nails in your shoulders, while she screamed that she'd never had it better. Well planned."

Brandon's sarcasm ripped at the already raw wounds blistering inside her. Jack had made a video of them? When? Her back against the door, nails in his shoulders . . . *Oh, God.* That first time they had sex, after he'd caught her masturbating in the tub. Had to be. Jack had filmed that without her knowledge and sent it to Brandon? And he'd arranged it all in advance. Unbelievable.

Her happiness curdled, froze. Her trust . . . evaporated in an instant. And he'd done all that for payback? Unforgivable.

Morgan lifted a trembling hand to her mouth. She was going to be sick. This was like a nightmare, gut-wrenchingly terrible, something she wished she could just wake up from. But it was too intense and vivid to escape. Brandon and Jack were playing out some drama here, with her squarely in the middle.

"You emailed him a video of us . . . W-why?"

Jack hesitated, clearly trying to gather his words. Or his lies? The question ripped through Morgan.

"You want to tell her about Kayla, or should I?"

"Brandon, shut up," Jack snarled. "She knows about Kayla."

Kayla? Who the hell was . . . Oh, Jack's ex-wife. Morgan had never heard the woman's name, but that had to be it. Yes, she knew about Kayla, knew that Jack had found his best friend and his wife having sex on video . . .

The full implication slammed into Morgan, stealing her breath, replacing it with pain so intense, she nearly doubled over.

She stared at Jack in dawning horror. "Brandon . . . he was your friend. He was the one in the video having sex with your ex-wife."

"While we were married," Jack snapped. "He betrayed years of friendship and trust."

And it had all hurt Jack's pride.

Morgan trembled with disbelief, with anger. With pain. Deke put an arm around her to comfort her. She elbowed him in the gut, clutched the sheet to her chest, and glared at them all.

Then she zeroed in on Jack. "You betrayed my trust, too. The things you persuaded me to do . . ." Her face flushed hot in remembrance. "The way you made me question everything about myself . . . Damn it, I believed in you. In us. God, I was an idiot! You must have laughed a hundred times."

"I never laughed. Morgan . . . *cher*, I never meant to hurt you. I—"

"You never even thought whether it would hurt her or not," Brandon accused. "You didn't care."

"That's not true." Jack eased toward her and reached out to her.

Morgan jerked away from Jack before he could touch her. Anger and anguish combined on his face, rolled through the taut, lean muscles rippling across his chest and shoulders.

No, it was an act. All for revenge. She wouldn't worry if he actually hurt. As Brandon said, Jack hardly cared whether he'd hurt her.

"*Swamp*, you son of a bitch. There's your safe word. Don't touch me again."

Her rebuff slashed pain across Jack's face, and he turned on Brandon.

"You're not exactly Mr. Clean here," Jack growled at her brother. "You're the one who seduced Kayla while I was married to her, made her believe you loved her—"

"So you seduced me in return?" Morgan shouted at Jack. "Pushed me to change my perception of myself and my sexuality. You made me believe you loved me, that I loved you, too. I said it to you while . . ." She gasped as the awful truth washed through her blood in an icy rush. "That must have been the ultimate revenge, having me tell you that I loved you during sex, just like Kayla said to Brandon. Did you know it would work out that perfectly, or just hope?"

"*Cher*, it was nothing like that. I swear. Honest. I—"

"Dear God! Did you do to Morgan what you did to Kayla?" Brandon broke in, his voice booming with incredulity. "Did you mess with her head and try to turn her into some submissive robot?"

"Does she seem like a robot to you?"

"Kayla couldn't handle what you wanted from a woman, and after you, she was afraid of every man. I no sooner had her, than she left me." Wearing a furious, incredulous scowl, Brandon grabbed Jack by the arm. "Have you done the same thing to Morgan, you bastard?"

"No!" Jack insisted. "Morgan *is* wired for what I need in a woman. She *is* my woman. I awakened her, which is more than you can say. I gave her everything her body yearned for, even a *ménage* when the thought of it twisted my guts in two, all because I wanted her happiness. What did you do besides ignore her sexuality, then leave her when some sick stalker followed her, masturbated on her bed, then shot at her in public? Yeah, that's love for you."

"He shot at you, sweetheart?" Concern transformed Brandon's angry face. He dropped his gun to his side.

"Put that away," she whispered, nodding toward the firearm.

With a reluctant sigh, one that communicated just how pissed he was, Brandon tucked his gun in the waistband of his slacks at the small of his back and turned to her.

When he tried to cup his hand around her shoulder, Jack snarled, "Don't touch her!"

Then he jumped in and hit Brandon with a right cross to the chin.

Brandon's head snapped back, and he came up rubbing his chin with one hand and forming a fist with the other.

Jack blocked Brandon's incoming punch. "I let you take Kayla from me. I didn't love her, and we all knew it. But you'll have to kill me before I let you take Morgan from me. I love her. I'll always love her." Jack turned to her then, his penitent frown ripe with a plea. "If you'll let me explain and apologize. You can't marry him."

"She's not marrying any of you!" screeched a half-wild voice from the open doorway.

Brandon turned and Jack leaned around her brother for a look at their new visitor, but Morgan didn't have to see to know who'd just arrived. She knew that voice.

"Andrew? What are you doing here?" She leaned into his line of vision, still clutching the sheet over her bare body.

Her blood turned to ice when she saw menace mutating his cultured face into a snarl and the threat in his stance as he blocked the door. Fury vibrated off him, zinging around the room like its own lethal force. Adrenaline and anger crashed through Andrew, judging from the way he twitched as he held a gun in his hands—a gun he pointed right at her.

Morgan gasped, her mind racing to comprehend this turn of events.

"Someone has to stop you." Andrew stared at her as if he barely knew her, taking in Deke and Jack, both shirtless and disheveled a few feet away . . . and drawing some accurate conclusions. "You fucked two men? I knew you were a whore, but this is even beyond what I believed you capable of. I can't believe I nearly married you. You dating Senator Ross's son infuriated me enough." Andrew tossed his unusually unkempt salt-and-pepper hair as he nodded at Brandon. "You visited him, agreed to marry him. You slept with him. And now you've taken up with yet another man. Your bodyguard, right? Did you ask him to dominate you, too?"

Andrew's sneer hung in the air, its hostility stinging her like a harsh slap to the face. She refused to be embarrassed by his words. But the gun pointed at her, making her heart pound, scared the hell out of her.

"Yes."

Jack glanced in her direction, then stared at Deke, some silent communication between them that she couldn't understand.

Andrew shook his head. "And now a morning spent cheating on your fiancé and sandwiched between these two testosterone-oozing lugs. For what? A few orgasms? You and I knew each other's minds and shared the joy of quality work, elevating tawdry sex to art, until you threw it away."

Brandon leapt toward Andrew, reaching out to swipe the gun from his jittery grasp. Andrew roared and scrambled away, firing two shots in Brandon's direction. Morgan heard herself scream as the retort of fire deafened her. Her brother threw himself to the ground and rolled away from the bullets.

Breath held, Morgan launched herself from the bed to check on Brandon.

"Back in the bed!" Andrew roared, turning the gun on her again. "Now!"

Easing back under the sheets, she covered her nudity again, shaking. Her hammering heartbeat nearly deafened her. Andrew was serious. Deadly serious. And Brandon . . . *Oh, God, had he been shot?*

Slowly, Jack bent to help Brandon up. Andrew's grip tightened on the gun, his mouth compressing into a grim white line.

Once on his feet, her brother turned to send her a reassuring glance. "I'm fine. Just do what he says, Morgan."

"And nobody else do anything stupid or heroic," Andrew snarled, tossing his arms around wildly, still clutching the chilling, shiny weapon.

Morgan forced herself to take a deep breath, tried to push calm through her body. She knew Andrew. Hysterics on her part would only up his dramatics. And he was an opera fan, a performing art where all the central characters frequently died and the audience applauded the tragedy of it all.

Please, God, no such tragedy for her. She had to save herself and stop Brandon, Jack, and Deke from doing something heroically fatal.

Morgan sucked in a breath and lowered her voice, trying to sound much calmer than she was. "Why are you here? My life is no longer your concern, Andrew."

"You ignored my notes and photos. You ran when I left my semen on your bed as a reminder of the place where we once connected. I tried to make you understand where you belonged and to whom you belonged. I could have forgiven you for Mr. Ross in time. You and I argued, and you might have thought I didn't intend to return for you. But these two . . ." He waved a shaking fist again, this time at Jack and Deke, gun clenched tightly in his grip. "I should have shot you at that strip club. I would have if the nasty den of iniquity hadn't been so crowded."

Andrew's words staggered her, making her mind race with implications. "So Reggie didn't . . . wasn't . . . ?"

Andrew rolled his eyes and sighed with impatience. "Pursuing you?"

"This is stalking, asshole," Deke said with a growl.

With a shake of her head, Morgan tried to shush him.

Thankfully, Andrew ignored him. "Reggie? Of course not. Didn't you see me at the strip club? I looked right at you. You almost fooled me with the disguise, but I'd know your eyes anywhere."

"I couldn't see through the crowded strip club," she murmured. "It was you? Given the pictures, I thought—"

Her ex-fiancé rolled his eyes. "Please. He taught me to take pictures and develop them. He had no idea I took pictures of you until just the other day."

Andrew sniffed, and Morgan knew he was insulted that she'd believed even for a moment that Reggie could stalk her as properly as he had.

"He didn't help you at all?" *Keep him talking, distract him. Stay calm. Find some way out of this damn dangerous mess.*

"He's too stupid. For a time, he helped me keep track of you, in the interest of flattering and protecting you. And once he figured it out, well, the stupid lug went to warn you, but he couldn't find you." Andrew shook his head, contempt twisting his face. "He upset that stripper whore last night and got himself arrested before he could warn you I was in town."

"You? You've been my stalker all along?"

Jack grimaced at her, then sent another glance to Deke. Out of the corner of her eye, she saw Deke nod. She tensed.

They were going to do something stupid and heroic—and get themselves killed.

"No," Morgan whispered at them.

"I am your savior!" Andrew shouted over her, then stiffened, his face darkening to a thunderous scowl. "Someone has to save you from your-self. When we first dated, you seemed so sweetly innocent. I overlooked your impurity because you were over twenty-one, and we hadn't known each other previously.

"After we argued about your crude bedroom ideas, I eventually real-ized that I might not have given you enough attention, and I started pur-suing you again, despite your involvement with Mr. Ross. I decided to flatter you and believed I could save you by marrying you. But . . ." He clicked the hammer back on the gun and gave a disdainful toss of his head toward Jack. "As soon as you met Mr. Cole, you began acting like a bitch in the throes of heat. He's a well-known dominant, and you all but licked him up with your gaze."

Morgan drew in a deep breath, resolving to stay calm—despite the fact that she both itched to strangle the bastard and run screaming from his gun. She ignored her temper and her sweating palms.

"I wanted Jack. He understood my need to submit, Andrew. He taught me there's nothing wrong with that." Whatever other deceptions lay between them, she'd always have that gift from Jack. "Your failure to accept me as I am only proves we're ill-suited. Go give some other woman your attention. Maybe she'll appreciate the obsessive bit. I don't. Get the hell out of my life."

"You're only proving what I feared. The only way to purge you of your wickedness is to kill you."

Morgan froze. Andrew raised the gun. Andrew—her former pro-ducer, her former fiancé, the mild-mannered artsy type wasn't just hyped up on momentary anger. He seriously planned to kill her.

"Now!" Jack shouted in the tense, churning air.

Deke grabbed her, yanking her to the floor in a tangle of arms and legs. Out of the corner of her eye, she saw Jack grab the gun at the small of Brandon's back, then push her brother into the corner behind Andrew, out of harm's way. Then she saw nothing, as Deke ripped her from the cocoon of the sheets and began to roll her under the bed.

An explosion thundered through the room. A moment later, some-thing struck her in the chest, whooshing the breath from her body with the force of the impact. The sting seared fire across her skin. In an instant, her body nearly imploded with pain. She cried out. But a second blast masked the sound.

She gasped for breath, a strange weightless, nearly floating feeling assailing her.

A cry, a thud, then . . .

"Morgan!" she heard someone shout as if from a distance.

Jack. It was Jack's voice. He sounded worried.

"Here . . ." she whispered, frowning against the pain. What was wrong with her?

"Shit!" Deke rumbled behind her. "She's hit!"

She was? Morgan's eyes fluttered open in time to see Deke put his shirt over her chest and press down. Painful, damn it!

"No . . ." she wailed.

"Where?" Jack demanded.

"Hell, I don't know. Her chest, I think. There's blood everywhere, front and back. Shit, she's bleeding fast. Call 911!"

# Chapter Eighteen

JACK dropped to his knees, watching Morgan's face pale into something damn near ghostly. The red of her blood gushed through Deke's gray T-shirt, turning it morbidly dark. The coppery smell of blood burned into his nostrils, exploded in his brain.

Son of a bitch, he wished he could kill that asshole Andrew all over again! For making her doubt her sexuality, for even thinking of hurting Morgan. And this time, he'd enjoy putting a bullet between the bastard's eyes.

But now, there wasn't time for anything besides saving Morgan's life.

Yanking the sheet off the bed, he wrapped it around her wound, applying pressure with one hand and reaching for the phone with the other. The 911 call only took a few moments, and the dispatcher promised to have someone there within minutes.

Jack only hoped Morgan hung on that long.

Now, all he could do was wait . . . and do a little damage control.

Casting a desperate gaze up at Deke, Jack was shocked to see his own grim concern mirrored there. Morgan had even left her mark on his hard-ass, tough-as-nails business partner.

"Take Brandon and get out of here."

"I'm not leaving her," Brandon said, now hovering above him, concern tightening his mouth.

"You stay, and the press will have a field day," Jack snarled. "Four men, one of them dead, two guns, and one naked woman all in the same hotel room. They'll start asking questions that the son of a man running for president shouldn't have raised. You leave, and I can play this like a bodyguard just doing his job. I'm friends with the locals. It will fly."

Brandon hesitated. Jack could tell his former friend was torn, and he didn't give a shit. He focused all his effort on stemming the flow of Morgan's blood.

But nothing helped. The blood just kept running, flowing . . .

"Hang on, *cher*. Stay with me. You can't give up, not now. *Je t'aime, mon coeur*."

"You love her?" Brandon's voice sounded thin, unsteady. He seemed shaken. "It's not bullshit. You really love her?"

Jack didn't have time to spare him a glance. "Yes, I love her, and I'm sure you'll find some way to use it to cut me off at the balls. Right now, I need you to get the fuck out of here."

"But she's—"

"If this turns into a media circus because of you and she dies, I'll make sure they have to pick up your remains with tweezers!"

Brandon fell silent for a moment, then nodded.

"Wait," Jack called. "The gun. You're not registered to carry in Louisiana, are you?"

And Jack had just killed a man using that weapon.

The elegant senator's son flinched. "Oh, God."

"Nine millimeter?" Deke asked.

"Yes." Brandon's voice shook.

"Jack?" asked Deke.

"In my duffle bag. Switch out the bullets. Fire a round into the grass outside the French doors or something. It's the best we can do, in case they run forensics."

"Those good ol' Cajun boys aren't going to look too closely. It'll work."

Sirens sounded in the distance. Deke swore and poured the bullets from Brandon's gun, switching them out with those in Jack's own. He thrust open the French doors at the side and quickly fired a round into the grass.

Jack flinched, heart pounding at the sound, the one that slammed home the fact he might lose the only woman he'd ever loved. The woman he wanted to keep for the rest of his life.

The woman who wasn't his.

"I'll call Alyssa. We'll find a place to hide Brandon. Touch base when you can," a shirtless Deke said, herding Brandon out the door.

Jack nodded, still applying pressure, afraid to lift the material, afraid to find out the blood was still flowing, afraid the bullet had hit some organ and was slowly killing her. Damn it, he'd flunked fucking EMT training.

"Hang on to her, man."

Jack glanced up. Deke stood solidly on his side, as always. No words necessary. No questions asked.

"Thanks," he croaked.

Now he only hoped that he could keep her alive so he could fight for her.

*   *   *

FOUR long hours later, full of questions and red tape and his guts shredding under the sharp blade of dread, night was falling. Jack reached the hospital. He had blood all over him—and he didn't give a damn. The police had just finished with all their long, annoying questions about Andrew's death. Through it all, he could only wonder, with a machete of fear stabbing him over and over, about Morgan's condition.

After barking an inquiry at the nurse's station, he sprinted to Morgan's room.

Heart pounding, he came to a dead stop in the doorway. *"Mon dieu."*

Wearing a pale blue hospital gown, she looked so still and lifeless and even paler than the white-white of her pillow. Even her sexy cinnamon freckles had faded to near nothing. The IV pumped fluid into her body through a tube stuck to the back of her hand. A bandage bulked up her right shoulder and, from the bulge in her gown, extended down to her rib cage.

If she died, it was going to be all his fucking fault. If he'd never started this stupid bid for revenge, if he'd just protected her, instead of screwing with her body, her mind . . . her heart, Morgan wouldn't now be fighting for her life.

"What's the news?" he snapped at Deke, hands shaking as he entered the room.

Brandon stood sulking nearby, arms over his chest, propped against a wall. He looked like a man with a lot of heavy shit on his mind. Jack related.

He sank into an uncomfortable chair the color of baby puke and couldn't help but wonder how on earth they had ended up wrestling over the same woman again? And why every time they did, the results were always so disastrous.

"It's good. They brought her back from surgery about twenty minutes ago and said she's going to be fine."

Fine. She was going to be fine. That's all that mattered.

"*Merci Dieu.*" He let out a ragged breath.

Deke spoke up. "It's a flesh wound. Bullet entered and exited cleanly, just below her collarbone. They've stopped the bleeding. They came and asked if any friends or family are AB positive and could give her blood." He shrugged an apology. "I'm B negative, man. Rare, but the wrong type of rare. Sorry. I need a cup of coffee. Want one?"

Jack shook his head.

Shit, he couldn't even help Morgan in this. He hated feeling so damn helpless. "I'm A positive."

As Deke left the room, Brandon shucked his jacket and rolled up his shirtsleeve. "I'm AB positive. I just told them I'll give. They're coming to get me in a few minutes."

A huge stroke of luck that Brandon had Morgan's rare blood type. Jack choked on a million replies that sprang to his tongue. He settled on the only one that would do for now. "Thank you."

"I care about Morgan, too. It's nothing."

It was everything to Jack. Brandon donating meant Jack had a shot at a future, even if Morgan never spoke to him again. Just knowing she was alive and well would sustain him.

In fact, Morgan's injury had made him realize a thing or two. Namely, that this vendetta he'd carried had both nearly made him and nearly destroyed him. It had to end. It was time to ensure this sort of shit never happened again. Time give Brandon back his life.

And to free himself.

Stumbling to his feet, Jack reached inside his coat pocket and withdrew a videotape. In an old package with a tattered white cardboard cover, it hung heavy in his hand.

"Here." He held it out to Brandon.

"What is this?" Brandon raised puzzled blue eyes to him.

"You know damn well what it is. I had this one in my office, which is right around the corner. I've got the spare in a safe-deposit box. I'll get it back to you next week. It's time I gave them to you."

Recognition dawned across Brandon's face. "The video with Kayla? No more threatening to blackmail me if I run for office?"

"No more," Jack answered tightly, then turned to sit.

"Seriously?" Brandon grabbed the arm of his coat. "Why? Why now?"

Jack faced his nemesis, his old friend, again. "Falling for Morgan proved to me real quick that self-control is just a high-minded ideal. You loved Kayla, and when my pride wouldn't let her go, despite her asking for a divorce, you claimed her the only way you could. In your shoes . . . I might have done the same."

"I loved her. She broke my fucking heart." Brandon's monotone reply revealed that he'd never recovered from Kayla.

For the first time in his life, Jack could understand that hit-by-a-Mack-truck feeling.

"I'm going to lose Morgan over this revenge," Jack muttered, raking tense hands through his hair. "Over something I should have let go of years ago. And if she rides off into the sunset to marry you, I don't want her to have any other reason to hate me. Just . . . take care of her."

Brandon rubbed at an apparent pain between his eyebrows and smiled with bitter irony. "I will, but I'm not going to marry her. Jack, she's not my fiancée, and I've never touched her in my life. She's my half sister."

If Brandon had said he was really a two-headed rhino in disguise, Jack couldn't have been any more stunned. "Sister?"

With a tight nod, Brandon began, "This can't leave the room. You've always been a man of your word . . . even when I haven't been."

"Your secret is safe."

"Thanks." Brandon sighed, stood, and paced. "My father impregnated her mother when she worked for him as a barely legal intern. He paid her handsomely to go away and never mention his name to anyone, not even to Morgan.

"About three years ago, when my father first started talking about a bid for the White House, he hired a consultant, who told him to dig out every skeleton in his closet and bury it even deeper. My father came clean to me about Morgan. I looked her up on his orders, with the intent to pay her off. But I liked her too much to give up being her brother. We kept in touch, saw each other. I was there when she taped her first show."

A smile lifted the corners of Brandon's mouth for a moment, before he turned pensive again. "When this business with the stalker started, I tried to help her. But protecting her from Houston became impossible, and when the asshole masturbated on her bed, I told her to come stay with me. We floated the story that she was my fiancée as a cover, since I couldn't tell anyone the truth."

And Jack had believed the lie, believed Morgan was his fiancée, then pursued her all the way to submission because of it.

Life was going to hurt like hell without her, but he couldn't be sorry he'd had her for a brief time. She clearly wasn't going to marry Brandon . . . but he also doubted she'd speak to him again.

"Bet having Morgan with you pissed your father off."

"You have no idea." Brandon's bitter smile spoke volumes. "Anyway, I was terrified when I got orders to go to Iraq for a three-week assignment. I knew she was alone and vulnerable. It even crossed my mind to call you, since you're the best damn bodyguard in the business." He sighed. "But I couldn't give you that sort of power over me. It never occurred to me that you were waiting for me to get engaged to get your revenge."

"For three years, yes. I wasn't going to give up."

"I don't blame you," Brandon admitted quietly. "I'm just glad that I only got as far as a debriefing in D.C. before the trip was postponed. I hope we're settled once and for all."

"We are." Jack sighed. "Thanks for the truth."

Silence descended. Jack stared at Morgan hard—as if he could will her awake.

She never moved a muscle.

"Is she being sedated?"

"I'm assuming so. She was awake about ten minutes ago, but now . . ."

Tension and hope gripped Jack's gut. "Did she say anything?"

"No. She just looked around, saw Deke and me, and shut her eyes again."

She hadn't asked for him. And why should she? Stupid to hope she would. From her point of view, he'd lied, used her, exploited her. Why should she believe that he loved her? And if she'd ever thought she loved him . . . well, his stunning conversation with Brandon earlier today would have cured her of that.

Losing Morgan wasn't anything less than he deserved. But the fierce urge to stave off the reality fueled a furious denial. Knowing he'd never touch her again was like a sharp gouge of pain knifing him right between the ribs.

"That's for the best, I guess. She won't feel any pain."

"True."

And she wouldn't wake up right now. Even if she did, would she really want him there?

No. She'd never want him near her again.

Jack shuffled his boot against the antiseptically clean floor, his chest crushingly tight. "I should go. Tell her . . ."

What? What the hell could he say to make this any better? It would take a fucking miracle to change her mind, and Jack didn't think he had any such miracle coming to him.

In the end, he settled on the simplest. "Tell her I'm sorry."

Shoving clenched fists into his stiff jeans, Jack forced himself to turn away from Morgan and walk out of her life.

# Chapter Nineteen

MORGAN paced across the hardwood floor of Brandon's living room. The surface felt cool beneath her bare feet but didn't soothe her searing thoughts.

"You're going to wear out the floor, little sister."

She flipped a gaze at Brandon over her shoulder. "Doubtful."

"Okay, then you're going to wear yourself out. It's barely been a week since you were shot."

"I've got to move around or I'm going to get stiff."

He sat back on the sofa, legs spread, elbows propped across the back. "I might buy that if it looked like mere exercise. This is nervous pacing. What's eating at you?"

Morgan didn't answer. Admitting the truth was too painful, made her look too stupid.

"Nothing," she finally murmured.

Brandon rose to his feet, until he towered over her. He'd definitely gotten the tall genes in the family, damn him. She was a midget by Hollywood's standards.

He grabbed her shoulders and turned her to face him, effectively ending her agitated waltz across the floor. "I've seen you obsess about

*Turn Me On* in the past. What you're thinking about today has nothing to do with that, though, does it? Reggie has apologized for selling you out. Andrew's funeral was conducted with a minimum of hype, and the press has no idea where you are. Already the gossip is dying down. You're healing nicely." His gentle stare probed. "I can only think of one thing that would make you this crazy right now. Or should I say one person?"

"I don't want to talk about it."

"You haven't wanted to talk about Jack since you left the hospital."

Morgan closed her eyes. "Don't say his name."

"You're being stubborn, little sister."

"*I'm* being stubborn?" She poked herself in the chest with an angry finger. "Excuse me, but I didn't start this shit. *He* did. But now I'm supposed to live with it."

"Live with what, exactly?" Brandon crossed his arms over his chest. "He shot and killed a man who would have ended your life without blinking."

That's it? That's all he acknowledged? "Yes, he saved me, and I'm grateful. But did you forget the little part where he lied to me and took me to bed to get back at you? He sent you a film clip of—" She gnashed her teeth. "I still can't believe that. He . . ." How the hell could she put the betrayal into words? "He acted like I meant something. None of that act was true."

"I think it was."

Morgan felt her jaw drop. "Why are you taking up for him?"

Brandon shot her a self-deprecating smile. "We used to be friends, until I fucked it up. Jack wasn't going to divorce Kayla without a good reason. Despite his . . . lifestyle, he was too Catholic. I pushed Kayla. And pushed and pushed. God, I wanted that woman. The one thing I never did was level with Jack and just tell him I was in love with his wife. And that she was in love with me. I just took her, and I didn't care how wretched he felt because holding her made me feel better. I think he was just repaying the favor, little sister, letting me see how it felt to be on the receiving end. If you should be pissed at anyone, it's me."

"Do you have any idea what he did to me? At all?"

"I hate to say this, but when I barged into that hotel room, you didn't look like you were suffering too much."

Morgan flushed twenty shades of red, she was sure, from both fury and embarrassment. "It wasn't the way he touched me." Though, at times, that had been hard to take, to accept how much she loved it. "It was the way he pretended to care."

A sudden knock on the door sent them both turning. Brandon cursed under his breath, then moved to open it.

"God, I hope it's not the press," she muttered. "Vultures."

Brandon cracked the door open, only as far as the security chain allowed. "What?"

No response. The door blocked Morgan's view, and she could only see Brandon raise his hand to take something from the visitor's grasp. Then he breathed what looked like a sigh of relief.

She looked down at the item in his hand. A videotape. The other videotape Jack had promised to bring Brandon?

"Is this what I think it is?"

The person on the other side must have nodded. *Who was it? Could it be . . . No.*

"Thanks. Do you want to come in?"

Morgan's heart started to pound. Oh, God. Maybe . . . Was it Jack? Would Jack come here, after a week of total, devastating silence? Despite his betrayal, she ached for him. Her heart was a hollow, gaping wound in her chest. She strained to hear the sound of his voice late at night when she lay in bed, unable to sleep. And her body nearly vibrated at just the thought of him. She throbbed. Overly sensitive and tight in all the wrong places with the mere remembrance of him . . .

God, what if he walked through that door now?

Brandon drew the door back to admit the stranger, but it wasn't Jack who filled the doorway.

"Deke . . ." Disappointment stabbed her without mercy.

"Hi, doll. Don't look too excited to see me."

"I am. I'm sorry." She did her best to paste on a smile.

"How you doing?"

She tried to shrug, then grimaced. Damn, would that shoulder ever stop hurting?

Yeah, and probably long before her heart did.

"I'm recovering," she said. "How are you?"

"Ready to get a miserable coonass off my back. Want to help me?"

"With Jack? I doubt there's anything I can do. He's made my role in his life perfectly clear."

"See, I don't think he has. Since you left, he snarls and growls and gets drunk, then sleeps it off and starts over the next day. He knows you're pissed. I told him he's too chickenshit to see you. He told me—"

"I can imagine what he said." Morgan grimaced.

"It's not pretty. He needs you."

"He needs a beating," she shot back.

"If you were dishing it out, he would take it, doll. At least then, you'd be talking to him."

Morgan didn't know what to say. Part of her wanted to beat the hell out of Jack. He'd made peace with Brandon at the hospital . . . then left her without a single word while believing that she was unconscious. She'd been groggy and far too overwrought to respond—but she'd been awake enough to hear Jack's every word.

That kind of crap didn't put him in the "nice guy" category. Bastard.

"Forgive me if I don't give a shit that he's annoying you and giving himself a daily hangover. It's the very least he deserves, Deke. I paid for his revenge with my heart and a piece of my soul."

"For what it's worth, so did he."

Deke's words were like a punch to the gut, like poking a stick at a wild animal. "Bullshit."

"He loves you. He just has no idea how to win you back and doesn't think he deserves the chance to try."

"At least we agree on something," she snapped.

But in her heart, hope surged. Was it possible that he stayed away, not out of disregard but guilt?

"Just talk to him, doll. You'd be doing me and Grandpa Brice a favor."

Morgan hesitated, so damn tempted. "Why should I want to do a favor for the old man who brought me nearly nonexistent lingerie in an underhanded attempt to throw me Jack's way?"

"Because he thinks you're perfect for his grandson. We all do. Even Jack. *Pleassseee*," Deke wheedled. "Talk to him. Just once."

"Grown men begging." She rolled her eyes.

But she feared she wasn't fooling anyone. The hunger to see Jack gnawed at her composure, her restraint. Yet the fear of getting sucked into his charisma again, of being duped by her own want, of stupidly clinging to him and giving him the power to hurt her again, kept her away.

Deke shrugged. "Whatever works."

"If he wanted to see me that badly, he knows where to find me."

"He's got the Catholic guilt thing down pat, Morgan. He knows he fucked up, and he's not going to push his love on you."

"He doesn't love me!" she shouted.

"He does," Brandon cut in. "He told me himself, in two languages. I've never seen Jack care too much about any one person in his life. I had no doubt when I looked at the man that he loves you."

Morgan sucked in a sharp breath. Was it possible she meant more to Jack than just a revenge fuck? Had she come to mean more than the means to fueling a vendetta?

"I can see your thoughts all over your face, doll. Granted, spending one morning inside you doesn't make me an expert, but—"

"I don't need to hear this." Brandon grimaced.

"I'm pretty sure I know where your head is at," Deke went on. "You aren't going to get answers by hiding here."

She mentally recoiled. First, the son of a bitch had to remind her about that awful, wonderful morning she'd spent squeezed between the two of them as they'd given her the ultimate pleasure. Her ultimate fantasy, despite Jack's reservations. Then he tells her that she's being a coward. Lovely.

She could feel Brandon's reproving gaze on her, too, and made a mental note to beat Deke's ass later.

Shaking her head to clear it, Morgan forced herself to focus. Even if Jack had put his fears aside, so much else had happened.

A protest leaped to the tip of her tongue. No way, no how, was she going to talk to Jack.

But . . . damn Deke, he was right. No one had the answers she wanted except Jack.

"Talk to him." Deke's quiet command went straight to her common sense and made mush out of it. "Come with me."

Her thoughts were so tangled, so jumbled. But one reality stood out for her: Jack was the strong, shrewd, sexual man her body and mind had been searching for all her life. She could either stay here and hide and always wonder what could have been. Or she could go talk to the man and find out where his avowals of "love" registered on her bullshit meter.

"Fine. But no promises that I'll be nice."

"None expected." Deke grinned, those indigo eyes sparkling with mischief.

"Give me ten minutes to get myself together."

Deke grinned. "Jack was nursing a bottle of Tennessee whiskey when I left. Better make it five."

*    *    *

CLIMBING into Deke's enormous Hummer for the long ride out to Jack's swamp cottage in Louisiana, Morgan reflected that, if she didn't know better, she'd assume Deke had chosen such a vehicle to compensate for a deficit in masculine proportions. But she did know . . .

Because of Jack. Because he'd granted her that fantasy.

It seemed silly to turn the events of the last two weeks over and over in her mind. She'd done it a million times. Jack had reeled her in, duped her by tantalizing her with the lure of fantasies she'd always wanted fulfilled. He'd delivered. No disputing that.

But for her, it had gone beyond pleasure. Way beyond. When she'd been with Jack, Morgan had believed heart and soul that it meant something to him. The knowledge that he'd done it all for revenge crushed her until she felt broken, unable to sleep, eat . . . breathe. Wondering how the hell she was supposed to go on with this pain.

"You're thinking too hard. I can almost feel the headache you're giving yourself."

She leveled a reproving stare at him. "As opposed to you men, who think of absolutely nothing but your little vendettas and your dicks?"

To his credit, he didn't wince. "Yes, I knew about Jack's plan. But I think it stopped being about revenge for him very quickly."

"Don't make his case for him. I don't want to hear it."

Deke's words only confused her, made her hope. She was going to see Jack for answers. Period. If she didn't get the answers she wanted, she'd go on with life—alone. Somehow. Not that she expected Jack to be able to convince her of his undying love. Honestly, how could such a bond form in mere days, when everything around them had been all danger and lies? Impossible, right?

So logical . . . except for the fact she'd fallen totally for Jack during their time together. And unlike anything she'd felt for any man previously in her life, this felt strong, unbreakable. Permanent.

Damn.

Deke blew through a yellow light on the outskirts of Houston, then pulled into the parking lot of an extended-stay hotel built like little condos with fresh paint and freshly planted flowers.

"You need to pick up your gear before heading out?" she asked.

"Not exactly."

Deke parked, then turned to face her. "Jack intended to drive the copy of Brandon's incriminating video straight to him. I ended up driving, since I didn't think Jack and Jack made a good team on the roads."

"Jack and Jack?"

"Jack Cole full of Jack Daniel's."

"So he's here?" she asked, her heartbeat suddenly zooming like a woman about to fall from a cliff.

Deke nodded.

"He came all the way to Houston to deliver the video and sent you to do it because he was too drunk? The son of a bitch chose to cozy up to a bottle, rather than possibly getting close to me?"

"No. When we got here, we did a little recon. When he realized you were staying with Brandon, he wouldn't go. He refused to bother you."

Of all the crazy, asinine notions . . .

Before Deke could say more, Jack opened the door of the room in front of him, gorgeously shirtless, dark hair disheveled. Sunlight glared in his face. He squinted and glared toward the Hummer.

"Did you deliver the damn video?" Jack shouted, trying to shield his eyes from the sun.

"Hmm. He's not slurring anymore," Deke commented. "Maybe he's actually semi-sober."

"This is ridiculous. Why am I here expecting answers from a drunk man who only pursued me so he could get back at someone else and get his rocks off at the same time? Take me back to Brandon's."

"Not yet. Ten minutes. Just give him that much."

Morgan said nothing.

"If you don't, I'll have to start pleading again."

She shot him a stare that should have told him that she was totally unmoved. But, as usual, Deke ignored her.

"I'll give you extra whine if you don't cave in . . ."

"Ugh! Fine. Ten minutes, then you're taking me back or I'm calling a taxi. And a hit man to finish off both of you. Pricks!"

"That's a girl." He planted a smacking kiss her on the cheek, then flashed her a million-watt smile.

Morgan just rolled her eyes. "Let's get this over with."

"I'll come around to get you, but hang tight for just a minute. I don't think he can see you with the sun in his face and these tinted windows. And I want you to hear something." Deke climbed down from the Hummer, then called to Jack, "Yep, it's delivered."

"You bring me a new bottle?"

"I brought you something else. Don't you want to know that I saw Morgan?"

"So she *was* there." Jack blew out a breath. Then he swallowed, jaw tensing. "How was she?"

"In better shape than you since she wasn't somewhere between drunk and hungover."

"Her shoulder?"

"Getting better. She was up and walking around. She looked good."

Jack nodded. A simple gesture . . . but the frown on his face tore at Morgan. Brows furrowed, eyes closed, jaw tight, he looked so damn sad. Regretful. Destroyed.

The sight took her aback, ripped at her heart. He actually . . . cared? That's what it looked like. He couldn't see her, had no reason to act something he wasn't or didn't feel.

Morgan swallowed.

"I'll bet she looked beautiful. She always did."

Deke stopped in front of Jack, lingering on the sidewalk in the noon-time sun. "Yeah, and she looked pissed."

"I expected that. I made a really stupid fucking choice when I didn't come clean with her. I had opportunities and I . . ." He shook his head, a gesture rife with regret. "I didn't take them."

"Yeah, that makes you a stupid putz, but that isn't the main thing she's pissed about."

"It's not?" He looked totally confused.

Jack didn't get it? How could he not get it? How could he totally not understand? Amazing.

Pushed by hope and confusion and her temper, she opened the Hummer door and leaped down. "No, you dumb ass, that's not what I'm pissed about."

"See, I told you I brought you something." Deke flashed Jack a smile. "Or someone."

"Morgan," Jack whispered, taking a step toward her, hands out-stretched.

"Nice of you to remember me."

The barb in her voice stopped him cold. He dropped his hands. "You're here to chew my ass out. I deserve it. I swear, I never meant to hurt you. I didn't think we'd really become so emotionally involved. But the minute I laid eyes on you—"

"Oh, stop with the romantic drivel. So I was a good lay, nice and submissive and—"

"Kids, why don't we take this inside so the nice strangers around the motel can't hear about your sex lives?" Deke shepherded them into Jack's room.

Morgan darted inside, past Jack, shocked that she'd been so stirred up that shouting in a parking lot about their intimate details seemed reasonable. God, that man got under her skin and fried her brain.

Inside, the white walls and nondescript pressed-wood furniture shouted "typical." The striped beige and ivory comforter lay strewn with the stiff white sheets across the bed. Brown indoor/outdoor carpet completed the utilitarian look. Thoroughly ugly. So how the hell had she wound up having one of the most emotional discussions of her life here?

She turned to find Deke shutting the door before he leaned against it. Jack hovered close to her, so close she could smell the mystery of his scent blending with the whiskey he'd been guzzling. But he made no move to touch her.

"You were more than a good lay, Morgan. Way more, and I knew I should come clean. A dozen times I told myself I should but . . ." Remorse bled into his gaze, tightened his mouth. "I love you, and I knew once I told you the whole story that I'd lose you. I couldn't bring myself to say it and make you hate me. It was going to come soon enough."

Morgan steeled her heart against the admission. But she wasn't quick enough. His words were like a surprise attack, and hope, pain, and yearning all joined the shock to wear her resistance down.

Tears stung her eyes. "You love me so much that when I was shot, you visited the hospital, had a nice cozy chat with Brandon about your ex-wife, then left him to deliver your apologies to me. And you *never came back.*"

Jack sucked in a sharp breath. "You . . ."

"Overheard every word at the hospital? Yes. But what I never heard was if you supposedly loved me, when you were coming back. It seemed awfully easy for you to write me off."

He finally breached the distance between them and gripped her uninjured shoulder. His touch slid over her like an electric shock, a jolt of heat, of desire. But more, even. This came with a blast of yearning that exploded from her heart, so strong it nearly brought her to her knees.

But Jack held her up. "*Cher*, I fucked up. I didn't have any right to try to win you back. Would you have believed a word I said? No," he answered for her. "And why should you take me back? I don't deserve it. I know that."

Was it really just as Deke said, that Jack felt too guilty to pursue his feelings for her? Was that the only thing that stopped him?

Maybe the more fundamental question was, did she want him back? Did she want Jack and all he could give her in her life each and every day?

Even his fingers around her shoulders made her feel more alive than she had in the last week. A wish burst inside her, straining against common sense. They were from different places, led different lives . . . Pointless rumination. If they were to become a couple, they could compromise, mesh lives, live part-time in Louisiana and part-time in Los Angeles. Something.

The more important fact was that inside, they shared something special, connected physically and emotionally. Sexually. Without him, Morgan had felt as if she'd been missing something significant.

No, more than that. She felt like she'd been missing half of herself.

Risk-taking had never been her forte, and taking the one she contemplated now scared the hell out of her. But if there was a chance, even a remote one, that she and Jack could get beyond this revenge of his and have something significant, even lasting . . . She'd be a first-class idiot not to find that out.

"Just answer me one question," she demanded finally. "*If* I was able to forgive you for this stupid-ass vendetta you used me for and I said I wanted you to talk to me, what would you say?"

Behind Jack, Deke pumped his fist in the air and nodded in approval. Lord, she'd forgotten he was there. Before she could tell him to get his ass out of the room, Jack hauled her against him.

"I'd tell you that you're what I've been searching for my whole life. I'd confess that I dreamed about you before I ever met you, and that the first time I got deep inside you I think I knew that you were meant to be mine. I'd tell you I love you."

The swell of emotion behind those choked words nearly undid her, and Morgan felt her resistance crumbling even more. The tears rushed back. Her mouth trembled. Her throat tightened. Her jaw shook with the effort to hold back the tears. How could the man get to her with a few perfect words? Damn it.

"*Cher*, I wish I could just growl a command at you and make you come back. But I can't just control your emotions. It's more important than growling at you to take off your little wet panties."

He was giving her the power. Totally. He might order her around in the bedroom, but he wasn't coercing her to give anything she wasn't willing to. He wasn't going to bully her into surrendering her heart. He *wanted* her to give it.

That fact shone from dark, red-rimmed eyes in a hollow, stubble-lined face that looked like he had felt nothing but hell for days.

The realization that he loved her and wanted her love in return slid over her like one of her mother's quilts, soft, comforting, warm.

"I didn't know what to say or do or how to get out of the mess I'd created." His self-deprecating laugh scratched across her senses, igniting her heart.

"'I'm sorry' is a good start," she whispered.

"I'm damn sorry. If I had it to do over again . . . I'd give you your interview, tell you that even though I hated Brandon, I wanted you more than anything in the world. Then I'd seduce you until leaving me was the last thing on your mind."

"Better plan."

"Smarter, that's for sure." Jack shrugged, dropped his hands. "But you'd have to forgive me."

"You'd have to promise not to pull something this brainless again."

"Promising that would be easy."

"You'd have to agree to be nice to Brandon."

Jack tensed. "We've made our peace. I don't respect what he did . . . but I didn't do much better. I don't know that we're ever going to be great friends again, but we'll get along. I could make that happen."

Morgan smiled. Insane, complex, drive-her-crazy man and his stunningly honest answer. "You'd have to promise to fulfill all my fantasies."

That perked Jack right up. He crashed into her personal space again and crushed her against his chest. Morgan felt safe, felt like she'd come home.

"That's a promise I'll have no trouble keeping," he whispered. "You got more fantasies I should know about?"

"Just one at the moment." She drew in a deep breath, tinged with the scent of Jack, solid and enigmatic all at once, the scent of hope and tomorrow and great sex to come.

"Yeah?" he murmured against her mouth. "Tell me, *mon coeur.*"

Morgan dropped her gaze, drew in a deep breath, and went for broke. "That everything we've been talking about could be real. I want to forgive you—"

"And I want you to wear my pendant." He fished it out of his pocket. "I've been keeping it here, close to me . . . to be close to you."

"Jack." Morgan just about dissolved into tears.

"I want to keep you, love you, have you with me always," he whispered.

In the background, Deke clapped and let loose a stadium-worthy whistle.

Jack started at the sound. Then he growled something ugly, set Morgan aside, and stomped to the door. He grabbed Deke by the arm. "And some fantasies are meant to be for two." He shoved Deke out the door into the harsh midday sun. "Go to your own room."

"And do what? You're more entertaining than the soap operas on TV right now."

"Fuck off." Jack slammed the door in his face, then sidled back to Morgan. "Where were we?"

She couldn't stop the smile curling up her lips. "With you having the fantasy that you could keep me and love me forever."

"Still having that fantasy." He cupped her face in his large, warm hands, and stared at her with dark, hungry eyes. "Can you make it come true, *cher*?"

"Thanks to you, I know who and what I am now." She brushed a solemn kiss across his mouth. "Your wish is my command . . . sir."

## About the Author

**SHAYLA BLACK** is the *New York Times* and *USA Today* bestselling author of more than seventy novels, including the Wicked Lovers series, the More Than Words series, and, with Lexi Blake, the Perfect Gentlemen series. For twenty years, she's written contemporary, erotic, paranormal, and historical romances. Her books have sold millions of copies and have been published in a dozen languages. An only child, Shayla occupied herself with lots of daydreaming, much to the chagrin of her teachers. In college, she found her love for reading and realized that she could have a career publishing the stories spinning in her imagination. Though she graduated with a degree in marketing/advertising and embarked on a stint in corporate America to pay the bills, her heart has always been with her characters. She's thrilled that she's been living her dream as a full-time author for the past ten years.

Shayla currently lives in North Texas with her wonderfully supportive husband, daughter, and two spoiled tabbies. In her "free" time, she enjoys reality TV, reading, and listening to an eclectic blend of music.